OF MIDGARD

BOOK TWO OF THE LOKI OF MIDGARD SERIES

LOKI
OF MIDGARD

THE TAMING OF THE TRICKST

JENNIFER MEINKING

Loki of Midgard: The Taming of the Trickster
Book Two of the Loki of Midgard Series
Copyright © 2020 by Jennifer Meinking

This is a work of fiction. Apart from obvious and recognized historical references, all characters and incidents in this novel are the products of the author's imagination. Any similarities to people living or dead are purely coincidental.

Published by

Soul Splash Press

Cover and Interior Design: Nick Zelinger, NZGraphics.com
Editor: Jen Zelinger, TwinOwlsAuthors.com

ISBN: 978-1-7337076-2-6 (print)
ISBN: 978-1-7337076-3-3 (e-book)
Library of Congress Control Number: 2019917303

First Edition

Printed in the United States of America

TO ALETHEA, *my free-spirited second daughter, who has taught me lessons of love, generosity, and kindness ... Thank you for always being ready with a hug, a smile, an act of service, and an encouraging word. You have grown so much in the last year, and I'm proud of you!*

TO SCOTT BUTLER, *who has taught me lessons of faith, endurance, and wisdom ... Thank you for always being a faithful undershepherd, a preacher of truth, and a Gloryhunter for Him. You are an inspiration to me and so many others, especially as you face battles that would make even the strongest falter.*

AND, FINALLY, TO HIM, *who has taught me lessons that span an entire lifetime, too numerous to count ... Thank you for sustaining me through the most difficult moments of my life, giving me the strength to persevere, and loving me even at my ugliest. Because of You, I have a future and a hope.*

PROLOGUE

The fire was dying.

What remained of the last log fell to the grate with a jolting crash, jerking him back to his painful reality. He had been so absorbed in his own memories, he had not even noticed the growing chill and darkness in the room. As the cold crept into his clothing, he scooted himself over slightly to stoke the glowing embers, then stood to retrieve more wood. His shoe slipped slightly on the worn photograph that had floated to the floor just before he first stepped into his own memories. He bent to pick it up. For what seemed like the millionth time, he traced the beautiful face he knew so well with one finger.

Now that he had committed himself to reliving the experiences that had brought him to this place, he resented the interruption that had forced him to step back out of his mind into the present. In a way, what he had remembered so far had brought him comfort and ignited again the love he had cherished. He had forgotten what it felt like to rejoice in the presence of another, to be enthralled with her every move. To know and to love. To be known and loved in return.

There was an old saying that it was far better to have loved and lost than to have never loved at all. He wondered if the author of that saying had ever actually experienced it.

Would he have made different choices if he had understood what was coming?

No, he did not honestly believe he could have stopped himself from loving her, even if he had known he would have ended up here eventually, consumed by agony and loss. Even if a hundred more years had passed, he would never have been ready.

He set down the photograph and threw more wood into the fire. Almost in protest, the embers kicked up swirling orange sparks, one of which attached itself to his hand and stung for less than a second before it went out. The rest of the sparks settled as the flames licked the logs. It was a beautiful display, even though it did not last. And he was glad to have seen it, immediately struck by the instant picture it painted of what he was currently facing.

The first time he had unlocked his mind to access the past, he had dragged himself into his own memories quite unwillingly, with fear and trepidation. But so far, forcing himself to pore over the double life he had lived, in all its glorious mess, had given him a reprieve from the pain pounding him at every turn. Like a splitting headache returning in force after easing temporarily, the ache in his heart set him to longing for further relief.

His anxiety to alleviate this new surge of emotional pain brought with it a hopeful eagerness that he would find the answers he sought through his mental journey.

Without even trying this time, he slipped back into the moment before the log had disrupted him, completely immersing himself in what he remembered next.

1

The youngest son of Odin hurried down a corridor inside the Théâtre des Champs-Elysées in Paris. He barely noticed the art on the walls or the elegant decor, as eager as he was to rejoin his American costar and spend the rest of the evening with her. He had grown weary of flip-flopping like a salmon out of water, questioning the wisdom of spending time with the talented singer but unable to stop himself. And so, Loki had finally admitted aloud to himself the strength of his feelings for Carina Green, although no one had heard his little dressing room pep talk. Now, he swelled with confidence that he would figure out how to pursue a relationship with her despite his station and responsibilities as a prince of Asgard.

Determined to enjoy her company as they celebrated their first successful performance together as Lukas Black and the Shooting Star, Loki banished Asgard from his thoughts and strode into the lobby.

And there she was, talking with Kristoff, his Norwegian friend and manager. The sight of her almost made him miss a step. Half of Carina's deep red hair was pinned up in curls while the rest settled around her shoulders. The violet hue of her beaded dress brought a warm glow to her skin. The hem was shorter than her usual style, cut at the knees to show off her lovely legs. He gulped and reminded himself not to stare, glancing around the lobby instead. Very few theater patrons lingered there; he must have taken longer in his dressing room than he had realized.

When he reached the pair, Carina took his arm, her brown eyes glinting with the engaging, feisty spirit he found so delightful. "You do clean up nicely, Mr. Black."

Usually, it bothered Loki when she lapsed into formalities with his human name, but her flirtatious tone lent a pleasing familiarity to her words.

"So do you, Miss Green," he said softly, feeling his green eyes flare, as they often did when he was happy or thinking of mischief.

Of course, for Loki, there was little difference between the two. The Norse people, influenced by ancient writings penned by his former enemy, had not been wrong about his nature when they named him the "god of mischief" almost a thousand years ago. Though many legends had unfairly turned him into an evil villain, some humans loved his stories, although not enough for him to justify revealing himself to their world, not even in 1924. The two men who did know his true identity had accepted him as he was rather than as he had been portrayed. The question haunting him was whether or not Carina would do the same. Loki frowned slightly at the thought but pushed it aside, thankful she had blushed and ducked her head at his words, or she might have seen and questioned his change in expression.

"Knock it off, you two. You're making me feel lonely," Kristoff grumbled, shuffling his feet and looking away.

"Shouldn't you be incredibly happy right now, Kristoff?" Loki pointed out teasingly. "Tonight could not have gone better."

"I would be if ..." Kristoff trailed off, smacking Loki on the bicep twice to get his attention.

"What?"

"Don't you see her?" Kristoff gasped, his blue eyes wide and his mouth hanging open as he pointed to a tall, willowy blonde walking purposefully through the lobby toward them.

"Pull yourself together, old chum," Loki whispered gleefully, never one to miss an opportunity for teasing.

Kristoff snapped his mouth shut. He adjusted his three-piece suit slightly as the woman reached them.

"Good evening, Miss Green, Mr. Black," she greeted them, then turned to Kristoff expectantly.

"Sch-Schmidt," he stammered. "I mean Kristoff. Last name's Schmidt."

Kristoff raised his eyebrows at himself and coughed, staring at the floor in embarrassment. It was all Loki could do not to burst out laughing. He knew exactly what was going on with his human friend. He had seen Kristoff flirt and even pair off with many women, but this one was decidedly different. She had a bold confidence about her that Loki imagined most human men would find intimidating.

"Kathleen Jones," she introduced herself, firmly shaking each of their hands. "I'm an American journalist from Chicago."

Just as Kathleen took a breath to continue, Kristoff interrupted with excitement. "Kathleen Jones? I've read some of your lifestyle and entertainment pieces! I love you! Well, I mean ... your work, that is."

He grimaced, looking at her shyly with one eye squinted almost shut. Kathleen smirked at him and raised one eyebrow. And Kristoff returned her smile with a grin so goofy, Loki wondered if he had looked that silly when he saw Carina for the first time. He glanced over at her. She stifled a cough with her hand, but he could hear the suppressed laughter in it.

Kathleen focused her attention on Kristoff, though she included Loki and Carina with an occasional glance. "The theater manager pointed me in your direction after the show, which was marvelous, by the way. You're their manager, correct?"

"Yes, that's right." Kristoff quickly recovered his composure, his business mind snapping him out of his stupor.

"I'm writing an extended exposé on entertainment in Paris. I'd like to request an interview. I think Americans would love to hear about tonight's show," Kathleen explained. "And not just in Chicago. The papers in Boston and New York will feature my piece, maybe even the ones in Santa Fe and Los Angeles."

Carina's face had paled at the mention of New York. She was no doubt thinking of her ex-fiancé and former accompanist, Klaus Mayar, who had traveled to New York to inform her father she had ended their engagement and refused to perform with him after he had repeatedly abused his position and her trust.

"When are you printing your piece? How long will you be in Paris?" Carina asked tentatively.

"A little while longer. Then I have a little personal traveling to do," Kathleen answered. "I usually submit my articles weekly, but I'd want to get this one submitted in a few days. If you plan to tour the States soon, the exposure could help spread the word."

"We hadn't talked about an American tour," Kristoff interjected. "I don't think we're quite ready for that."

"Oh, you need to talk about it," Kathleen chuckled. "There's a lot of money to be made in America."

"Be still, my heart," Kristoff whispered to Loki. "She has business sense. I think I'm in love."

Loki stifled a laugh, this time unwittingly drawing the attention of the journalist to himself.

"Is something funny?" Kathleen asked with a mischievous twinkle in her bright blue eyes. "What did you say, Mr. Schmidt? I also like to laugh, you know."

"I was admiring your business sense, actually," Kristoff answered smoothly, although he nervously ran one hand through his sandy hair. "And just Kristoff is fine. I take it you have connections in the entertainment industry in the States?"

"I do," she affirmed, a sly smile spreading across her face.

"How about this, Kathleen? Oh, may I call you Kathleen?" Kristoff asked.

"You can call me Kat," she corrected him.

"Kat? I like it." Kristoff nodded his approval, then continued, "Why don't you join us for dinner, Kat? There are several restaurants around here perfect for an interview."

"Oh, could we go to a club?" Carina asked excitedly. "That encore made me want to go dancing!"

"You? At a nightclub?" Kristoff asked, his eyes widening in surprise.

Loki knew Carina's father would not approve of such a suggestion, which made him want to indulge her wish all the more.

"I'm open to either," Kathleen said. "I do have questions for all three of you. Although, I should point out, it might be hard to do an interview in a club, so a restaurant would be better."

Carina's face dropped, though she quickly hid her disappointment. Only Loki had seen it.

"Why don't you two have dinner?" Loki suggested, winking at Kristoff. "And I'll take Miss Green dancing. I'm not really in the right frame of mind for an interview tonight."

"I'm fine with that," Kristoff spouted.

"Would you be open to an interview in the morning?" Kathleen asked eagerly.

"Kristoff and I have business to attend to in the morning," Loki replied.

"Could we meet for lunch?" Kathleen countered.

Kristoff and Carina both looked at Loki, who nodded.

"Why don't we meet at noon?" Carina asked with her own sly smile. "Kristoff, would you make the arrangements with Miss Jones tonight?"

"I am the manager, aren't I?" Kristoff quipped dryly.

"Shall we go then?" Kathleen asked, turning to Kristoff expectantly.

Kristoff grinned at Carina and winked at Loki, then put his hand on the small of Kathleen's back to escort her to the doors. The two of them seemed unaware of anyone else around them, engrossed as they were in their animated conversation.

"And perhaps you can help me brainstorm logistics for an American tour," he was saying as he held one door open for her.

Loki chuckled. They were perfect for each other.

"I think Kristoff finally found the girl of his dreams," Carina observed.

"Mm-hmm," he acknowledged absentmindedly, then turned his attention back to her. "Did you really want to go dancing? Or was that just to help Kristoff get a date?"

"Knowing Kristoff the way I do, he'll insist it's a business meeting, not a date," Carina responded.

Loki laughed. "I do believe you're right. But he fancies her. That was fairly obvious."

"Indeed," Carina remarked. "I just hope she doesn't hurt him like Astrid did."

"You know about Astrid?" Loki asked in surprise. He had almost forgotten about Kristoff's hustling ex-girlfriend.

"It's a long story, but I'm afraid I introduced them," Carina explained sadly. "She broke both our hearts when we found out what she was really like. Kristoff has never been serious about a woman since."

Loki did not like the level of intimacy in Carina's voice. He did not look at her but clenched his jaw and stared straight ahead as he asked, "Were you hoping he would be serious about you?

Carina laughed. "Heavens, no! Kristoff has always been like a big brother to me. I have a feeling Kathleen Jones might be just what he needs."

"Perhaps," Loki sighed with relief.

"Anyway, to answer your question, yes, I really do want to go dancing. Can we get out of here before someone else tries to grab us?"

As they stepped into the Paris night, Loki asked her, "Wherever did you learn to dance like you did tonight?"

"I've had dancing lessons for years, mostly ballroom and ballet, but I did learn quite a few popular dances. Father won't be happy if he hears I did the Charleston on stage."

"That was the Charleston?"

"Don't make fun," she chided. "I wasn't exactly dressed for it."

"You are now," he observed, admiring her. "You look quite fetching."

"Thank you," she giggled. Then she grabbed his arm with excitement as he hailed a taxi. "I've heard they have the best jazz in Montmartre. We'd have our pick of dance halls and nightclubs."

"How do you know so much if your father never lets you do anything?" Loki asked as a cab pulled up to the curb.

"I read, Luke," Carina boasted, sliding into the car as he held the door for her. "A lot."

"So do I," he chuckled, happy she had dropped the formalities and called him by his human nickname again.

The ride was lengthy, but Carina made the time pass quickly. She pointed out several landmarks, speaking wistfully about one particularly magnificent building.

"That's the Palais Garnier, home of the Paris Opera and Ballet. Someday, I'll perform there," she predicted.

"Opera?" Loki asked in surprise. "Or ballet?"

"Neither," she laughed. "Sometimes, they do other types of concerts. I can dream, can't I?"

"It is impressive," he acknowledged, looking out the window. "It looks like a palace."

"You should see the inside," she sighed dreamily. "It's like nothing I've ever seen. One of my favorite novels is set there."

"Which one?"

"*Phantom of the Opera* by Gaston Leroux," she replied.

"I haven't read that one," Loki confessed. "Tell me about it."

The rest of the trip to Montmartre, she recounted the plot with gusto. Loki listened intently, far more interested in her enjoyment of the story and her thoughts on it than the actual story itself.

Suddenly, she stopped talking.

"What's wrong?" Loki asked.

"Klaus hated it when I analyzed whatever book I was reading," she answered quietly. "He pretended to be interested at first, then just got increasingly more annoyed."

"I'm not Klaus," Loki reminded her gently.

"No, you're nothing like him," she agreed. "In fact, you're nothing like anyone I've ever known."

"Carina ..." he started to say, then stopped abruptly.

He was waffling again. All of her signals told him she had feelings for him. But how would she react if he told her who he really was? Was he just fooling himself that they could be together?

"Yes?" she prodded, confused by his silence.

The taxi driver stopped the cab, giving Loki the perfect opportunity to avoid continuing that conversation.

"We're here," he stated. "You'll have to lead the way on this little expedition. I don't know this place at all."

They strolled down a few streets, noting the neon signs of several nightclubs against the deepening sky. Some places advertised live bands or musicians. All of them seemed packed to the windows with people. The faint sound of brass instruments and lively piano music trickled out into the evening, enticing them to join the partygoers. Loki did not register which nightclub they decided to enter, but the jazz blaring from every crevice immediately infused him with vigor and spunk. The live band featured six talented musicians who filled the club with energy and passion. Loki recognized the saxophone, trumpet, trombone, banjo, drum set, and clarinet, in addition to the piano, which the banjo player occasionally played.

A change came over Carina. She pulled Loki into the fray, weaving through the crowd to find a suitable spot on the dance floor. Loki already knew the Charleston and the foxtrot, but Carina showed him how to do the shimmy, the buzzard lope, and the bunny hug. They even danced the tango. He found each dance fascinating, but the Texas Tommy was his favorite by far. When the music picked up the pace, the moves Carina had showed him seemed to pour from his soul into his feet. The two of them kicked, twirled, and twisted their hips and knees as the band increased the tempo again. Carina flipped over him once or twice and even slid through his legs once, but he never missed a beat. The song ended with crashing finality, leaving them both breathless. To Loki's shock, the other dancers had cleared the space around them and stood watching with awed amazement. As the last note of the song faded, the unexpected audience erupted in a roar of cheers.

One of the musicians yelled out, "You two need to go on stage!"

Another musician hollered back at him, "They did, you idiot! That's Lukas Black and the Shooting Star, the hottest new act in Paris!"

Loki and Carina took a bow as laughter filled the club and every eye in the place seemed to lock on them again. The band started another song, inciting a frenzy of movement all around them, which allowed them to slip away unnoticed.

Now that his adrenaline was beginning to wane, Loki suddenly remembered he had a midnight appointment. The clock behind the bar told him he had time, but not as much as he wished.

"Are you hungry?" Loki asked Carina. When she nodded, he led her to a cozy table. "Why don't we eat something, then head back to the hotel? It's late, and you need your rest."

As much as he wanted to spend more time with Carina, he knew he could not miss that appointment.

2

"You know, I think this has been the best day of my life. I've never had so much fun." Carina smiled at Loki, intertwining her fingers with his as he slid beside her into the backseat of the taxi.

"Same here," he replied, hating how the minutes had ticked by so fast. He wished there were more miles between the Montmartre district and their hotel, just to prolong these moments with her.

"It'll be an easy day to remember, especially as an American," Carina continued. "I had forgotten until now, but today is the Fourth of July."

"Isn't that your country's independence day?" Loki asked.

"You've read American history!" Carina exclaimed, clearly pleased.

"Some," he replied. "I hope to see America someday, after all."

"Me too," Carina agreed softly. "I've never been farther west than New York state."

"That's farther west than I've been," Loki remarked woefully.

"We'll just have to remedy that," Carina teased.

Loki smiled at her, then watched Paris pass by the taxi window while he absentmindedly caressed Carina's hand with his thumb. She did not pull away, as she had the last time he had done it. She seemed very relaxed and content, and he wished again for more time together. Once they reached their hotel, Carina would go to her room. And Loki would head back to the lobby to meet Kristoff and the two self-exiled Asgardians, Baldur and Hod, one of whom happened to be his long-thought-dead older brother.

Loki's sharp mind replayed the plan he had hatched to smuggle his childhood friend, Sigyn, off of Asgard to reunite her with her former suitor, Kvasir. The two had been separated by nearly a thousand years of wrong perceptions, including Sigyn's belief that she had been in love with Loki. Then Kvasir assumed Loki had married the nobleman's daughter and later dishonored her by cavorting with Midgardian women, neither of which was true. The sticky situation nearly cost Loki his life, in more ways than one. He grimaced when he remembered the times Kvasir had tried to kill him, then shuddered as he thought of how close he had come to losing Carina forever.

"What's wrong, Luke?" Carina asked, squeezing his hand slightly, her face concerned.

"Oh, nothing," he replied with an uneasy smile. "Just … sorry tonight has to end."

She eyed him with a touch of suspicion, falling into silence for a few minutes before speaking again. "I've talked almost nonstop about myself and my interests all night. Tell me something about you."

"Like what?" he asked, looking at her quizzically.

"What do you like to do for fun?" she asked.

"This," he said simply.

"What does that mean?" She wrinkled her nose in a teasing, confused expression.

"I don't know," he laughed. "You look so cute right now, I've completely forgotten the question."

"Oh, come on, Luke," she pouted, punching him lightly on the shoulder with her free hand. "Tell me something about you. Something real."

"How real?" he teased.

"Are there levels of real?" she laughed.

He paused for a moment, becoming very serious as he decided to test the waters. "I was actually thinking about how I almost got engaged," he said abruptly.

"What?" Her body stiffened as the laughter in her voice died. "When?"

"About two weeks ago."

"Why didn't you?" She tried to remove her fingers, but he tightened his grip on her hand.

"I grew up with her, but I didn't love her. Our families wanted us to marry," he confessed.

"An arranged marriage?" Carina asked, her tone lightening slightly.

Loki sighed. "No, no one forced me. I was heartbroken over someone else, so for a short time, I courted the girl."

"I don't think I'm ready for this much real," she whispered.

Loki fell silent, released her hand, and stared out the window again, unsure of what to say next. "I just thought it would make everyone happy if I married her."

"Except you," Carina pointed out.

Loki looked at her hopefully but guardedly. "Exactly. I still didn't call it off until I realized she was in love with someone else."

"Was this the woman you almost got killed over?" she asked hesitantly, as if she was compelled.

"He was never *that* close to killing me, but yes," Loki clarified. "We've put all that behind us."

"Is she with him now?"

"She will be very soon," Loki responded somewhat vaguely. "I promised her I would help them run off together. She tried to persuade me to fight for the one I had lost, but ..."

"But what?"

"Even if she cares for me ... I just don't know if ..." Loki took a deep breath. "There are some serious obstacles."

"Oh."

It was the heaviest word Loki had ever heard Carina speak, and he had no response. He had come so close to confessing all, but she had not responded with the encouragement he needed. His words were not coming out right. What was she thinking? The complications once again crowded his mind, heavily shadowed by his doubt.

Gloom settled over them as they got out of the taxi and walked into the hotel. They rode the lift up to their floor in uncomfortable silence, while Loki desperately willed her to say something.

Anything.

He could not bring himself to speak first.

She walked woodenly to her door and fumbled with her key. Loki hovered nearby, shifting his weight from foot to foot, then reluctantly took several steps toward his own door.

"Luke?" she spoke up quietly, stopping him in his tracks. "Why can't you be with that other woman?"

"What other woman?" he asked, bewildered.

"The one you're in love with, the one you've given up on," she said nonchalantly.

She did not look at him as she put the key in the lock and turned it. The short click and ensuing creak of the door almost drowned out the sound of quiet sniffling. He stood there in the hallway, his mind in a state of confusion.

Is she crying? he asked himself as she bid him good night and started to close the door behind her.

A sudden thought dawned on him. How could he have been so dense? He had spoken in terms too veiled. She seemed to have no idea he was really speaking of her. In one fluid movement, he leaped at the door and stopped it from closing.

"Carina, wait! Do you think—"

"I said good night," she cut him off stiffly, trying to close the door. He held it still.

"I think you misunderstood me," he objected.

"Is that so?" she retorted. "Well, I don't see why your personal escapades should matter to me anyway. You're free to do what you want."

"Is this some kind of game to you?" he demanded angrily. He suspected she was bluffing, but her haughty manner and careless words hurt him. "Why are you acting like this?"

She opened the door wide, raising her voice slightly. "You want to talk about games? Who's been flirting with me, holding my hand, and making eyes at me all day? Who was dabbling around with another woman two weeks ago? And who's in love with yet another one he can't have? The great Lukas Black, that's who! You must be quite the ladies' man."

Her voice oozed with scorn, but tears were forming in her eyes. Loki had taken several steps toward her during her tirade, watching her intently and processing her words as she backed away from him with each step.

"Is that what you think?" Loki asked incredulously, stung she would view him that way.

"Stay where you are!" Carina spat as her back reached the far wall inside her room. "I refuse to be your next conquest."

The door suddenly slammed behind them. They both jumped. The jolt shook Loki out of his wounded feelings. He immediately grasped the humor in the situation. Carina stared wide-eyed at him as he began to laugh.

"What's so funny?" she demanded, wiping angry tears from her eyes.

"How can someone so smart be so stupid?" he gasped, gloriously happy. If she was jealous enough to completely lose her reason, she just might love him.

"How dare you!" she huffed, stomping toward him and lifting her hand.

She fumed in exasperation when he grabbed her wrist in midair before she could slap him.

"Oh, no, you don't," he reprimanded her. He released her wrist, then quickly gathered her into his arms and held her tightly. "Carina, you goose," he said softly, his voice low and tender.

She trembled against him and tried to pull away, but he was too strong. "Let me go, Luke," she demanded, her voice muffled.

"No!" he stated defiantly.

"Please?" she asked, her anger finally abating.

Loki released her and watched as she hurriedly wiped her tears away. He did not touch her again but waited patiently for her to calm down.

"What are you grinning at?" she sniffed.

"It's kind of funny, don't you think?"

"I don't find anything funny right now."

"Well, I find it hilarious. You think you're just some sort of challenge to me? It's not even logical," he chuckled.

She paced the room, jabbing her finger at him. "It's perfectly logical! Why else would you suddenly tell me all this, unless you're on the rebound? Did you expect me to feel sorry for you and cave to your advances?"

"Of course not," Loki growled.

She ignored him, stuck in her conclusions. "Why do men do this? Using a woman's sympathy to worm their way into her bedroom? It's despicable! And to think that I actually ..."

She threw her hands in the air near the end of her tirade, then clapped them over her mouth as she registered what she was about to say.

Loki reached her in two strides.

Guessing what she had almost confessed gave him the boldness he needed. If he did this right, it should rectify all. She inhaled sharply when he cupped her face gently with both hands, just as he had done earlier that day. This time, his determination left no question as to what he intended to do. An unspoken statement seemed to hover in the air as he pulled her to him. She put her hands on his chest in a half-hearted attempt to stop him, but her lips yielded to his immediately, softening like butter as she slid her hands up and around him.

He released her almost as quickly as he had kissed her, still holding her tightly around her waist. "There! Is that the kiss of a man looking for his next victim?"

"I'm not sure," she murmured breathlessly, her eyes searching his face as she fingered the hair at the nape of his neck. "Maybe you could run it by me again?"

He grinned, then bent his head to kiss her longer and more deeply the second time. When he finally released her, she swayed dizzily. He steadied her quickly, helping her sit down on the sofa across from the bed. Sitting shoulder to shoulder beside her, he suddenly felt painfully shy.

"You're even better at that than you are with words," she said shakily. "No one has ever kissed me like that."

He chuckled but did not look at her. "I've never kissed anyone like that."

He could feel her staring at him. "I find that hard to believe," she challenged, somewhat bitingly. "Lukas Black, the ladies' man, who juggles three or more women at a time, has never kissed anyone like that?"

"Are you still stuck on that?" He shook his head, protesting, "Kristoff and my brother are ladies' men. Not me."

"Even so, that was no ordinary kiss. Why did you do it?" she asked shyly.

Ready or not, he knew he had to finally tell her how he felt. He would deal with the complications later.

He sighed deeply and stammered, barely above a whisper, "Because ... I ... I'm ..." Finally turning to face her, he took a deep breath and forced the words out. "Because I'm in love with you."

"You are?" she gasped as a gorgeous smile transformed her face, like the sun breaking through the clouds after a dreary waterspout. Then she furrowed her brow. "I'm really confused. Why didn't you say something before now?"

"I was stupid. I admit it," Loki answered, a pleading tone creeping into his voice. "But truly, I love you as I have never loved anyone."

When she only searched his face again, he hunched over with his elbows on his knees and stared at the carpet. His heart was out there in the open. The seconds of silence were terrible.

"Did you fall in love with me before or after you almost got engaged?" she finally asked quietly.

"Before," he sighed, wishing she would just let that go. "The simple truth is I almost married someone else because you were marrying someone else. She was the rebound, not you. And certainly not some other woman."

"Oh, so I'm this mystery woman you can't have?" she teased as she nudged him with her shoulder.

"You knew it all along?" he cried, glancing at her. "You just wanted to make me say it?"

"No, I really was confused!" she insisted. "I wanted it to be me, but thinking it might be someone else made me livid."

"I noticed," he remarked dryly.

"On the other hand, if it was me, it sounded like you had given up."

He studied his hands, once again afraid to look at her. "It's only ever been you since the first time I saw you. And yes, I have lost hope several times. I'm not really sure of anything except ... the more time I spend with you, the more I cannot bear to part from you."

"Then don't," she whispered, turning his face toward her and seeking his lips again.

The intensity of her kiss awakened a hunger within him, which made him instantly and acutely aware of how the

evening could unfold if he yielded to it. He rested his forehead
on hers and tried to catch his breath.

"It's getting late. I should go," he murmured, afraid he
would push things too far if he stayed much longer.

"I'm not tired," she murmured back, caressing his nose
with hers. "You can stay ... if you want to."

The temptation was so strong, it staggered him. "I want
to, but—"

She silenced him with her mouth. And Loki found himself
responding with breathless ardor as he relished the sensation
of her fingers in his hair. He pulled her onto his lap, ignoring
how dangerously close he was to losing all of his resolve from
moments ago. Instead, he toyed with the idea of allowing nature to take its course. On the other hand, how could he take
her past the point of no return, when she was not his for the
taking?

Ah, but she could be mine, he thought.

His conscience quietly reminded him an upstanding
Asgardian man would never compromise the honor of a lady,
but he had broken other Asgardian laws and standards. She
certainly was not Asgardian. And he was not on Asgard
anyway. They did things differently here. He loved her. Why
not express it? The passion in her kiss indicated she wanted
him to do so. Wasn't that enough?

She suddenly slipped her hands under the suit coat he still
wore to pull him closer, momentarily distracting him from
his internal battle. He almost panicked when he realized he
had accidentally dropped his clothing illusion, but then he
relaxed. He had only disguised the color of his Midgardian
suit and shirt, and she had not noticed his mistake. If he had
chosen to wear illusionary garments over his Asgardian gear,

there would be a completely different scenario playing out. It was a poignant reminder he had not told her who he really was. He had, in fact, deceived her. Out of necessity, yes. But if he followed his heart and continued on his present course, would she despise him later? Or accuse him of trying to conquer her again?

As he wrestled with the decision he must make, she moved her hands to the back of his neck, never taking her mouth from his for long. He did not really want to consider the fragility of their budding relationship and all the uncertainty between them, still looking for any excuse to pursue his growing desires.

Her hands slowly and agonizingly glided down his shoulders and chest. He suddenly came to his senses. This was not a question of love or desire but of respect and timing.

Loki mustered every ounce of self-control he had to gently take her hands, choking out, "No, no, Carina! We have to slow down."

He looked deeply into her eyes as he said it, lest she misunderstand, but he was grieved by the rejected, embarrassed look on her face. He had hurt her, but if he had not stopped things before they progressed any further, he knew the hurt would have been far deeper.

"We're only kissing," she contended hesitantly, though the sudden gleam in her eyes almost stopped his pounding heart and caused him to cast aside all propriety. But the look was immediately followed by confusion and uncertainty as she added, "Didn't you just say you wanted to stay?"

"I do. Oh, I do," he breathed, shutting his eyes again and squeezing her hands slightly as he fought his desire for her.

"And that's exactly why I should leave before I compromise your honor."

When she pulled her hands away from his, he tentatively and fearfully opened his eyes. But the hurt look on her face had been replaced with one of understanding and awe.

"You're so different," she murmured, cupping his cheek tenderly. "Most of the men I know would not hesitate to push an advantage."

"I love you, Carina," he stressed, stroking her cheek with his knuckles. "You are worthy of my respect."

She leaned into his touch and shut her eyes tightly as her body trembled. She appeared to be fighting a surge of her own desires. When she opened her eyes, she nodded in resignation, as if to confirm she agreed with what he had already realized. It was too soon, and neither of them was ready.

"You're right," she exhaled, easing herself off his lap to sit beside him. "I do want your respect, just as much as your love."

"That's the closest you've come to saying how you feel about me," he pointed out shyly.

"Oh, Luke! Haven't you figured it out by now?" A smile played around the corners of her mouth, her eyes more luminous than he had ever seen them. "I am hopelessly in love with you."

Although he really did know by that point, hearing her say she loved him affected him deeply. He was not aware he had been holding his breath, until all the air shoved itself out of his lungs in two surprising words. "Since when?"

"What?" she asked incredulously, then started laughing when Loki blushed. "Very well, I'll tell you. I had a crush on you the very first time I saw you perform in the streets."

"Really?" Loki grinned, already enjoying her story.

"You were so handsome and charismatic. Even then, I sensed you were different from the men I knew, but I couldn't get close enough for you to notice me."

"I probably would have completely forgotten what I was doing if I had," Loki admitted. "Remember my reaction the first time I saw you? I was a complete idiot. And you laughed at me."

She giggled. "Only because I was pleased that my plan worked so well."

"What plan?"

"I'm the one who put it in Father's head to hire you to perform that night so I could meet you, although I didn't tell him that."

"You little minx!" Loki exclaimed, immensely pleased. "But if you had feelings for me, why did you agree to marry Klaus?"

She sobered instantly. "I was a silly girl with a crush. I wasn't prepared for the attraction to be so obviously mutual and intense. It frightened me, so Klaus seemed safer—"

Loki could not help but snort in derision.

"I know, I know," Carina sighed. "Marrying him was what my Father wanted for me, so I said yes when my heart screamed no. I actually cried myself to sleep that night, then secretly went looking for you the next day."

"You did?" Loki was stunned.

"When Kristoff told me you had left Germany, I decided to accept my lot and forget you."

"He never told me you came to him," Loki grumbled.

"I made him swear not to, out of embarrassment. And I never told him why I was looking for you, although I daresay he probably figured it out. He didn't tell me you two planned to meet in Paris either. I was shocked when you showed up on my doorstep the other day."

"I shocked myself," Loki chuckled. "When I found out you were there, I just had to see you again."

She smiled at him lovingly. "I'm glad you came when you did. I think I realized it was more than a crush when you swept up all that broken glass and fixed my hand after my temper tantrum. By the time you walked me back to my hotel that night, I knew I was in love with you."

"Is that why you cried in the hotel lobby?"

"You saw that?" she muttered.

"It broke my heart," Loki confessed. "I didn't know what to do."

"Neither did I," she admitted. "I felt so utterly hopeless and trapped. It's been a lot of ups and downs in just a few days, but my love for you has only grown."

He kissed her again, almost crushing her in his exuberance. She broke away this time.

"Luke, if you don't leave right now, you won't be leaving at all," she sighed shakily.

"What have you done to me, Carina Green?" He gazed at her lips and bit his own in agony as desire coursed through him again. "And what on earth do we do now?"

She took a deep breath, then rose from the sofa and walked to the door, opening it for him. "We both get some sleep."

He nodded and made himself walk out into the hall.

As he passed her, she kissed him on the cheek, whispering, "Go with my respect, my gratitude, and my love."

Loki allowed her words to sink into his soul. When Kvasir had taken the identity of William Shakespeare over three hundred years ago, he had written poignantly about love. But one specific phrase danced in Loki's mind.

He kissed her hand, lingering only slightly. "Parting truly is such sweet sorrow. Good night, Carina."

"Sleep well, Luke," she murmured, her eyes shining as she reluctantly but resolutely shut her door.

Loki fell against the wall outside Carina's door with a heavy thud and drew one long, shuddering breath.

What have you done, Loki? he berated himself viciously.

All of the complications of a relationship with her hurtled through his mind yet again, but his heart breathed her name with every pounding beat, drowning out the voice of uncertainty. She loved him. She respected him. And he knew he would die for her.

"I would love to hear this explanation." Kristoff's sarcastic voice from down the hall startled Loki.

Baldur and Hod were with him. Loki had completely forgotten about their meeting.

"Where have you been?" Hod squawked at him angrily. "We've been waiting downstairs for twenty minutes, man."

"I think it's fairly obvious, Hod," Baldur snickered, his dark eyes dancing with fun. "How was she, little brother?"

"Wait, did you two …" Hod smirked, gesturing to Carina's door and back to Loki.

"No!" Loki growled, stomping toward them.

"Very human of you, though I don't blame you," Hod

laughed, ignoring Loki's denial. "That Sheba is fine! I'd probably hit that myself."

Before Hod could utter another word, Loki had the shorter man by the throat and pinned against the wall. "I did not take her. And you will not touch her either."

Kristoff raised his eyebrows in barely restrained amusement.

"Hey, hey!" Hod struggled to free himself, choking slightly. "Can't you take a joke? It's your business! Do what you want."

Baldur chuckled. "He's telling the truth, boys. Did you see that whipped look on his face? Oh, little brother, have you got a problem."

"Don't say it, Baldur," Loki warned, letting go of Hod, who rubbed his neck and glared at him. "Don't you dare say it."

Baldur regarded him solemnly but with respect. "This is true love, little brother. It takes extraordinary discipline to deny your own desires, especially on Midgard."

Loki groaned and ran his hand through his hair, remembering how she had kissed him. "She's pure and precious, like silver. I will not tarnish her."

"Oh, this is getting serious!" Hod exclaimed. "You sound just like Kvasir."

Baldur nodded. "They are a lot alike, those two."

"I don't want to talk about this anymore," Loki huffed, walking toward the lift. "I have a promise to keep."

"Oh, so now we're on a time schedule?" Hod scoffed, following after him and the other two men. "Didn't seem to bother you twenty minutes ago!"

"Drop it, Hod," Loki warned.

He did not look at any of the men as they rode the lift to the ground floor, trying to engage his mind with what they needed to do. Once they were outside the hotel, the coolness of the night cleared Loki's head.

"Where are we going, then?" he asked Baldur.

"The Eiffel Tower," Baldur informed him. "That direct connection I told you about is right near the base. It leads to a cave on the South Sea of Asgard."

"Too bad it isn't closer to the palace," Loki murmured. "That would have saved me a lot of trouble."

"Listen closely," Hod instructed Loki as they approached the glowing monument. "Since we're pressed for time now—"

"Let it go," Loki groaned, cutting him short. "I'm sorry, alright?"

"That's all you had to say," Hod shot back with a grin. "Anyway, I'm going back with you. I know the way, so it will be faster than trying to give you directions."

"Hod, quit picking on my brother," Baldur laughed quietly. "You were planning to go with him all along."

Suddenly, the four men stopped. As they neared the entry point Baldur had spoken of, a figure approached them from the dim light under the tower.

"You're late," Kvasir stated flatly.

"Would anyone else like to take a jab at me for that?" Loki demanded.

The other men stifled their laughter.

"Where were you?" Kvasir pressed.

"Whooee, don't bring that up," Hod said, shaking his head. Then he blurted out, "We caught him coming out of that American singer's hotel room."

"Hod!" Baldur reprimanded. "You just said not to bring that up."

"That's because I didn't want anyone else to do it before I did," Hod hooted, nudging Kristoff, who also burst out laughing.

Loki glared at them both but could not stop himself from smiling.

Kvasir sized Loki up with a knowing nod, the smirk on his own face replacing the nervousness that had been there.

"What are you doing here, anyway?" Loki questioned Kvasir before anyone else teased him further. "This wasn't the plan."

"Oh, we forgot to tell him, Kvasir," Baldur confessed, slapping his forehead.

"I'm going with you," Kvasir informed Loki, putting up his hand when he began to protest. "You told me to face my fears, did you not?"

Loki nodded, already impressed with the change in Kvasir.

"So then, you will not fight my battles for me. She'll face us both, and then she will truly be free to choose."

The other four men stood silently, regarding Kvasir with awe and respect.

Then Hod broke the moment, complaining, "Just how are we supposed to hide four people from Heimdall and Odin?"

"Don't you mean five?" Loki corrected him. "If we're all going now, we aren't leaving Kristoff behind."

"I'm not going, Loki," Baldur said quietly. "I would endanger the whole mission. And I have no desire to go back."

"Baldur, I don't understand this," Loki exclaimed. "How can you live with yourself, knowing so many people mourn your death?"

Baldur shook his head. "Someday, you might face the same decision, little brother. Only then will you understand."

"Me?" Loki repeated, shocked at the suggestion. "I don't think I could ever fake my own death like all of you."

"I never have," Kristoff corrected him, which brought laughter and a relief from the tension.

"We've wasted enough time." Hod winked at Loki, who glared at him, not missing the final jab at his tardiness. Hod continued, "We still have the problem of concealing four people on reentry."

"I could displace the light and make us all invisible, but I've never tested my skills to that level," Loki offered.

"It won't be enough," Hod said, shaking his head. "The cave is remote, but Heimdall would sense that much heat signature, especially Kristoff's."

"I've got something for you," Kvasir said, holding out a small black object. "Just a little something I invented when I planned to sneak Sigyn away from Asgard."

"What does it do?" Loki asked.

"It's a cloaking mechanism. It will conceal heat signatures within a ten-foot radius of the device, plus make the user, and whomever he wants, invisible to anyone of his choice."

"Say what?" Hod asked, scratching his head.

"Watch," Kvasir said. He pressed a tiny, flashing red button on the side of the object and vanished.

"Is something supposed to be happening?" Hod asked. "You look weird, but I can still see you."

Kvasir reappeared. "Only because I wanted you to," he informed Hod.

Kvasir pressed the button again twice. This time, Loki saw him, although shimmery in form. But Hod's surprised exclamation told Loki that Kvasir had vanished to Hod's eagle eyes. The other men laughed, for they could still see Kvasir in some fashion and enjoyed Hod's shock.

"That's some gadget," Loki said with admiration when Kvasir clicked the button once more to turn off the cloaking.

"Loki, I want you to do this," Kvasir said, tossing it to him. "This tool will be far more effective with abilities like yours."

"Did you use this when you were hunting me down?" Loki asked, holding it up to inspect it.

"Only when I didn't want you to see me," Kvasir chuckled. Then he grew serious. "If this goes well, it's yours."

"What if we get separated?" Kristoff asked. "I didn't plan to get stranded on an alien planet today."

"On Asgard, *you're* the alien," Hod pointed out dryly.

"Exactly!" Kristoff spouted. "And I'm not welcome there, am I?"

"Would you rather not go?" Hod taunted him.

"Didn't say that," Kristoff growled.

"Relax, both of you!" Loki exclaimed. "Kristoff has a point. We won't be able to see each other."

Kvasir clutched his forehead, then slid his hand into his hairline, grabbing a few tawny tufts in frustration. "Loki, weren't you paying attention? Just program it so we can all see each other, but no one else can."

"How?"

"I understand why Hod was confused, but I thought you would have figured it out by now," Kvasir quipped.

"Come say that to my face," Hod said angrily, but Baldur already had a grip on him to keep him still.

"Well?" Loki demanded.

"With your brain waves, Loki," Kvasir sighed in exasperation. "That woman you were with has made you addle-headed. Try it. Do it with everyone but Baldur."

Loki telepathically transferred his instructions to the device while he clicked the button. The men he had silently named turned shimmery, as Kvasir had during the last test of the device, but Loki could still see them. "Baldur, did it work?"

"I can hear you, but I can't see any of you," Baldur replied.

"It doesn't work on sound, so we'll have to be quiet," Kvasir admitted.

"Don't you control sound, Luke?" Kristoff asked.

"I can only displace or manipulate it," Loki said. "I can't silence it completely."

"You hear that, Hod? You'll have to be quiet," Baldur teased his friend, rubbing his black curls affectionately.

"Get off me," Hod spat angrily, smacking Baldur's hand. But then he grinned. "This is the most fun I've had in years!"

"That makes one of us," Kristoff groaned nervously.

"Come on, human, stick with me. This is about to get wild!" Hod cried, waving them all to follow him to the south pillar of the tower.

Just a few feet away was a hidden door, which was tightly locked. Baldur picked the lock easily, ushered them through, and stood guard outside. Loki cautiously flared just a touch of light. Stairs led to yet another locked door, behind which hid a stark room lined with strange equipment and electronics. More doors hinted at other mysterious passages or rooms.

"What is this place?" Loki muttered.

"It's an underground bunker from the Great War," Hod

whispered fiercely, hushing him. "It belongs to the French military."

Kristoff stood aghast, looking around, then hurried to catch up when Loki signaled him. Kvasir and Hod led them through a series of tunnels that looked less man-made, then stopped abruptly. Multicolored light shimmered on a rock wall in front of them.

"How did this get here?" Loki asked. "The Eiffel Tower is less than forty years old. And this bunker is fairly new, isn't it?"

"I built this portal for Sigyn," Kvasir answered. "This city was here long before the tower or the bunker, although it wasn't always called Paris. When I came alone, I made my way north as far as I could go, then west. Eventually, I came back, but the tower and the bunker were here by then. Somehow, the portal survived, so I told the other Asgardians about it. But it hasn't been used in a long time."

"You built it?" Loki asked incredulously. "How?"

"With the same malleable ore the Bifröst is made from. I simply programmed a direct connection from the cave on Asgard to here," Kvasir explained. "If you're powerful enough, you can override the connection with your brain waves to take you somewhere else. But then it becomes indirect, and you can't return without dark magic."

"How do you know all this?" Loki demanded.

"I've made my fair share of mistakes," Kvasir said vaguely. "And believe me, I've paid the price."

"Are we done with the science lesson?" Hod exclaimed. "Let's go already!"

Kvasir nodded, putting his finger to his lips and signaling Loki to push the button. Loki did, then clapped his hand over

Kristoff's mouth to keep him quiet since his human friend had never traveled this way and might unintentionally shout. The strong, magnetic pull sucked them through the portal into a dark cave. The only sound was a slow, rhythmic dripping.

Loki released Kristoff and shivered. "I hate caves!"

"Why?" Kvasir asked, moving toward the entrance.

"Oh, just that little scene you wrote about me being bound forever in a cave with my nonexistent, murdered son's entrails," he whispered fiercely. "Unbelievably bad form, Kvasir."

Kvasir just shrugged and grinned sheepishly, whispering back, "Yeah, sorry about that."

"We can talk normally now," Hod said. "Heimdall is watching elsewhere."

"You can see him?" Loki asked in disbelief.

"Super sight, man," Hod reminded him with a grin, tapping his temple and winking one golden eye at him. "Plus, Heimdall's my brother, you know."

"I didn't know that," Loki remarked. He turned his attention back to Kvasir. "But honestly, Kvasir, what is it with you and caves? You even wrote your own death scene in a cave."

"In my mind, I did die here," he said sadly, looking around. "So many memories …" Suddenly, he sank to the cave floor with his legs crossed and dropped his head into his hands. "I can't do this."

"Oh, yes, you can," Loki scolded, pulling him back to his feet. "You insisted on coming, and we aren't turning back now. And I'm not quoting any more Shakespeare either, so get ahold of yourself."

"What if …"

"No more what-ifs! Do you want to live another thousand years in darkness, wondering what could have been?"

"No," Kvasir whispered, sounding very much like a child.

"Look!" Hod gasped, pointing to the cave entrance. "Someone walks the sand!"

"We can't see as far as you can," Loki said impatiently. "Who is it?"

"It's a slender woman with wavy blond hair, about a quarter of a mile away," Hod said excitedly. "Her face is turned the other direction. She's singing to herself."

"It has to be Sigyn!" Loki burst out. "Kvasir, she's nearby!"

Kvasir went white as a sheet, clutching Loki as he sank back to the floor. He looked utterly sick, panic rising in his voice. "What do I do? What do I do?"

"What do you do?" Hod screeched, smacking Kvasir's jaw. "Pull yourself together, man!"

Kvasir shook himself, then stood. "Thanks, little buddy. I think … maybe … I can do this."

"I'm gonna allow that just this once," Hod said, shaking his finger at Kvasir. "But don't you ever call me little buddy again."

"Well? Go to her," Loki cried, pushing Kvasir toward the cave entrance as he hesitated.

"Not yet! What if someone sees me?" With both hands, Kvasir braced himself against the rock face that formed the entrance and resisted Loki's pushing.

"There's no one else around for miles!" Hod yelled. "And even if there were, we're all still invisible. She's turning back the other way. Get out there!"

"I can't," Kvasir sighed, trying to retreat, his face contorting with every known emotion. "I can't handle another rejection."

"You were the one who wanted to come," Kristoff said in exasperation, helping the others block his way. "Isn't it just like rejection if you never try? Be a man ... er ... be an ... Asgardian?"

Kvasir suddenly laughed. "This is why I like humans. Very wise words, friend."

He straightened his clothing and snapped his neck to the right and to the left, then strode out of the cave before he could change his mind.

The other three men exchanged eager looks. Then Hod spouted, "I gotta see this!"

He hit Kristoff and Loki both on the chest, then dashed out of the cave after Kvasir, with Kristoff and Loki right on his heels.

Kvasir stopped and called over his shoulder, "I would have come out a lot sooner had I known you were coming with me!"

"Where's the fun in that?" Loki said once they reached him.

Kvasir grinned and punched him good-naturedly, then continued down the long stretch of white sand. The farther they walked, the more confident Kvasir's steps became and the higher he held his head. Kristoff and Hod lagged behind Loki and Kvasir. They could see Sigyn clearly now, walking toward the beach house, which was still a good distance away. She suddenly stopped to look out to sea.

"Reveal us," Kvasir urged Loki quietly. "But keep Hod and Kristoff hidden. I don't want them to scare her."

"Shouldn't I stay hidden as well?" Loki suggested.

"No, she needs to see us both," Kvasir stated emphatically.

Loki gestured to Kristoff and Hod to show them what he was doing, warning them to be quiet, then manipulated the device to get the desired effect. The ring on Sigyn's finger immediately turned bright green, catching her eye. She whirled around as if she knew she was not alone, covering her mouth with her hands when she spotted Loki and Kvasir standing almost shoulder to shoulder about fifty feet away. She looked from Loki's grinning face to Kvasir's uncertain one, then gathered her skirts up in one hand and ran toward them.

"Steady," Kvasir warned Loki, who had already anticipated what was coming and stepped away from him slightly.

The word had barely faded in the air when she threw her arms around Kvasir, knocking him to the ground.

"You came for me!" she cried in Asgardian, covering his face with kisses while he laughed.

Then she scrambled to her feet, blushing furiously and biting her lip as she stared at the sand.

"Hello, Sigyn," Kvasir said softly as he stood up and brushed himself off. "It's been a long time."

Then they were both talking at once, their words jumbling over each other, as they tried not to interrupt but laughed because they could not help it.

Loki took several steps back, grinning wider than ever. It was terribly awkward but sweet. He walked back to where Hod and Kristoff had stopped. They were both rubbing their eyes.

"Sun's in my eyes," insisted Hod when Loki raised his eyebrow at him.

"I'm, uh ... you know ... allergies," Kristoff sniffed.

"To what? Sand?" Loki asked incredulously.

"It's just ..." Kristoff remarked, gesturing toward Kvasir and Sigyn.

They were walking together, arm in arm, deep in conversation. Every once in a while, Kvasir would throw his head back and laugh.

"Oh, so it's awkward when it's me, but you're tearing up like a little girl when it's him?" Loki scoffed indignantly.

"Look!" Hod cried, pointing.

Kvasir had fallen to his knees in the sand and seemed to be waiting for something. Sigyn's hands were frozen over her mouth as tears streamed down her face. All three men stopped breathing for half a second, then sighed in relief when she finally nodded, her formerly fearful face wreathed in smiles. Kvasir leaped to his feet, grinning from ear to ear. He picked her up and twirled her over his head. She stretched out her arms and tipped her head back as they spun in the sand. And just as Sigyn had told Loki, what seemed like ages ago, Kvasir did not drop her. He gently lowered her to her feet, then bent her backward to kiss her.

"Wow," Kristoff muttered. "I think we all know what that means."

"Yeah," agreed Hod. "Show's over."

"Shall we, gentlemen?" Loki suggested, waving for them to follow him as he picked his way through the sand toward the happy couple.

"Hello, Loki," Sigyn said shyly, wiping her eyes as she clutched Kvasir's arm.

"Hi, Sigyn," Loki replied, winking at her. "May I be the first to congratulate you both?"

"It's all because of you," she declared. "I can't thank you enough."

"Same here," Kvasir agreed, nodding at him with respect.

"You two need to catch me up on all of this," Sigyn implored. "You almost act like friends. Kvasir, did you really try to kill him?"

"He sure did," Hod answered for him as he and Kristoff joined them. "Three times!"

"Where is that voice coming from?" Sigyn asked, bewildered.

"Oh, right," Loki muttered, clicking the device button to reveal the other two men to Sigyn.

"Is that a Midgardian?" Sigyn gasped, switching suddenly to English.

Kristoff looked shocked, but Loki was not surprised. All Asgardians studied English for diplomacy, as it was a common tongue throughout the galaxy. And Sigyn was well-trained. She knew it was ill-mannered to speak Asgardian in front of a foreigner.

"What? Is it that obvious?" Kristoff asked Hod.

"Yeah, it's that obvious," Hod chuckled to Kristoff, then winked at Sigyn. "You're quite grown up, Sigyn. Good to see you again."

"You haven't changed a bit, Hod," Sigyn said, then turned to Kvasir. "Three times, Kvasir? Isn't that a bit excessive?"

"I've lived in darkness for centuries, Sigyn," Kvasir said seriously. "There's a lot I have to tell you."

"We'll get to that," she said, kissing his cheek. "All that matters is that we're together again."

"Yeah, it's awkward now," Kristoff grumbled, looking away.

"I'm out," announced Hod, pulling Kristoff with him. "We're going back to the cave. Don't be long. Heimdall may turn his gaze on us, and he can't know Kristoff is here."

Loki tossed Hod the device. "Better use this, just in case."

Hod and Kristoff vanished, surprising Sigyn again. "You do have a lot to tell me!" she exclaimed.

"Well, Kvasir, what's the new plan?" Loki asked, hands in his pockets. "Since you ruined the old one."

"May I tell him?" Sigyn asked Kvasir, who nodded. She bounced with excitement. "We're eloping on Midgard!"

"I gathered that. I guess it didn't take much to overcome your objections," Loki laughed.

"I'd be a fool to refuse him a third time," Sigyn asserted confidently. She paused and stroked Kvasir's cheek with one finger. "No, I was a fool the first two times."

Loki shuffled his feet, embarrassed by the show of intimacy. "Are you coming with us now?"

"No, not now," Sigyn giggled. "My parents are taking me to see your trials. We'll arrive at the palace the morning of your birthday. Kvasir says there is a direct connection to Norway there."

"Yes, there is," Loki confirmed, then addressed Kvasir. "Am I still sneaking her away from Asgard to meet you in Norway?"

Kvasir nodded. "If you're still willing. I don't want to interfere with your rite of passage. I know how important that is."

"I'll manage," Loki assured him. "This is just as important."

"Good, we're agreed then. I want to get everything ready for our new home together." Kvasir nuzzled Sigyn's nose with his, then kissed her again.

Loki kept his eyes on the sand, wishing he had followed Kristoff and Hod back to the cave.

"Loki?" Sigyn prodded softly. "Will you be alright?"

"He'll be fine, love," Kvasir answered, as if Loki were not standing there. "Apparently, he has a lover on Midgard."

"The Midgardian woman?" Sigyn gasped.

"First of all, she's not my lover, at least not the way the term is understood on Midgard," Loki corrected Kvasir. He was tired of explaining this. "We haven't—"

"I see," interrupted Kvasir, a wide grin on his face and a twinkle in his eye. "Who could refrain that had a heart to love, and in that heart courage to make 's love known."

"I'm not doing this again, Shakespeare," Loki groaned. "And you know very well that's the exact opposite—"

"Yes, Loki, I know," Kvasir interjected with another smirk. "And I respect you all the more for it."

"Why does he call you Shakespeare?" Sigyn asked Kvasir.

Kvasir chuckled, looking at her fondly. "It's a long story, one I greatly look forward to telling you." He drew her hands to his mouth and kissed them. "But for now, we must leave you here. 'Ever has it been that love knows not its own depth until the hour of separation.' Will you wait for me, sweet Sigyn?"

"It's only a little longer, Kvasir," she reminded him. "I've waited for almost a thousand years, though I did not know it until Loki showed me."

"Again, thank you," Kvasir said to Loki.

Then Kvasir hugged Sigyn one last time and followed Loki back the way they had come.

4

Kvasir walked backwards until he could no longer see Sigyn, then reluctantly faced forward. "My heart is full, my friend, fuller than I ever thought possible," he told Loki.

"Did you just call me 'friend'? Just a few days ago, you hated me," Loki challenged, a smirk playing about the corners of his mouth.

"I didn't hate you quite as much as I made out," Kvasir admitted. "Otherwise, I would have just killed you on Asgard. But then, I also loved Sigyn too much to cause her such grief."

"Instead, she endured a different grief," Loki pointed out. "As did you. I suppose your writings became an outlet for your suffering?"

Kvasir stared at the sand thoughtfully as they walked. "You know, when I wrote those stories about you, I never once considered you would someday read them."

"Then why taunt me with them when we fought in Belgium?"

"I was blind with rage that you weren't as worthy of her as I thought you were," Kvasir answered. "Of course, I was wrong about that too."

Loki stopped abruptly and grabbed Kvasir's arm. "That makes no sense! You turned me into a villain in prose, then claim you thought me worthy?"

Kvasir gripped both Loki's arms in return, though he kept his voice calm. "Your merits, what Sigyn loved and I believed I lacked, ate at me like a festering sore. As the jealousy in my soul grew, so did the darkness in my writing," Kvasir explained, abruptly letting Loki go. "But did you not notice I wrote nobility in you as well? In some of my stories, you tried to make up for your mistakes, even doing good. And not a few of the humans loved you for it."

"I suppose," Loki remarked, remembering what Carina had said about the Norse version of Loki the night he had met her.

"You know the stories about you didn't start with me, don't you?" Kvasir added. "There were oral traditions and different versions long before I penned anything."

"Where did the oral traditions come from?" Loki wondered aloud.

"Who knows," Kvasir answered. "Our people probably started the tales, and they changed with each telling. Even Odin's stories are told differently, depending on who tells them. And each storyteller portrays his as the correct version. It's human nature, I suppose."

"And you took advantage of that?" Loki asked, somewhat playfully but with a touch of rebuke.

"I did, indeed," Kvasir confessed. "Among other things I regret. Telling Sigyn everything will not be easy, especially in regard to my past lives."

"Well, don't regret your writings," Loki offered magnanimously. "They are treasured by several cultures. In a way, you gave them a gift."

"I appreciate that, Loki," Kvasir said, his gray eyes misting over slightly. "But I am sorry for the trouble I've caused you. And I'm grateful for what you've done for Sigyn and me. You have truly put an end to my misery, as I asked you to in Belgium. But I never thought it would be by reuniting me with the one I love more than my very life."

"You *are* a poet, Kvasir," Loki observed. "That reminds me, I don't think that quote back there was Shakespeare, though similar. Another of your identities?"

Kvasir laughed. "No, that was written by a human friend of mine, Kahlil Gibran, in a book of prose poetry fables he published last year. He lives in New York now, but I met him in Paris fifteen years ago when he studied art there. I'm not the only good writer on Midgard, you know."

"What's your identity now?" Loki asked curiously.

"I haven't had one since Edgar Allan Poe," Kvasir answered.

"Edgar Allan Poe? Surely not! I thought he was an American," Loki challenged. "And married."

"And I have been both, for a time. Anyway, all my former wives have died, and what friends I have now know me as Kiv."

"That's relatively close to your real name," Loki observed.

"Yes, well, I got tired of faking my death and coming up with a new identity. It got too complicated, what with changing my appearance and inventing a backstory for each life I lived," Kvasir explained.

"Just how did you manage changing your appearance anyway? Do you also manipulate light? And how do the other Asgardians hide that they don't age as humans do?"

Kvasir laughed. "What you do naturally, I figured out how to do scientifically. I've been selling appearance generators to

Asgardians and other immigrants to Midgard for hundreds of years. It's good business."

"And these Midgardian women you married, did they know who you really were?"

"Only a few of the earliest ones," Kvasir replied. "I am not proud of some of the deceptions I've spun."

"Well, I'm impressed," Loki asserted. "From what I've read, your last 'death' was quite the performance."

"It wasn't actually me," Kvasir admitted darkly, "but some poor soul who resembled my Poe identity somewhat and had been beaten and drugged to delirium. I am ashamed to say that when I saw the chap wandering the streets of Baltimore near an Irish pub, I saw an opportunity for escape and took it."

"You killed him?"

"Hardly!" Kvasir objected. "I changed my appearance to an unknown passerby and contacted a doctor I knew. Once we got the man to a hospital, I took the appearance of a nurse attending the doctor to keep an eye on things. I've been around long enough to know there was no saving him, though the attending physician tried. The man's brain was bleeding, and he had several internal injuries. The sensationalism of the day took it from there once he had died, but I might have helped it along."

"How?" Loki asked curiously.

"Oh, I had bribed the doctor quite handsomely. I even gave him an elaborate story to tell. He was quite willing to go along with it. He, at least, knew I was still alive, but he took the truth to his grave. I almost wonder if he convinced himself his memoir of my death really happened. I did enjoy reading it, as well as some of his later writings about me," Kvasir chuckled.

"Weren't you supposed to marry again?"

"She never could make up her mind," Kvasir scoffed. "And after my supposed death, she denied we were ever engaged, even though the wedding was supposed to be ten days later. By the time she died, I had relocated to Paris."

"Did you write that poem 'Annabel Lee' for her? The one they published after your supposed death?"

Kvasir snorted derisively. "She certainly thought so. But no, I was remembering Sigyn when I penned that."

"I should have known," Loki sighed. "Surely you know how you influenced literature as Poe? Even Jules Verne imitated you."

"Aye, but it was a difficult life, one that made me realize I couldn't do it again. And now, being relatively unknown and mysterious makes this all very convenient for me. I won't have to 'die' this time, just disappear. Sigyn and I may not even stay on Midgard for long."

He stopped suddenly, about twenty feet from the cave entrance, where Hod and Kristoff waited.

"I can only say that because of you," Kvasir said gratefully, placing his hand on Loki's shoulder. "Is there anything I can do for you in return? Perhaps help you win the heart of this woman you love?"

"She's already told me she loves me," Loki informed him.

"Then what's the problem?"

"I'm assuming Sigyn told you my rite of passage is almost upon me," Loki guessed.

"She did. I find it strange you didn't mention it before," Kvasir remarked. "But it's only three months. It's nothing."

"And after? You know I cannot bring her here." Loki half hoped his firm statement would end the conversation but could not help but wonder if Kvasir would know the answer to his dilemma since he had lived on Earth for so long.

"True," Kvasir pondered, stroking the trim beard on his chin. "Although you've already brought one Midgardian here."

"Only for a little while and hidden. To be with Carina, I would have to completely disappear to Midgard, something I cannot do."

"Why not? I see no conflict," Kvasir argued.

"How can you not?" Loki returned with frustration. "I am a prince of Asgard. Do you know what Odin would do to me if I abandoned my people?"

"You don't strike me as an Asgardian who lives by Odin's approval or even fears him. I thought Loki does what he wants," Kvasir taunted him.

Loki glowered at him. "Just what's that supposed to mean?"

"Do you serve the throne, or do you serve yourself?" Kvasir asked.

"That's unbelievably helpful, Kvasir," Loki spat sarcastically. "There's no easy way to answer that. Obviously, the noble play would be to take my place as Thor's stooge, serve the throne, as you say, and sacrifice what my heart desires, which I would otherwise pursue without hesitation if I only served myself."

Kvasir smirked. "Thor's stooge? I think now we're getting somewhere, O Undecided One."

"Don't toy with me!" Loki practically shouted. "You have no idea what I've lived under for centuries, how I've strived for approval, what I've put aside to be what they expect me to be. You just said you saw no conflict and even encouraged me to be with the one I love, all while pointing out how selfish that is. Do you think I haven't considered how it would break my parents' hearts if I did what I want and disappeared to marry a Midgardian? They've already lost one son that way!"

Loki had been talking furiously, his stride matching his torrent of words. When he realized Kvasir had drawn out his innermost thoughts, he stopped abruptly and faced his grinning, former enemy.

"Marry?" Kvasir snickered. "Who said anything about marriage? Although that is the most logical end to this. If you haven't touched her, you must be thinking that way."

"Great Odin's Raven!" Loki gasped. He had only hovered on the idea at the very edges of his subconscious. And it had slipped out of his mouth just as subconsciously. "Is that even a viable option for me? To marry a Midgardian, as you did?"

"I'm not the only one. Most of the exiled have entered into marriage with Midgardians," Kvasir informed him. "Baldur's done it more than any of us. He even has living children. Stronger genes, I assume. Mine have all died."

Loki felt a gnawing horror in his stomach. He had not even thought about what implications there could be for half-Asgardian, half-human children.

"I'm so sorry," he uttered sheepishly. He usually would not pry into someone's grief, but he had to know the answer to this new question burning in his mind. He stared at the ground in discomfort and stammered, "Was … was there something wrong with them?"

Oddly enough, Kvasir laughed. "No, of course not. The human bloodline weakens Asgardian life spans and immunities. Some of our children live regular human lives;

some longer. I had one daughter who lived for five hundred years. People thought she was a witch. I would rather not discuss that though."

Loki recognized a note of pain in Kvasir's tone. Though curiosity welled up in him, he squelched it.

"Anyway, it sounds to me like you know what you want but are loath to claim it," Kvasir observed. "You will have to make a choice. I think you know that. Didn't you say something like that to Sigyn?"

"I did. And yes, I know. But there's another problem," Loki pointed out painfully. "The woman I love doesn't know who I really am."

He heard Kristoff shout from the cave, "You have to tell her!"

Loki frowned. Apparently, Hod had been eavesdropping and filling Kristoff in on the conversation.

"Kristoff is right. Telling her the truth is your first hurdle to overcome. Relationships without trust are absolutely miserable. I should know," Kvasir informed him. "When you have that taken care of, we'll go from there."

"I'm not sure I need your help," Loki grumbled as they entered the cave.

"You do," Hod informed him with glee as he and Kristoff reappeared. "Absolutely and without question, you do."

Loki faced the three men grinning at him. "I'll think about it," he offered, more to shut them up than anything. "Can we get back to Midgard now?"

When Hod handed him the device, Loki cloaked them all, in case any soldiers had entered the bunker while they were gone. The strong pull was over quickly. The foursome hurried through the dark tunnels and out the hidden door of the empty bunker, where Baldur stood gazing at the few visible stars.

"How'd it go?" he asked with a huge grin when he saw Kvasir's elated expression.

"As expected," Loki answered.

"She's agreed to marry me. Loki will sneak her away from Asgard during his trials, and they'll meet me in Norway," Kvasir added.

"Trials?" Kristoff asked.

Baldur looked solemnly at Loki. "Are you really old enough for the rite of passage already?"

Loki nodded, smirking slightly. "You forgot my birthday, big brother?"

Baldur grinned good-naturedly. "No, just how old you are. I'm surprised you didn't mention it the other night."

"Why would he?" Hod remarked. "It wasn't relevant to our first plan. If we'd stuck with keeping it gradual, Loki would have completed his rite of passage. But Romeo here just had to come tonight and speed things along."

Kvasir grinned. "You have to admit this is a better plan."

"Fair enough," Baldur replied. "But this complicates things for Loki. What if he's caught?"

Loki shrugged. "I'll be fine."

"What are you guys talking about?" Kristoff interjected.

"I'll explain later," Loki told him. Turning to Kvasir, he asked, "Do you know where the other portal is?"

"Yes. I'm leaving for Norway first thing in the morning," Kvasir confirmed. "There's so much to do!"

Loki grinned to himself. At least he would not have to worry about Kvasir's meddling.

Then Kvasir stuck his forefinger in Loki's face. "The next time I see you," he admonished, "I expect to hear you've told her who you are."

Kristoff and Hod nodded condescendingly at Loki in agreement.

"She doesn't know who you are?" Baldur exclaimed, shaking his head in dismay. "Little brother!"

"Alright, I'll take care of it!" Loki snapped.

Kristoff whistled slowly at Loki's outburst, while the other men simply smirked at him.

"See that you do," Kvasir grunted.

"I said I would," Loki grumbled childishly.

"Now then, can all of you make it up to Norway for the wedding?" Kvasir included them all in this request. "Baldur, you'll do the ceremony?"

"Why don't Hod and I go with you to Norway, and we'll work it all out there?" Baldur responded.

"Would you?" Kvasir asked eagerly. "I could really use the help!"

"Let's call it a night for now," Baldur suggested. "Loki ... we'll see you on the other side."

"What about me?" Kristoff grumbled as the three Asgardians ambled off, leaving him and Loki alone under the tower.

"I was hoping you might bring Carina up for the wedding since I'll be on Asgard," Loki informed him. "But for now, don't you have a short London tour to plan?"

"I almost forgot," Kristoff groaned. "I really need some sleep."

Loki laughed. "You and me both, old boy."

As they hurried back to the hotel, Loki remarked, "I never asked how your date with Kathleen Jones went."

"You mean my business meeting? It was hardly a date," Kristoff protested.

Loki snickered. Carina had been right. He raised an eyebrow at his human friend.

Kristoff sighed. "I wish it had been a date. She's incredible, Luke. Smart, gorgeous, driven. I can't wait to see her again."

"Are we going to be planning your wedding next?" Loki teased him.

"Let's not rush things, eh?" Kristoff retorted, a panicked look on his face. "But what about you? Aren't you a little worried about jumping into things with Carina after she just broke up with Klaus?"

"Of course I am!" Loki snapped. Then his voice softened. "But you were right. I love her. And she loves me."

"I thought so!" A self-satisfied grin spread over Kristoff's face. "I'm not supposed to tell you this, but she came to me after you left Germany."

"She told me," Loki admitted.

"Oh, did she? Well, before I left, I actually suggested Paris as a tour possibility to Klaus. I might have even made a few calls to help things along."

"Kristoff, I'm shocked," Loki chuckled. "What about the lecture you gave me, once you got to Paris, about getting myself in deeper?"

Kristoff snorted. "Haven't you ever heard of drawing out a confession?"

"You Midgardians are far more devious and manipulative than I ever gave you credit," Loki said with admiration. "Did you know Carina gave her father the idea for me to perform because she had a crush on me and wanted to meet me?"

Kristoff burst out laughing, but sobered quickly. "May I give you a piece of advice?"

"You're going to give it to me whether I want it or not, aren't you?"

"Naturally," Kristoff grinned. "Tell her who you are as soon as we're done in London. Then be patient with her. She might need some time to think about everything. She has a lot more at stake than I did when you told me."

"Worried how my big reveal might affect the London show?" Loki challenged him, hitting him playfully.

"Alright, fine, yes," Kristoff muttered. "But that doesn't change what I said. And don't do it all big and scary like you did with me either. You have to be gentle with women."

"You didn't exactly believe me until I did that," Loki reminded him as they walked through the hotel lobby and got onto the lift.

"True," Kristoff acknowledged. He drew a deep breath, then smacked Loki hard on the back as the lift doors opened. "You'll figure it out, buddy. I have faith in you."

Loki paused as they neared Carina's door, then forced himself to keep walking to his shared room with Kristoff. He would see her soon enough.

As both men settled into sleep, Loki abruptly disturbed the stillness. "Kristoff! I almost forgot something important."

"What?" he answered sleepily.

"After we're done in London, I have to go back to Asgard for a while."

"Of course," Kristoff replied. "How else will you get Sigyn?"

"No, I mean after the wedding. I have to return right away for my rite of passage."

"Oh yeah, Baldur mentioned that," Kristoff muttered, stifling a yawn. "I'm guessing that's some sort of becoming-a-man thing on Asgard."

"Yes," Loki acknowledged. "I've been fully grown for hundreds of years, but this makes it final and legal. Then I can travel the Nine Realms without sneaking around, fight in battle, and maybe finally be taken seriously as a prince."

"That's great, buddy," Kristoff mumbled, clearly trying to stay awake. "How long will you be gone?"

"About a week for the first time, then for three months," Loki answered.

"Three months!" Kristoff yelped. His linens rustled, and the bed creaked slightly as if he had bolted upright. "Are you crazy? Klaus could do an insane amount of damage in that time frame. You're planning to just leave me here to deal with it on my own? What about Carina? What about touring?"

"What else can I do?" Loki spouted, linking his hands behind his head as he stared at the ceiling. "The rite of passage is a sacred requirement of all Asgardian men. It's not like I can just skip it."

"Are you sure about that?" Kristoff asked slyly.

"Don't even go there, Kristoff," Loki warned him, leaning on one elbow as he peered at his friend in the dark. "It's one of the most significant times of my life. We're talking about honor and glory. Don't you understand that?"

"Are you trying to persuade me or yourself?" Kristoff pressed him, settling back into his bed.

"There's nothing more to say. I'm doing it," Loki spat with finality, flipping onto his back again. "And don't tell any other humans either, especially Carina. I'll make up some excuse for my absence."

"You said you were going to tell her who you are," Kristoff challenged. "When I said give her time, I didn't mean abandon her for three months."

"I'll figure something out," Loki growled.

"The other Asgardians already know all about this rite of passage, don't they?"

"Yes," Loki said cautiously.

"Maybe I'll have a talk with them," Kristoff mumbled.

"What are you up to?" Loki asked suspiciously.

But Kristoff was already snoring, leaving Loki awake with his frustrations as an idea played in the back of his mind.

Does Kristoff have a point? he asked himself. *What would happen if I spent my rite of passage on Midgard?*

No other Asgardian had ever done that, to his knowledge. If he laid his plans carefully, no one on Asgard need ever know. The tremendous risk gave him a thrill that almost choked him as he began to talk himself into it. Asgardian law forbade anyone to track him during the allotted time period, including Heimdall. Nor was anyone permitted to ask him about his experience when it was all over, not even the king or queen. All of Asgard would judge the success of the endeavor by how he had changed. The trials would only last several days. If he came back to Midgard immediately after, he could learn far more than he would in the solitary Asgardian forest. He would still emerge a man. He would still have plenty of time for reflection. He felt his eyes flare with mischief at the thought of fooling everyone.

Yes, I'll do it! Loki thought, his exhilaration ebbing as sleep took him. *Just to prove I can.*

A cool, soft hand stroked his hair. Loki opened his eyes to see Paris sunlight streaming into the room and Carina's beautiful brown eyes inches from his face. She sat on the floor beside his bed, her chin resting on the mattress.

"Good morning," she murmured.

"Hi!" he answered, surprised by her presence. "Where did you come from?"

"Kristoff let me in," she explained, standing up. "He went to get coffee. Kathleen Jones should arrive soon."

"What time is it?"

"Almost noon, Sleeping Beauty."

"Did anyone go to the theater this morning?"

"No, Kristoff called the manager and told him we would have to wait for the new contract until after London."

"Because of me?"

"No, he said it was a negotiating tactic. They'll pay more once our new act gains popularity or something."

Loki grimaced to himself, knowing it really was because of him.

"Kristoff says you finished whatever business you had early, then went back to bed," Carina continued.

Loki nodded. He sat up, then yawned and stretched slightly. "I didn't even hear you knock."

"You were practically comatose," she teased him. "I'm just relieved you don't snore."

Loki growled playfully and threw one of his pillows at her, which she easily caught, then used to pummel him. He grabbed the other one to defend himself against her onslaught. They were both laughing so hard, they did not hear the door open.

"That's it!" Kristoff blurted with a scowl. "You're getting your own room in London, pal." He set two cups of coffee down on one of the dressers, then walked into the bathroom grumbling to himself, "Pillow fights? Good grief! How old are we?"

That only set them off laughing again, but they tossed the pillows aside.

Carina sat gingerly on the end of Loki's bed while he slipped on his robe. He was thankful he had started sleeping in Midgardian clothing, keeping his battle gear tucked away in his luggage at night. If she had seen him in his Asgardian attire, there would be no end to the questions, but he was still a little embarrassed about his silk pajamas.

It could be worse, he silently told his reflection in the large mirror over the dresser. *You could have slept in nothing at all.*

Out loud, he said, "Carina, look what you did to my hair."

It stood up all over his head in black tufts.

"I like it like that," she asserted.

He felt even more embarrassed and kicked at the leg of the bed. "It's not fair for you to see me like this while you look like perfection."

"Nonsense, I think you look adorable." She patted the spot next to her on the bed. "I'll fix it for you, if you want."

Loki's eyes widened, and he gulped. If she knew the thoughts stirring in his mind … *Stop it, Loki*, he rebuked himself.

Kristoff walked out of the bathroom right at that moment.

"Where's Kathleen?" Carina asked him.

"Downstairs, which is where I'm headed," Kristoff answered. "I just brought your coffee up." He looked Loki over disdainfully. "Luke, you'd better get yourself cleaned up. You look awful."

Loki glared at him, then raised his eyebrows at Carina, who was stifling a laugh as she stood.

"I'll go down with you," she said to Kristoff. Then she kissed Loki on the cheek and whispered, "I still think you're adorable, but I guess you're on your own."

When Loki joined them in the lobby less than ten minutes later, having rushed to pull his look together, Carina took his arm.

"Are you two a couple as well as a performing pair?" Kathleen asked in that bold, American way of hers.

Loki and Carina glanced at each other with uncertainty, waiting for the other to answer first.

Kristoff rolled his eyes, then opened his mouth to speak.

"You could say that," Loki spoke first, as whatever words Kristoff had been about to say died in his throat. "But only since yesterday. And we would like to keep that private for now."

Carina nodded her agreement, smiling gratefully at Loki.

"That's a shame," Kathleen sighed. "It would have made my piece far more interesting. I should point out that people will notice before long. Considering Miss Green just ended her engagement to Mr. Mayar, tongues are bound to wag."

"She has a point," Kristoff said, rubbing his chin thoughtfully. "It might be smarter to address it head-on and leave no room for gossip. The tale of your little barroom brawl is already making its way around Paris, though it wasn't big enough to make the papers."

Seeing the alarm on Carina's face as she no doubt imagined her father reading a discussion of her personal life, Loki spoke up again. "That may be true, but at least it won't be in print for the world to read. Let's leave the personal discussion out of it, please."

"Very well," Kathleen sighed. "I despise yellow journalism, so I will respect your privacy. If word gets out, it won't be because of me."

And true to her word, Kathleen rarely deviated from professional and business matters throughout the interview, with just a few questions about their impressions of Paris or their opinions on performing.

After lunch, Kristoff led the way to the theater, talking with great animation to Kathleen, who strode independently beside him but ducked her head toward him as they talked. Carina and Loki stayed a few paces behind them.

"Carina, are you afraid of your father?" Loki asked.

"A little," she answered. "I love him, and I respect him, but some of the people he does business with have turned him into something he never used to be."

"I hope you never feel that way about me," Loki said quietly.

"Then never give me a reason," she answered just as quietly.

They walked in silence for a little while before Loki spoke again. "What do you think he'll do when Klaus reaches him and tells him his twisted tale of woe?"

Carina shuddered. "I think he might talk to you, but if it doesn't go his way ..."

"I can handle myself, and I can handle him," Loki assured her. "I'm worried about you, especially regarding Klaus."

"I have the beautiful dagger you gave me, though a few more lessons wouldn't hurt," she said playfully. "But won't I have you?"

Remembering his decision to return to Midgard for his rite of passage, he smiled down at her and kissed her very lightly on the tip of her nose. "Yes, you'll have me."

"That wasn't very professional, Mr. Black," she teased him. "I'll have to ask you to keep all displays of affection to more private surroundings than the street."

"What did you have in mind, Miss Green?" Loki murmured, deepening his voice flirtatiously.

Carina blushed, then answered seriously, "Luke, until this thing with Klaus and my father blows over, Kathleen is right. We have to be careful and guard our reputations. I know you'll treat me as a gentleman does a lady. You always do. But we need to be strictly professional in public."

"And when we're alone?" Loki asked hesitantly.

"After last night, I know you'll be a gentleman even when we're alone. But it's probably best we don't put ourselves in a compromising situation again."

Loki sighed. He knew she was right. If he had stopped things sooner, perhaps she would not have felt the need to address it.

"Did I push it too far last night?" he asked nervously.

"Oh no, Luke," she insisted, holding his arm tightly as she stared up at him. "Quite the opposite. I'm the one who got carried away."

"It wasn't just you. And I loved every second of it," he sighed so softly, he was not sure if she even heard.

But then she answered silkily, "And that's why it meant so much when you chose to leave. Putting aside your own interests showed your love more than words and kisses."

"I'm glad," he said simply, not sure how to respond and relieved when they arrived at the theater.

The conversation had been decidedly uncomfortable, but at least they understood one another. He poured everything he felt for her into the songs they sang together for their final performance in Paris. The crowd was even louder than it had been the night before, chanting for another encore. But Kristoff addressed the audience this time, encouraging them all to see Lukas Black and the Shooting Star in London or when they returned to Paris. There were groans and cheers, as Kristoff walked off stage, throwing a last wave at the still-thundering crowd. Finally, it was all over.

Waiting for Carina outside her dressing room, Loki pondered all that had happened and how he would get back to Asgard once they were in London. Would he have to return to Paris? He dared not risk the amount of dark magic required to reopen his original point of entry in Montparnasse, which had long since faded. The Eiffel Tower Bifröst connection was an equally dangerous option, given its location. Suddenly, he remembered the Asgardian underground club. Surely someone there would know about any portals in London.

The door to Carina's dressing room opened, pulling Loki from his thoughts. She stood in the doorway, looking back.

"There are a lot of memories here," she commented. "I feel a little sad to leave it behind."

"Cheer up, my star," Loki said softly, daring to kiss her cheek since no one was around. "We'll make more memories."

"Oh, I like that," Carina answered shyly.

"Which part? The kiss? The thought of making more memories with me?" Loki guessed. "Or perhaps just my good looks?"

"No, silly. Well ... actually, yes ... to all of the above. But I meant I like the nickname you just gave me," she snickered. "I think you deserve more than just a kiss on the cheek for that."

"What about what you said earlier?" Loki reminded her, though his pulse had already quickened.

Without answering, she pulled him into her dressing room, wrapped her arms around him, and kissed him soundly.

When she released him, he fell against the wall dramatically. "Not fair, Carina! Now it's my turn."

"No, just one is all we should risk," she laughed, grabbing his hand and pulling him down the hall before he could kiss her again. No one had seen them. "Come on! I'm sure Kristoff and Kathleen are waiting for us."

"Kristoff *and* Kathleen?" Loki repeated in confusion. "Why would she be waiting for us? The interview is over."

"Didn't you hear Kristoff invite her to join us after the show?"

"I only heard him ask her to find him after the show," Loki admitted. "That's why he didn't meet us back here."

"Oh, well, she's coming to dinner with us," Carina informed him. "I don't know how you missed it."

"Me either. Maybe I was daydreaming about you," he teased. When she blushed, he continued, "I'm surprised you agreed to that. Aren't you worried about what she'll write?"

"She seems honest enough," Carina said. "It should be fun."

"If you're not worried, then neither am I," Loki declared. He winked as he playfully asked, "Where are we dining tonight, fair lady?"

"The same place Kristoff took Kathleen last night," Carina answered. "He couldn't say enough about it when we were waiting for you this morning. It's called Les Deux Magots. A lot of artists eat there."

"If he liked it so much, why didn't we go there for lunch?"

"He suggested it, but Kathleen said it would be too busy," Carina replied. "Tonight, it's perfect."

As they entered the lobby, Loki spotted the two of them quickly. He noted how eagerly Kristoff spoke with Kathleen as they waited. And she seemed just as interested in what he was saying. They only stopped their discussion long enough to greet the two performers, continuing to talk for the entire taxi ride to the restaurant. Loki hardly minded since he tuned them out to talk with Carina.

When they arrived, the bright lights over the awning of Les Deux Magots twinkled with an inviting warmth that promised a charming evening. Loki caught a glimpse of two regal statues and elegant decor inside the packed café just as the foursome decided to dine outside.

Loki ordered grilled salmon. Everyone else opted for duck, which was served with tiny potatoes. After they had eaten, they all strolled north to the bank of the Seine and enjoyed the clear night air for a bit.

They had not lingered long when Kathleen reluctantly stated, "I suppose I'd better head back to my hotel. I have an early day tomorrow."

"We'll take you," Kristoff offered.

"Don't be silly," she laughed. "Our hotels aren't anywhere close to each other. Besides, you mentioned you're all taking the earliest available train to Calais, so you have to be up before I do."

"At least let me hail you a taxi," Kristoff countered. When she nodded, he flagged one down and offered his hand to help her get into the vehicle.

Loki and Carina stayed back a few paces, too far to hear their final goodbye. But as the three of them headed back to their own hotel, Kristoff stared moodily out the taxi window.

Carina nudged Loki. "He seems sad," she whispered, gesturing to Kristoff.

"Mm-hmm," Loki acknowledged. "Don't worry, I'll cheer him up."

"How?"

"I can hear you," Kristoff interjected crabbily.

"Hey, remember that place the other night?" Loki asked him cheerfully. "Where you got so zozzled, you don't even remember how we got back?"

"Neither do you!" Kristoff retorted.

Carina shifted uncomfortably.

"Well, I remembered I left something there. I'm going to have to go back to get it," Loki replied. "Want to go with me?"

Carina narrowed her eyes and stared straight ahead, clearly irritated. "What about me?"

"We'll drop you off at the hotel first. It's no place for a lady," Loki informed her.

"Then it's no place for you either," she huffed.

Kristoff grinned wickedly at Loki. "I saw at least one other woman there that night. I'm sure she would be fine if we all go together."

"Kristoff!" he whispered through clenched teeth.

"Do you not want me to go? Are you hiding something?" Carina demanded.

"Not at all," Loki assured her. "It's just a rough way down, and it's a little weird."

"Down?"

"It's in the catacombs," Kristoff informed her, obviously cheering up.

"The catacombs?" she said excitedly. "Now you have to take me!"

"We do?" Loki asked innocently, glaring at Kristoff. What was he doing? He had told Loki himself to wait until the last night in London to reveal his identity.

"We do," Kristoff confirmed, desperately trying not to burst out laughing at the look on Loki's face. "There's something you need to know though, Carina."

"What's that?" she said excitedly, as Loki instructed the taxi driver to change their destination.

"Everyone there is so obsessed with Norse mythology, they all call each other Norse names," Kristoff said.

"Like I said," Loki added, "a little weird." He was relieved Kristoff was not just trying to push him into revealing his secret.

"I think I'm going to like this place!" Carina announced. "What do they call you, Kristoff?"

"I've only been there once," he admitted. "And I was passed out most of the time. I didn't get a nickname."

"What about you, Luke?" Carina asked.

Loki cleared his throat, brought his fist to his mouth, and coughed, "Loki."

"Loki?" Carina laughed. "Then I shall be Sigyn."

Without thinking, Kristoff blurted out, "You look nothing like Sigyn!"

He immediately winced as he realized what he had just said.

Loki threw daggers at Kristoff with his eyes, but Carina did not notice.

"Why? Because people tend to think of her as a blonde?" she asked innocently. "I've seen artwork portraying her as a redhead. And Sigyn was Loki's wife, so I want to be Sigyn."

"Actually, that relationship was grossly exaggerated," Loki corrected her. "They were never married."

"But that ruins their whole love story!"

"Maybe they didn't have a love story and were just good friends," Loki suggested.

"No, the legends say they were in love, but Loki had multiple affairs. Even so, she was the picture of faithfulness and loved him to the end," insisted Carina.

Loki felt sick to his stomach. Would Kvasir's writings always haunt him?

"You have a point, Carina," Kristoff interjected. "Quite frankly, he didn't deserve her."

"Don't you ever shut up?" Loki snarled at him.

Kristoff buried his mouth in his sleeve to hide his laughter and stared out the window.

Carina stared incredulously at Loki. "He's right!" she exclaimed. "I wouldn't have tolerated his shenanigans. I would have left him or even killed him."

Kristoff made a wheezing sound, clearly enjoying the little exchange too much.

"You're making me feel like a villain," Loki grumbled. "I'm nothing like that."

"No one said you were," Carina said soothingly as she leaned against him. "If I play Sigyn and you play Loki tonight, we'll just know you are the better, more honorable Loki, the one you grew up reading about. And then, I won't have to kill you."

Kristoff snickered.

"Kristoff, have you had too much to drink?" Loki demanded, decidedly irritated by the whole conversation.

"No," he choked, trying to hide his laughter. "I just find this whole thing hilarious. You would too, if you were me."

"That's probably true," Loki admitted, chuckling a little himself.

He relaxed and enjoyed Carina's warmth against him, though he resisted putting his arm around her.

The taxi dropped them off at a nondescript nightclub Loki remembered passing when Baldur and Hod had taken them to the catacombs to confront Kvasir. Since entering the underground labyrinth was dangerous, those who did so regularly did everything in their power to ensure the entrances were not easy to find. Even Kristoff looked lost after the taxi peeled away, though he had been there once. Loki had an impeccable memory, however, and led them straight to the gaping black doorway of the secret entrance they had used last time. Recent rain had left pools of murky water oozing down the old stone stairs. Loki would have rather used his talent for light manipulation to illuminate their way, but since Carina was with them, he settled for Kristoff's electric torch. When they reached the bottom, the flickering beam revealed fresh, muddy footprints. They soon overtook two men in hiking gear.

"Where are you headed, friends?" asked the older of the two, a pleasant-faced man with gray hair.

"I would guess a party," quipped the younger one, his honest brown eyes alight with interest. "Be careful not to mess up those fancy clothes down here."

"We aren't going far," Loki replied, his tone guarded but friendly. "What about you?"

"Just exploring the mines," the older man answered with a warm smile. "We don't run into too many people down here."

Loki wanted to ask what he meant by the mines, but he feared his lack of knowledge might betray them.

"You think you packed enough gear?" Kristoff joked, eyeing the large traveling packs both men bore.

"I sure hope so," the younger fellow jested back. "It's a long way back from where we're going."

The two men waved cheerfully, bid them to enjoy their time in the catacombs, and turned down a side corridor.

"Where are these mines?" Loki asked Kristoff.

"You're in them," Carina answered for him.

Kristoff shook his head and grinned, as if he knew a torrent of information was about to pour out of her mouth.

"The old mines date way back. They include the catacombs but extend beyond them," she informed Loki, gesturing the way the men had gone. "Some people call the whole thing the catacombs. But it's not really accurate."

"What did they mine?" Loki inquired. He had been fascinated by mining as a boy, but he had never shared that with anyone.

"Paris stone and gypsum," Kristoff answered.

"Lutetian limestone is the proper name of Paris stone," Carina corrected. Kristoff just snorted as she continued, "Much of Paris was built with it. And gypsum has many uses."

She elaborated on a few, impressing Loki with her knowledge. As the trio made their way through the final corridor of bones and skulls, Loki was further delighted by Carina's toughness and her fascination with the whole endeavor.

Once they reached the hidden door of the Asgardian underground club, unyielding eyes peered at them through the opening.

"Loki," the Asgardian bouncer, Tyr, acknowledged. Then he nodded at Kristoff. "Loki's human. Sorry, can't recall your name."

"Kristoff," Loki reminded him.

"Right. Who's the human girl? She can't come in here."

"She's one of my humans," Loki responded, winking and shaking his head slightly at Carina, who had raised an eyebrow at the questioning.

"Hmm," Tyr muttered, pondering this. "I don't know. Baldur and Hod aren't here to vouch for you."

"I've come for something I left behind the last time," Loki said. He gestured emphatically toward Carina. "You can't expect me to leave the lady out here."

"Tell me what it is, and I'll fetch it for you."

Loki sighed. "It's information. Private information. Something I should have asked the last time I was here."

"Like what?" Tyr growled.

"Look, Tyr," Kristoff interjected, "if you're so worried about a harmless girl, Loki can just go in alone, and I'll stay out here with her."

Loki resisted the urge to snort at how thickly Kristoff laid on the guilt. He pasted a downcast expression on his own face. Now that they were actually there, he did not want Carina left outside, even with Kristoff.

As if on cue, Carina smiled demurely at Tyr and blinked innocently. "Come now, gentlemen, this fine doorman is just doing his job. I wouldn't want him to bend the rules on my account."

"Is she a friendly, like Kristoff and Joyce? Does she know?" Tyr asked tentatively, as if he was close to changing his mind.

"Yes, yes, she does," Loki lied.

The door swung open. Tyr grinned at them. "I guess it's okay since you're with Baldur's little brother."

Carina's mouth dropped as she stepped into the room and saw the huge bulk of the massive Tyr, as well as the strange people and surroundings. "Baldur's little brother?" she whispered to Loki. "Do these people make up their own stories?"

Loki laughed nervously. Before he could answer, Freya appeared and wrapped her arms around Carina. "Finally, another woman! But you're not Asgardian, are you?"

"I'm supposed to be Sigyn," Carina said with uncertainty. She looked down at her clothes. "I didn't dress the part. I didn't know Luke would be bringing me here tonight."

"Who's Luke?" Freya asked sweetly.

"She means me, Lady Freya," Loki interjected. "It's my human name. She just knows that one better."

"Of course," Freya said with a nod, then looked around. "And what's this about Sigyn? Is she here? I haven't seen her since she was a baby."

"She's just pretending to be Sigyn."

"Well, please, just be yourself," Freya chirped. "You don't have to pretend to be an Asgardian to be welcome here. I'm Freya. That's my twin brother, Frey, over there."

Frey waved and shouted, "How's your mom, Loki?"

Loki chafed inwardly at Frey's familiar tone. He did not care to be reminded that the Asgardian had courted his mother so many years ago. But Frey was the most likely to have the information he needed.

Stuffing his consternation down, Loki suddenly realized Kristoff had spotted James Joyce and crossed to the other end of the room. They were already deep in conversation, leaving Loki with a dilemma. He could not risk Carina overhearing what he needed to discuss with Frey.

"Freya, I need to speak privately with your brother on a business matter. Would you keep an eye on my human?" Loki asked nonchalantly, hoping Freya would catch the subtle hint not to discuss nonhuman matters with Carina.

"Wait a moment, Loki." Freya stopped him with one perfectly manicured hand on his arm. "Isn't this the Shooting Star?" Then she spoke to Carina before Loki could answer. "Of course, I knew I recognized you. You sing divinely! Won't you sing us something?"

"She doesn't do free concerts," Loki said hurriedly, pulling her with him, away from Freya.

"Don't be absurd, Luke," Carina whispered. "They were kind enough to let me in here. It's the least I can do."

Then, to Loki's shock, she climbed up on one of the sturdy tables, skirt and all. She began to sing something he deduced was an Irish bar song once James Joyce joined her in singing from across the room. Kristoff jumped in on the chorus just as someone began pounding the accompanying notes on an old upright piano that had seen better days.

The Asgardian audience hooted, cheered, and clapped as Carina twirled around and kicked up her heels. How she managed all of those moves in her dress, Loki could not fathom. He reluctantly tore his fascinated gaze away, remembering why he had come. He pulled Frey aside and got the information he needed about the London connection to Asgard just as Carina came down hard on the table, almost in a split, arms outstretched. She quickly bounced back to a standing position and bowed for the clapping Asgardians. Loki hurried to help her come down from the table, but she leaped over his outstretched hand and landed perfectly on the floor, prompting another round of cheers and hoots.

"I've never seen you do anything like that," Loki praised Carina as Kristoff and James Joyce joined them.

"And that was without a single drop of liquor," she bragged. "I don't need to get drunk to have fun."

"Teach us your ways, O Sage," Kristoff quipped sarcastically, eliciting a round of laughter. "By the way, Carina, this is James Joyce. I believe you've heard of him."

"Oh yes," she gushed, her eyes shining. "I absolutely loved your short stories in *Dubliners*!"

"Ah, and have you read *Ulysses* yet?" Joyce asked.

"Not yet," Carina admitted. "But I have seen your play and read your novel *A Portrait of the Artist as a Young Man*."

"What did you think of it?" Joyce asked.

"I can't help but wonder if the protagonist was really you."

Instead of answering, James Joyce turned to Loki. "Keep this one. She has the voice of a siren, the face of an angel, and the mind of a scholar."

Loki beamed at Carina, who blushed and curtsied. Kristoff rolled his eyes but grinned.

Joyce turned back to Carina and handed her his calling card. "Stop by my home before you leave for London tomorrow, and I'll give you a copy of *Ulysses*. As for tonight, it's high time I returned to the wife."

"Did you finally marry Nora, you renegade?" asked Freya, who had been eavesdropping.

"It's only a matter of time," Joyce harrumphed. Then he tipped his hat and left.

"Your human is welcome here any time," Tyr exclaimed, shaking Loki's hand vigorously as they prepared to leave. "Bring her back, Loki, you hear?"

Loki dipped his head in acknowledgment as Carina stifled a delighted laugh. As they ran back through the catacombs to catch another taxi, even Kristoff was in high spirits.

By the time they reached the hotel, Carina was fast asleep on Loki's shoulder, her hand locked in his. He gently pulled her out of the cab, then carried her all the way up to her room while Kristoff managed the lift and all the doors.

"I wonder if I'll ever find love like that," Kristoff said wistfully, obviously touched but a little envious.

"What about Kathleen?" Loki grunted.

"I don't even know if she likes me," Kristoff said with a shrug.

"Oh, please," Loki scoffed. "She didn't ask us to call her Kat. Just you."

"I doubt she'd mind if you did," Kristoff remarked. "Probably just an oversight."

"You're missing the point," Loki insisted.

"Well, she did ask me to stay in touch. But that could just be for business. Besides, she's American. I'm Norwegian."

"Why would that matter? You're a world traveler. So is she," Loki scoffed. "At least you're both human."

"Right, sorry, old boy. She's human, and you're not." Kristoff gestured toward Carina as Loki lowered her into her bed and pulled the blankets over her. "What are you going to do?"

Loki looked down in wonder at her as she slept. "I have to find a way," he said softly. "But if we bend too far, I'm afraid we'll break."

Loki gazed across the English Channel as the ferry plowed through the salty water. He was enjoying this trip even more than the first one. Carina had been immersed in her new book at first. But when Loki teased her that she might not even notice if she were swept overboard, she laughed and joined him at the rail, admiring everything she saw.

As the ferry approached the White Cliffs of Dover, Carina pointed toward the plains. "Your ancestors might have fought mine right over there."

"I rather doubt that," Loki said with irony.

"What do you mean?"

Loki immediately realized he had walked into a quandary. He was supposed to be Icelandic, with Viking blood flowing through his veins.

"You never mentioned you had any British heritage," he said quickly. "How could your ancestors fight mine?"

"Some of my ancestors were Anglo-Saxons, whom the British also descended from," Carina clarified. She looked at him inquisitively. "Didn't you know that?"

"I wasn't thinking quite that far back," Loki chuckled. "Besides, your father has Scandinavian roots, if I recall correctly. So that means your ancestors fought each other." He paused as a delightful thought occurred to him. "Is that why you're both so ornery?"

"Maybe," she laughed, then grew serious. "I've never been to London."

"Never?"

"Father has several times, but he always left me in New York or Stuttgart. I wonder if it's anything like I imagined."

"You'll like it," Loki encouraged her.

"As good as that book is, I'm so glad you didn't let me miss this," she exclaimed, leaning her head back against him slightly, taking care not to appear too intimate. "That reminds me … last night was fun, especially pretending you were Loki."

"What if it hadn't been pretend?" Loki asked cautiously.

She straightened up and looked at him with a strange expression on her face. "Are you teasing me again? Like you said last night, you're nothing like Loki."

"Not the villainous version, certainly," he muttered.

"You sure don't look like him," she teased him. "Especially not the Loki in my newest book. He's quite frightening, but you're …"

"Better looking, I hope?"

"Devastatingly so," she said very quietly.

Loki chuckled shyly, looking out across the channel the way they had come as the ferry glided into the harbor. "I don't know why they drew him that way. Most of the stories describe him as handsome, even beautiful. Kristoff told me once you're practically in love with him."

"I am not in love with Loki!" she sputtered indignantly, instantly drawing his gaze. "Fascination is not the same as love. Besides, you can't love someone who isn't real."

Loki winced as her words sliced through him. Though he knew she was referring to a character and not really to him, doubt crowded his thoughts as thickly as the people who were waiting to disembark. He looked out to sea again to hide his consternation. She said something, but he did not register her words. When he turned his attention back to her, he realized he was alone at the rail. With a start, he pushed his way through the people swarming around him and unsuccessfully tried to spot her. An irrational panic came over him, and he understood why Kvasir had faltered in the cave. What if she only loved him as Lukas Black and rejected him as he truly was, the real Loki? The fear of loss squeezed his chest with a pain so tangible, he stumbled.

"Luke, what's wrong?" Kristoff was suddenly there, grasping him under the arm.

"Where's Carina?" Loki demanded, shaking him off in embarrassment. "I lost her in the crowd."

"She's right there." Kristoff pointed to her clearly visible red hair as she moved with the throng getting off the ferry. When she turned back to smile brilliantly at them, Kristoff urged Loki, "Hurry up, or we just might lose her for real."

Loki grabbed his arm. "Kristoff, wait."

"Alright, buddy, what's really going on?" Kristoff looked at him with concern.

"I can't tell her," Loki confessed. "She just told me she can't love someone who isn't real. And then when I couldn't find her—"

"What?" Kristoff exclaimed. "That's the stupidest thing I've ever heard. You're as real as I am, and she loves you! Pull yourself together, old boy. You're acting like ..." He stopped suddenly as a realization hit him. "Okay, okay, I see what's happening. Just relax. You don't have to do anything you don't want to do."

Loki palmed his face with one hand. "Yes, I do. I know I do."

"Well, far be it from me to tell you your business—" Kristoff started to say.

Loki burst out laughing. "You're always telling me my business."

Kristoff's lips twitched. "I was going to say, do you want her to find out from someone else?"

"Like you?" Loki growled.

"You know me better than that, Luke," Kristoff retorted with a hurt tone. "You'll know when the time is right. Until then, try not to think about it. And remember, if you never take the risk, you'll never know."

"When did you get to be so smart?" Loki clapped Kristoff on the back, just like he always did to Loki.

"I've always been smart," Kristoff said haughtily.

Carina waited for the men as they got off the ferry. She grabbed Loki's hand almost immediately.

"Where did you disappear to?" he asked with some irritation. "You scared me."

"I told you it was time to get off the ferry," she returned. She frowned slightly at his rough tone and slipped her hand from his. "Didn't you hear me?"

"I guess I missed that," he admitted. "When I turned around, you were gone."

"Oh, I'm sorry," she chuckled. "I didn't mean to worry you. I can take care of myself, you know."

"Nobody's lost," Kristoff pointed out. "Can we get moving?"

Carina laughed and took Loki's proffered hand as Kristoff hailed a cab. London became new and fresh to Loki as he saw it through Carina's eyes. By the time they arrived at the Savoy Hotel, all the fear he had experienced, though brief, did indeed seem ridiculous. He chided himself for faltering.

Carina's excitement over the Savoy was contagious. She grabbed his arm and pointed out every new and wondrous thing she spotted. Her reaction was in stark contrast to Loki's silent awe when he had gaped at the elaborate chandeliers, rich draperies, and gilded columns leading up to sculpted archways and ceilings. But even Carina was stunned into silence by the opulently wealthy people trickling through the ground floor of the hotel.

Though Carina had her own room, the three of them spent most of the afternoon relaxing in the larger suite the men shared, despite Kristoff's insistence in Paris that Loki would have his own room. After a cozy British supper of bangers and mash at one of the pubs, they joined the nightly party at the hotel. Kristoff used the event as a networking opportunity. He introduced Loki and Carina to London's elite, whether he knew them or not, and encouraged them all to see Lukas Black and the Shooting Star at the Savoy Theatre one of the three following nights.

The next morning, Kristoff took them on a whirlwind taxi tour of London, pointing out such landmarks as Tower Bridge, Westminster Abbey, and several of the more popular palaces that tourists viewed. Loki was immediately struck by how different the royal structures were from the palace in which he had been raised. Odin's palace towered over Asgard's capital city in golden splendor, while most of Great Britain's palaces stretched over well-kept grounds in stately elegance.

His interest in the architecture was fleeting, however. Loki itched to get out of the cab, preferring to explore rather than be limited to their view from the taxi window. Carina, on the other hand, seemed fascinated with the history and magnificence of each place, content to admire from a distance.

As they finished the tour and drove back to the Savoy Theatre for a quick rehearsal, Carina playfully whispered, "You seem terribly bored, Luke."

Loki was slightly taken aback. He thought he had done a better job of acting interested, not wanting to spoil Carina's delight. He shrugged and flippantly remarked, "Oh, I've just seen my share of palaces."

"I thought you were only here for two days last time and didn't do much touring?" Carina pressed him.

"I've traveled a lot," Loki answered quickly. "I would have rather explored one or two for a few hours than try to see every single one from a distance in one morning."

"Which ones would you choose?" Carina asked.

Loki grinned as he recalled what he had read about England's colorful history, especially King Henry VIII and his string of wives. Without hesitation, he replied, "The Tower of London and Hampton Court Palace."

Carina laughed. "Are you into Tudor history?"

"I'm not a fan of the drama and intrigues of the royal court back then, but you have to admit there's something fascinating about that period," Loki admitted.

"Yes," Carina agreed thoughtfully. "I'm actually an admirer of Lady Jane Grey, the Nine Days Queen."

"Why?" Loki asked, genuinely interested but also delighted to catch another glimpse of the studious and philosophical side of her multifaceted personality.

"She was incredibly intelligent and kind, they say. And she was so brave when she faced her execution. A woman of great faith and principle. Somehow, I don't think she would have trembled in fear at the things I have."

As she said this, Carina turned away from Loki, but he caught the look of regret on her face. Kristoff had been listening from the front seat. He caught Loki's eye, then started a conversation with the driver about the Imperial War Museum's move from the Crystal Palace to the Imperial Institute in South Kensington.

Loki used the opportunity to gently turn Carina's face so she would look at him. "Do not think she never felt fear, my star. Remember how she faltered at the chopping block when she could not find it with her hands?"

Carina's eyes widened. "You've read about Lady Jane Grey?"

"I've read about a great many things and people," Loki chuckled. "She only faltered for a moment, but she regained her courage and stared down her fear. I've seen you do the same. You are a strong and brave woman, just as intelligent and kind as she was. Perhaps you would have been kindred spirits, had you not been separated by time."

Carina's eyes shimmered, but her lips curved upward. "And you are a poet, Mr. Black. Perhaps William Shakespeare would have been your kindred spirit."

"I'm often shocked by how alike we are," Loki murmured.

"Are?"

Loki grimaced. He had slipped with his words three times

on this trip! If he did not get a handle on himself, Carina would figure out his identity before he could tell her.

"He may be gone, but I'm still here, aren't I?" he quipped.

"I'm glad of that," she said softly.

They arrived at the theater, leaving no more time for that conversation, much to Loki's relief. They spent the rest of the day rehearsing for their first performance in London. And as all three of them expected, their act was every bit the success in London as it had been in Paris.

The morning of their second performance in London, Kristoff left for one of his own appointments, leaving Carina and Loki alone in the men's suite.

"Well, what should we do until rehearsal?" Loki pondered aloud, trying to ignore his own mischievous thoughts.

"I've wanted to visit the London Zoo since I was a little girl," Carina said shyly. "I know it sounds childish, but would you mind taking me there?"

"I would love that!" Loki exclaimed with a wide grin. "I don't know why I didn't think of it."

He was almost giddy with the anticipation of spending hours with just her. Rather than take a taxi, they boarded a bright red, double-decker bus plastered with advertisements. It was a new experience for both of them. The open air of the top deck, the higher vantage point, and the perimeter seating made the ride far more interesting than a taxi ride would have been.

When they arrived at the zoo, they strolled hand in hand, admiring the animals in the exhibits. Carina lingered at each enclosure, reading every description and bit of trivia. Loki did not rush her. While she indulged her thirst for knowledge, Loki contented himself with watching the people. Mothers chased after unruly toddlers or pushed prams to quiet their babies. A young couple kissed right in front of him before wandering off to the next exhibit, not caring who might see. In a way, he envied their freedom and anonymity. He was thankful he and Carina were lost in the crowds for once, if only for a few hours. No one seemed to know or care who they were, and he would enjoy it while it lasted.

A small girl a few feet away from Loki dropped a brown stuffed bear with black button eyes. Her mother had not noticed, intent as she was on keeping track of the girl's older brother. As the tot tried to grab her toy, the mother tugged at her to keep walking. The child did not cry or protest, but her large brown eyes met Loki's green ones for an instant. Loki immediately felt drawn to the little tyke. He had always liked children, entertaining them on Asgard with stories and tricks. And they were often as drawn to him as animals were. But he had not had the opportunity to be around many Midgardian children. He smiled at her, pleased when she shyly smiled back.

"Excuse me, ma'am!" Loki called after the mother as he picked up the stuffed animal. "Your little girl dropped this."

"Oh, thank you," the frazzled woman responded, snatching the bear and hurrying off after her son.

The little girl pumped her short legs to keep up with her mother but turned long enough to wave and smile at Loki just before they disappeared into the crowd.

"That was kind of you," Carina said softly, a strange expression on her face.

"Eh, she was a cute kid," Loki replied nonchalantly, slightly embarrassed she had witnessed the moment. "She reminded me of you."

"How so?"

"Her eyes were like yours. Big, brown, and full of spirit," Loki answered, blushing slightly.

Carina kissed his cheek. "That's sweet, Luke. Oh, look, there's the new aquarium that opened in April!"

He grinned as Carina pulled him inside, wondering what it would be like. No one kept aquatic animals on Asgard, save for the carp that swam in the garden ponds. These fish were all types, colors, and sizes. Watching them swim in their tanks had a calming effect on Loki, making him feel peaceful and almost lazy. He wished they could stay longer, but Carina was ready for the next sight.

After a quick lunch, since the weather was quite fine, they decided to leave the zoo and take the hour-long walk to Buckingham Palace. As they passed through Trafalgar Square, Loki chuckled to himself, thinking how Paul Derval, owner of the Folies Bergère in Paris, would enjoy feeding all the pigeons there, as many people were doing. Carina did not take much notice of the birds, fascinated as she was by the sculpted lions at the base of Nelson's Column. They did not linger long but soon passed under the Admiralty Arch, an impressive structure serving as a gateway to the Mall, the ceremonial road leading to Buckingham Palace through St. James Park.

The beauty of the grounds and fountains had a profoundly relaxing effect on Loki. He led Carina over to a bench with a perfect view of the lake, from which they could also see the back of the palace. A swan and several large birds with enormous beaks swam on the shimmering water, their white bodies reflected perfectly from the surface.

"Let's just sit here for a while," Loki requested, taking

advantage of the somewhat secluded spot to put his arm around her.

"Look at those pelicans over there," Carina said, pointing to the giant birds. "They're so different from the swan."

The two of them watched in silence as they cozied up to each other on the bench.

Reluctantly, Loki suggested, "Shall we continue to the palace?"

Carina sighed and snuggled closer to him. "It's not open to the public. I doubt we could get much closer, even on the other side."

"Fine with me," Loki replied with a grin.

"Debutantes are introduced at court there," Carina informed Loki rather wistfully. "They're presented in full court dress, with three ostrich feathers in their hair."

"And I bet not one of them was ever introduced in two different societies," Loki reminded her. "And they certainly didn't have the great Lukas Black as an entertainer."

Carina playfully nudged him with her shoulder. "Certainly not. But ever since I heard that the king and queen host command performances, I've wanted to be invited inside. Maybe someday, we'll be popular enough to merit an invitation."

"We'll add that to your list, right below performing in that opera house in Paris," Loki told her.

"Are you making fun of my dreams?" Carina asked, though her playful tone told him she was not serious.

"Never," he responded, his own tone in earnest. "I plan to be part of making those dreams reality."

She smiled at him so beautifully, he simply could not resist the magnetic draw of her mouth and found himself kissing her, oblivious to the few other tourists walking nearby.

When he broke away, he started to apologize, but she placed one finger over his lips to shush him. "Look around, Luke," she whispered. "No one cares. But I'm glad to know I still hold your interest."

"More than you could ever know, my star," he answered.

She hugged him, then turned to look at Buckingham Palace again. He slipped his arms around her from behind and rested his chin on the top of her head. They did not speak. As Loki reflected on all their time together and how it had drawn them ever closer, it was a welcome relief to simply hold her in his arms. Until that moment, they had kept their relationship closely guarded and professional, even when only Kristoff was around.

Loki began to wonder about the change in his human friend since they left Paris. He rarely spoke of the bold American journalist from Chicago, nor did he take any notice of the pretty girls he usually pursued quite readily. Loki briefly considered he might simply be preoccupied with the show and its profits, but then he remembered catching Kristoff watching wistfully whenever Carina would linger a little too closely to Loki.

He must miss Kathleen, he thought, then checked his watch. "We should head back, Carina. Are you ready for rehearsal?"

"No," she sighed. "But if we must, we must."

They took a taxi to the theater, then sailed through their rehearsal and second London performance. Though Loki had cherished the time with Carina, his anxiety grew as the hours passed, for it meant drawing ever closer to the last night and the truth he dreaded telling her. But he was resolved, as Kvasir had been at the end.

Loki and Kristoff stood in the hotel lobby after a late, gourmet breakfast, discussing whether to visit the Tower of London and Highgate Cemetery or to take a picnic to Hampton Court. Carina seemed preoccupied and unusually quiet, not even offering her own preference or opinion.

"I'd rather save the picnic for tomorrow," Loki asserted. "Then we won't be rushed. As it is, if we don't leave soon, we won't have much time before we have to be back for rehearsal."

"I see your point," Kristoff agreed. "And since tonight is your last performance in London, we'll need to discuss where we're going next."

Loki shifted his weight nervously. Tonight, he would tell Carina the truth. Then they would only have a few days together before he slipped back to Asgard again. He had not even figured out what he should say yet.

"I need something from my room," Carina announced suddenly.

"We can go back upstairs before we go," Loki offered.

"No, you stay here," Carina insisted. "I shouldn't be long."

She hurried off without another word, fussing with something in the folds of her skirt.

Loki and Kristoff exchanged surprised glances.

"Has Carina talked to you yet?" Kristoff asked Loki as they waited.

"About what?"

"She got a telegram from New York earlier this morning."

"What did it say?"

"You'll have to ask her," Kristoff said with a shrug. "She didn't tell me."

"But she told you she got a telegram?" Loki asked, hurt that she had not told him.

"No, they handed it to me at the front desk since her room is under my name. I gave it to her right before we came down for breakfast, but I never saw her look at it. She hasn't said a word about it since."

"She didn't say much of anything at breakfast, come to think of it," Loki agreed. "Should I ask her about it?"

"Yeah!" Kristoff drew out the word mockingly, eyebrows raised and hands in his pockets as he lifted his shoulders to emphasize how obvious it was. "It's probably from her father."

"How does he know she's here?"

"I left forwarding instructions at our last hotel, in case any requests or messages came in. Anyway, I'm sure she's read it by now."

"She *has* been up there for a while," Loki observed. "I think I'll go check on her."

"Good, go!" Kristoff urged him, his tone worried.

Loki knocked several times at the door of her room, but she did not answer.

Maybe she isn't in there, he thought.

He enhanced the sound waves and heard soft, rustling movements. He considered picking the lock, but Carina quietly opened the door and moved aside to let him in, trying to hide her face.

"Is there something you want to tell me?" he asked her softly, observing the redness around her eyes.

She threw herself into his arms and sobbed quietly on his chest, her shoulders heaving. Then she tore herself away and shoved a crumpled piece of paper into his hand.

He smoothed it out, clenching his jaw as he read the words.

Come to NYC immediately STOP
Will address Paris on arrival

"What do you make of it?" Loki asked her, noting Joseph Green's name in the signature line.

She began pacing the room, taking a shuddering breath every now and again from crying so hard. "It's exactly as I feared. My father wants me to go to New York. He must be furious! What if he forces me to marry Klaus?"

"You don't have to go," Loki said fiercely. "You're a grown woman."

"What else can I do?" she cried. "He's my father! I'll have to face him eventually and take responsibility for what I've done."

Loki took her shoulders a little more forcefully than he intended, cringing when she flinched. "You've done nothing wrong! And I will not stand idly by while your overbearing father forces you to marry that beast."

"Will you go with me?" she pleaded hopefully, placing both hands on his face.

"What about tonight? We have to finish here," Loki reminded her, taking her hands in his.

"We'll leave in the morning!"

"How long is the trip?" Loki asked hesitantly, calculating in his mind how much time he had left before he had to go back to Asgard.

His mother might already have returned from Vanaheim, and Thor and Odin were due back from their diplomatic mission soon.

"The fastest steamer makes the Transatlantic Crossing in four and a half days," she responded enthusiastically. "I would love to show you New York! I feel I could face anything with you by my side. If Father could just see how much we love each other ..."

Her voice trailed off when she saw the pain on Loki's face.

His heart had sunk lower than he ever thought possible. "Carina, I ... I can't go with you."

"Why not?" she demanded petulantly.

"There isn't enough time. I have to return home," he groaned.

"When were you going to tell me you were leaving?" Carina demanded.

"I planned to tell you tonight, after we performed, when the timing was right."

"Are you going back to Iceland or Norway?" Carina asked, becoming more agitated. "And for how long?"

"Neither," Loki said hesitantly, leaving her second question unanswered. "I guess I might as well tell you now."

"Tell me what?" Carina huffed.

"I'm not who you think I am."

"What do you mean?" she whispered, her face white as she backed away from him and sat down heavily on the bed.

"Loki is real, Carina," Loki blurted out, then silently berated himself for how unnatural he sounded.

"What does Loki have to do with—"

"Loki is me. I mean, I *am* Loki, the real Loki."

"That's not funny," she gasped. "Why would you joke at a time like this?"

"It's no joke." He knelt before her and took her hands again, pleading with his eyes. "I don't live in Norway, and I'm not really from Iceland. I'm ... from Asgard."

"But of course!" she shot at him sarcastically. "The mythical city in the sky, connected to Earth by a rainbow bridge."

"Only in a manner of speaking," Loki responded. "It's actually a completely different planet on a higher plane."

"Oh, so you're an alien," she stated flatly, removing her hands from his and standing up abruptly to cross the room.

"Kristoff used that term when I told him. I suppose it's true, though I don't like how harsh it sounds," Loki admitted, standing up and following her.

"You roped Kristoff into this?"

"Carina, please listen! I never planned to fall in love with you, but I did. And I've hated deceiving you," Loki said, placing his finger on her mouth to shush her before she could retort back at him. He continued, "I'm telling you the truth now. I am Loki but not the villain you've read about. I'm turning 1,400 years old very soon. I do want to go with you to New York, but I've run out of time. I must return to Asgard for a series of trials to take my place as the youngest son of Odin."

"Loki wasn't Odin's son. They were blood brothers," she whispered, her eyes distant and glazed.

"Just another twisted version," he insisted. "And it's wrong. Odin is my father. Even a select few of the legends tell it so, though they all got my mother wrong."

"It doesn't matter," she said, shaking her head as her eyes focused on him again. "Clearly, you've gone mad."

Loki sighed with frustration. Kristoff's warning sounded in his mind. Revealing himself as Loki of Asgard in all his battle splendor would indeed be the wrong choice. And since she had seen enough of his skills, he knew it would not phase her in the slightest if he demonstrated them again, even at a higher level. Then he remembered she had met other Asgardians, though she had not known it.

"Do you remember the club in the catacombs?" he asked.

"What about it?"

"Think about how strange everything seemed to you. Even the people. Most of them were Asgardians, what you humans call the Aesir." He paused. "Well, some were Vanir, I guess."

"Oh, so now you're a god?" she snapped.

"No, not a god. None of us are gods," Loki replied. "We're like faster and stronger humans that live longer. I don't believe in any god, though I meant what I said in Paris. If there were a god like that ..."

He trailed off when he saw she was staring at him fearfully, her face still white and her eyes wide.

"Carina, I know this is a shock to you. And it's not how I wanted it to happen. But you cannot tell anyone what I've told you. Kristoff and James Joyce are the only humans who know my true identity," Loki explained.

"I have no intention of telling anyone," she huffed. "Despite whatever mental breakdown you're having, I couldn't bear it if they locked you away."

"You don't believe me, do you?" Loki said quietly, ashamed to feel tears pricking at his eyes.

She shook her head. "Please stop, Luke. You're breaking my heart."

"I never wanted to hurt you, my star. And I'm so sorry I deceived you. Can you ever forgive me?"

She silently turned her back on him.

"Please don't shut me out! Surely, you must know how much I love you," he pleaded with her, his voice breaking.

"Do you?" she asked him icily, whirling around to face him but keeping her arms tightly crossed.

"How can you even ask that?" he gasped as he gripped the bridge of his nose to stop the painful tears. They trickled out anyway.

A brief, unreadable emotion flitted over her face. He reached for her, but she stiffened as he pulled her into his arms. She did not resist his kiss, but she did not return it either. Her lips remained cold and frozen. She watched him warily as he pulled away after just a few seconds. Several more tears escaped from his eyes, but she just stood there, emotionless. He would have preferred she had slapped him again.

A knock sounded at the door. Carina breezed past Loki to open it and waved for Kristoff to enter.

"You better do something about him," she demanded, pointing at Loki. "He's lost his mind."

"You told her, didn't you?" Kristoff asked Loki with resignation.

Loki nodded, his face contorted with pain.

"Don't even start with that, Kristoff," Carina huffed. "I don't know what game you two are playing, but it's not funny. And your timing is terrible."

"Oh, Carina, don't be like that," Kristoff groaned but stopped when she held up her forefinger, her eyes wild.

"Not another word, from either of you!" Carina warned through clenched teeth. "We will get through tonight's performance; then I'm going to New York, as my father demands. Now, both of you get out of here before I refuse to perform at all!"

She shoved them both out and slammed the door.

"Well, that went well," Kristoff quipped nervously.

Without a word, Loki punched him hard in the shoulder, sending him into the wall across the hall.

Kristoff groaned and picked himself up gingerly. "Yeah, I deserved that. Now what do we do?"

"It's over!" Loki cried, turning away from him in despair. "You heard her. She's going to New York, where her father will probably force her to marry that—"

"Luke, you cannot let that happen," Kristoff interrupted, his face horrified. "What about that poor girl's future? Don't you love her?"

Loki whirled around to face him. How dare he question that, especially right after Carina had! "Of course I do!" he asserted fiercely. Then his shoulders slumped in defeat. "But what future could she have with me?"

"Whatever future you make," Kristoff retorted, refusing to back down. "You cannot give up now!"

"What would you have me do?" Loki demanded. "Chase her across the Atlantic and jeopardize everything on Asgard?"

"If that's what it takes," Kristoff insisted. "Fight for her! Or you're no better than Kvasir was a thousand years ago."

"You are my friend, Kristoff, and I know you speak these words as a friend," Loki growled. "But you cannot possibly understand my position as Odin's son. There is nothing left for me here."

"Where are you going?" Kristoff called after him as Loki headed for the emergency stairs.

"Out!" he yelled back. "Don't follow me. I'll be back at the theater in time for rehearsal, if she can stand the sight of me by then."

As soon as he was outside, Loki used Kvasir's device to hide his presence, lacking the emotional strength to do it himself, and ran hard for the Palace of Westminster.

Maybe there's a way, Loki thought, clinging to one sliver of hope.

Frey had told him the Bifröst portal was hidden on the banks of the Thames, very close to the north end of the palace, where he could clearly see the famous clock tower, Big Ben. The portal was well-hidden to prevent humans from finding it by accident, but he located it easily since he knew where it was. Loki had never used a Bifröst connection to travel within Midgard, but he had to find out if there was a portal to Asgard in New York. If Carina could come to accept who he was, perhaps he could risk going with her to New York by eliminating the lengthy steamer trip back to England or France. Perhaps he could still protect her. Perhaps she could still be his.

As his thoughts crashed into each other, he steadied himself and thought only of the underground Asgardian club in Paris. And just as he expected, the cool, dank air of the catacombs hit him as soon as he passed through the indirect connection.

Tyr ushered him inside the hidden club, which was almost empty, no doubt due to the time of day.

"Do you live here, Tyr?" Loki asked him, surprised he still guarded the door.

"No, I just started my shift," Tyr laughed. "Why are you here? I thought you went to London with your singer friend."

"I did. I just came from there through the London portal," Loki replied.

"You used the Bifröst to travel within Midgard?" Tyr yelled.

"Is that a problem?" Loki was taken aback.

"No, I just wanted to see your reaction," Tyr laughed, slapping his enormous upper thigh. "Classic."

Loki rolled his eyes. "Tyr, I don't have much time. Have you seen Frey?"

"Not since yesterday. Why?"

"I need to find out where the Bifröst connection is in New York," he explained, somewhat frustrated.

"There isn't one," Tyr replied.

"How can that be?"

"The lands to the west were wild and untamed when we first started building connections to Midgard. As far as I know, no one ever bothered."

"Not even in the last two hundred years?" Loki asked incredulously.

"No one's come from Asgard that recently except you," Tyr informed him. "The only direct connection to anywhere in the United States is through the main Bifröst bridge, through Heimdall. There might be connections to other realms."

Loki groaned, then brightened as he thought of a possible solution. "I could go from London to New York, right?"

"How would you return?" Tyr asked.

"I'll figure it out, Tyr, thank you," Loki said, figuring he would have to use dark magic.

He wondered briefly why Asgardians condemned such practices. Loki had only experienced minor physical pain the few times he had muttered the incantations from the ancient text in Odin's vast library. The warning it gave of the high price meant little to him now. He could handle some momentary pain. He really had no other choice. Besides, dark magic was relatively convenient.

Tyr stared at him with a strange expression, almost as if he knew what he was thinking. But he simply stated, "Loki, you worry me sometimes."

Loki flashed him a charming grin. "No need to worry, Tyr. By the way, where does the London portal connect on Asgard? I never asked Frey."

Tyr scratched his head. "I don't know, actually. You could ask him when he comes in tonight."

"There isn't time," Loki informed him. "I need to get back to London."

"But—" Tyr called out.

That was all Loki heard. He was already out the door and slipping through the portal. The visit had been so fast, he needed very little dark magic to get back to London. He had so much on his mind and such pain in his heart, he hardly noticed the grappling twinge that always accompanied his use of dark magic now.

Once the air and sunshine of London hit him, he hurried back to the hotel, staying invisible to avoid talking to anyone. He changed into his Asgardian gear, packed his suitcase, and left the luggage where Kristoff would be sure to find it. Loki glanced around the suite just once before leaving, a peculiar melancholy settling over him as he remembered the laughter he had shared with Kristoff and Carina in that very spot just a few days ago.

Loki disguised his Asgardian clothing, then walked to the Savoy Theatre, where he obtained permission from the manager to practice early. He sat down at the piano. All of his emotions poured out of him as he pounded and stroked the keys with his eyes tightly shut. He had no idea how long he played, but he was almost spent when he noticed Carina watching and listening from the front row. He stopped playing abruptly, unable to read anything but confusion on her face. She seemed decidedly different than a few hours earlier in the hotel room. Her mannerism puzzled him. He had no idea what to expect or even how long she had been there.

"I half expected you to be in a bar," she said curtly. "But you're not like Klaus, so it makes more sense to find you here."

He just stared at her, remaining silent.

She got up and moved toward the stage, climbing the stairs slowly. She cocked her head. "What's wrong with your eyes?"

He still said nothing, frozen at the piano. He had not even been aware his eyes had turned gray and dull again. He sat there hating his face and his eyes for betraying the uncertainty and pain he felt.

"Are you not speaking to me now?" she demanded, sitting beside him at the piano.

"Is there anything left to say?" he responded, his voice strained as he looked away from her.

"You tell me."

"What would you like me to say?" Loki asked, glancing at her for just a moment.

Her eyes were angry, but pain lurked beneath the anger. "The truth," she said simply.

"I told you the truth!" he insisted.

"I heard you in the hallway," she declared. "Whatever you were trying to tell me before, I don't think it was an act. I almost wish it was, but Kristoff spent the last two hours trying to convince me he's actually been to this Asgard."

"Where is he now?"

"In the lobby," she replied, jerking her head toward the doors. "I asked him to give us some time."

"For what?" Hope surged through his heart.

"There are my green eyes," she said softly.

He sighed, embarrassed. "My eyes change color with certain moods. I have to figure out how to stop that from happening."

Her mouth twitched slightly. "I wish mine did. They're always boring brown."

"There's nothing boring about your eyes." Loki almost smiled when she blushed at his compliment, but he knew now was no time for flirting. He just had to get through to her somehow. "Once, I said I showed people what they wished to see. Do you remember?" he coaxed her.

"Yes, the night we met. And I said believing was seeing."

"We were saying exactly the same thing. But I cannot make people see what they do not wish to see," Loki said sadly. "I just hope you believe me before it's too late."

"It may already be too late," she breathed so softly, he almost missed it.

"Don't say that," he begged her. "I might have figured out a way to go with you to New York, but I couldn't stay long."

"How?"

"Would you even believe me if I explained it?"

"I don't know what to think or believe, Luke ... or whoever you are. Maybe it's best for us to spend some time apart. I'm brave enough to go to New York alone to face my father. You do whatever it is you need to do, wherever it is you're doing it. And then ..." Her voice trailed off in uncertainty.

"What?"

"I don't know," she whispered.

She stood abruptly and hurried to the lobby to retrieve Kristoff. When she returned, the three of them delved into practice without another word about the incident over Loki's true identity. Kristoff eyed Loki several times, his gaze concerned, but there was no opportunity for the two of them to talk alone. Loki and Carina acted cordially and professionally toward each other, but the tension and anguish between them was palpable.

During their performance, they sang their usual duets with such pain and so many unanswered questions, the audience was entirely still at the end of the last song. Even Loki's normally bright color enhancements had taken on darker hues. Neither Loki nor Carina had emerged dry-eyed, and the people seemed to sense that something deeper was happening. Surprisingly, they lapped it up like thirsty animals, wiping their own eyes as sniffles sounded throughout the still theater. Then, almost as one, they all leaped to their feet, applauding vigorously.

When Loki joined Carina for their final bow, he squeezed her hand three times as a message he could not trust himself to say aloud. He kissed her cheek in front of the entire theater, his lips accidentally catching one of her salty tears. Then he abruptly turned heel and disappeared into the wings.

He found Kristoff in the lobby. "I'm off to Asgard now," he whispered so no one would overhear.

"I'll walk out with you," Kristoff said, tipping his hat to the theater patrons with whom he had been talking. Once they were outside, he asked, "Now what? Your performance was heartbreaking."

"She still doesn't believe me. She wants us to be apart for a time."

Kristoff sighed. "I'm sorry, Luke. I tried."

"I know, and I'm grateful."

The two men clasped arms for just a moment. Then Kristoff pointed out, "If she goes to New York, I won't be able to bring her to Norway."

"She may never want to see me again anyway."

"Don't think like that," Kristoff encouraged him. "I'll find Baldur, Hod, and Kvasir in Norway and tell them what happened. We'll help you in any way we can."

"Thank you. I'll see you in about a week then," Loki said, then turned to leave.

"Loki?" Kristoff called softly.

Loki stopped in his tracks and slowly faced Kristoff, shocked to hear his real name.

"Did you say goodbye to Carina?" Kristoff prodded gently.

"Why would I do that?"

Kristoff raised his eyes at him incredulously. "I'm going to pretend you didn't just say that."

Loki sighed. "Kristoff, she doesn't want to see me."

"You really don't know much about women, do you?"

Kristoff retorted with a smirk. "Would you just trust me on this one?"

Loki groaned, but he followed Kristoff back inside and to Carina's dressing room door. It was eerily quiet. Kristoff knocked firmly. There was no answer.

"I don't think she's in there," Loki remarked.

"Call her," Kristoff commanded.

"What?" Loki asked, feeling irritated with his friend. But when Kristoff raised his eyebrows insistently and gestured to the door, Loki decided to humor him and called, "Carina?"

The door opened just a crack. "What is it?"

Loki could not see her, but he knew by her voice that she had been crying. When Kristoff nudged him hard, Loki answered hesitantly, "I came to say goodbye."

"Goodbye, then." The door clicked shut.

Loki dropped his head and turned to leave, but Kristoff shoved him back toward the door.

Loki shot him a look, but Kristoff narrowed his eyes and mouthed, "Try again."

Loki rolled his eyes, but he knocked again.

"If you're going to leave, then leave!" she spat from inside.

Loki's own stubbornness kicked in, and he snapped, "Fine, then!" But at the stormy, no-nonsense look on Kristoff's face, Loki swallowed his pride and said, "Please, Carina, I would really like to say a proper goodbye, especially if you don't ever want to see me again. May I come in?"

The door swung open. She stood there with a confused look on her tearstained face. "I never said I didn't ever want to see you again."

Loki did not address her statement but merely repeated, "May I come in?"

"You can say what you need to say from there," Carina insisted.

"I'll go somewhere else," Kristoff offered.

Carina sighed, then ushered Loki inside. "Please wait there, Kristoff."

She shut the door, then turned to Loki, folding her arms tightly across her chest. "Well?"

Loki gulped, then began, "I really am sorry I lied to you about who I am. I didn't think any of you humans would trust me or give me a chance because of all the twisted stories about me. I wish I had told you the truth before now, but would you have accepted me as I am if I had?"

Carina's eyes filled with tears, but she clenched her jaw and looked away. "Did you intend to use me and leave me all along?"

"No, never!" Loki exclaimed. "If I had, I would have taken advantage of you in Paris."

Her face flushed crimson. "Please don't bring that up. I'm embarrassed enough that I fell for all that."

"Everything I said I felt about you was true!" Loki cried, taking a few steps toward her. "Why else would I still be here, begging you for another chance? Is there anything I can do to earn back your trust?"

He expected her to move away, but instead, she threw her arms around him and buried her face into his chest. Surprised but pleased, he returned her embrace. But as she changed her position slightly, one of the invisible buckles on his leather jerkin caught her hair, causing her to gasp in pain.

"What ... what is this?" she demanded, frantically feeling his illusionary shirt.

Loki gently freed her hair from his buckle, then stepped back and allowed his illusion to fade away, revealing himself in his Asgardian clothing, although without the glamour and power he had used with Kristoff.

He turned around, arms outstretched. "This is me, Carina. As I truly am."

She covered her mouth with both hands, staring at him as he quickly renewed his illusionary black suit, green silk shirt, and black tie. Then she stammered slightly, "I ... I really need some time to consider all of this."

"Kristoff said you might need time," Loki acknowledged. "I will respect that and take my leave. But if you should ever need me, I'll do everything I can to be there. Kristoff will know how to find me."

Carina nodded, her face softening slightly, but her eyes remained unreadable as she hugged him tightly again.

He kissed her forehead. "I hope this isn't the last goodbye, my star." He opened the door, then turned back to say, "I love you."

She did not answer.

Loki felt as though his heart would crack into a thousand jagged pieces, but he forced himself to leave her there.

Back in the hallway, he squeezed Kristoff's shoulder to thank him for pushing him to speak with her. He could not trust his voice. And since nothing more needed to be said, the two walked silently together to the Savoy Hotel doors. Kristoff went inside, but Loki ran for the Palace of Westminster.

He tested the portal's direct connection first and was pleased to find it brought him deep within the Asgardian wilderness, where he would be going to start his rite of passage, which he would likely do as originally planned now that Carina needed him to keep his distance.

Would he ever see her again? Would she come to resent him or, worse, forget about him? Even the Asgardian sunlight seemed to grow dark and cold with that thought.

He memorized the area, then popped back to the dark London night. As he passed through the portal again, he thought of his own room on Asgard and was pleased to find himself standing in familiar surroundings. He threw himself onto his bed, not bothering to undress. Despite his internal anguish, he slept soundly until a knock at the door woke him.

"Loki, are you in there?" his mother, Frigga, called.

"Yes!" he answered.

"Where have you been?"

"Right here, Mother," he said, opening the door.

"No, you haven't," Frigga scolded as she swept into his room. "I returned last night. The staff say they haven't seen you or heard from you since I left. And you didn't answer your door this morning."

"I've been in and out," he insisted. "I'm obviously here now."

She looked closely at him. "Well, your eyes are just as dull, so I guess you haven't been with your mystery woman."

Loki ignored her comment, sensing she did not fully believe him. "When do Father and Thor return?"

"Tomorrow," she answered.

Loki grimaced, rattled by his miscalculation. If he had gone to New York, he would surely have been caught.

"Sigyn's family will arrive for your birthday celebration in a week," Frigga continued excitedly. "Then the trials begin!"

"I know when my trials begin, Mother," Loki groaned.

"Are you ready?"

"I am. Was there anything else?" he asked pointedly, in no mood for company.

"Aren't you hungry? You're not going to make me dine alone again, are you?" she pouted.

"Oh, is it time for dinner already?" Loki asked.

"Were you taking a nap?" Frigga teased him, gesturing to his crumpled clothing and tousled hair. "Isn't it time you toughened up a bit?"

"You think me soft?" Loki growled.

"No, dear," she laughed. "Just a little friendly teasing. I've missed you!"

She hugged him tightly, and for a moment, Loki wanted to tell her everything.

Instead, he joined her for dinner and pretended to listen as she filled him in on all the news from Vanaheim. He had gotten so used to Midgardian food, he had little appetite for the Asgardian fare before him. This, of course, concerned Frigga, who seemed intent on getting him to eat more.

"Mother, you don't make any sense," he chuckled. "You tease me for being soft but try to fatten me up when I need to stay fit for my trials."

"I'm sorry, my son," she sighed. "I hope it will not be too long before I see happiness in you again."

"Me too," he muttered, pushing his plate away.

He walked with Frigga to the library, where they read together until she asked him to escort her to her quarters.

Back in his own room, sleep eluded him. His body's insistence that it was daylight on Midgard intensified his worry over Carina's plight. She would be on her way to New

York by now. He knew it would still be several days before she arrived, but imagining her facing both Joseph Green and Klaus alone was too much. Loki reminded himself she had handled herself just fine before he ever met her, but it did not help. For the first time in his life, he used his own brain waves to force himself to sleep.

The morning of Loki's 1400th birthday dawned bright and dazzling.

Everything had taken on a far more festive and exciting air once Thor and Odin had returned several days ago, leaving Loki little time to dwell on how Carina was faring on her journey. He had gone back to regular sparring with his brother, not needing to study any further. He always enjoyed the snatches of time he could grab with Thor, as long as no one teased Loki about the noticeable differences between the two brothers.

Loki had not been there at the landing pad to greet Sigyn's family when they arrived. Frigga had insisted he give his input on preparations for his birthday feast taking place that evening, pulling him away from the preferred solitude of the library. He did not mind the planning. He rather enjoyed giving his opinion and showing a little of his creative side. But he had wanted to set aside a little time to himself before the festivities started. Since his mother clearly had other ideas, he surrendered himself to her good intentions. But when she tugged him toward the banquet hall to start the decorating, he protested vehemently, having no desire to be involved with such a task beyond deciding the color scheme, which he had already done. Once his mother left him in the kitchen, he breathed a sigh of relief and helped himself to an apple. He bit into it and almost choked when Sigyn burst through the doors and cornered him.

"I've been looking all over for you!" she exclaimed, embracing him eagerly. "Many happy returns!" She looked around at the busy staff, then whispered, "When do we leave?"

"Sigyn, we can't talk here," Loki whispered back fiercely.

"Well, where can we?" she demanded impatiently.

"Come on!" He gestured for her to follow him to the banquet hall, where several servants were moving tables and potted plants under Frigga's supervision.

Green and gold silk billowed from the alabaster archways that led to the large balcony overlooking the capital city. Loki paused for a moment and nodded in approval at how his mother had used the first two colors he had requested. He wondered how she would pull in the black, but he knew she was more than capable.

With amusement, Odin and Thor watched Frigga boss the servants around, though they did not dare interfere. Sigyn's parents were seated at one of the long banquet tables, also watching the whole process. Both Loki's trusted guards stood at attention by the great oak doors. They discreetly signaled to him that they were keeping a watchful eye on Sigyn's father, just as they had promised. Of course, Loki knew Lord Berg had nothing to do with Baldur's fake death, but he had kept his oath to Baldur and withheld the truth. If Odin was suspicious of Berg, perhaps the powerful nobleman was still a threat for other reasons. Regardless, Loki suspected the imminent disappearance of Sigyn would cause significant problems with Lord Berg.

"Sigyn and I are going for a walk," Loki announced as soon as Frigga expressed her satisfaction with the placement of a large flower arrangement.

He started to close the large doors before Lord Berg could protest or make a snide remark. Thor winked at Loki ostentatiously and moved to engage Berg in conversation. At the same time, Lady Annette placed a restraining hand on her husband's arm. Seeing this, Loki knew they were not likely to be disturbed.

"Do you want your ring back?" Sigyn asked as they made their way outside. The green gem glowed brightly on her finger.

"Not until you are safe with Kvasir," he informed her.

She blushed and sighed happily. "Now will you tell me when we leave?"

"Be patient, little one," he told her.

"Little one?" she tittered. "You haven't called me that in eight hundred years."

"That's about when I realized you were all grown up," Loki admitted, "and quite obviously crushing on me."

"I readily confess, I feel foolish for how I acted after Kvasir disappeared," Sigyn said softly. "Seeing him again was … better than I'd ever imagined. You were right all along."

"Of course I was." Loki smiled, pushing his own pain aside in his happiness for his childhood friend.

"Do you have a plan for getting me to Norway? I've never been smuggled before," she chirped.

"Yes, but we must be very careful. And no one can know I'm involved. It has to look like you left me," Loki instructed her. "I will come for you by night, while Asgard sleeps, before my trials have ended. But I don't know which night will be best to make our move, so you must be ready every evening."

"And we'll continue our charade until then?"

"Yes."

"That won't be hard," she stated. "Apparently, I've had a lot of practice acting lovesick when you're around."

Loki laughed for the first time since he had parted from Carina, but thinking of her at that moment immediately sobered him. She should have arrived in New York by now.

"You don't seem happy, Loki," Sigyn observed. "Do you regret what's happened? I assumed you had finally won the heart of your Midgardian."

"I thought I had, but—"

"Something stands between you?"

"She thought I was Midgardian like her. When I told her the truth, she asked me to part from her."

"For good?" Sigyn gasped.

"I don't know," Loki muttered.

"Did you lead her to believe you were Midgardian?"

"Yes, that's how it's done on Midgard. You might have to assume a human identity, you know."

"Kvasir will teach me," she said confidently. "But Loki, all you have to do is show her who you really are. Not tell her, show her. She loves the real you, I'm certain of it."

"And why is that?" Loki asked.

"How could she not? She just has to be shown, as you showed me with Kvasir."

"Maybe I will," Loki replied, smiling down at Sigyn. "If she gives me the chance."

"Take the chance," Sigyn corrected him. "Isn't she worth the risk?"

Her words resounded in his mind throughout his entire birthday feast, through all the toasts, dances, stories, and revels. They resounded still as he drifted off to sleep that night.

But the next morning, he put them aside for the series of oral tests on Asgardian and interplanetary history. Most people found this part of the trials terribly boring. Only the royal family, Sigyn's family, several visiting dignitaries from other planets, and a few other nobles came to the huge palace ballroom to fidget through it. Loki passed the first set of trials with excellence, easily outscoring Thor. Of course, Loki wasted no time in lording that over his older brother, but Thor only grinned and told him to refrain from bragging until the final day.

The celebratory feasting for his first day of trials flew by faster than he expected. Frigga had left the green silk in the archways but replaced the gold silk with black. Since she had used black table runners, gold charger plates, and green centerpieces for his birthday feast, she arranged the tables with green runners, black chargers, and gold candelabras set with ivory taper candles. Frigga never liked to use the same decor twice in a row, and Loki found he preferred this new look to the decorations for his birthday feast. Loki also approved of all of the culinary choices, from simple fruits and gelatin salads to roast pheasant stuffed with chestnuts. He did not eat as much as usual, for he sorely missed Midgardian fare, especially ice cream. Sigyn had been seated beside him, with her parents across the table, much to Loki's chagrin. But he refused to allow them to ruin his enjoyment, which was tempered only by how his heart ached for Carina to be in Sigyn's place.

As a courtesy to their foreign guests, who were staying at the palace, the Asgardians only spoke English, the common tongue. As the banquet drew to a close, Loki wished again that Carina had been there. She would have enjoyed some of the more intellectual conversations.

After all the guests retired for the evening, Loki wandered off by himself, not quite ready for bed and still thinking of the human girl who held his heart. All was quiet on the palace grounds, and the outside air was pleasant.

Perhaps tonight would be a good night to squirrel Sigyn away, Loki thought.

As he drew near the old tree, a dark shadow appeared and Kvasir's voice spoke quietly, "Where is Sigyn?"

"She's in the palace, you fool," Loki hissed. "What are you doing here? You'll ruin everything!"

"It's your birthday, isn't it?" Kvasir answered defensively.

"My birthday was yesterday," Loki corrected.

"I miscalculated then," Kvasir responded. "Anyway, I thought I could help get Sigyn out of here. And Kristoff has a message that can't—"

"Who goes there?" the strong voice of Lord Berg sounded from a high window.

"Can he see me?" Kvasir whispered as loudly as he dared.

Loki quickly grasped the cloaking device he kept in his pocket and pushed the button to hide Kvasir.

"It's only me. I'm just out for a walk, Lord Berg," Loki called back.

"Sigyn had better not be with you," he snapped. "I thought I saw two people."

"No, you must have seen my shadow," Loki insisted. "Sigyn's in her room, I'm sure. You can check if you'd like."

"Don't think I won't!" he yelled, then disappeared.

"I despise that man," Kvasir spat, when he was sure Berg had gone. "Now what?"

"This just got complicated. I have no idea what he was doing there," Loki informed him. "Now it has to be tonight. There's too much risk to wait. What message does Kristoff have?"

"Oh, it's from your Carina," Kvasir replied, his brow furrowed with worry. "He can explain once we're through, but he said it's urgent. That's part of why I came."

Loki sighed, worry creasing his own brow. "Very well. I'll be back with Sigyn as soon as everyone is asleep. Be back here by midnight, Asgardian time. And for all that's sacred, hide yourself this time!"

Kvasir nodded, taking the invisibility device Loki held out to him.

Loki hurried back to his own room, taking the long way. He nearly collided with Lord Berg, who was returning to his own room after checking on his daughter.

"Well?" Loki demanded.

"She's there," Lord Berg admitted. "She was fully dressed, as if she planned to go out or had been out."

"Maybe she had," Loki said with a shrug. "But she wasn't with me. If you'll excuse me, Lord Berg, I face my abilities test tomorrow, and I need my rest."

The man grunted but let him pass. Loki turned just once to see the man still watching him suspiciously. He waved cheerfully, then returned to his room with a scowl. He quite agreed with Kvasir. The man was insufferable.

When eerie stillness finally settled over the palace, Loki cloaked himself with his own powers and crept out of his room. He made himself visible once he reached Sigyn's door and tapped it quietly.

When she opened it, he slipped into her room and whispered, "It has to be tonight, Sigyn. Now. Your father suspects something."

"I know," she whispered back. "He showed up at my door and asked me some odd questions."

"What questions?"

"Why I was still dressed, if I had been outside, and if I had seen any strangers lurking about the palace," she responded nervously.

"Kvasir was at the tree earlier. Your father might have seen him, but I can't be sure. Grab what you plan to take. Hurry, little one!"

She flew across the room and grabbed a small satchel, which she threw over her shoulder. With more effort than usual, he managed to cloak both Sigyn and himself with his own powers. They tiptoed very quietly past her parents' room, looking behind them every so often as they made their way to the old storeroom.

Once they reached the tunnel, Sigyn heaved a sigh of relief.

"We're not safe yet," Loki shushed her.

They slipped quietly through the tunnel and out the old stone door. At the tree, Loki removed Sigyn's invisibility but kept his own, in case Lord Berg was watching. As soon as

Sigyn was visible, Kvasir revealed himself. She threw herself into his arms and welcomed his kiss.

"Can't that wait?" Loki huffed.

"Loki?" Kvasir asked the air. "Where are you?"

"I'm here," Loki hissed, staying hidden. "I thought I sensed someone watching just a moment ago. We need to go now."

Kvasir grabbed Sigyn's hand and pulled her through the tree, neglecting to cover her mouth in his haste. She shrieked involuntarily as she passed through, her cry cut off suddenly as she vanished. Loki jumped through the tree himself as Lord Berg shouted his daughter's name from several hundred yards away. Lights turned on in the palace and guards clamored in the distance.

The Nordmarka forest near Christiania had not changed. The sun shone just a little more brightly through the dense green leaves, making the air feel refreshingly heavy and lazy. Sigyn looked around her in wonder, still clutching Kvasir's hand. Baldur and Hod stood there grinning, but Kristoff looked grim.

"We're blown!" Loki shouted, revealing himself at once. "Why did you scream, Sigyn?"

"I couldn't help it," she gasped. "Did they hear me?"

"I think they heard that scream all the way in Valhalla! You should have covered her mouth, Kvasir," Loki groaned.

"I know, but it can't be helped now," Kvasir defended himself.

Baldur straightened his shoulders, his face resolute. "I thought it might come to this. Go back, Loki. We'll destroy the tree on this end. You'll have to take care of the other side."

"Won't destroying one side be enough to stop anyone from following them?" Loki asked.

"Yes, but a one-sided portal is far too dangerous to leave like that. Hurry now!"

Loki wondered what he meant, but time had almost run out. And as Baldur nudged him toward the tree, he realized he had not asked about Carina's message.

"Wait!" Loki insisted just as Kristoff opened his mouth to speak. "Kristoff, you have a message from Carina?"

"Yes, she's in trouble!" Kristoff cried.

"What?" A thousand emotions rushed through Loki as his protective instincts took over.

Kristoff shoved a piece of paper into Loki's hands. "I got this yesterday. Find a way to get to her as soon as you can."

"We'll hold the wedding for you," Kvasir informed him, squeezing his shoulder and slipping him the cloaking device.

"You don't have to do that," Loki protested, sliding the device and the paper into the hidden breast pocket of the Asgardian banquet tunic he still wore.

"Nevertheless, we shall. There's no more time," Kvasir urged. "Go!"

Loki sprang through the tree, invisible again, and knocked over Lord Berg, who had been about to go through the tree himself. Loki knocked the nobleman out with one solid blow to the head. He never saw it coming.

Loki revealed himself and knelt beside the unconscious Berg, faking great concern, just as the guards arrived at the scene.

"What happened?" one of the guards demanded. "We heard a scream and a shout."

"I don't know," Loki lied. "I just got here myself and found him like this."

Berg moaned as he regained consciousness and tried to sit up.

"Lie still, Lord Berg," Loki soothed him. "Can you tell us what happened?

"I saw Sigyn ... with Kvasir ..." he groaned, sitting up anyway and holding his head.

"The poet who disappeared centuries ago?" Loki asked, feigning surprise.

"You know very well whom I mean," Lord Berg growled. "They were over there, and now they're both gone. Vanished."

"He must have dashed his head on that tree," Loki informed the guards. "Get him inside."

The tree shuddered as they made their way back, and Loki knew Baldur had done his part. Odin and Thor met the entourage at the main palace doors. The guards took Lord Berg to his room, where the king bade them return to their posts. Odin's personal healer examined the nobleman while Frigga sat with Lady Annette, who wrung her hands and cried silently. The king and his sons watched grimly, waiting for the healer's prognosis.

"You have a mild concussion," the woman said, rising to her feet. "It is important that you rest."

"I'll do nothing of the sort," Lord Berg thundered. "My daughter has been kidnapped by that scandalous poet!"

"No, not kidnapped, Lord Berg," Frigga said quietly. She had not spoken up until now. "Lady Annette, would you like me to read the note you found in Sigyn's room?"

Lady Annette said nothing but held a crumpled paper out to Frigga.

Frigga took it, smoothed out the paper, then read aloud, "My dearest parents, I have eloped with the man I truly love. I know you would want me to be happy. If you leave us alone, we may return in time. Love, Sigyn."

Odin sighed deeply. Lady Annette sniffed pitifully, but Lord Berg looked downright murderous.

"There's another inscription," Frigga added, peering at the paper. "Dear Loki, I have left your ring where you will be sure to find it. I'm sorry."

Thor walked over to Loki to pat him sympathetically on the shoulder. "Ah, brother, your first heartbreak. And just when you had learned to love her."

Lord Berg looked sharply at Loki, who was desperately trying not to grin at Sigyn's cleverness. "Where would she hide your ring?" the nobleman demanded.

"Was it not with the note?"

Everyone looked at Lady Annette, who shook her head.

"It glows whenever I am near it," Loki said with a shrug. "Wherever she left it, I'll find it."

He knew exactly where it was. Sigyn had tried to give it back, but Loki had gestured for her to give it to Kristoff right before passing through the Bifröst tree. The Bifröst tree! He had almost forgotten.

"Father, don't you think it's time we cut down that old, dead tree Lord Berg ran into before someone else gets hurt?" Loki suggested.

"That is no old, dead tree," Odin said gravely. "It is a portal to Midgard, one I have long overlooked. I have no doubt that is how Sigyn and Kvasir made their escape."

"I'm going after her," Lord Berg announced, rising to his feet.

"No, Berg!" Odin commanded. "They have likely destroyed the other end by now. In your current state of mind, you would not like where you would end up."

"Then command Heimdall to send me through the Bi-fröst," Lord Berg insisted.

"Did you not listen?" Lady Annette finally spoke, pleading with her husband. "If we ever hope to see her again, we must let her go. If you hadn't forbidden her from seeing him all those years ago, we might still have our daughter."

She broke down in tears again, while Frigga comforted her. Loki pasted his most sorrowful look on his face. He even cast an illusion of several fake tears glistening in the corners of his eyes.

"I will not be made into the villain here!" Lord Berg exclaimed, glaring at Loki. "I don't know how, but I know you had something to do with this."

Loki boldly met his angry gaze and said nothing, the perfect picture of wounded innocence.

"Don't give me that look! You've made a grave error, boy. I would have made you king," Lord Berg snarled.

"King?" Thor growled in surprise and anger.

Odin fixed Berg with his good gray eye. "Choose your next words very carefully, Lord Berg, for your last ones bordered on treason."

All the fight went out of Berg, and he slumped back into his chair. "Odin, my king, I am no threat. I only grieve over the loss of my daughter and her future."

"I know. But this is no time to lay blame, either of you," Odin said gently to both defeated parents. "Loki has nothing to gain from this. He is a victim as much as anyone. What's done is done. And the past must stay in the past."

Lord Berg opened his mouth, as if to speak.

Odin held up his hand to silence him. "I will have Heimdall

watch over your daughter, as often as I can spare him, once Loki's trials are complete."

"Thank you, my king," Lord Berg said, but his eyes were as hard as lead as he motioned to the door. "Please, if you would all leave us to our grief ..."

Outside the guest room, Thor walked ahead with Frigga, but Loki pulled his father aside. "He will try to go through that tree, Father."

"Of course he will," Odin agreed, a twinkle in his gray eye. "I have already given the order to destroy it at first light."

"Why not now?"

"It will be a lengthy and difficult task, safer in the morning. Until then, I have stationed an armed guard." Odin paused, then asked, "Is this concern for Lord Berg or for Sigyn?"

"I am concerned what Lord Berg will do to Sigyn and Kvasir if he catches them. But I also worry about the safety of Asgard. What did he mean by making me king?" Loki asked.

"Lord Berg spoke out of turn, but I suppose it is time you knew. Regardless of whatever ill feelings you bear toward him, he has long been your advocate," Odin responded. "He believes you are more suited for the throne than Thor."

"Only because he expected me to marry his daughter," Loki said bitterly.

"Do you grieve, my son?" Odin asked. "Or are you relieved?"

"Both," Loki answered truthfully, although his grief was not for Sigyn. "If Sigyn is happy, I am content. I do care for her."

"This should not have happened during your trials. I have the power to delay them for a few days, if you prefer," Odin offered.

"No, Father," Loki protested. "How would that look to our guests? I will continue."

Odin smiled fondly at him as they parted ways. "Your wisdom grows by the day. Good night, my son."

Loki struck his fist against his chest twice and bowed, greatly pleased by his father's praise, then turned on his heel and strode to his own room. As soon as he was alone, he pulled out the paper Kristoff had given him and read it with great consternation.

> *Wedding in three weeks STOP*
> *Alien god needed STOP*
> *Beware of hit*

Loki slammed his fist into his wall in anger and frustration, cracking the alabaster. What could he do? He could not fathom how Joseph Green could force his daughter to marry Klaus Mayar. Carina's father had certainly seemed like a reasonable man, though possessive and overprotective of his daughter. How could he not know what kind of man Klaus was? And why would Carina not inform her father how the scoundrel had behaved? Something far more sinister must be happening. Carina was clearly under duress and could not speak or act freely. Did Klaus have some sort of power over her? What did "beware of hit" mean?

A soft knock at his door startled him out of his brooding thoughts. He composed himself quickly and opened it to reveal Frigga standing there.

She raised one eyebrow, immediately noticing the damaged wall. "May I come in?"

"I'm tired, Mother," he protested. "Does Father know you're here?"

"He does not," Frigga replied. "He's busy with Thor. And I need to speak with you alone."

"About what?"

"Clearly, you are agitated," she answered, gesturing to the wall. "Tell me what's going on. Did you help Sigyn escape?"

"Mother!" he chided.

"Well, did you? Was that your promise to her?"

"I cannot fool you, can I?" Loki stomped over to a chair and slumped into it. "Does Father also suspect?"

Frigga chuckled. "He might, but I doubt it. He has certain blind spots when it comes to his youngest son."

Loki made a wry face. "I would say he has many. I sometimes wonder if he notices me at all, except when it suits his purpose."

"None of that, Loki," Frigga chided. "He notices more than you think. He is proud of your progress, and you know it. Now tell me, when did Kvasir return to Asgard?"

"I will not betray him, Mother. His exile was self-imposed. He has broken no laws."

"Well then, I will assume it was before you gave Sigyn your ring. Why then did you encourage her to flee?"

Loki sighed. "I just wanted her to be happy. She truly does love him. I think you suspected that as well."

"Yes, I did," Frigga admitted. "Still, I thought you could make each other happy. As your father has said, what's done is done. I wish Sigyn nothing but joy."

"If Berg goes after them, he'll ruin her life. Again," Loki pointed out.

"I'm more worried about you." She looked at him carefully. "Something else troubles you."

Loki sighed. "I cannot tell you what troubles me unless all of this stays between us."

"I swear it," Frigga pronounced solemnly, "as long as your secret does not endanger you or Asgard."

Loki peered at her, deciding she was in earnest. "Very well, I confess. I did see the woman I love while you were in Vanaheim, though accidentally. I sort of ran into her while I was out."

Frigga raised her eyebrow again but waited for him to continue.

"The man she was planning to marry is a selfish brute. He even dared to abuse her."

"*Was* planning to marry?"

"Yes, she caught him with another woman. After I fought him in defense of her honor, she ended their betrothal."

"You fought him?" Frigga sounded impressed but worried. "Did anyone see this?"

"It was fairly private, Mother. I kept our royal reputation intact. After that, something else happened. Then she asked me to part from her, so I respected her wishes."

"Something else happened? Oh, Loki, you didn't—"

"If you're asking if I took advantage of her, no, I did not. I love her too much to compromise her honor."

"Then what happened to make her dismiss you so callously?"

"She wasn't callous," Loki insisted, somewhat indignantly. "I lied to her about who I am. When I told her the truth, she couldn't handle it. She asked for time to think."

"Then there is hope for you yet," Frigga observed. When Loki just looked at her sadly, she tentatively asked, "All of this happened while you were promised to Sigyn?"

"No, I was never promised to Sigyn, nor she to me. You were right. It was all just a cover for planning her escape with Kvasir. As I told you, Sigyn knew about the one I love."

Frigga sighed deeply. "Who is this woman?"

"I'm not ready to answer that question," Loki said guardedly.

"Why? Because she's of common blood?"

"You are quite perceptive, Mother."

"Does she love you?"

"She said as much, but now I'm not sure. I did betray her trust, after all. And to complicate it further, I received word tonight she may be in danger."

"Oh? How so?" Frigga asked casually, though there was a note of alarm in her voice.

"I'm not sure, but it sounds as though her father intends to force her to marry the brute after all."

Frigga frowned. "Arranged marriages are illegal here, even for commoners."

"It's not an arranged marriage. But there is something sinister going on, I'm sure of it."

Frigga walked over to Loki and kissed the top of his head. "You would save her?"

"And if I do, what then?"

"Her origins matter not to me. If you love this woman, she will be accepted."

Loki snorted derisively. "Not by Father."

"You are not being fair to your father. He loves you and wants you to be happy as much as I do," Frigga scolded him.

"And did you know he is considering naming me king instead of Thor?" Loki demanded.

"Who told you that?" Frigga gasped.

"Ah, then you do know," Loki challenged her. "And I am not as free as you want me to believe."

"You must put Lord Berg's words out of your mind," Frigga insisted. "Thor is the rightful heir to the throne."

"I know that, Mother," Loki snapped. "Do not remind me yet again how I am not Thor's equal!"

Frigga sighed, hurt flitting through her eyes. "Your father believes you are every bit as kingly as Thor. Perhaps more so! But he has not yet made a decision to overrule the line of succession."

"All of this aside, nothing can be done now, can it, Mother? I am bound by law to finish my trials and then embark on my rite of passage. My hands are tied."

Before Frigga could speak, a sudden shout and clash of arms outside interrupted their conversation. They both dashed to the window but could not see what was causing the commotion.

"Lord Berg is gone!" a voice cried.

Loki rushed outside, but his mother ran toward the sound of Lady Annette's wailing. Odin and Thor had reached the tree before Loki. His two trusted guards lay in their own blood, though not dead.

"Get them to the healer," Odin barked at several other guards who had rushed out at the noise. Then he strode toward the palace with Thor right behind him. "Send more guards to cut this tree down and burn it before someone else goes through!"

In the noise and confusion, Loki saw an opportunity and acted quickly. He clicked the button on the device Kvasir had returned to him and slipped through the tree while it stood unguarded, risking a bit of dark magic in addition to his own brain waves to transport him to New York, focusing on wherever the closest place to Carina might be.

He found himself in darkness, afraid his technique had failed him.

"**D**on't lie to me, Carina! You sent a telegram, didn't you?"

"What makes you think I sent a telegram?"

Her defeated tone and Klaus's angry voice were both muffled. A door creaked open, footsteps sounded, and light illuminated the room as the door slammed shut.

Loki blinked away the sudden glare in his eyes, still hidden. Relief flooded him. He had not stranded himself after all. He was in a study very similar to Joseph Green's in Stuttgart. Since the heavy drapes were still drawn, Loki had no idea what time of day it was.

"Quit stalling! A telegram arrived from Norway yesterday, addressed to you," Klaus answered, shaking a paper in her face. He read aloud, "'Understood.' That's all it says."

Loki cursed Kristoff inwardly for placing Carina in greater danger, though he was grateful his friend had been short and cryptic in his response.

Carina tried to hide a slight smile. "If that arrived yesterday, why are you bringing it up now?"

"I had to wait until Joseph wasn't around, didn't I? And he might come up here any minute!"

"Exactly! And if my father hears you berating and threatening me like this, even these lies you force me to tell won't save you," Carina seethed at him.

Klaus grabbed her arm as she tried to move past him. "You were trying to get a warning to that freak magician or his buddy, weren't you? I told you what would happen to them if you breathed one negative word to them or your father."

"I haven't," she cried in fear. "Please let me go."

Klaus released her, surveying her quietly. Loki fought to refrain from pouncing on the man as he took Carina's face in his hands to forcibly kiss her, though she tried to turn away from him.

Klaus ignored her obvious disgust. "I'm not as bad a sort as you think I am, darling. We were friends once, weren't we? If you would stop being so hostile, I would not have to use such extreme measures."

"If you hadn't used such extreme measures, I wouldn't be so hostile," she retorted, staring him down.

"Oh, really?" Klaus said sarcastically. "And would you be marrying me if I hadn't threatened to send hired guns after your boyfriend? You forced my hand, didn't you?"

She dropped her eyes.

"Carina, I don't like being the bad guy." Klaus switched to a gentler tone, though his voice held an undertone of warning. "We would both be happier if you could bring yourself to love me."

"I will never love you," she whispered fiercely.

"Still mooning over Black, are we? Where is he now?" Klaus spat, gritting his teeth. He grabbed her shoulders and shook her. "I try to be nice, and this is what I get? What did that telegram say, Carina?"

When she did not respond, Klaus raised his hand to strike her but nearly lost his arm as Loki grabbed it and yanked it back.

"Luke!" Carina gasped, gaping at him with wide eyes. "Where did you come from?"

Klaus quickly recovered and backed against the wall, cowardly holding Carina in front of him. "Get out of here, Black! Or I will break her arm, then tell her father and the police you did it."

Loki's favorite dagger flew from his hand, nicking Klaus's ear just before embedding in the wall by his head. "Touch her again," Loki growled. "Next time, I won't miss."

Klaus grabbed his ear. Feeling the blood oozing out of it, he threw Carina to the side. She cried out as she landed, which distracted Loki enough to give Klaus time to pull the dagger from the wall. As Klaus threw himself at Loki, he only narrowly missed slicing him. But Loki released two more daggers in seconds and drove Klaus back. Carina drew her own dagger before Loki could stop her. She thrust it into Klaus's upper arm, then collapsed into a trembling heap when he roared with pain and anger. Loki dropped his daggers and used the opportunity to land an uppercut to Klaus's jaw, knocking him backward.

Loki yanked his first dagger from Klaus's grip just as he slumped unconscious against the wall. Then he rushed over to Carina, slipping the dagger into its hiding spot.

"Did I kill him?" she asked, trembling.

He laughed, pulling her to her feet. "No, you just stuck him. Beautifully, I might add, although you put yourself in danger with that stunt. Are you hurt?"

"I'm just shaken up," she admitted.

"Good. Don't ever scare me like that again!" he scolded her as he retrieved his other daggers from the floor.

She laughed shakily. "How did you get here so fast? I only sent that telegram yesterday."

"Carina? Klaus? What's all that ruckus up there?" bellowed Joseph Green from a lower level.

Carina gasped and clutched Loki's arm as he stood defensively in front of her. "Get out of here. He'll think you stabbed Klaus!"

"Not if he doesn't see me," Loki told her. "It's quite impossible, humanly speaking, for me to have been here. Would he recognize your dagger?"

"Yes!" she cried. "When he found it in my room, I told him it was a souvenir from Paris. Should I take it out of his arm?"

"He'll bleed all over if you do that, and I don't have time to give him medical attention, especially if he wakes up and tries to fight me again. Let your father handle it," Loki instructed her quickly. "We need to go."

"Where?" Carina cried.

"There's no time," he urged as Joseph's footsteps approached the door. "You'll just have to trust me."

Before she could respond, he covered her mouth in case she screamed and hid them both with Kvasir's device. Then Loki whisked her through the quickly fading temporary portal with as much dark magic as he dared. As soon as she filled her lungs to scream, her knees buckled. He quickly released her mouth to support her, reducing the sound of her cry to a whisper as he did so. This expended mental energy, combined with the magnetic pull of the portal, almost knocked him out. But he somehow managed to stay conscious as they teleported back to his room in Asgard.

Loki rushed her over to his bed, then collapsed beside her in agony. The searing pain coursing through him made him briefly question his continued use of dark magic to travel, especially as much as he had needed. But when the pain quickly faded, Loki brushed those thoughts aside, justifying his choices under such dire circumstances.

As he regained his own strength, he grew aware of Carina almost hyperventilating beside him, her eyes wide as she stared blankly at the pattern on his bedspread. "Are you alright, Carina?" he asked, worried she might faint.

"Yes," she gasped, though she tried to hide her shaking hands.

"Are you in pain?" he pressed her, concerned the dark magic might have affected her.

"No, I ... I don't understand what just happened," she stammered. "What did you do to me? Where are we?"

"We're on Asgard."

Carina's eyes widened as she started to sputter loudly, but Loki gently placed his hand over her mouth again. "You must try to be quiet! No one can know you're here."

When she nodded, he removed his hand.

"Won't someone see me?" she objected, keeping her voice low.

"You are invisible to everyone but me."

"I'm invisible? How is that possible?" she gasped.

"How is any of this possible?" Loki challenged her. "I just took you from New York to Asgard in a matter of seconds."

Carina took a deep breath and closed her eyes to calm herself. When she opened them again, she looked around as if finally noticing her new environment. "This place … it looks like a palace."

"It is a palace," Loki chuckled. "These are my quarters."

Carina surveyed the large room with great interest, taking in the draperies, four-poster bed, chaise lounge, and elaborate area rug spread over the marble floor. "You really do love green, don't you?"

"Not everything I told you was a lie," Loki admitted. "I described Loki the way I did so you would see the real me." He led her to the window and gestured for her to look out across the sleeping city. "And now, you can see my world."

She gazed out across the alabaster buildings, her face a picture of wonder and admiration. Familiar with the sight himself, he watched her with delight, feeling the color rush back into his eyes.

"I've never seen anything so beautiful," she breathed. "The way the moon hits the walls of the city … they gleam, almost like snow."

"In the sun, it looks more like gold," Loki added proudly. "It's the way we treat the alabaster stone."

"The architecture is quite unusual," she continued, not taking her eyes off the view, which took on a magical air as Loki imagined how it must appear to her. He gazed at her tenderly as she elaborated, speaking as if she were in a dream. "The buildings remind me of seamless organ pipes. From here, I can imagine some gentle giant sculpting each towering column to a point. I've never seen so many spires in one place. It's so … futuristic! Like something Jules Verne might describe. Do people live in the tops? I don't see any windows."

"No," he answered. "Why would they?"

"Why build up if you don't plan to use it?" she chuckled. "That's a lot of wasted space. But never mind that. Is that the edges of a wild forest over there?"

He looked where she pointed, though he knew what he would see. "Yes, that's where I'll be going for my rite of passage soon."

"What's that?"

"A time of solitude in the wilderness," he murmured, staring at the distant tree line with some trepidation. "There are many mysteries in that forest. I'm supposed to find them, to prove I'm a man."

"Aren't you a man?" she glanced at him, then back out the window.

"Not to my people, not in every sense," he replied. "Until I complete the rite of passage, I'm just a young prince most people don't take seriously."

Carina furrowed her brow suddenly, then sat down heavily on his chaise lounge. "I don't understand. How can this be happening? How can you be Loki, *the* Loki?"

He sighed, unsure if she expected an answer. He had been growing nervous about how much time had passed since Lord Berg disappeared and assumed his presence would have been expected by now.

But before he could think of what to say, she drew her knees to her chest and muttered, "This is a dream. It has to be a dream."

"Fine, you go back to sleep then," he reassured her. "I'll be back in a little while."

"Where are you going?" She scrambled off the comfortable chair and ran to him. "Don't leave me here alone."

"There are things happening here that I don't have time to explain right now," Loki insisted. "I really must go. Please trust me. Stay here and try to rest."

"How long will you be gone?" she pleaded with him.

"Only a little while," he assured her. "When I return, we can get caught up."

He clicked the button off the invisibility device to reveal them both, then showed her how to hide herself. He warned her to stay away from the window just in case, then left the room.

He went in search of Odin and Thor, fearful he might have been discovered, though not just because of his absence. Legends told of Asgardians who could sense the use of dark magic when the usage was greater than a certain level. He had never before dared to test those rumors. Until tonight. And he imagined both Odin and Heimdall must be in that number. And if Heimdall realized what he was up to, he would not hesitate to inform the king. Since no guards had come to fetch him, he hoped his secret was still safe.

Loki found his father and brother closeted in Odin's main office. He braced himself as he joined them.

"Where did you disappear to?" Thor demanded. "Mother said you ran outside when the commotion started. I thought I saw you, but then you vanished."

"I did vanish. I went on an investigation of my own throughout the palace grounds," Loki replied.

"And what did you find?" Odin inquired.

"Nothing more than you already know," Loki informed them. "My efforts proved futile, I'm afraid."

Odin nodded, turning his attention back to Thor. Feeling

immense relief, Loki concluded the cloaking mechanism had hidden the dark magic, as well as Carina and himself.

That really is one handy gadget, Loki thought.

"As I was saying, Lord Berg has vanished, seriously wounding two guards," Thor said angrily. "We must act before he does! Seize his estate! Question his servants!"

"Thor!" Odin warned. "Look to your temper. Berg seeks his daughter, not war. Heimdall will locate him, though I am certain he regrets his rash decision."

"What do you mean?" Thor demanded.

"A Bifröst portal with no destination leads to a place of lawlessness and despair, unless you have the power to override it. If war comes, we will be ready. But we will not seek it out," Odin commanded, holding up his hand to silence Thor just as he opened his mouth. "I will say no more on the subject. Go now, my sons. Get some sleep."

Once they left their father to himself, Thor asked Loki, "What do you make of this?"

"Father is right, Thor," Loki replied. "Lord Berg acted rashly, out of grief. We must provide comfort for Lady Annette. She's lost everything in a matter of hours."

"Bah, leave that to Mother," Thor scoffed. "My hands itch for battle."

"Then spar with me, one last time. Tomorrow morning, before my abilities test," Loki offered in an attempt to placate him.

Thor cheered up instantly, clapping Loki on the back. "That will be a fine warm up for you, brother. And very amusing for me."

"Hilarious," Loki muttered, then bid Thor good night.

He stopped in the kitchen to grab some food for Carina,

who he assumed would be hungry soon. He spun around several times, not sure what she would like, but finally settled on a golden apple, green grapes, hearty brown bread, and chunks of soft Asgardian cheese. He was nearly caught by some guards as he hurried back to his room. He balanced the food in one hand as he opened the door. Panic seized him momentarily; Carina was nowhere to be seen. But then, to his great amusement, a piece of cheese lifted itself off the plate he carried.

"Carina, did you hide yourself from me?" he accused her playfully.

A bodiless snicker sounded as the cheese wafted away on the air, then disappeared as she popped it into her mouth.

"I was bored, and I didn't feel right going through your things, so I played around with your little invisibility machine for a while," she explained, her voice slightly muffled as she chewed. "Is this Brie de Meaux?"

"In a way," Loki replied. "I've tried Brie de Meaux. I'm sure it came from Asgard because of a story my father once told. He never said when or where, but some monks sheltered him once, back when he used to wander Midgard in disguise. He happened to have some Asgardian cheese, so he shared it with them. They loved it so much, he brought an Asgardian farmer on his next trip to teach them how to make it."

"That's quite a story."

He grinned in the direction of her voice. "I don't know much about Asgardian travel to Midgard in the old days, but I've always loved that story. It made me feel connected to your world somehow. As much as I love Asgardian cheese, I do wish one of your people would teach our farmers how to make Gouda or Cheddar."

"As advanced as Asgard seems, they've never figured that out?" Carina razzed him.

"There's never been a need. I don't think Asgardians experiment nearly as much with food," Loki mused. "Honestly, I prefer Midgardian fare most of the time."

"Well, this food doesn't look much different," Carina observed, then abruptly changed the subject. "The only thing I don't like about this doohickey is I can't tell if it works when I'm by myself."

"Then why did you bother playing with it?" Loki teased.

"Oh, I was just curious if I could see myself, so I experimented with a few things," Carina answered. "Nothing very impressive. I could only see my hand in front of my face one time. But I couldn't see myself in the mirror. That was strange."

"When could you see your hand?"

"I had to think to make myself invisible to everyone but me," she answered.

"That didn't work in the mirror?" he asked curiously. When she responded in the negative, he mused, "Must be something with light or brain frequency. I'll have to ask Kvasir sometime."

"Well, I'm glad to know it works on you," she pointed out.

"You aren't supposed to use it against me," Loki chided her, secretly impressed that she had.

"I'll try to remember that," she snickered. Seeming to sense he was proud of her, she boasted, "I think I've mastered this little device."

"Good," Loki praised her, placing the plate down on the small table near his bed. "You'll probably need it while you're here, maybe even tomorrow."

She appeared and grabbed some grapes. "Thank you for the food, by the way. I love grapes, especially green ones."

"So do I." He shook his head when she offered him one. "I'm not hungry."

"So, what happens tomorrow? And when exactly is tomorrow? It's still night here." She jumped onto his bed, sitting cross legged and waiting expectantly for him to answer her questions.

"It's after two a.m., I believe, so I guess it's already tomorrow. I spar with my brother in a few hours, then—"

"Who is your brother? You never told me his name," Carina interrupted. "Is it Baldur, as Tyr said?"

"Baldur is my oldest brother," Loki explained. "But no one here knows he's still alive. I was talking about Thor. He's just a little older than me."

"The god of thunder?"

"That's how he's called on Earth," Loki affirmed.

"And what happens after you spar with Thor?" she asked.

"I face the second level of my trials to prove I can control my skills and abilities as an Asgardian."

"Your magic?"

"It's not really magic," he corrected. "Kristoff called my abilities superpowers. It's a rather excessive description, but accurate."

He brought the plate with him as he sat across from her on the bed.

When he set it down between them, she grabbed the bread but made a face with her first bite. "Do they only make rye bread here?"

"No, that's just all I could find tonight. Here, try the apple," he offered, holding it out to her.

151

"Will this make me immortal?" she teased, though she took it eagerly.

"I'm afraid not," Loki answered with a grin. "I'm not immortal myself."

She took a bite, the juice foaming slightly around the corners of her perfect mouth. She shut her eyes and murmured, "Oh, this is so good."

Loki bit his lip and looked away. Her obvious delight in the apple made her almost irresistible to him. He forced himself to control the urge to gather her into his arms and focused on the apple itself. "Now do you see why I said apples should never be cooked?"

"If I had access to apples like these," she said, wiping her mouth, "I would actually want to see how they taste in a pie."

Loki shuddered, making Carina laugh, though she stifled it with her hand. As she polished off the apple, he explained everything to her as he had to Kristoff, also filling her in on all of the events since they had parted in London.

"And now, it's your turn," Loki told her. "Did Klaus blackmail you?"

She nodded. "But first, he tried to win me back. He was there to meet me as soon as I got off the steamer, with flowers and a syrupy smile, as if nothing were wrong. When I brushed him aside, he apologized for what happened in Paris, but he was so condescending! He had the nerve to say he and Father both believed I had ... and I quote ..." She made a haughty face and attempted to imitate Klaus's voice as she continued, "'succumbed to the clever manipulations of a talented master of deception.'"

"Oh, please," Loki scoffed. "Though I must admit that's the nicest thing Klaus has ever said about me."

She chuckled, then continued, "When that tactic didn't work, Klaus said he had thugs watching you and Kristoff. He said if I refused to marry him or told Father the truth, he only had to send word and they'd bump you off."

"Despicable," Loki muttered. "And an utter lie, at least as far as I'm concerned. He couldn't possibly have anyone watching me."

"I didn't know that," Carina stated somewhat defensively.

"Of course you didn't," Loki reassured her. "Sending that telegram must have been a huge risk for you."

"It was," Carina agreed. "I don't know what Klaus would have done to me if you hadn't shown up."

"Maybe you would have killed him," Loki teased her.

Carina shuddered. "What if it had come to that?"

He reached for her hand. "It didn't. You're safe now."

She squeezed his hand and smiled. "Thank you for rescuing me." When he nodded to acknowledge her gratitude, she winked at him and asked, "But how will I ever get my dagger back?"

Loki stifled a laugh. "I'll take you back to Midgard after the final level of trials, when I head to the wilderness for my rite of passage. There's a portal there that links to London."

"What's the final level?"

"Single combat with my choice of weapons," Loki answered, enjoying the concern on her face.

"Like the gladiators of Ancient Rome?"

"Oh no, it's rarely lethal," he assured her.

"That isn't very comforting," she retorted. "What will we do after we arrive in London? Go back to New York?"

"If that's where you want to go, but I have a wedding to

attend in Norway first," he said. "I was hoping you'd go with me."

"Whose?"

"Sigyn's," he reminded her. "Don't you remember what I told you?"

"I'm still piecing it all together," she admitted. Then she smiled wickedly. "If I understood correctly, you're not married to Sigyn, as the stories say. But you almost got engaged to her?"

"Do we really have to go over all this again?" Loki groaned. Then he too smiled wickedly. "Although, I must admit, I did enjoy elements of the last time you got jealous of Sigyn."

She blushed. "I remember."

He leaned toward her, but she held out her hand and shook her head.

"Don't you need to sleep at some point?" she pointed out.

He frowned, disappointed. "You're probably right," he said, getting up and crossing the room to his chaise lounge. "You take the bed. I'll sleep over here."

"Is there any chance someone might come in here?" she asked. "Maybe I should stay over there and use this thing to hide myself."

"I would hardly be a gentleman if I let you do that," Loki protested. "I locked the door. No one will disturb you, but yes, do hide yourself."

"You won't be comfortable over there. It's morning in New York. I'm really not even tired," Carina protested, but her sudden yawn contradicted her words. When Loki raised his eyebrows at her, she admitted, "I guess I haven't slept well since London."

And sure enough, she was asleep almost as soon as she had settled into his bed. Despite his own exhaustion, he watched her from the chaise lounge until his eyes finally drifted shut.

Several hours later, a quite visible Carina shook Loki awake, not the pounding on the door he should have heard.

"You're visible, Carina," he whispered fiercely, stretching as he stood up. "You must have deactivated the device in your sleep!"

"Loki, I'm tired of waiting!" Thor bellowed in Asgardian from the hallway.

"Is that Thor?" Carina whispered as she disappeared again, apparently forgetting to remain visible to Loki. "What did he say?"

"He's tired of waiting for our sparring session," Loki answered. "I overslept, so now there's no time for me to get you any breakfast. I'm sorry!"

"I'll be fine. May I go with you?"

"No, you have to stay here," Loki muttered.

"Please? I want to watch. I'll be quiet!"

Loki reluctantly agreed. He could not see her or feel her as they walked down to the armory. Yet, knowing she was there and watching gave him an edge he had never before had in any sparring session. For the first time in his life, he bested Thor in swordplay.

"Ho, brother, what did you eat today?" Thor praised him. "Your skill has indeed grown!"

"Still think you'll have to peel me off the arena floor tomorrow?" Loki challenged him, reminding Thor of his taunt from their last sparring session.

"Perhaps not," Thor conceded. "I don't envy your contender, whomever they choose. What weapons will you use?"

"Swords and daggers, of course," Loki replied, wiping the sweat off his forehead and neck.

"It's what you're best at," Thor agreed. "Shall we go once more? Or perhaps switch to axes and hammers?"

Loki snorted. "Just so you can take away my moment of triumph?"

Thor laughed, "No, brother, it belongs to you. In fact, I shall tell the story of how you vanquished the Mighty Thor tonight at Father's table. The ladies will swoon, and you will soon forget Sigyn in their company."

Loki winced, thankful Carina could not understand their conversation. He hoped she would not ask him about it later. "Don't do me any favors, Thor. I'll find love in my own time."

"I'm still telling the story," Thor insisted. "But I won't throw any maidens your way if you don't want them. More for me."

Loki laughed. "Do you need more?"

"I was willing to share," Thor said with a shrug. "You turned me down."

"Yes, well, I prefer a woman with more than a pretty face. Anyway, I had better get washed up and ready for the next test."

"Indeed! Today should be decidedly less boring than yesterday," Thor stated, clapping Loki on the shoulder. "You really are doing well, brother."

The two brothers clasped arms for a moment. Loki flashed Thor a smile, then walked alone back to his room, hoping Carina followed. He left the door open to allow her to get back inside when she caught up. He slipped into his bathroom, washing off all the sweat and grime. Out of habit, he wrapped his towel around his waist and stepped back into his room to grab his clothes. He nearly jumped out of his skin when Carina gasped.

"Did you forget I was here?" she asked.

"I wasn't thinking," he admitted sheepishly. He still could not see her but noticed she had shut and locked the door to his room.

"At least you thought to grab a towel," she snickered. "You certainly look human right now."

He made a face in the direction of her voice, then ducked back into the bathroom and got dressed quickly, thoroughly embarrassed. When he stepped back into the room, she was visible again, though shimmery.

"Who can see you now?" he asked.

"Just you. At least, that was the objective," she declared. "Shall we test it? I wouldn't mind seeing Thor again. He is very handsome, you know, though he also looks nothing like the drawings."

Loki scowled, already embarrassed by her reaction to seeing him almost naked and now angered by her praise of Thor.

"By the look on your face, one might say you're jealous of your brother," she observed softly, drawing near to him.

"Everyone compares me to him," Loki retorted defensively. "And now, even you are making me feel inadequate."

"Well, you beat him, didn't you?" She placed her hands on his shoulders and looked up at him coyly. "Besides, I only meant it from a purely aesthetic position. I've never been attracted to burly, blonde men."

"No?" Loki challenged her. "What then?"

"Dark hair, green eyes, lanky with solid muscle," she described, squeezing his biceps playfully. "Someone who moves like a panther instead of barreling down anyone in his path. That's more my kind of man."

"Anyone I know?" he murmured, delighted by her praise. His heart raced as he drew near to kiss her.

She placed her hand on his mouth and gently pushed him back. "Oh no, you don't. When do I get to wash up?"

Loki frowned, feeling foolish for not considering her needs. "Go ahead. I'll find you some women's clothing from what Sigyn left in her guest room."

"I don't want to wear her clothes," Carina pouted.

"Would you rather stay in that dress for two days?"

"No," she admitted, looking down at herself. "And I suppose there's no hope this could be washed?"

"There would be a lot of questions if some woman's dress and undergarments turned up in my laundry," he teased with a roguish grin.

She blushed but sighed. "Very well, I'll handwash them and hang them up to dry." She peeked into the bathroom, her eyes widening at the enormity of the porcelain, clawfoot tub. "I'm going to enjoy this!"

She shut the door and started her bath water. Loki smiled to himself, trying not to imagine her undressing and sliding into the warm water.

He sauntered casually down the corridors and ducked into the guest room Sigyn had occupied. He was rifling through her abandoned luggage when he heard a frightened gasp.

He froze.

"Your Highness," squeaked a guilty looking maid. She had

slipped in so quietly, he had not heard her. "What are you doing here?"

"Looking for my ring," Loki answered confidently. "What are you doing here?"

The maid looked at the floor, rooted to the spot. "I was sent to pack up Lady Sigyn's things."

Loki grinned. He knew she was not telling the whole truth. "Did you plan to try something on in the process? Perhaps claim something for yourself since no one knows what she took with her?"

"Please, my prince," the maid pleaded, trembling in fear. "Are you going to turn me in?"

"Come now, don't be afraid," Loki comforted her. "You know I don't mind a bit of mischief. Perhaps we can help each other."

"How so?"

"I'll keep your secret if you will keep mine. I'll even let you take a dress for yourself," he offered.

"Your secret, sir?" The maid looked confused.

"I find myself in need of a dress," Loki explained. "And some undergarments."

"Your Highness?" The maid looked decidedly uncomfortable.

Loki chuckled. "Relax. They're for a woman I know who doesn't have anything."

"How kind of you, Your Highness," the maid replied. "And you wish your charity to remain anonymous?"

"Something like that," Loki said nonchalantly. "Sigyn isn't coming back. She has no need of these things. Help me choose something practical but pretty, then choose one for yourself."

The maid curtsied, then rummaged through the luggage while Loki stood by and watched. She held up the blue dress Sigyn had worn when Loki had tried to kiss her.

"No, not that one," Loki protested.

The maid laid it aside for herself, then held up a red dress. Loki shook his head. She showed him another blue one, then a black one. None seemed right for Carina. Finally, she held up a long purple day dress that Loki had never seen Sigyn wear. The garment was decidedly not Midgardian fashion, but he thought Carina would like the color and the style, which had a fitted waist with a flared, ombre skirt and no sleeves.

"Perfect," Loki exclaimed. He could not wait to see how it looked on her.

The maid rolled the proper undergarments and the dress into a tight little ball and handed it to Loki. She quickly packed up the rest of Sigyn's things and hid the dress she had chosen in her maid's uniform. Loki made himself invisible and followed her out the door. He knew she would never speak of it for fear of discovery herself.

Back in his room, he knocked respectfully on the bathroom door. Carina did not answer.

"Carina, it's me," Loki called softly.

"Oh, come in," she called back.

"I don't think I should," Loki objected bashfully.

"I'm completely immersed in bubbles!" she protested with an incredulous laugh. "I saw more of you than you could possibly see of me. But if you'd rather not, just open the door a crack and slide the clothes inside. I'm not ready to get out."

Loki stood outside the door, fighting with himself. Knowing she was in there bathing was hard enough for him. If he actually saw her, covered in bubbles or not, he feared his own response to such a sight would not be exemplary.

Respect, he reminded himself silently.

He gulped and shut his eyes tightly, then cracked the door. Taking a deep breath, he shoved the clothing through, quickly pulling the door shut, lest he change his mind. Draping himself across his bed further inflamed him as the sweet scent she had left on his sheets filled his nostrils and threatened his resolve. Thoroughly frustrated, he sat down at his desk and tried to read one of the books his mother had given him for his birthday.

The bathroom door opened.

"It doesn't fit quite right," Carina complained, pulling at the dress. "She must be taller and thinner than I am."

Loki smiled softly. "I never cared much for purple until you wore that one dress in Paris. Truly, it is your color. You look absolutely beautiful."

Carina's face brightened, though she looked shyly at the floor. "Thank you."

He stood and took a few steps toward her, but they were both startled by three solid raps at his door—the knock of a palace guard.

"Here's your chance to test your invisibility," Loki whispered, walking over to open the door.

"They're ready for you, Your Highness," the guard informed him.

He gave no sign he could see or sense Carina, though Loki could still see her in his peripheral vision. He nodded to the guard, then closed the door.

"He didn't see me," she stated, quite pleased with herself. "May I go?"

"Why? So you can see Thor again?" he grumbled.

"That's not going away any time soon, is it?" she remarked ruefully, though the laughter in her voice betrayed her lack of remorse. "Now you know how I feel about Sigyn."

Loki smirked. "Were you trying to make me jealous?"

"Maybe a little," Carina admitted sheepishly. "I know you said you had to act the part with her, but I don't like thinking about the two of you together."

"Well then, don't think about it," Loki responded with a pleased grin. "At least I know you still care."

Carina reached up and smoothed back a stray lock of hair from Loki's forehead. "Of course I do. Were you worried?"

"As a matter of fact, yes," Loki muttered, closing his eyes at her touch. "But there isn't time to talk about that now."

"You'll let me go?" Carina asked excitedly.

"Come on," he sighed. "You'll have to find your own seat. Don't make a sound, and don't bump into anyone!"

11

Loki followed his four-guard escort down the tree-lined, gravel path leading to the outdoor arena next to the palace, his confident strides kicking up a pebble now and then. He did not have to muffle the crunch of Carina's footsteps since the guards made their own racket of rattling armor and measured marching. As they approached the looming triple archway of the arena entrance, he glanced behind him to make sure Carina had stayed with them. He quickly gestured for her to enter through the stone arch to the left. She slipped around his entourage to follow several stragglers walking up the stone stairs to find a seat in the stands. The guards filed through to the right to take their places with their fellow soldiers.

Loki placed one hand on the sculpted column nearest him to steady himself, then entered through the center arch. The trumpets sounded to announce his arrival. He waited for half a second for the herald to shout his name and title, then remembered he was not a royal spectator this time and would be doing it himself shortly. From the royal box, Thor made a fist of triumph as Odin nodded to acknowledge his youngest son and Frigga smiled serenely. Loki straightened his shoulders, reminding himself to focus, and waved to the crowds as he took his place in front of the nobles who would judge his abilities. He saw Carina's shimmery form perched at the top row of the stands, away from the other people but where she could still see. Many more Asgardians had come to see this demonstration, but he had used his abilities so often in performance settings on Midgard, he experienced no nervousness. He planted his feet firmly on the dirt floor. He could not be more ready.

A white-haired, handsome noble sporting a heavily embroidered, blue velvet doublet instructed in English, "State your name and title."

Lord Bragi, a distinguished member of Odin's war council, had also presided over Loki's first day of trials. As the head of the judging committee, he sat slightly elevated in the center of the wooden platform, with two judges on either side— Lady Winsletta (who was Bragi's wife), Lord Trebent, Lady Gladys, and Lord Shronner.

"Loki, prince of Asgard, son of Odin," Loki responded in a clear, strong voice.

He was too far away to see Carina's facial expression, but he did notice she leaned forward when he announced his title.

"State your natural-born abilities," Lord Bragi droned.

"Manipulation of light and sound," he answered confidently.

His mother had warned him to never speak openly of his ability to read minds or influence thought, as it would cause fear and concern. Odin and Thor had emphatically agreed with her since they knew his loyalty. At times, Loki wondered if Odin ever planned to use him and his convenient but dangerous gift as a weapon or for spying.

"This should be entertaining," Lord Bragi noted with a pleased smile, bringing Loki's thoughts back to why he was there.

Focus, Loki! he urged himself again.

The other nobles nodded approvingly, exchanging eager smiles with each other. The spectators murmured with anticipation until Bragi silenced them with a wave of his hand.

"Demonstrate," the nobleman commanded. "Begin with light."

Loki used the sunlight to form a glowing ball of white light, dividing it into one red ball, one yellow ball, and one blue ball. He juggled those three balls, making more in purple, green, and orange as the primary colored balls passed each other over his head. He was an artist, mixing light instead of paint, with the air around him as his palette. He continued to juggle, splitting each solid color into three shades respectively until he was juggling eighteen colored spheres of light. Then he began reducing the balls one by one, throwing them high as he juggled the others. When each ball vanished in a flare of glittering sparks and sharp bursts of sound, the audience oohed and aahed, ignoring Bragi's attempt to keep the arena quiet. When only the original three remained, Loki split them into blasts of color. He sent them flying through the air, stopping them inches away from the faces of his immediate family in the royal box, drawing a gasp from the rest of the spectators, who then sighed with relief when he brought the spheres back to himself. Loki played as though the colors had splashed all over his clean white tunic, eliciting a laugh from the crowd. With a snap of his fingers, the colors vanished. With another snap, he vanished himself. When he reappeared, he had created two illusionary versions of himself, which bowed with him before the nobles.

"Which one of you is the real Loki?" Bragi asked with great interest.

"The one in the middle," all three Lokis spoke at once. Then the real Loki stepped forward, and the illusions vanished.

"Impressive," Lady Gladys cried.

"Begin your sound demonstration," Bragi commanded.

Loki recited a beloved Asgardian poem that had been translated into English but changed his voice to sound first like Odin's, then like Thor's. When he finished reciting, he made his voice sound like rushing water, the howl of a wolf, and the whinny of a stallion. His last sound was an eagle crying from an eyrie, which he sent echoing through the arena. Several people held their ears, including Carina.

"That will do," Bragi said, rotating his pinky finger in his own ear as if to rid it of the piercing noise.

Loki bowed, then stood waiting for his marks, which he was pleased to hear were higher than the previous day, though not quite as high as Thor's had been. Loki had expected as much. The people had been awed, even frightened, by the thunder, lightning, and drenching rain Thor had summoned months ago. But as Loki's scores were very close to his brother's, he was delighted. He just might emerge Thor's equal after all. All Loki had to do was win his match the following day.

The people mobbed him, congratulating him on his performance. But as he was too busy looking for Carina, he only registered a sea of faces and brightly colored clothing, as well as the boisterous praise of some barrel-chested men and the gushing voices of several enamored women, which he ignored. The experience overwhelmed him; only Midgardians had shown him such approval before now. His guards quickly extricated him from the mob of well-wishers. Once freed from the fracas, he spotted Carina, who had hovered as close as she dared without mingling with the people. He discreetly signaled for her to follow him as the guards escorted him back to his quarters.

Once they were both safely in his room, he selected his banquet clothes, opting for all black under the battle gear he was expected to wear, then slipped into his bathroom to change.

Through the closed door, he informed Carina, "You'll have to stay here during the banquet. The risks are far too great for you to participate, even as a silent observer."

"But I haven't eaten all day!" she complained.

Loki came out of the bathroom and kissed her forehead. "I'll bring you something to eat as soon as I can get away. Please understand, my star. I could get into serious trouble for bringing a Midgardian to Asgard."

She nodded, relenting, but kept her arms folded as he locked her in his room.

The feasting went far too long that night, leaving him no time to worry about his last test, especially since his thoughts never strayed far from the woman waiting in his room. He barely registered whom he talked to or even who attended. Thor kept his promise and described how Loki had beaten him in their match that morning, loudly lamenting how he needed to step up his own training to remain the best in battle. Loki rolled his eyes but enjoyed the attention, especially his father's approving nod. As Thor had predicted, several of the single noblewomen who used to ignore Loki began to eye him with sudden interest, much to his chagrin. He maintained his distance, then finally excused himself. Thor protested greatly but was soon distracted by yet another opportunity to tell one of his tales. Relieved to escape the thunderous noise of the crowded banquet hall, Loki raided the kitchen for leftovers. He was nearly caught several times by guests or guards but managed to get back into his room without further difficulty.

He found Carina reclining on his bed, lost in one of the new books he had left on his desk.

Loki set down the heaping plate of banquet food he carried and locked the door. "I hope you didn't lose my place," he teased her. "Which book are you reading?"

"Well, if you don't know, it must have been quite some time since you picked it up," she teased back, not even looking up. "It was the only one on your desk written in English. It's called *The Fall of the Sparrow*. I've almost finished it."

"Don't tell me how it ends," Loki warned. "That was a birthday gift, so I've barely started it."

"When was your birthday?"

"The day before yesterday."

"Happy birthday," she said automatically, still not taking her attention away from the book.

"I thought you would be starving by now," Loki stated, taking the food over to her. "Look what I brought you."

She held up her hand. "Last page!"

When she closed the book, Loki handed her the plate, which was loaded with tender slices of suckling pig, a generous helping of seasoned turnips smothered in chicory sauce, green gelatin salad, and two soft white rolls.

"How much do you think I eat?" she spouted, but she tore into the food while Loki watched with amusement. Between bites and murmurs of how good the food tasted, she asked, "How was the banquet?"

"It was a typical Asgardian banquet." He was not sure if she was happier to see him or the food, now that she was not distracted. "Did you enjoy my show earlier?"

She looked up from the food and commented, "Funny you should use that word. I loved every minute of it, but it did make me wonder if this is all just that."

"What?"

"An elaborate show. Maybe I'm just on a huge movie set, and these are all very good actors."

Loki rolled his eyes. "Why would I go to such trouble? I thought you finally believed me!"

"I thought I did yesterday, but it's just all so confusing when I think about it," she objected. "I don't want to be deceived."

"I could easily deceive you, and you would never even know it," he informed her haughtily.

"What does that mean?" she asked indignantly.

"I didn't reveal this at the trials because it's a dangerous gift, but I can tap into people's brain waves and influence thought if I choose," Loki confessed.

"You read minds?" she gasped, somewhat sarcastically, but with a touch of fear.

"I never do it without permission. My mother has the same gift. And possibly my father, although in a different way. It's a secret we share in my family."

"Was your mother the queenly one sitting by Thor today?"

"Yes, and beside her was my father, Odin, king of Asgard."

"I thought so. He looks every bit as I imagined him. Black eye patch, ravens, and all," Carina admitted. Then she paused thoughtfully before continuing. "How are those ravens still alive if Sleipnir is dead?"

"They're descendants of Huginn and Muninn. Sleipnir had several children as well. My father is raising a colt from his lineage, though he is not as fond of me as his grandfather was."

"Does he also have eight legs?" Carina asked.

"Odin only chooses colts born with eight legs," Loki stated.

"Well, if this is all an act, you've chosen excellent actors, yourself included," Carina sighed.

"Do you really think I've hatched some elaborate scheme, with a different language and everything?" Loki asked, raising his voice slightly.

"I don't know," she muttered.

"You don't know?" he repeated incredulously. "You saw the city last night!"

"Maybe it was a very realistic painting," she mused.

"And a different one this morning?" he shot back sarcastically. "You went outside twice today! How could I fake that?"

"Really well-done movie sets," Carina answered. "I've never been on one, but they sure know how to make films look real. Costumes, scenery, the whole ball of wax."

Loki narrowed his eyes. *Is she serious?* he thought. Aloud, he asked, "Do you realize you're deliberately deceiving yourself?"

"How so?" she demanded.

Loki had been sitting across from her, but he got up in frustration and paced the floor.

What's it going to take for her to accept who I am? he thought. *Haven't I shown her enough?*

"You came so close to accepting the truth. In fact, I thought you had. But now you're denying all of the evidence around you because it challenges what *you* thought you knew," Loki expounded sternly. "Don't let your intelligence get in the way to the point that you convince yourself of something stupid."

"Stupid?" she repeated angrily.

"Yes, stupid. Next, you'll be saying I faked taking you through the portal," he accused her, placing his hands on his hips.

"Maybe I dreamed it," she huffed. "I must have blacked out at some point."

"You are a stubborn girl," he grumbled.

She snorted and opened her mouth to retort, but just then, a soft knock sounded at his door.

"Can I have just one moment's peace?" Loki erupted.

"That's no way to talk to your mother, Loki!" Frigga scolded him from the other side of the door.

"What is it, Mother?" he called, surprised she was speaking English.

"Is someone in there with you?" she demanded.

Carina gasped and vanished, leaving the partially eaten plate of food on his bed.

Loki opened the door wide and showed his mother the seemingly empty room. "I was playing around with sound," he lied.

Her sharp eyes caught the plate on his bed. "Why did you leave the banquet just to bring food back to your room? Something wrong with the company?"

"I tire of all the noise and raucous jokes," Loki replied, truthfully this time. "Was there something you needed? And why are you still speaking English? It's just us."

"I've been speaking English all day, and I will be again tomorrow. It annoys me to keep switching," Frigga said, arranging her skirts as she sat down on his chaise lounge. "Now, I've been thinking about this secret love of yours, Loki dear. I think I've found a solution."

Loki hid his irritation, remaining silent as he folded his arms across his chest and leaned as nonchalantly as he could against his desk. She clearly intended to stay longer than he wished, and he dreaded what she might say in front of Carina. But if he insisted that Frigga speak Asgardian, she would be suspicious as to why. He resisted the urge to look toward his bed, remembering he would not be able to see Carina there.

"Has her father forced her to marry the other man yet?" Frigga continued.

"No, why?"

"Do you intend to rescue her before he does?"

"I've been told she has already escaped their clutches," Loki answered. "The danger seems to have passed."

"That is good news!" she said with relief. "So then, I think we should invite all the common folk to the feast we'll have when you return from your rite of passage."

"What for?" Loki asked cautiously.

"Don't you see? It's the perfect way to introduce this girl to us in a nonthreatening way. Surely, she'll come to her senses about your identity quickly. We can arrange it so everyone thinks you met her and fell for her at the banquet."

"What good would that do?" Loki asked. "Sounds like some ridiculous fairytale."

"Well … that way, no one would know you've been sneaking around. Once you are pledged to her, we can even take her under our protection. Nobles were not always nobles, after all, and it will further endear your father to the people if one of his sons takes a common bride," Frigga explained. "At least, that is what I shall tell your father after you speak with him of your desire to marry her."

"Scheming again, Mother?" Loki said casually, hiding his embarrassment at what Carina was surely hearing.

"I'm doing this for you, Loki," Frigga defended herself, rising to her feet and coming close to him. "If you love this girl as much as you say, I will love her as well. Your father will heed my influence. Why shouldn't she be a princess, beloved by all of Asgard?"

"You're a hopeless romantic, Mother," Loki groaned.

"I would see you happy," Frigga said softly, smoothing his hair back from his forehead. "You desire to marry her, do you not? I can see the green has returned to your eyes."

He shut them tightly, for hope had indeed risen in his heart. Perhaps he had been wrong all along. Perhaps Carina could be his bride, maybe even his queen.

"I'm so glad you've fallen in love with an Asgardian, common or not, rather than the daughter of a visiting dignitary," she continued. "Or, perish the thought, a Jotun or a Midgardian. I really don't know which would be worse."

Loki's hope died almost as quickly as it had sprung. But all he said was, "A Jotun, Mother? Why would you even bring that up?"

She sighed. "Yes, that one is rather farfetched. But Midgard is certainly fresh on my mind, now that Kvasir and Sigyn have fled there. It's a beautiful place, and Midgardians can be charming, but neither Asgardians nor Vanir should mingle with them."

"Nevertheless, it's happened, Mother," Loki said nonchalantly, as if they were discussing the weather.

"I am aware of that," Frigga said breezily. "Children born of those unions never really belong in either world. It's not a life I would wish on anyone."

Loki could barely hide how uncomfortable he was. He shuddered inwardly, still appalled at her suggestion that he could ever be with a Jotun. Most Asgardians looked down on Midgardians, perceiving them as weak and short-lived. But Jotuns were despised more than any other race of the Nine Realms, even more than the fire giants of Muspelheim. Loki had never even seen a Jotun, but the tales described them as horned monsters with thick hides the color of a stormy sky. But then some of the tales also claimed Midgardians were plain, with stringy hair, inept brains, and beady eyes. He wondered what else had been exaggerated over time and what was actually true. And that led him to consider how all of the old prejudices and hatreds between the races had started. He filed that away for further thought since his mother seemed intent on lecturing him at the moment. He was surprised she had called Midgardians charming. Clearly, she did not share all of the same prejudices as her subjects or even her husband. Why had she brought it up? Did she suspect? Was she trying to send him a veiled warning? She had always spoken plainly to him in the past. Why would she change that now?

"Loki, are you even listening to me?" Frigga demanded.

"Of course I am, Mother," Loki lied. He had no idea what she had just said.

And she knew it. "Your eyes are changing so much, I can't

decide what you're thinking. Daydreaming about this love of yours, perhaps?"

"Perhaps," Loki repeated with a smirk. Since his eyes kept betraying him with Carina so near, he manipulated the light to place a gray film over his eyes. The illusion was surprisingly painful, most likely because he had to apply it directly to each iris. It was the only way to fool his mother. He hoped he would not have to hold the color change for long.

She peered at him closely, making him squirm slightly. "She really must be quite a woman to distract you so."

"She is," he affirmed. "But why did you bring up all that intermarriage nonsense? You should know I have no interest in monsters or Midgardian maidens. Next, you'll be suggesting I could fall for fire giants, dwarves, or elves."

Frigga sighed. "My dear son, there are many things I wish I could explain to you. Surely you know not everything you've heard or read is true."

"Why are you being so cryptic?" Loki huffed.

Frigga gazed at him, her expression unreadable. She seemed about to divulge something. Then her face smoothed into the look Loki recognized as her way of ending a difficult conversation.

"Never mind. You have your secrets. I'll keep mine," Frigga declared.

"Well then, as fascinating as this pointless topic is," Loki stated, "I do finish my trials tomorrow. And Father has surely missed your presence. May I retire now?"

Frigga kissed him on the cheek. Just before she left his room, she prompted him, "Think about what I said."

"Which part?" Loki asked warily.

"The feast, of course, and welcoming your mysterious Asgardian commoner into our family."

Loki nodded, then bid her goodnight. As soon as he had closed the door and made sure her footsteps moved down the hall, he rested his forehead against the door with his arm above his head. What had just happened? And how would Carina respond to what she had surely overheard?

He spoke to the empty room. "You can come out of hiding now."

"No," Carina stated flatly, sounding on the verge of tears.

He walked over to the bed, trying to feel where she was.

"What's wrong, my star?" he asked hesitantly.

His responses to Frigga must have hurt her, especially since their conversation had been charged before his mother's strange warnings. Would she let him explain?

"Don't call me that," she whispered fiercely from somewhere nearby. "I'm a Midgardian, remember?"

"That does not matter to me," he said softly. "Please, I need to see your face."

The plate lifted off the bed. Loki smirked in triumph at Carina's mistake. She must not know that invisibility only applied to objects when the device holder already had them in hand. He quickly calculated where her arm would be and grabbed it, making her drop the plate onto the floor.

"Look what you made me do!" she cried. "Let me go."

"Not until you show yourself."

When she made herself visible, he released her. Rather than vanish again, she grabbed the pieces of the plate and started to gather up the food.

"Leave it before you cut yourself," he told her. "I'll call a servant to clean it up."

"With me in here?" she huffed, ignoring his instructions and scooping up the rest of the leftovers.

"You're angry," Loki stated matter-of-factly. He did not quite know what to do.

"Why should I be angry?" she retorted, rising to her feet and plopping the broken plate and bits of food into the large, widemouthed vase by his desk.

"That's not a trash can!" Loki cried in dismay.

"I don't care!" she huffed.

"Well, I do!" he snapped, reaching into the vessel to clean it out.

"Then you should have put a plant or something in it," she scoffed.

"You don't put a plant in a piece like this!" he retorted. "My parents gave me this vase. It's over three thousand years old. I'll never hear the end of it if it gets ruined!"

"Well, excuse me, you conceited high-hat!" she burst out. "How was I supposed to know?"

He whipped his head around to glare at her, then gasped sharply in pain as the jagged edge of the broken plate jabbed him. He drew his hand out. A few drops of deep red blood welled up from the small cut.

"Oh no, you're hurt!" she exclaimed.

"It hurts less than your words," he answered angrily, turning his back on her and grabbing his kit to take care of the cut.

"And what about yours?" she defended herself sharply. "Now I know why you have to hide me. How could you, a prince of Asgard, be seen with someone like me? I'm sorry I'm such a burden that fills you with shame."

"What?" he exclaimed. Her assumptions stunned him, though he knew they were logical, based on his own assertions to his mother. He examined the cut he had sealed, thankful it was not in a place that would affect his final test.

"At least I completely believe you now. That should comfort you," she huffed.

"It doesn't," he grimaced. He paused as her words registered. "Oh, now you believe me?"

"Everything makes perfect sense now," she berated him, although she kept her voice down. She paced the floor, flashing her eyes angrily at him. "You must have told your mother, the queen of Asgard, no less, that you supposedly love me—"

"Supposedly?" Loki interrupted indignantly.

"But you never told her what I was. And why would you, with how your mother spoke of people like me?" she spouted indignantly. "How *you* spoke of people like me!"

"Neither of us said anything inherently bad about Midgardians," Loki defended himself.

"It's obvious you look down on us and all those other types of people you mentioned," Carina pointed out. "Are all Asgardians such snobs?"

"Are you calling my mother a snob?" Loki growled.

"She sure acted like one," Carina insisted.

"You didn't like it when I insulted your father," Loki chastised her. "I'll ask you not to insult my mother."

Carina's face softened, as did her tone. "Do you really think yourself above us all?"

Loki wrinkled his face in confusion. "I was raised to believe Asgardians were better than other races, though not to treat them with unkindness, except for Jotuns and fire giants. They've destroyed many of our kind."

"And that's exactly where prejudices lead," Carina observed. "You can grow beyond your upbringing, you know."

Loki looked down at his lush, green area rug and inspected one of the entwined golden circles in the pattern. "You think less of me, do you?"

"Did you think less of me for trying to convince myself none of this was real?"

"Not really," Loki answered.

"And neither do I," Carina asserted. "I just think you're capable of higher thinking." She planted herself in front of him, all of the anger seeping from her body as she gazed at him with compassion and understanding, mingled with a disappointment that pained him. "Is this what you've been battling all this time? Do you really believe it's impossible for us to be together?"

He looked away. "Why would you want to be with me? I'm a conceited high-hat and a snob, remember?"

She sighed deeply. "I didn't mean it. This temper of mine really flares up when I'm angry or hurt."

He silently went back to clearing the debris out of the vase, taking it to the bathroom trash.

"Your kind bleeds red?" she asked casually, as if trying to ease the tension.

But her choice of words aggravated him. He did not like this distinction, this separation, and he suddenly understood that his upbringing had indeed been wrong. Despite this realization, he found himself quite unwilling to let go of her sharp tone and words, though he knew he had hurt her just as deeply.

"Stop it with my kind and your kind!" he blurted out. "I don't care where we came from. We're no different! Yes, I bleed red. And I have feelings just as you do."

He fell silent, stewing over the names she had called him, which cut his heart far deeper than the plate had his hand.

"I'm sorry I hurt you," she said quietly, her eyes downcast when he finally looked at her. "Will you forgive me?"

The hurt and anger fled from him in an instant. He walked over to her and lifted her chin so she would look at him. "I forgive you. And I'm sorry for my harsh words."

"And?" she prompted, smirking at him slightly.

"And for the things I said to my mother about Midgardians, and ... I don't know what else," he answered, frustration creeping into his voice. "I'm just ... really sorry."

"I forgive you then," she relented softly.

He sighed with relief. "I was already starting to disagree with my people about Midgardians. I like your world. And I have never been ashamed of you. *Ever!*"

"No?"

"No," he repeated emphatically. "I don't want to fight anymore."

"Lovers quarrel," she answered, reminding him of his own words from weeks ago as she wrapped her arms around him. "Anger passes in time."

"I thought we weren't lovers," he murmured, embracing her tightly with his cheek resting on her head. He yearned for her even more now that they had argued and made it right.

"Not in every sense. Not yet." She pulled away, searching his face with doubt in her eyes. "Is there any hope for us?"

"There's always hope," he encouraged her, though his own heart was heavy. "But I do have obligations and responsibilities here."

"And I cannot stay here, hidden away until I wither and die," she said dolefully.

"I would never ask that of you. I'm planning to spend my rite of passage time on Midgard," he confessed. "With you. For three solid months."

"To what end?" she sighed. "You would just return here again, for who knows how long. I can't live like that, never knowing when you'll be here or there."

He stepped back. "Please don't say another word. We should both sleep before either of us says more we'll regret."

She looked as though she would argue but changed her mind and meekly walked over to his bed, where she buried herself in his blankets and pillows. Her form turned shimmery. Loki smiled to himself, pleased she still wanted him to see her. He settled himself on his chaise lounge, shifting until he was comfortable. He was finally drifting off to sleep when he felt something press against him. He opened his eyes to see Carina there, but because the device was still on, her body emitted no warmth.

She laid her head on his chest, looked up at him shyly, and whispered, "I feel safer over here."

He kissed the top of her head and held her in his arms as she snuggled against him to find a comfortable spot.

"Okay, you can stay," Loki murmured, too groggy to think much about it. "Just this once."

12

Asgardian sunlight warmed Loki's eyelids, waking him from a sound sleep. Had he heard someone banging on his door? Or was it just a dream? Carina lay against him, still shimmery and fast asleep. Suddenly, he spotted Thor leaning against the armoire with a huge smirk on his face. He sat up with a start. Surprisingly, the movement did not wake Carina.

"I dare say, brother, you're going to sleep away your entire rite of passage," Thor chuckled, taking a few steps toward the chaise lounge. "Rough night? Too much ale?"

Loki was still partially trapped under an invisible, sleeping Carina. He discreetly tried to nudge Carina awake. Still, she slept, sighing slightly.

Thor stopped suddenly. "What was that?"

Loki yawned as if he had made the sound, then barked, "What are you doing in here, Thor?"

Carina's eyes flew open. She froze, a terrified look on her face. But Thor remained entirely unaware of her presence.

"You didn't answer when I knocked. It's not my fault you left your door unlocked!" Thor defended himself.

"Thor, how many times do I have to tell you?" Loki griped. "If the door is shut, I don't want you in my room."

"Father has summoned us," Thor informed him. "Secretly. That's why I'm here instead of one of the guards."

Carina had stealthily moved away from Loki, eyeing Thor with trepidation. Loki scrambled to his feet, sending her an apologetic look. He knew she would not have understood Thor's words, but he could not translate or explain.

"You look terrible," Thor muttered. He tugged and pulled at Loki's attire, smoothing out wrinkles and fixing his collar. "I'm grateful you slept in your clothes, at least."

"Quit fussing at me. You're worse than Mother," Loki grumbled, smacking his hands away.

"Let's go. He's not in a good mood," Thor commanded as he strode out the door.

Loki had no choice but to hurry after him. Out of the corner of his eye, he saw Carina's shimmery form trailing behind them.

"What's this all about?" Loki asked when he finally matched Thor's strides with his own.

"He won't speak until we're both there," Thor said ominously. "But I can tell you something strange is going on."

Instead of Odin's offices, Thor led Loki straight to the carved, gold-inset doors of the throne room. Together, they walked past the marble pillars and golden statues of previous kings lining the wide corridor leading to the opulent throne. And there sat Odin, in full royal robes. His black eye patch and pet ravens intimidated most Asgardians, but when he gripped his great staff, only a great fool would not fear him. This morning, he was more king than father.

"My sons," he greeted them solemnly.

"Father," they returned in unison, striking their chests twice and bowing.

"There is a presence on Asgard that does not belong," Odin announced grimly. "Heimdall has sensed it, but it has eluded him."

Loki pushed down his rising panic and refused to allow himself to even glance where Carina lurked. How could he have overlooked a fact he knew all too well? Without the protection of the device, both Odin and Heimdall could sense any presence that was not Asgardian. He should have been more careful! The unyielding eyes of the statues seemed to bore into his back, piercing through his skin. Though he felt exposed, he swallowed hard and erased every emotion from his face but passive concern.

"Lord Berg?" Thor asked, his face reddening with growing anger.

"No," Odin replied. "Lord Berg is in the very place I expected him to be. His misery there has only begun."

"Will you retrieve him?" Thor growled.

"Not yet. He is surrounded by darkness and anger. We have him under surveillance. Lady Annette has not been informed, and I wish to keep it that way. Her grief is deep enough."

"What do you think it is, Father?" Loki asked innocently.

"We have not been able to trace it, but we know it's not one of our visiting dignitaries. Whatever heat signature it gives off has flickered out every time we get close to pinpointing its location," Odin answered, rotating his staff in one hand, as he often did when contemplating a difficult situation. "We got close enough last night to determine it was near or even in the palace, so you must be extra cautious. Have either of you seen anything suspicious?"

"No, but I have heard a few strange sounds here and there," Thor said.

Before Thor could say anything more, Loki interjected, "Father, is it possible someone or something wandered into Asgard from the old tree before you destroyed it?"

"Possible, but unlikely. Because of this and the situation with Lord Berg, I have closed the Bifröst to be on the safe side. No one enters or leaves Asgard until we are assured there is no further threat," Odin informed them.

"For how long? Political unrest grows on Vanaheim. Our uncle struggles to maintain control. He couldn't even attend Loki's trials," Thor protested. "I must return before winter, and I had hoped to take Loki with me."

"I expect everyone will be able to resume travel long before Loki returns," Odin reassured him. "This is merely precautionary. To allay suspicion and avoid making the people skittish, I will have the Captain of the Guard announce that we are doing emergency maintenance on the bridge. And I will handle our foreign guests privately. Sooner or later, whatever is here will have to reveal itself. Heimdall and I will be watching and listening more carefully now. I want you two to do the same."

Loki dreaded asking his next question but knew he must, to find out what Odin knew as well as to divert suspicion from himself. "Father, are there other paths on and off Asgard that would pose a risk to our people?"

"Only one that I am aware of, built by none other than Kvasir, but it has been long inactive," Odin replied. "It's in a cave by the South Sea, near Lord Berg's property, actually. Heimdall has reported nothing suspicious from it in years."

"Should we not destroy that portal as well?" demanded Thor.

"No, that would be irresponsible," Odin responded sternly. "If someone were to stumble upon the other end on Midgard—"

"Why should we care about Midgard when Asgard is at risk?" Thor thundered.

Loki blinked at his brother's blatant disrespect and braced himself for what he knew would follow.

Odin leaped to his feet, straightening his shoulders as he stood. "Those are not the words of a king, Thor, but of a foolish boy who does not understand we protect all life, not just our own!"

Thor was silent, but the muscles in his arms tensed with anger as static electricity jumped between his fingers. Distant thunder sounded.

"Please don't make it rain, Thor!" Loki whispered through clenched teeth. "My single combat test is today."

Thor glanced at Loki and relaxed slightly.

Odin fixed Thor with his gaze and continued, "Once Loki has embarked on his journey, I am sending you with a full battalion to guard the cave entrance, as well as Lord Berg's property. Lady Annette has agreed to remain here with your mother for now."

"And how long must I remain at the South Sea?" Thor inquired grumpily.

"Until I summon you!" Odin snapped. "I need you to investigate discreetly, if you can manage that. And nothing more will be said by either of you, to anyone, including each other. Am I understood?"

Thor and Loki nodded and bowed, though Loki could sense Thor's anger simmering under the surface. Thor turned heel and strode out of the hall, but as Loki turned to follow, Odin stopped him with a subtle motion of his hand.

As soon as Thor was out of earshot, Odin spoke. "Loki, if you were not facing your rite of passage, I would prefer to send you on this errand. But this is Thor's chance to prove to me he is capable of more than waging battle. There is far more to being a king than fighting enemies and forcing others to do your bidding."

"I understand, Father," Loki said.

"I know you do, my son," Odin replied, his voice thick with hidden meaning that did not escape Loki's notice. "But we will not speak of that now. You must follow my orders and not speak of this to your brother."

"As you wish, Father," Loki said, bowing again. "I rather doubt Thor is in the mood to speak to anyone. I'm glad he will not be my challenger today."

Odin chuckled, then dismissed Loki with a wave of his hand. Loki walked slowly to the giant doors of the throne room, where Carina hid behind a pillar, despite being invisible.

To give her time to slip out of the hall, he paused and turned to address Odin once more but spoke from his heart. "Father, there is no one more loyal to you than Thor. You have taught him well. He will make you proud." Loki paused, then added, "And so will I."

Odin merely nodded, but his one good eye was suspiciously shiny.

Certain Carina had made her exit, Loki nodded respectfully at his father once more, then stepped into the hallway and swung the doors shut with a resounding boom.

Back in his own quarters with the door locked, he turned to Carina with seriousness.

Before he could speak, she quietly asked, "Do they know I'm here?"

"You could understand?"

"Not the words. Only tone and body language."

"They know something or someone is here. They will close in on you sooner rather than later," Loki affirmed. "You cannot be visible again, nor should you speak, just to be safe. I will return you to Midgard tonight. You'll have to attend the banquet now."

"But you didn't want me to last night," she argued. "Why the change?"

"I'll be leaving for the wilderness straight from there. I was going to sneak back for you, but I don't want to let you out of my sight."

"Won't it be crowded? What if I bump into someone?" Carina countered.

"We don't have a choice," Loki stated with finality. "This is the safest way to get you out of here. I will not risk speaking to you, so you must watch me closely and follow my signals."

She nodded, then whispered, "I heard your father say something that sounded like 'king' several times. And you also used the word. Odin seems angry with Thor, and Thor with him. Are you going to be the next king instead of Thor?"

"I do not know," he responded. "I believe my father may be considering it, but much depends on Thor."

"Do you want to be king?"

"I haven't thought about it much," Loki replied honestly. "It would be wiser for me to put it aside for now. Nor should we continue talking."

She wrapped her arms around him and buried her face into his chest. He could not feel her warmth but returned her embrace, feeling as though she were slipping away from him yet again even as he held her. He reluctantly let her go, signaling for her to change back into her own clothes and to hide Sigyn's in the large pack he began preparing for his journey.

Once everything was ready, Loki called a servant to take the pack to the banquet hall. After he had gone, Loki and Carina settled together on his chaise lounge, staring out the window in silence and clinging to what Loki feared could quite possibly be their last moments together.

The guard's knock at the door came too soon. But reluctant as he was to part from Carina, Loki was ready for this defining moment in his life.

As he strode purposefully toward the arena once more, he knew he must keep his mind clear for the moment he faced the contender chosen for him. The hum and excitement of the crowds drifted into the armory as Loki chose his weapons. Satisfied with his choices, he stood waiting to be announced in the arena entrance closest to the sparring stations, armed with fencing swords in each hand, as well as an Asgardian dagger sheathed to each of his boots. The stands were so packed, he could barely see where Carina had stashed herself. After he took his place in the center again, the herald announced his opponent, the tall and swarthy Lord Vega, an intimidating master swordsman with bright blue eyes and a black goatee streaked with gray. The nobles in charge of his trials had chosen the best, to leave no room for accusations of nepotism.

When the horns sounded to begin the match, Loki and Vega advanced rapidly toward each other until their swords met in several skilled blows.

Vega complimented Loki, "Fine footwork, my young prince."

Loki lunged forward, but Vega parried then thrust forward with one sword aimed at Loki's chest. Loki barely avoided being nicked.

Impressed but not surprised, he commented, "And that was a perfect riposte."

Vega dipped his head in appreciation. Their swords became a flurry of majestically moving blurs as the spectators roared with each clash of steel. The two Asgardians were too engaged for any more talking.

Suddenly, Loki stumbled over a rock he had not seen and fell on his back. Vega hovered over him with one sword at his throat as the crowd collectively gasped. Just at that moment, Loki caught a glimpse of the hidden Carina with her hands clasped over her mouth in silent horror. The sight invigorated Loki so much, he drove Vega off with sheer adrenaline, knocking both swords out of his hands. The nobleman landed on his back in the dirt. Unable to reach his own dropped swords quickly enough, Loki reached for his daggers as the master swordsman scrambled to his feet. In one swift movement, Loki rolled over and swung one of his legs to connect with the backs of Vega's calves, knocking him back down to the ground. Loki quickly straddled his chest with both daggers poised at his throat, just as he had done with Kvasir. Lord Vega held his hands up, yielding and acknowledging the prince as the victor.

The crowd began chanting Loki's name as both men jumped to their feet. Loki sheathed his daggers and held both fists up in the air, roaring with triumph and exulting in their adoration.

Is this what it's like to be a king? he thought with ecstasy.

Time seemed to freeze as he looked to where he had last seen Carina, but she was not cheering or clapping. She merely stared at him with a strained, fearful expression. Confused, he dropped his arms and cocked his head slightly, but she looked away. He retrieved his swords as the Captain of the Guard made the announcement about the Bifröst. The crowd buzzed with irritation and questions to each other, already forgetting the spectacular display Loki and Lord Vega had given them. Slightly disappointed it was all over, Loki headed for the baths near the sparring stations, signaling first for Carina to follow the throng of nobility moving toward the palace.

As soon as Loki arrived at the final banquet in his honor, which was slated to last into the evening, Thor rushed to greet him.

"Well done, brother," he thundered, lifting him off the ground in a bear hug. "I never doubted you for a second!"

Loki spotted Carina in the banquet hall close to the green silk draped near the balcony, then lost sight of her as more and more people poured into the hall. Thor ushered his younger brother to the buffet tables, where Loki filled his plate with roast pheasant, candied yams, green beans tossed with almonds, and a large chunk of Asgardian cheese. He glanced at Thor's heaping plate, then snorted when his older brother loaded up a second.

"Is that for someone else?" Loki teased. "All of Vanaheim, perhaps?"

"Hardly," Thor retorted, balancing both plates in one hand to grab his full tankard of mead.

Loki merely rolled his eyes and made his way to the royal table. As he seated himself and sipped a goblet of ale, he noticed Lord Bragi and Lady Winsletta seated in the spots formerly reserved for Sigyn's parents. Since they were speaking with his mother, Loki just nodded at them, then turned his attention to his food.

Through every toast and speech, Loki tried unsuccessfully to catch another glimpse of Carina, reassuring himself that she was fine. And since his longing to share his triumph with her had to remain unsatisfied, he wanted to at least make sure she was impressed with him, if she was watching. He laughed harder at Thor's antics than ever before, clapped Thor's warrior friends enthusiastically on the back when they spoke with him, and to any eye, was every bit the prince he was expected to be.

As the sky darkened and filled with stars, Odin finally stood and struck the floor with his staff to silence them all.

"Friends, Asgardians, distinguished guests, we are gathered here to honor the last of my sons, Prince Loki of Asgard, brother of Thor," Odin proclaimed. He motioned for Thor and Loki to join him. "A father could not be prouder of his sons, nor a king be blessed with more loyal subjects. We say goodbye to Loki tonight as he follows the path Thor returned from months ago. But we have no doubt he will be just as victorious as his older brother, showing his mettle a thousand times over!"

With every mention of Thor, Loki's heart sank a little, but he tried to brush aside the fierce need he always battled to prove himself Thor's equal. Even on one of the most significant nights of his life, he shared the spotlight with

Thor. Frigga watched him carefully, her eyes shining with the same suspicious sheen as Odin's eye had earlier. Far behind her, Loki saw Carina picking at the unattended and decimated food tables while Odin had everyone's attention. The sight of her, shimmery as she still was, brightened his heart. He grinned widely at her stealth and resourcefulness. When he noticed Frigga still watching him, he winked at his mother, as if his smile were due to Odin's words.

Even with Carina in the corner of his vision, Midgard seemed far away as the chants and cheers of his people once again filled Loki's ears. They lined up on either side of the banquet hall, making a pathway for him. Loki had packed everything he had been advised to take on his three-month trek into the wilderness, plus a few extra things he might need on Midgard. But now that Odin had hinted he was indeed thinking of his youngest son as a kingly prospect, Loki once again seriously considered doing exactly as he was expected and fulfilling his rite of passage in the wilderness, after he attended the wedding and took Carina home.

Once he had reached the outermost set of doors, he hoisted his long, sturdy pack onto his back and took the walking stick his mother held out to him.

"When you return," she whispered as she hugged him briefly.

Loki knew immediately what she spoke of, and it dampened his mood considerably. Why must he be forced to choose between the woman he loved and his homeland?

Thor and Odin were the last ones to bid Loki goodbye. He clasped arms with his brother and respectfully bowed to his father since practically all of Asgard watched the moment.

Then he set forth toward the forest, not looking back until he was sure even the stragglers had returned to the banquet hall. When he finally turned around to make sure Carina was following him, there was no sign of her.

"Carina?" he whispered fiercely. "Are you there?"

No answer.

Did she miss the signal? he asked himself with alarm.

He hid his pack near a bush slightly off the road and sped back to find her. As he was nearing the palace, a clump of wet dirt hit him squarely in the shoulder. He looked wildly in that general direction.

"Here," Carina hissed. She was tucked away underneath the great arched bridge leading to the palace.

"What are you doing under there?" he chided her quietly as he climbed down to retrieve her.

"I couldn't get out," she whispered defensively, rising to her feet and brushing the dirt off. She gestured to the fork in the road immediately after the bridge. "By the time I broke through, I couldn't tell which way you had gone."

Loki nodded apologetically, cursing himself for assuming she could easily follow him. He was immensely grateful she had been savvy enough to wait for him to return for her since the road on the right led to the heart of the capital city and villages beyond.

He scooped her up without a word. The water under the bridge had dampened her hair and clothing. She clung to his neck wearily as he took the left passage leading to the wilderness and carried her to where he had left his pack. He gently lowered her to her feet, grabbed the pack, and motioned for her to follow him. Under cover of darkness, they made the long trek to the forest. Though Loki had memorized the area where the portal had been built, everything looked different by the light of the moon. By the time he located the small, hidden dugout in a grassy knoll, Carina was once again nowhere to be seen.

He retraced his steps, silently berating himself for not paying better attention. He finally spotted her shimmery form crumpled in a heap around a bend about one hundred feet from where he had discovered her absence. He rushed to her side. Her eyes were shut tight, her breathing shallow as she shivered uncontrollably. The night had grown much cooler. Since he was dressed for it, Loki had not thought of how it might affect her, especially damp as she was. He scooped her up again, but her body was limp. Her arms hung like deadweight, her head lolling back. He gently set her down inside the dugout and covered her with a thermal blanket he had packed, keeping her away from the dirt wall laden with Bifröst ore. He hastily built a roaring fire, then brought her as close to the crackling flames as he dared. He propped her up on his lap, wrapping his arms around her to envelop her in his own body heat. Feeling a hard lump against him, he found the cloaking device hidden in her dress. Concerned it might be keeping her cold and knowing Heimdall would not be watching, he clicked it off. Still, she did not move, though he was relieved to feel her breathing.

He held her even more tightly, pressing his cheek against hers, and willed her to regain consciousness. Her body grew warmer, and her breathing became deeper. He rubbed her arms vigorously, desperately trying to wake her. To his relief, she finally stirred. Then her eyes popped open, and she looked around in panic.

"It's okay. You're safe," Loki soothed her, allowing her to move away from him. He got up and unpacked some of his rations, informing her, "We can talk now."

She nodded but did not speak, intent on eating and drinking what Loki had given her.

"You really gave me a scare," Loki told her, sitting beside her again. "Are you okay?"

"I think so," she said, wiping her mouth after another swig of water. "Can I go home now?"

"To New York?" Loki frowned. "What about the wedding?"

"Oh, you still wanted me to go?" Carina asked, refusing to look at him.

"Why wouldn't I?" Loki insisted, feeling somewhat hurt. "Even if I do my rite of passage here, I can spare a little time before I come back."

"That's just it," Carina replied, finally looking at him. "You'll be returning here. And where does that leave me?"

Loki frowned again, turning his face away this time. He felt as though his heart would tear in half. Seeing her lying helplessly on the ground had terrified him, despite his effort to focus on reviving her. The cheering and the adulation of his people had long faded in his mind. What had he been thinking? They did not need him. Thor would make a fine king with more training from Odin. He turned back to face her, admiring her profile as she stared into the fire.

"Watching you today was very eye-opening for me," she continued, her arms around her knees. "I'm a little afraid of you."

"Afraid of me? Why?"

"I don't even know what you are, really," she answered, tucking her chin into her knees as if she knew her answer was not satisfactory.

"I'm still the same guy," he said as he nudged her shoulder with his. "But whatever I am, whatever I've been … I'm yours, if you'll have me."

"Have you? How could I have you?" she asked incredulously, her eyes blazing as she glanced at him. She stood abruptly, folded her arms, and stared at the fire dancing on the steadily burning wood. "I could never compete with the glitz and the glamour of Asgard or the thrill of ruling an entire planet. You would never be content with just me."

"Yes, I would," he retorted curtly, almost childishly.

"You say that now, but I saw the look on your face when the people chanted your name. And I see the conflict in you right now. I have no doubt you've decided to stay here and become everything you were meant to be." She shook her head sadly and sighed with resignation. "And you probably should. I fear the man I fell in love with is long gone."

"I'm right here! And I am still Lukas Black." Loki rose to his feet and gently took her by the shoulders. "But could you ever bring yourself to love me as Loki, as I truly am?"

"I do love you, the real you," she admitted, but his hopeful smile faded when she continued, "but I need someone I can depend on, someone who will share my life and my dreams." She looked down, then spoke so softly, he almost missed it. "I think it's best if …"

"If what?" he prompted her, a lump already forming in his throat.

"If we never see each other again. You'll forget me in time."

"No," he whispered, as tears he could not stop streamed down his face, for her words had hit him like a sledgehammer. His voice broke. "You don't mean that."

"What choice do we have?" she cried, her own tears flowing. "You belong here, and I don't."

"Carina, don't do this!" Loki fell to his knees, his chest burning from the pain of losing her. Words poured from him like hot lava as he grabbed her hands. "I've been a fool! I'll renounce my title, my homeland, my family, everything, just for the chance of one lifetime with you."

"You'd do that?" The pain fled from her face as her eyes widened in wonder. "For me?"

"Yes, a thousand times, yes!" he cried. "Please, I can't live without you."

She lowered herself to her knees in front of him. "If you would make such a sacrifice for me, then I know without a shadow of doubt that you truly love me, just me."

"I have always loved just you, my star," Loki said softly, raising her hands to his lips and speaking against them. "How many times must I tell you that?"

"At least twice every day," she commanded, her eyes sparkling with mischief.

He chuckled in response, then looked at her intently. The decision over which he had agonized was made. "Then … will you marry me?"

"What?" she gasped. "Where? When?"

"On Midgard, as soon as possible," Loki implored. "Just say you will."

"On one condition," she answered, rising to her feet and pulling him up with her.

"Anything!" he cried eagerly.

"Stop all this nonsense talk about being anything less than what you are," she entreated with a mischievous grin that crept over her face like the sunrise.

He frowned, confused. "I thought you wanted me to renounce my life here."

"How could I claim to love you while forcing you to deny yourself?"

"Were you testing me, Carina Green?"

"No, I honestly thought I had to set you free," she replied earnestly.

"To be set free from you would be a prison of its own," Loki informed her.

"I didn't realize how much pain it would cause you until now. You are indeed a man divided, partly because of me. I would see you whole. If removing myself from the equation isn't the way, then somehow I must help you embrace all of what and who you are meant to be."

"But, Carina, if I remain Loki, how will we live? You said—"

"I know what I said! I haven't figured it all out, but we'll find a way," she said confidently. She placed one hand on his cheek. "We'll make a way!"

He was overwhelmed by her strength and wisdom. When he felt the brilliant green rush back into his eyes, he removed the painful light manipulation that had kept them gray. She smiled when she saw it and flicked her gaze to his lips and back to his eyes.

As he bent his head down to kiss her, he whispered, "You fiery, impossible woman. How I love you!"

"Well, I think you need a fiery, impossible woman, Loki of Midgard," she responded, holding his face in her hands.

"Asgard," he corrected, though hearing her call him by his real name for the first time, even incorrectly, had made his heart leap.

"Only when you're here," she teased him, pulling him so close, their lips almost touched. "The rest belongs to me, and I'll call you what I want."

"Agreed," he murmured. Then he kissed her with wild abandon.

She returned his passion as if she too had missed the feeling of their lips melded together seamlessly. The overwhelming joy in his heart drove everything but Carina from his mind. His fingers crept into her hair as they slowly sank to the ground by the dwindling fire. The taste of her lips, the scent of her hair, and the gentle touch of her fingers awakened a fierce, heady desire within him. He kissed her jawline hungrily. As she lifted her chin in response, he dared to burrow hard into her neck. She gasped and held him there, murmuring his true name with an intense longing that made him feel reckless. He did not want to stop, but he knew he must.

"I'm sorry," he gulped, tearing himself away. "I shouldn't have done that."

"Why not? We're getting married," Carina said playfully. She ran her fingers teasingly over his collarbone, making him shiver. "I'm yours, aren't I?"

"Not yet, my star," he whispered, trying to hide the longing in his own voice. He could barely breathe. "We're not … lovers … yet."

She leaned forward and drew him closer. "Don't you want us to be?" she whispered bewitchingly into his ear.

"Don't tempt me, Carina! I want you more than I can stand," he groaned, holding her at arm's length. "But I will not take you until you are my wife and I am your husband."

She regarded him with a mixture of surprise, respect, and a little angst. "Do all Asgardians have such old-fashioned notions?"

"We take marriage very seriously," he said, kissing her forehead tenderly as he willed himself to calm down. "Please don't feel rejected. You are precious to me and worthy of my respect. And since you kept yourself from Klaus, I think this is what you really want."

"I never loved Klaus," she sighed. "But I respect you as much as I love you, so once again, I concede. Are you sure this is what *you* want?"

"Yes, I want to show my commitment to you. You are worth waiting for, my star," Loki assured her, tracing her lips with one finger. "Now, tell me your Midgardian customs before we return to London. I want to do this right."

"Well, most men ask a woman's father for her hand in marriage before even proposing to her," she informed him. "But we're obviously past all that."

Loki frowned. "I don't answer to Joseph Green, but I will speak with him if you would like. I just don't want to delay things too much. It did occur to me that I can better protect you from Klaus when you are my wife."

"Is that the reason you're marrying me?" Carina teased.

"Are you serious?" Loki asked in alarm.

"No," she laughed. "I just want to hear you say why again."

"Because I love you, and I want to pledge my life to you," he told her tenderly. "Shall I speak to Joseph or not?"

"It wouldn't change my answer," she pondered aloud, "but it might make things easier if we had his blessing."

"Where do you think he is?"

"I'm not sure," Carina admitted. "I've been gone for at least two days, maybe three. He must be looking for me by now."

"Where would he look?"

"If he suspects I tried to find you, he'll contact Kristoff," she replied. "I'm sure he saw the telegram. Klaus dropped it on the floor during the fight."

"Kristoff is in Norway, waiting for me," Loki informed her. "If he's heard from your father, he might know where he is."

"How long will it take us to get to Norway from London?" Carina asked.

"We really don't even need to go to London, come to think of it," Loki informed her. "I can take us straight to Norway. Or even Germany."

Carina grimaced. "On second thought, I'm afraid he would forbid us. Maybe it's best to speak with him after we're married. Then he'll have to accept you."

Loki grinned. "I would prefer that. So then, what is actually required for marriage on Midgard?"

"We'll need a marriage license, witnesses, and an officiant," Carina said excitedly. "If we get married without my father, I suppose I'll have to give up my dream wedding, but you're worth it."

"What was your dream wedding?" Loki asked curiously.

"A beautiful white dress, flowers and candles everywhere, elegant music and food, and at least a hundred guests," she sighed dreamily.

"A hundred?" Loki groaned in dismay. "How long does it take to plan something like that?"

"I had already started planning it before I left Germany, thinking it would be with Klaus," she answered. "I hadn't found a dress yet, but we were going to get married at our house in Stuttgart in a little less than three weeks."

"Three weeks?" he complained. "I was thinking something simpler. And much sooner."

"Like what?" she asked, but her face fell in disappointment. Though she had offered to sacrifice her vision, Loki could tell she was hiding how much it meant to her.

He lifted her chin with his hand. "You'll have your Midgardian wedding somehow," he encouraged her. "But if I only married you by the laws of your world, I would not be bound to you by the laws of mine. And I truly want you to have all of me."

"Then what do we do?"

"Marry me in an Asgardian ceremony first," Loki declared.

"Here on Asgard?" she gasped.

"No, in Norway. Baldur is marrying Kvasir and Sigyn soon after I arrive," Loki told her. "He could marry us at the same time, and we'll add the legal requirements for Midgard. Then, after we are husband and wife, we can speak to your father about a second wedding."

"I rather like this plan of yours. I just hope Father will be reasonable." She leaned forward and kissed him on the cheek. "What are we waiting for?"

Loki put out the dying fire, hoisted his pack onto his shoulder, then grasped Carina tightly with his other arm. In seconds, they were through the portal and standing in the spare room of the Norwegian townhouse Kristoff shared with his older sister, Helga.

13

Loki's sharp ears picked up the curious sound of Helga giggling in the kitchen. To his surprise, he heard her say in almost perfect English, "Baldur, if you don't give me some space, I'll never finish getting lunch ready!"

Baldur's rich voice responded playfully, "That's the idea, you decadent pastry, you! Let them fend for themselves."

Loki put a finger to his lips, greatly amused, and beckoned for Carina to follow him. He was grateful he did not have to switch to Norwegian since Carina would not understand it.

"Don't listen to that charmer, Helga," Loki teased as they walked into the kitchen. "What's a wedding without food?"

Baldur had his long arms around Helga's waist, but he stepped away from her quickly and leaped at Loki.

"You're back, little brother!" he shouted.

"This is Baldur?" Carina asked, looking up at him in awe.

Baldur kissed her hand gallantly. "At your service, Shooting Star."

Helga hugged Loki warmly. "It is so good to see you, Luke! Oh, I suppose it's Loki, isn't it?"

"It's better to call me Luke, especially around people who don't know who I am," Loki grinned, thankful someone else had made her aware of his true identity. "Have you got any cinnamon buns on hand, Helga?"

"Not today, dear boy," she chuckled, much to Loki's disappointment.

Kristoff dashed into the kitchen at the commotion, followed by Kvasir and Sigyn. The limited space in the room did not stop the joyful reunion. Everyone talked over each other with questions no one heard or answered. Kristoff hugged Carina, then Loki. When Kvasir clasped Loki's shoulders, grinning widely, Carina stood off to the side, watching shyly and somewhat fearfully, though she bristled when Sigyn kissed Loki on the cheek.

Then Sigyn turned to Carina with a warm smile. "Is this your Midgardian, Loki? She's lovely!"

"This is Carina Green, the Shooting Star," Loki introduced her, linking his arm with Carina's and intertwining their fingers together. "Carina, this is Sigyn."

"She's very beautiful," Carina whispered fiercely to Loki, eyeing Sigyn. "Are you sure you haven't made a mistake?"

Before Loki could respond, Kvasir addressed her. "I caught your show in Paris, Miss Green. Magnificent!"

Sigyn pouted slightly, saying over her shoulder, "You never say that when I sing."

Kvasir grabbed Sigyn around the waist and kissed her cheek from behind. "You, my love, are exquisite."

As Sigyn nestled into the arms of her betrothed, Carina relaxed noticeably.

"And that's Kvasir," Loki told her. "Sigyn's intended."

"Of course! You two are the ones getting married!" Carina cried. "Congratulations!"

"Thank you," the happy couple said in unison.

"Where's Hod?" Loki had just noticed the short-tempered Asgardian was missing.

Kristoff sobered immediately. "He's on guard duty."

"Guard duty?"

"The men have been taking turns guarding the house," Kristoff explained. "Klaus Mayar sent a contract killer after me. Oh, and in case you didn't know, you're also targeted, Luke."

"Carina told me," Loki replied. "Have you seen anything suspicious?"

"No, not yet," Kristoff said grimly. "But you should also know Joseph Green has his own men looking for both of you."

"Oh no!" Carina gasped, clutching Loki's arm.

Kristoff laughed. "It's not what you think! We've been communicating by transatlantic telegram, which is costing me a pretty penny. But what I can gather is Joseph had been doing a little digging of his own before Klaus even arrived in New York. He has quite the network, you know."

"Why would he do that?" Carina asked.

"I guess he didn't fully trust Klaus after all."

"But he trusted Klaus enough to marry his daughter?" Loki scoffed.

"Don't get ahead of the story!" Kristoff insisted.

Loki and Carina exchanged glances.

Kristoff continued, relishing the attention, "Last week, Joseph heard Klaus was a suspect for a few robberies in Germany and—"

"I knew he was running out of money, but I had no idea he was stealing from people besides me," Carina gasped, interrupting him.

"There isn't enough evidence for those crimes, apparently. But the New York police pegged him in connection with a bank robbery there."

"What?" Carina gasped again. "He robbed a bank?"

"So it would seem. When Joseph found Klaus unconscious with your dagger sticking out of him, he wasn't sure what happened but hoped it was self-defense and that you were safe somewhere. He found my telegram on the floor and deduced you'd been in contact with me."

"Where is Klaus now?" Carina asked.

"He tried to run, but he didn't get far. He's rotting in a New York jail cell until the trial. Looks like he'll be an unwilling guest of the American judicial system for a long time."

Carina threw her arms around Loki in relief. The others had settled around the kitchen table, listening, while Helga finished setting food out for everyone.

"That still doesn't explain why Joseph put Carina in harm's way with Klaus," Loki pointed out.

"I suppose he was still piecing it all together when I arrived in New York?" Carina suggested. "He did stay fairly close most of the time."

Loki was not quite satisfied but decided to move on to his next burning question. "Did Joseph mention my part in it?"

"No, I doubt he knows you were involved," Kristoff said. "I didn't even know until you showed up with Carina just now."

"Then why is he looking for me?"

"He figured if Carina were on the run, she would try to find you, which clearly she did," Kristoff replied. "He just wants Carina to come home."

"I wonder why Klaus didn't say anything," Carina said to Loki.

"About what?" Kristoff asked her.

"Loki showed up out of nowhere the day I stabbed Klaus," Carina answered. "He stopped him from hitting me and knocked him out. Then he took me to Asgard."

Everyone in the room paused mid-bite, looking at Loki and Carina with shock.

"I guess it's your turn to fill us in," Kristoff said. "Hod will want to hear this. I suppose we can let him off duty for a little while."

Kristoff slipped out, then returned with Hod.

"There he is," Hod cried, clasping Loki's arms in Asgardian greeting. His golden eyes looked from Loki to Carina. "Yeah, I definitely want to hear this story."

He grabbed some of the food, then leaned against the wall and listened with great interest as Loki described what had happened in the study that day. Then Carina took over and told them all about the trials. It thrilled Loki to hear her speak so highly of him. She was a master storyteller, keeping their rapt attention with every word. They gasped as she told of her close encounters with being discovered and her collapse on the path to the wilderness portal.

"And then, by the fire," she finished, "he asked me to marry him."

The sharp crack of a gunshot clipped the air, slightly muffled by all the cheers and congratulations.

Kristoff yelped and fell over, clutching his shoulder. "Sniper!" he cried. "Everybody down!"

The women threw themselves to the floor with startled

screams. The men instinctively shielded them with their own bodies.

"Can you see anything, Hod?" Baldur urged.

Hod had already rushed to the open kitchen window and slammed it shut. "One shooter. And he's on the run!"

"Go! All of you!" Kristoff said weakly, trying to stop his own bleeding as Helga crawled over to assist him.

"What about the women?" Kvasir demanded. "Isn't four Asgardians against one sniper a little overkill?"

"I have a rifle, and I know how to use it," Helga informed him indignantly. "You don't know who or what you're dealing with! We'll lock the windows and doors, just in case."

"She's right. There's no danger to them at the moment, anyway," confirmed Hod as he yanked open the kitchen door. "Hurry now!"

The other men dashed out the door and vaulted over the short wall protecting Helga's garden. The eagle-eyed Hod was the only one who could see the fleet-footed gunman they chased through Christiania. Hod barked directions as they ran, while people jumped out of their way or hollered at them. Finally, the Asgardians cornered the culprit in an alley. He fumbled with his pistol, trying to reload.

"You didn't get the memo, did ya, jack?" Hod jeered. "Your boss is in the can. There's no way you're getting paid."

The man pointed the now-loaded handgun at Hod, but his eyes were on the imposing Baldur, his face uncertain.

"I wouldn't if I were you. You shoot him, you deal with me," Baldur said with a sly grin. "You've already shot his favorite human. I think he just might kill you for that."

"He was my human first," Loki growled. "I'll kill him!"

"You're out of options," Kvasir told the man, who jerkingly moved the gun barrel to each man as if unsure where to aim. "Why don't you put the gun down? Even if you got a shot off, you would be dead before the bullet hit its target."

"He's dead anyway," Loki snarled. "We didn't even need all of us to take this one out."

The shooter slowly put down the weapon and raised his hands into the air. Hod slipped behind him in a flash, twisting his arms behind him with his uncanny strength.

"I'm only a hired gun," the man protested. "It's nothing personal."

"You're not a very good one," Loki taunted. "You easily could have killed Kristoff … or any of us. Why didn't you?"

"I wasn't supposed to!" the thug barked. "He doesn't want any of you dead. Not yet, anyway."

"Who doesn't?" asked Baldur.

Loki smirked to himself. They all knew who was behind the attack. The question was whether or not the goon would openly reveal it or any other information they could use.

"Don't pretend you don't know! Black, at least, knows," the man snarled. He jerked his head backward toward Hod. "Obviously, so does this guy."

"Klaus Mayar," Loki informed the others, playing as if they were unaware. Then he taunted the gunman, "How disappointed he'll be to hear you failed."

"I didn't fail," the man spat.

"How's that?" Loki asked nonchalantly.

"I was given very specific instructions. For Schmidt, for you, Black, and for the girl," the man bragged.

Loki took a menacing step toward him, fists clenched. "What about the girl?"

"I'm the only one who's found my target so far, but now that I know where Miss Green is, all I have to do is send word to my associate watching the house in Germany."

"Then what?" Loki spoke calmly, despite the smoldering anger in his eyes.

The thug stared right back at him, a wicked smile spreading over his face. "We'll hold her somewhere you'll never find her and do whatever we want to her. She's such a bearcat, I'm gonna enjoy that part."

Loki smashed his fist into the gunman's stomach as Hod held him still, but before he could cave in the man's face, Baldur pulled him back.

Kvasir put a restraining hand on Loki's arm. "You need him alive."

Loki's head cleared. He nodded and reached for his wallet as the man groaned and gasped for air. "How many of you are there? And how much were you promised?"

"Just ... three of us ... for now," the man wheezed. "We get ... a thousand American dollars each ... when the job is done." As he recovered from the blow, a greedy look gleamed in his eyes. "You want me to call it all off? It's gonna cost you."

Loki desperately wanted to snap the man's neck, but he knew he needed him to stop the other two out there. Police sirens sounded in the distance.

"What do you mean 'when the job is done'?" Loki demanded.

"Ah," the man sneered, "that information has an even higher price. I've told you enough."

Loki grimaced. They were running out of time. "Send word to your buddies and call it off," he told the man menacingly, pressing a wad of money into his hand. "It's over."

"Are you kidding me?" the man scoffed, quickly counting it. "This is the wrong currency and less than half of what we were promised."

Loki abruptly stepped up to him, his face mere inches from the shooter's. "Listen, you mangy cur! It's either this now or nothing but handcuffs and a jail cell in a matter of minutes."

"Fine," the gunman sighed with resignation. The sirens were close now. "You won't see me again."

"What about the others?" Loki challenged him.

"I'll call it off," the man muttered begrudgingly.

"Good, because if we so much as think we're being followed, we'll come for you so hard and so fast, you'll wish you'd never been born," Loki threatened.

The man nodded, his eyes furtive as the sirens drew closer. As soon as Hod released him, he took off running, leaving the gun on the ground.

The four Asgardians turned to face the policemen as they pulled up in two squad cars. Loki immediately recognized one of them as the cop who had witnessed two drunk vagabonds' unsuccessful attempt to mug him the last time he had been in Norway.

"Look who it is, fellows!" the policeman said to the other three cops in Norwegian. "Are you okay, Mr. Black?"

"I'm fine," Loki answered, slipping into flattery. "And so relieved you're here, officers! We were chasing the guy who shot our friend, but he got away."

"Someone's been shot?" exclaimed the policeman.

"Yes, and we need to get back to take him to the hospital. There's the gun, and the guy who shot him went that way," Kvasir declared, pointing in the opposite direction than the man had fled. "If you hurry, you might catch him."

The first policeman shouted his appreciation as another grabbed the gun. Then all four scrambled to get back in their cars.

As they sped off in the direction Kvasir had indicated, Baldur chuckled, switching back to English. "You know he went the other way, right?"

"He needs time to call off the rest of his dogs," Kvasir pointed out. "They'll catch him soon enough. Meanwhile, Kristoff needs medical attention."

"I'm glad you, at least, kept your head," Loki said, clapping Kvasir gratefully on the back.

"What are you talking about?" Kvasir laughed. "You were fantastic!"

Loki smiled as they ran back to the house. Had Kvasir really tried to kill him just six weeks ago? The two of them had come a long way in a short time. His thoughts turned to Kristoff, who had once joked Loki would be the death of him someday. He cringed inwardly at how close he had come to fulfilling that, feeling the blame keenly.

And he realized with a start just how much his Norwegian manager and friend meant to him.

14

"The bullet struck right under the clavicle on the left shoulder," Helga informed the men when they returned. "It's still in there."

"We need to get him to a hospital," Kvasir urged.

"Nonsense," Helga scoffed, her blue eyes flashing. "I was a field nurse during the war. I've seen far worse."

The women had already moved Kristoff into the guest bedroom, from which Helga had apparently been barking orders to the other two women. Carina removed the last of several sterilized surgical tools from a pot of boiling water in the kitchen, while Sigyn finished preparing strips of soft white cloth and gauze. She was unusually quiet and avoided everyone's eyes. Loki peered at her, remembering how she used to act that way as a child, usually when she had done something she was ashamed of and felt compelled to tell on herself.

Helga removed the washcloth Kristoff had been using to apply pressure to his wound, then checked the bleeding.

"It's not the first time I've been shot," Kristoff muttered, wincing with every jostle or touch. "Those doctors down at the infirmary couldn't do better than Helga can."

"Can you remove the bullet?" Loki asked Helga.

"What do you think I'm getting ready to do?"

"I can seal the wound," Loki offered. "No stitches."

"Cauterization?"

"In a manner of speaking, yes, but not as painful. It's an Asgardian technique. I used it on Carina once."

"No scar," Carina testified, showing her completely smooth hand.

"I vote for that," Kristoff quipped. Despite his pale face, the large beads of sweat on his brow, and the dark circles forming under his eyes, he seemed in unusually good spirits.

Helga peered up at Carina's hand and nodded at Loki. "The rest of you get out of here and let me tend to my brother."

Everyone left, and the room grew still and quiet. Helga selected two forceps and a scalpel, setting them down on the clean cloth she had placed on the table next to the bed. She gave Kristoff some vodka to drink and a piece of cloth to bite since she had no other anesthetic available.

"I sure do wish I had some Dakin's solution," Helga remarked as she poured vodka over the wound, which made Kristoff grunt in pain.

"What's Dakin's solution?" Loki asked curiously.

"It's an antiseptic we used during the war," Helga answered. "Sodium hypochlorite and boric acid. Now, if you want to talk, talk to Kristoff. This is going to hurt."

Helga gently dug into the wound with a pair of forceps and the scalpel, trying to see where the bullet might be. Her poking and prodding brought several muffled groans from Kristoff, but he held as still as possible. Loki filled Kristoff in on what had happened with the gunman to distract him, also using his light manipulation to illuminate the muscles under Kristoff's skin so Helga could see exactly where the bullet was lodged.

"That's most helpful," Helga breathed, putting down the scalpel and grasping the elusive bullet with the second set of forceps. "It just missed the bone."

Kristoff breathed a sigh of relief through the cloth as she pulled out the small piece of oblong metal and dropped it into a small dish. She poured more vodka on the wound to clean it again, which brought another grunt from her brother.

"Your turn," she told Loki, holding sterilized gauze on the wound to staunch the last spurt of blood.

Loki took out his kit, allowing Helga to watch as he sealed the bullet hole.

"Astounding!" she exclaimed.

"This one might scar a little," Loki warned Kristoff. "But it will heal faster and won't be as painful as stitches."

"What about wound care?" Kristoff asked as Helga wrapped it with more gauze and clean cloth.

"Just don't be an idiot and open it back up," Loki laughed. "You can wash and all that. But you'll have to take it easy."

"Bed rest?" Kristoff groaned as Helga helped him put on a button down shirt.

"You got shot in the shoulder, not the abdomen or the leg," Loki taunted him. "Don't get into any fights, and you should be fine."

"Thanks, Dr. Black, Nurse Helga," Kristoff laughed, tentatively testing his shoulder rotation. "That was some impressive teamwork."

"Dr. Black? How about a career change, Luke?" Helga teased him.

"Not on your life," Loki protested, but he laughed with them.

Helga busied herself with cleaning up after the procedure, insisting Kristoff stay in bed for at least twenty minutes. She ignored her brother's vehement protesting and shooed Loki out of the room. He ambled into the living room, where he was greeted by somber faces. Carina was fast asleep on the sofa. She woke with a start when Loki cheerfully announced Kristoff would fully recover, expecting to see relief transform all their faces.

"It's not that," Sigyn sighed. "There was another guy, and I let him get away."

Ah, so that's what was bothering her, Loki thought.

"It wasn't your fault," Kvasir comforted her. "You never would have had to deal with it if I had stayed here."

"I just can't figure out how I didn't see him," added Hod.

"He had to have sneaked into the house when you weren't watching," Baldur guessed. "Before the first guy shot Kristoff."

"I still should have sensed him," Hod insisted.

"Could we get back to what happened?" Loki asked warily.

"I caught him rifling through Kristoff's study when Helga sent me to get the vodka," Sigyn explained. "I screamed, and he chased me into the kitchen, where Carina knocked him out with Helga's frying pan."

Loki glanced at Carina with open admiration before asking, "Where was Helga?"

"She ran upstairs to get her gun," Carina yawned. "But Sigyn had already tied him up with vines when she got back."

"What?" Loki exclaimed. "Vines?"

Carina seemed wide awake now. "You should have seen it! Helga had this cute little plant in the corner, but when

Sigyn touched it, these huge vines shot out of it and wrapped the guy up in a vise grip."

"She has the gift of growth," Kvasir informed Loki, who was staring at Sigyn in shock. "Didn't you know that?"

"I never asked," Loki admitted.

"It seems to me that's something you should have known," Kvasir returned. "You grew up with her, didn't you?"

"She never used her gift around me," Loki grumbled, irritated by Kvasir's probing.

"You didn't?" Kvasir asked Sigyn. "Why not? It's a wonderful gift!"

"Thor saw me use it once and made fun of me," Sigyn replied quietly. "After that, I never used it around anyone in the royal family."

"Thor can be a real schlub," Loki remarked.

Kvasir peered at Loki. "And you never asked. It must run in the family."

"I'm not marrying him. I'm marrying you," Sigyn said hotly. "Now leave him alone."

"Yes, ma'am," Kvasir replied meekly, though he winked at Loki.

"And so it begins," Hod remarked dryly.

Kvasir laughed as Sigyn ducked her head shyly and whispered, "Thanks for defending me, though."

Loki grinned to himself, but prompted, "What happened after the vines?"

"He was still unconscious, but he started choking and turning blue," Sigyn continued the story. "I tried to release the coils a little, but I hadn't ever used my gift in reverse. The plant shriveled up completely. He came to and ran off. Helga got a shot off, but she's fairly certain she missed."

Loki sighed. "Well, it can't be helped. At least we know where all three of them are now. But don't worry, Sigyn. I don't think we'll be seeing any of them again."

Helga joined them, followed by Kristoff, who walked without help into the living room. The others exclaimed over Kristoff and gathered around him as he sank into a faded, comfortable-looking armchair.

When Loki caught him up on the altercation with the intruder and told him about Sigyn's gift, Kristoff snickered wickedly and asked, "Can she make Hod taller?"

Hod fixed him with his intense, golden gaze. "You're lucky you just got shot, man!"

"Relax, Hod," Kvasir grunted. "How do you feel now, Kristoff?"

Kristoff gave a brief summary of his medical treatment. The doorbell interrupted him as he began to laud his own bravery, emphasizing the lack of any anesthetic. Helga left to answer the door, then returned to the room a few seconds later with a tall blonde.

"Kat!" Kristoff exclaimed, standing and wincing slightly as he moved his sore shoulder the wrong way.

"You stay right there," Helga scolded him.

"Did I interrupt a party?" Kathleen asked, her intelligent blue eyes sweeping the room.

"More like a surgery," Kristoff quipped. His huge grin indicated he was immensely pleased to see her.

"Surgery?" Kathleen repeated quizzically.

"Oh, uh, I got shot, but that's off the record," Kristoff replied, blushing.

"Shot?" she cried, her face full of concern.

"It's only a graze," Kristoff lied. "I'm fine, really. Anyway, the party comes later. We're getting ready for a wedding."

Kathleen looked decidedly confused, as if she did not know which question to ask first. "Sounds like my timing is unfortunate. I'll come back another day."

"No!" Kristoff exclaimed, then blushed again when she raised an eyebrow at his forcefulness. He changed his tone to be more professional. "I'm sure you came all the way to Norway for something. Is there something I can do for you?"

Kathleen shifted uncomfortably. "I had hoped we could speak privately, but—"

"Oh, absolutely," Kristoff interrupted eagerly. "Just step into my office."

"But shouldn't you be resting?" Kathleen objected.

"Yes, he should," Helga muttered indignantly.

"Really, I'm fine. I had very good medical care," Kristoff replied, winking first at Loki then at Helga, who did not look happy as the visitor followed Kristoff to his little corner office.

Once they had closed the door, Hod nudged Baldur. The two of them snickered.

"What's so funny?" Helga demanded.

"Isn't it obvious?" Baldur replied. "He's completely smitten."

"Totally twitterpated," added Hod.

Helga frowned somewhat haughtily. "I don't care how much he fancies her. That woman is up to something."

"Now, Helga," Baldur chided her gently, crossing the living room to hug her tightly. "You can't hold on to your baby brother forever." When Helga merely crossed her arms and huffed, he turned to Kvasir and Sigyn. "Are you two ready for a wedding? Looks like Kristoff will be just fine."

Hod hooted, "Oh, that American journalist will make sure he's fine."

Helga glared at them both as Baldur joined Hod in uproarious laughter.

Loki just smiled fondly at Carina, who hid her grin behind her hand. "Are you ready to marry me?" he asked her quietly.

"Today?" she whispered back.

"Why not? We have witnesses and an officiant. Thanks to Kristoff, I'm an official resident of Christiania on paper, so I'm fairly certain we can get a marriage license here. I'll ask him to be sure."

When she nodded, smiling brightly at him, Loki pulled Baldur aside. "Would you marry us when you marry them?"

"It's fine with me, but you need to ask them." Baldur gestured to Kvasir and Sigyn, who were staring at each other with a sudden nervousness mingled with excitement.

"Is it finally time?" Sigyn whispered. "After all these years?"

"Have you changed your mind?" Kvasir asked her, his face uncertain. "It's not too late to turn back."

Sigyn looked at Loki, then back at Kvasir. "I still choose you."

Kvasir kissed her happily but pulled away when Loki cleared his throat awkwardly and asked, "Do you mind if Carina and I join you?"

"What?" Kvasir growled, looking at Loki with a bizarre, uncomfortable look. "We're not really into—"

Loki groaned and covered his face with his hand, embarrassed by how his timing had made the question sound. "The wedding, Kvasir," he clarified. "Carina and I would like to take our vows as well, if that's alright with you?"

Everyone else burst out laughing. Kvasir looked at Sigyn when the laughter had finally died down. She nodded her approval, then jumped up to hug both Carina and Loki.

"I'm so happy for you, Carina," she exclaimed. "I hope we'll be like sisters."

Carina smiled, still a little unsure of how to respond to Sigyn, then looked up at Loki and reminded him, "You still haven't told me what your Asgardian marriage traditions are."

"I'll just let you see for yourself," Loki told her with an impish grin. "Sigyn can help you get ready."

"When exactly is this happening?" Carina prodded him.

"By the light of the stars," he answered her.

"We need to go shopping!" Sigyn grabbed Carina's hands and pulled her toward the front door, giggling the whole way. "What fun we'll have!" she gushed just as they disappeared.

"Shopping?" Loki repeated, looking at the other men in confusion. "Should I go with her?"

"I'll go," Helga offered. "This is a woman's thing, Luke, dear. You likely won't see her again until it's time to take your vows."

She slipped on her shoes, grabbed her handbag, and hurried to catch up with the girls. Kristoff and Kathleen came out of the study just as Helga shut the door.

"Where did everyone go?" Kristoff asked in bewilderment.

"Shopping," Kvasir said dryly.

"For what?" Kristoff asked. "I thought Sigyn was ready days ago."

"She was," Kvasir responded. "But Carina isn't."

"You're marrying her tonight?" Kristoff questioned Loki. "Her father won't like that!"

"Carina and I decided to speak with him after the fact," Loki reassured him. "He'll just have to accept it."

"I hope you know what you're doing," Kristoff replied nervously.

Loki ignored his comment. "Carina says we need a marriage license."

"I can help you with that," Kristoff said.

"Now can I write your love story? In my next article?" Kathleen asked excitedly. "Oh, congratulations, by the way."

"Always business, aren't you, Kat?" Kristoff teased her. Then he turned again to Loki. "Speaking of business, how would you and Carina feel about booking an American tour? Kathleen came to tell me several program directors contacted her after they read her exposé, asking how to get in touch with your manager."

"I'm open to it, but can we talk about that after the wedding?" Loki laughed. "And Kathleen, you can print whatever you want about us in a few weeks. How about that?"

Kathleen nodded. "I'm staying nearby," she said. "Let me know when you're ready to talk. People are going to eat this up!"

"Did you take a taxi over here?" Kristoff asked her.

"Yes, why?"

"I'll drop you off at your hotel," Kristoff offered. "I have to take Luke to the courthouse anyway."

"Sure, I'll take you up on that," she said with a bright smile.

Behind their backs, Loki jerked his thumb at the two of them, winking at the other men, who snickered as he followed the couple out to Kristoff's car.

"Are you free tonight?" Kristoff asked, as Kathleen got into the passenger seat of his car while Loki splayed out in the back.

"Possibly. Why?"

"Would you be my guest at the most interesting wedding you'll ever attend?"

"Can I write about it?" she asked playfully.

"No!" Loki growled.

"No," Kristoff repeated, meeting Loki's glare with a fiendish grin. "It's a top secret tradition from Luke's homeland. If you'd rather not go, I understand. It wouldn't really benefit your career."

"I'd love to go," she replied, winking at him. "I'm not always all business, you know."

Kristoff flashed her a lopsided smile, then proceeded to engage her in conversation about her work and places to which they both had traveled. Loki tuned out their discussion, preferring to focus on his imminent wedding. His thoughts quickly turned to his father as he contemplated the type of husband he would be. For thousands of years, Odin and Frigga had chosen to make their marriage work in spite of the pressures of running the kingdom planet of Asgard. He remembered Thor's words about their parents' mutual love and respect for each other and how things had not always been so.

The car stopped in front of the Saga Hotel Oslo, snapping Loki's thoughts away from Asgard and back to where he was.

"I'll pick you up after nine, then," Kristoff called to Kathleen as she exited the vehicle.

She bent down to look at him through the open window. "I'll be ready."

As they pulled away from the hotel, which was a wedge-shaped stone building, Loki caught a glimpse of the other women. They had just walked out of one of the quaint little shops on a long, interesting-looking street named Bogstadveien. He smiled to himself when he noticed Carina's face wreathed in smiles, glowing with nervous excitement. Loki almost wished he could join her, but his business at the courthouse could not wait.

Once they arrived at the solemn stone building, Loki and Kristoff stood in line for what seemed like centuries. Since Kristoff was unusually quiet and distracted, Loki watched the people hurrying around or impatiently standing in line awaiting their turns for whatever business they had there. He noticed at least two couples and guessed they were also purchasing marriage licenses.

"Shouldn't Carina be here for this?" Loki asked suddenly, worry furrowing his brow.

What if they deny me a license? he thought.

"Technically, yes," Kristoff answered. "But since time is short, we'll give it a shot without her. If they won't budge, we'll have to go find her and hope they don't close before we can get back."

Loki nodded. Then, seeing an opportunity for teasing, he casually remarked, "What else happened this afternoon? You and Kathleen both looked a little flushed when you came out of your study."

"Nothing happened," Kristoff insisted rather glumly. "It was just stuffy in there. Her visit was strictly business, as always."

"She could have called you or wired you a telegram from Paris," Loki pointed out. "Instead, she travels all the way up here? And finds out where you live?"

"I gave her my address," Kristoff replied.

"Well, why is she staying?"

"She said she has family nearby."

"Oh really? Is she Norwegian?"

"Yeah, on her mother's side, she has an aunt, grandparents, and some cousins she visits every summer. Not in Christiania. She never got around to telling me where exactly. And she has an uncle here in town."

Loki laughed. "Then why didn't she call you from there?"

"I don't know," Kristoff sighed with a little annoyance. "I'm telling you, she's all business with me."

"Come on, Kristoff! She came to see you."

"You really think so?" Kristoff asked doubtfully.

"I know so," Loki declared. "I thought you were the one who knew so much about women. Even I know they don't come around unless they like you."

"Why would she make an excuse to come see me?" Kristoff asked.

"She's proud," Loki answered. "And it's quite possible she's as clueless as you are. Everyone else can see the attraction between you. Why can't you?"

"Sounds like another couple I know," Kristoff chuckled, nudging Loki.

"Well then, I'd say that's a very good sign," Loki quipped.

Kristoff grinned broadly. "Maybe you're right! Thanks, pal."

Just then, they were called for their turn. And as anticipated, the stern-looking woman at the desk informed them Carina must be present to obtain the license. Though Kristoff tried to flatter her and explain the situation, she merely looked down her nose at him and coldly repeated herself, suggesting they return the following day with the bride.

"Now what?" Loki asked as they turned away. "We don't have time now to get Carina. I could spin an illusion of her. Would that work?"

Kristoff had not heard, his attention focused on something in another direction. "Follow me," he instructed Loki. Then he hurried in the direction he had been looking and called out, "Liam! Liam Borsheim!"

A tall, thin man with straw blond hair and piercing, ice blue eyes stopped as he was about to exit the lobby. "Kristoff Schmidt!" he exclaimed, his formerly serious face transformed by a delighted smile. "How's my favorite section leader?"

"I was your only section leader," Kristoff remarked dryly.

"Well, the other guys said you were the best they ever had, and I believe them, Sarge," Liam laughed.

Loki looked at Kristoff curiously, deducing they must be old war buddies.

Kristoff grinned, but remarked, "Enough about that. We're almost out of time."

Liam frowned, his face instantly settling into its former seriousness. "Why do I feel like you're about to ask me another favor?"

"Because I am," Kristoff confirmed. "You recognize this fellow, don't you?"

Liam eyed Loki warily but stuck out his hand for a handshake. "Lukas Black, the magician who needed citizenship and travel papers. Yes. It's a pleasure to finally meet you."

"The pleasure is mine," Loki responded politely with his most charming smile. "It seems you are the man to thank for the legal documents Kristoff procured for me."

The man looked pleased but narrowed his eyes slightly. "You're welcome, but let's get to the point. You didn't come to

227

thank me. I'm assuming there is a problem you need me to fix?"

"Not at all," Kristoff reassured him. "They wouldn't give him a marriage license because the bride isn't here. And the wedding is tonight."

"Nothing like waiting until the last minute," Liam sighed. "These things take time, you know."

"We just arrived in town a few hours ago," Loki explained. "She's been out shopping for things for the wedding or she'd be here."

"Sounds poorly planned," Liam remarked dryly.

"Come on, old friend," Kristoff persuaded him. "What can you do to help? For old time's sake? We've really got our backs to the wall here, as Field Marshal Haig put it."

Liam grimaced. "I wondered when you would bring that up. I've got nothing but love for you, brother, and I'll never forget what you did that day, but this has to be the last time. After this, we're even."

Kristoff shoved out his hand to take Liam's in agreement. "Just means I'll have to save your sorry life again so I can lord that over you."

Liam laughed, slapped Kristoff on the back, and motioned for them to follow him to his office.

Loki felt he might burst from repressed curiosity. "You saved his life?" he whispered to Kristoff.

"Yeah, in France," Kristoff whispered back. "Liam and I were the only Norwegians in our unit at the time." His eyes glazed over slightly with sadness, but he shook it off and continued, "Norway stayed officially neutral, but some of us smuggled ourselves into the Allied forces."

"Why?" Loki asked curiously.

"My great-grandfather was British, so Helga and I didn't agree with the Norwegian government's position. We both felt we had to get involved. Her husband, Erik, and a few others felt the same."

Liam unlocked his office door, motioned them inside, and sat down behind his desk. He had overheard. "As did I, but Kristoff climbed up the ranks fairly quickly. He was a sergeant and a section leader, but that didn't stop him from taking a bullet with my name on it."

"Really?" Loki breathed, casting an admiring glance at his friend.

"Sounds more impressive than it was," Kristoff muttered. "I was only in charge of twelve men. And the bullet just nicked my arm. I took one in the leg that was far worse."

"Don't let him fool you," Liam protested as he pulled some paperwork out of a drawer. "It would have hit me in the chest if he hadn't jumped in and pushed me out of the way."

"Can we just finish our business?" Kristoff groaned. "How do we expedite this?"

"It usually takes some time to process, but you came to the right person," Liam stated proudly. "I really don't know why you didn't just start with me."

After answering a series of questions and filling out paperwork, Loki finally clutched the piece of paper that represented a new life with Carina, feeling a little light-headed. Liam informed them what additional documents he needed on file and promised to sign the license in the morning as their authorized municipal officiant since Baldur would not qualify. Kristoff assured Loki he would take care of the rest. Loki hoped they would not have to follow the same tedious process for their wedding in Germany, but at least Carina would be there.

Silence fell over both men as they drove back to the house. Loki did not mind Kristoff losing himself in his thoughts. He would rather not talk anyway. Everything seemed far more real now that he had the license.

When they arrived and walked inside, Baldur and Hod teased Kristoff mercilessly about Kathleen's visit, especially when Loki told them she was attending the wedding, all of which Kristoff handled fairly good-naturedly.

Kvasir kept silent through all the teasing. "It's really happening," he suddenly stated, his tone somber and filled with wonder.

"You're not getting cold feet, are you, Kvasir?" Kristoff asked.

"Are you kidding? I've longed for this day for a thousand years!" he exclaimed, his face brightening with anticipation. The other men sighed with relief, then brightened as well when Kvasir asked, "Are there any snacks in this house? It's going to be a late night."

They raided the kitchen, then set up a game of poker at the table. Loki played one hand, then opted for a brief nap when his eyes started closing involuntarily. When he woke, he ambled back into the kitchen, where the men dealt him back into the game. They were so involved in razzing and besting each other with each hand, they all jumped when the front door slammed and feet pounded up the stairs.

"The women are back," Hod announced unnecessarily, for they could all hear Sigyn's giggle and Carina's bell-like laughter as Helga admonished them to hush and hurry.

When Helga came downstairs, she fussed at them for the mess in the kitchen, but Baldur appeased her by cheerfully offering to clean it up himself. Although she was visibly pleased by his offer, she shooed them all out, ignoring Baldur's protests.

"I wonder what time it is," Kristoff remarked as he glanced at his own wristwatch. "Wow, it's already half past eight."

"Sunset should be right around nine," Baldur predicted, pulling the living room curtains aside to look at the sky. "You boys had better get ready."

Loki stood in the guest bedroom, staring at the jumbled mess of clothing on the bed. He had packed several Asgardian garments as part of his ruse, and Kristoff had also brought back his luggage from London, which still contained his Midgardian clothing. All of the choices had Loki frozen in indecision, unsure of the best thing to wear and wishing the white suit he had worn while performing with Carina had been real.

Kvasir knocked on the door, calling, "Loki, are you ready yet?"

Loki opened the door and pulled Kvasir inside, groaning, "I have no idea what to wear."

Kvasir laughed. He looked confident and daring in a three-piece, solid black suit complimented by a sky blue vest and bow tie that brought an indigo hue to his gray eyes. "You sound like a woman, Loki, and you'll make us all late like a woman."

Loki grinned. "Better not say things like that around Sigyn."

"We don't have time for this," Kvasir grumped. "Just spin an illusion."

"No illusions," Loki protested. "I want this to be real."

Kvasir frowned, sorting through the heaps of clothes Loki had thrown on the bed. "Are you marrying her as Loki or Lukas Black?"

"Tonight, I marry her as Loki, the Asgardian way, but I'll sign the document Lukas Black," he informed him. "After I explain things to her father, we'll have a Midgardian wedding for show. At least, that's the plan."

"Sounds needlessly complicated," Kvasir observed, holding up the best of the Asgardian gear to inspect it.

"That's rich, coming from you," Loki retorted. "Are you going to help me or not?"

"Here, wear these! Now, hurry up!" Kvasir commanded, tossing him the garments he had chosen before stepping out of the room.

After Loki finished dressing, he admired himself in the mirror. The dark green tunic opened slightly just below the collar. Gold trim laced over the breast in a V-shaped pattern. The black pants had subtle green stripes on the sides, with a matching belt that pulled it all together. Loki spotted his black cape, which he did not remember packing, and added it to his ensemble. High black boots with sheathed daggers completed the look. Satisfied, he called Kvasir back into the room to see his handiwork.

"How do I look?" Loki asked him, telling himself silently that Carina would like how the outfit accentuated the green in his eyes.

"Like a prince," Kvasir answered, clapping him on the shoulder. "Although I have no idea why you thought you might need all that on your rite of passage."

"Perhaps I subconsciously planned for this instead," he admitted.

"Perhaps," Kvasir agreed. His face paled suddenly as he glanced in the mirror. "How do I look?"

"Like a successful playwright," Loki told him, clasping both Kvasir's arms in friendship. "Steady, man. We are about to become the happiest Asgardians on Earth."

Kristoff, Hod, and Baldur waited for them in the living room. They all nodded with approval at how fine the two grooms looked.

Kristoff handed Loki the ring he had lent to Sigyn. "You'll be needing this."

"Where are we doing this?" Loki asked Baldur, starting to feel nervous.

"We thought the edges of the Nordmarka would be perfect," Baldur replied. "There's a great spot near the old portal."

"That does sound perfect," Loki agreed with a wide grin. He had attended his fair share of Asgardian marriage ceremonies. Despite his sudden nervousness, he looked forward to experiencing it for himself.

Kristoff threw his car keys to Baldur. "You take the men up and get them ready. I'll pick up Kathleen and bring the women out in Helga's car."

"When did Helga get a car?" Loki asked in surprise.

"I bought her one when I got back. I told you we were making plenty of money," Kristoff answered. "Hod, are you coming with me or going with Baldur?"

"Are you kidding?" Hod laughed, his golden eyes filled with mischief. "And miss a chance to tie these two reprobates to a tree?"

"Baldur it is," Kristoff laughed. "I'd trade places with you if it weren't for Kathleen. You Asgardians have some strange customs. This is going to be unforgettable, although I think someone should have warned poor Carina."

"Sigyn might have," Loki replied. "By the way, does Kathleen know who we really are?"

"No, and it's best she doesn't," Kristoff replied, already on his way out the door.

"Well, that's just fantastic," Loki grumbled to Baldur. "I wanted you to use my real name."

"Just change the sound so she hears your human name," Baldur suggested. "And anything else that sounds too Asgardian. Should be easy for you."

Loki nodded thoughtfully. He must be more anxious and excited than he realized. He normally would have thought of that.

The crisp, cool air of the Norwegian summer evening soothed Loki's nerves somewhat as they piled into Kristoff's car. The soon-to-be groom's thoughts were such a jumbled mess of anxiety and exhilaration, the drive to the Nordmarka seemed much shorter than he remembered. Before Loki registered they had arrived, he had mechanically followed his friends to the portal tree, the charred remains of which looked forsaken and lonely. Loki stared at it, filled with nostalgia and a slight stab of grief. The old tree represented so much, including bringing the star of his heart into his life. He looked up through the tree tops at the twinkling stars in the deepening sky, wondering if any of them might be Loki's Torch or even Carina, the constellation after which his bride-to-be had been named.

Baldur and Hod set up two torches next to two younger trees standing close to each other. They were not too deep in the forest, but it was so late at night, no one worried about being seen. And with Heimdall watching Lord Berg from Asgard, as well as guarding the Bifröst, it was unlikely he would turn his gaze to Midgard.

Kvasir and Loki obediently backed against each tree respectively and allowed themselves to be tightly bound and blindfolded. Loki tested his bonds, making sure they were fast and sturdy. The seconds ticked by torturously, but Loki did not have to wait long, for he soon heard the other car approaching and footsteps crunching on the path leading to the area.

Loki could not see his bride, but he could feel her take her place next to him, waiting for what would happen next. He knew she would also be blindfolded. They were not permitted to see or speak to each other at this part of the ceremony.

As silence settled over the group, Baldur cried out, "We are here to try both Kvasir and Loki to see if they be guilty of pursuing love and seeking holy matrimony! If found guilty by the witnesses present, they will be sentenced with an unbreakable bond only death itself can sever. I present to you Sigyn and Carina, their alleged betrothed. Ladies, join hands with the accused."

Loki felt Carina feel for his hand, then intertwine her fingers with his. His bonds were situated high enough to allow him to bring her hand to his mouth to kiss it.

"Does anyone here bring testimony against them?" Baldur continued.

Hod spoke up, more solemnly and eloquently than Loki had ever heard him. "I have seen tenderness and affection in both of these couples, as you all just saw when both men kissed the hands of the women they love. They have set aside their own needs and desires to protect the purity of their brides. As they have chosen this noble sacrifice, an act of true love, so they would also lay down their very lives for them."

"You have heard this testimony," Baldur shouted. "Does anyone else bear witness against either man?"

"Yeah, I do," Kristoff spoke up, his voice merry and full of mischief. "I've personally watched these two men up close. They're both utterly lovesick."

"Would you be so kind as to elaborate?" Baldur inquired, his own voice taking on a wicked edge.

Loki groaned inwardly, wondering what his friend might say to humiliate him.

"Hmm… Shall I elaborate on how our renowned magician dropped his mouth open like a codfish the first time he saw Carina?"

Snickers sounded throughout the small audience. Carina squeezed Loki's hand.

"Or perhaps on how love drove our prolific writer almost to murder and then to reluctant friendship?" Kristoff continued.

With the encouragement of the spectators, he proceeded to elaborate on both, amidst alternating laughter and hushed awe. Encouraged by Kristoff's boldness, several others popped up with comments or stories until Baldur had to quiet everyone down to continue the ceremony.

"How do you plead, Kvasir?" Baldur asked solemnly.

"Profoundly guilty," Kvasir answered confidently.

"How do you plead, Loki?"

"Oh, I'm definitely guilty," Loki responded happily.

"Witnesses, how do you find the accused?"

"Guilty!" the guests cried, laughter lingering in their voices.

"You are hereby sentenced, Kvasir, to oneness with Sigyn, and Loki, to oneness with Carina. To claim your husbands and say your vows, oh, brides," Baldur continued gleefully, "you must first rescue them from their bonds while blindfolded. For you will not always see clearly, nor will married life be devoid of trials. The men are permitted to give you guidance as necessary, for you must work together when difficulties arise. When you have at last found a way through whatever keeps you from your love, you will be rewarded."

Loki tensed with anticipation. This had always been his favorite part to watch. Carina released Loki's hand and felt her way around the ropes binding him to the tree.

She fumbled with the knots for a few seconds, then whispered, "Do you have your daggers?"

"As always," Loki chuckled. "There's one hidden on the outside of each boot."

Her cleverness delighted him, but her intention to cut the ropes away from him while blindfolded slightly alarmed him. Loki shivered as he felt her hands move down the side of his right leg, then grasp the dagger from his boot. He involuntarily shifted slightly against the ropes as he felt cold steel on his chest.

Sensing his consternation, she whispered, "Trust me."

The ropes tightened briefly and fell away as the guests cheered. As soon as his arms were free, he felt for her face as she felt for his. He heard the guests cheer for Sigyn and assumed she had also freed her betrothed, though he had no idea how. Loki's fingers brushed against cloth on Carina's face.

He removed her blindfold just as she removed his. He blinked twice to adjust his vision and stared at his bride in awe.

Carina stepped back to look at him. Her eyes sparkled like the stars and burned with a fire rivaling the smoldering torches. Her red hair was loosely braided and laced with white flowers, though a few tendrils had escaped to frame her face. The simple white dress she wore shimmered in the torchlight, cinched at the waist and flaring out in soft folds to form the long skirt. The translucent sleeves were slit at the shoulders and flowed down over her arms, just past her fingertips.

"Great Odin's Raven," he gasped, his voice catching as he drank in the breathtaking vision before him.

She giggled but placed her finger on his lips. "None of that strong language, Loki," she teased him. "Although I might use it myself. You look so dashing, I'm positively weak at the knees."

Her words pleased him, but he was so full of emotion, he could not speak.

"You've lost your tongue again, haven't you, Mr. Black?" Carina teased him.

Loki nodded, gulping as Baldur instructed both couples to stand by the torches and take each other's hands. Thankfully, Loki's tongue loosened just as Baldur began to lead them in their vows.

"I, Loki Odinson of Asgard, fully commit myself to you, Carina Green of Midgard," Loki repeated dutifully, only slightly aware of Kvasir as he took his own vows with Sigyn. "I will devote myself to caring for you as a faithful husband, forsaking all others. I solemnly swear to serve, love, and respect you, working with you toward unity. For only death shall part me from you."

He beamed silently at Carina as she repeated after Baldur, hardly hearing Sigyn's voice to Kvasir as he committed Carina's promise to his memory. "I, Carina Green of Midgard, fully commit myself to you, Loki Odinson of Asgard. I will devote myself to caring for you as a faithful wife, forsaking all others. I solemnly swear to serve, love, and respect you, working with you toward unity. For only death shall part me from you."

"Gentlemen, have you each brought your bride a token?" Baldur asked the men.

Loki drew out his ring and placed it on her finger, where it shone with a brilliant green glow. "Please accept this token of my love and fidelity. Wear it as a reminder of the vows we have taken this night." Then he whispered, "Until I find a ring that fits you better."

She whispered back, "Oh, but this is quite a ring. I might not give it back."

Kvasir had also presented Sigyn with a ring of his choosing, speaking soft words none of them could hear.

"Ladies, have you each brought your grooms a token?" Baldur asked the women.

While Sigyn presented Kvasir with the ring she had chosen for her groom, Loki watched in amazement as Carina reached into the folds of her dress.

"How did you ever find a ring for me on such short notice?" he whispered.

She smiled sweetly, showing him the black band set with tiny green stones. "Let's just say it found me."

Though he wanted to ask her more questions, Loki grinned and remained quiet as she slipped it on his finger, repeating almost the same words he had used. He was surprised it fit perfectly.

"By Asgardian law, I, Baldur, the eldest son of Odin, declare your marriages sealed. Husbands, give your wives a taste of the happiness you will bring them," Baldur commanded.

Carina peered at Loki in confusion. Instead of explaining, he grabbed her and bent her backward, kissing her deeply as everyone hooted and hollered.

"Oh, that's what he meant," she said breathlessly when he released her. "We Midgardians just say 'you may kiss the bride' at that part. Then the couple shares a polite kiss. I think I like your Asgardian way better."

He laughed and lifted her up in the air, not taking his eyes from hers. He did not twirl her, as Kvasir did Sigyn, but set her down on her feet, then scooped her up in his arms and kissed her again.

"I'm quite impressed you cut me loose while completely blindfolded," he praised her, putting her down again. "However did you do it?"

"I don't reveal my secrets either, Master Magician," she teased as she pulled him in for another kiss.

"Alright, you two," Kristoff interjected, strolling up to them with Kathleen on his arm. "The rest of us are still here. You're entitled to all that, but we don't want to see any more."

Loki and Carina laughed together, then accepted the congratulations of them both.

"How did you like the wedding, Kathleen?" Carina asked.

"It was unusual but very beautiful," she answered. "I really wish I could write about it. I understand your culture keeps their traditions from the outside world, Mr. Black?"

"Yes," he replied. "And I thank you for respecting that. You can write about our second wedding in Stuttgart, if you wish."

"I'd like that. Will it be a big wedding?" Kathleen asked with interest.

Carina smiled at her. "We haven't decided. It's really more of a formality since we're already married."

Loki kissed his new bride on the top of her head, his mind already wandering to the moments awaiting them later that evening.

Baldur and Hod helped Helga retrieve all of the food from the car, setting it all down on blankets in picnic style. Amidst the laughter and congratulations that went around as they all enjoyed each other's company, Loki thought of a dilemma.

"Carina," he whispered, "I didn't plan for where we could go to be alone tonight."

"Where are Kvasir and Sigyn going?" she asked lightly. "Just ask them."

"You don't just ask someone about that," he whispered fiercely, his face already turning red.

"We do," Carina tittered. "Watch." Then she turned to Sigyn and asked sweetly, "Sigyn, dear, where are you two going on your honeymoon?"

"We thought we would spend a little time in Paris since our new house here isn't quite finished," Sigyn answered, snuggling closer to Kvasir. "We'll stay at the hotel tonight and leave in the morning."

"The same hotel where Kathleen is staying?" Carina asked.

"Yes," replied Sigyn. "Baldur and Hod are also staying there. I'm sure you could get a room as well."

Carina made a face at Loki and whispered, "See? There you have it."

As the group began packing up the leftover food and blankets, Kristoff pulled Loki aside.

"I guess you decided to skip that rite of passage thing?" Kristoff asked, grinning at Loki from ear to ear. "From what the other Asgardians say, that's paramount to treason. Baldur never completed it either, but then he's dead to Asgard. If you're staying, I, for one, approve of your decision."

"Because it benefits you?" Loki said, making a wry face at him.

"Naturally," Kristoff agreed with a sly grin.

"Well, I'm not skipping it. I'm merely doing it here," Loki argued.

"Whatever you say, pal," Kristoff said. "It suits me just fine. If you were going back right away, I would have wasted my money."

"What money?"

Kristoff's grin grew even wider, as if he were about to burst with secret news. "I hope you don't mind, Luke, but I got you two a wedding present. I bought you tickets for the Bergen Railway."

Carina overheard and gasped with delight as she joined them. Loki did not even bother to hide his own wide smile.

"You're sneakier than I am," he teased his friend. "However did you pull that off? And when?"

"We all have our secrets," Kristoff laughed. "But I don't mind sharing mine. One of the ticket agents is a friend of mine. I called him while you were napping and picked up the tickets before I brought the women over. It sounds easier than it was."

"You never cease to amaze me," Loki praised him.

Kristoff continued, "I thought about sending you to Tromso or Alta for the northern lights, but it's not the right time of year."

"Do we have time for this?" Loki asked. "We have another wedding to plan after I speak with Joseph Green. I still have to find him. And what about this American tour?"

"Joseph already left New York," Kristoff informed him. "I sent word to him that Carina is safe and coming home soon."

"Why would you do that?" Loki growled.

"Because I know Joseph. He would have found out soon enough. If I didn't tell him first, there would be hell to pay," Kristoff retorted. "Besides, I told him I would let him know if I heard from Carina. It's not right to worry him further."

"Thank you, Kristoff," Carina said softly, placing one hand on Loki's arm to relax him. "Please don't tell him we're married yet."

"Nope, that one's on Luke," Kristoff grinned. "But I'll back you up if there's trouble."

"Again, thank you," she replied.

"Anyway, stay in Bergen for three or four days, then Joseph will likely be in Stuttgart by the time you're done there. We'll discuss the tour when you get back," Kristoff stated.

"That will need to be planned quickly. Don't forget, I have to return to Asgard in three months," Loki reminded his human friend.

Carina frowned, but Kristoff shrugged. "There's time. We'll start working on it while you're in Bergen. Kat will be here for a few weeks."

"Oh, really?" Loki said, a teasing note in his voice, as Kathleen also joined them when she heard her name. "You'd better not take her up to Lillehammer before you take me."

Kristoff glared at him, but Kathleen chuckled.

"My mother's family actually migrated to America from Lillehammer, Mr. Black," she informed him. "I have relatives there, so I've been several times. It's one of my favorite places on Earth."

"Same here!" Kristoff exclaimed, his eagerness blending with nervousness. "If you want to save on taxi fare, I'll drive you up there ... if you want. I'd love to show you this gorgeous overlook on the way. Not many people know about it."

"I just might take you up on that," Kathleen said, smiling warmly at Kristoff.

"Looks like I've been replaced," Loki quipped.

Carina gently pulled him to where the others were just finishing the clean-up, leaving Kristoff and Kathleen alone until it was time to return to Helga's house. Loki glanced back once to see Kathleen listening intently to something Kristoff was saying. His happiness for his friend's progress with Kathleen was slightly tempered by the fear he might lose his best friend. The fact that he just got married himself did not enter his mind. Regardless, he sensed things were changing. It was exciting and disconcerting all at once, but he did not dwell on it any further once they left the Nordmarka to return to Christiania.

As Kristoff pulled up to the house, Loki asked him, "When does our train leave?"

"Boarding starts at eleven," he responded. "I'll give you the tickets and the money you'll need once we're inside. It wasn't easy for my friend to get them either, so don't miss that train."

"Thank you, Kristoff. It really is a wonderful gift," Loki said as they entered the house. "How would I go about getting that hotel room Sigyn mentioned?"

"Eventually, I'm going to have to teach you all this," Kristoff teased him. "And make you track and manage your own money. But tonight, it would be faster if I just do it. Go pack your suitcase."

Loki threw all of his Midgardian things in his suitcase while Carina went upstairs with the women to gather her own belongings. He set his luggage down by the door, then joined the other men in the living room.

Kristoff sauntered out of his study and addressed Loki apologetically. "Every hotel in Christiania is booked."

Loki groaned in frustration.

"You're welcome to the guest bedroom here," Kristoff said. "It won't be comfortable, but you'll have the whole trip to Bergen to be together."

Hod spoke up. "Can't they have our room for the night, Baldur? We're leaving tomorrow anyway."

"I don't see why not," Baldur chuckled. "Do you think Helga would mind putting us up, Kristoff?"

"I might mind," Kristoff quipped. "I know you two have some unspoken thing going on."

"It's not that unspoken," Baldur laughed. "Your sister is delightful."

"I'm honestly glad to see her happy again," Kristoff sighed. "Don't break her heart, Baldur, or I'll find some way to break your tree trunk of a neck."

"That's not going to happen," Baldur said happily. "We're just taking it slow."

"Which is a big deal for you, man," Hod interjected.

"I know," Baldur replied with wonder. "It's different this time. We understand each other." Then he handed Loki his key to the room. "Leave this on the dresser. We'll just get our luggage and check out after you two leave for Bergen."

"Thanks, Baldur. Anything else?"

Baldur winked. "Just one more thing. Bed her well, little brother. You've waited long enough."

Loki chuckled as Kvasir protested, "What, a month? I've waited nearly a thousand years!"

"Yes, but you've had a few Midgardian wives in there, Kvasir," Baldur reminded him, much to Kvasir's chagrin. "I'm fairly certain this is Loki's first time."

Loki flushed crimson but grinned when Kristoff defended him.

"Not for lack of opportunity! There were plenty of women willing, but he turned them all down one way or another." Kristoff's tone turned wistful and serious. "He's a better man than I am. I never even considered waiting, and now that I've finally met someone I really care about ..." His voice trailed off in regret as all the men grew heavily silent.

Loki stood, walked over to Kristoff, and squeezed his shoulder. "It's never too late for a fresh start, Kristoff. You could at least wait for Kathleen."

Kristoff did not answer but grasped Loki's hand on his shoulder in acknowledgment. Sigyn walked into the living room with her luggage, followed by Helga.

"Where are Kat and Carina?" Kristoff asked.

"They'll be down shortly," Helga answered. "You'll have to buy Carina a few things on your trip, Luke."

"I don't mind," Loki responded, eager to whisk away his new bride.

"Oh, right," muttered Kristoff. He ducked into his study

and returned with an envelope stuffed with cash, which he handed to Loki. "Your tickets are in there. Don't lose them!"

"Relax, old boy," Loki chided him. "I'm not completely irresponsible!"

Kristoff leaned over to whisper, "I know where your head is, buddy. Enjoy tonight. You've earned it." As Carina and Kathleen entered the room, he continued so Carina would hear, "But do not, under any circumstances, miss that train."

Loki opened the door to the rather simple hotel room, which had a large bed centered on one wall and a smaller cot next to it. He set their luggage down as Carina breezed past him to draw the curtains closed.

She was ominously quiet.

"Is this okay?" Loki asked her, unsure of how to interpret her silence. He locked the door, temporarily turning his back to her. "I can sleep on the cot if you're not ready."

He did not hear her walk back over to him but became acutely aware of her hand on his back as she circled around him. He watched her with uncertainty, his nervousness overriding his longing for her. She reached up to caress his cheek with one hand and ran the other through his hair.

"I'm just feeling shy," she confessed. "Maybe even a little scared."

"Of me?" Loki asked tentatively, reaching out with his own hand to touch her face. He never wanted her to feel afraid of him again, as she had on Asgard.

"Not really. Something just feels different," Carina said thoughtfully. She dropped her hands to her side, looking at the ground as she continued, "I was never completely sure where things would lead before, even though I never had to be the one to draw the line. Tonight, I know what's about to happen, what's expected of me."

"No, not expected," Loki corrected her, lifting her chin up so she would look at him. "Just because you're my wife doesn't mean I no longer respect you. You're mine to cherish and protect, that's true. But that doesn't give me the right to take you whenever I want. I will never force you to do anything you're not comfortable with, so if you're not ready, I'll wait until you are."

Carina cocked her head and gawked at Loki with wide-eyed amazement. "This isn't what I thought it would be."

"What do you mean?"

"I was beginning to think you might throw me on the bed and have your way with me," she admitted sheepishly.

"What? Why?" Loki was slightly offended but more curious than anything.

"I could feel the tension building in you on the ride over here," Carina pointed out. "I'm flattered you're so intensely attracted to me, but it was a little frightening."

"Well, in my defense, you were pressed up against me. Don't you know what that does to a man?"

"I guess not," she muttered. "But it wasn't the first time we were jammed in a car together."

"The first time was pure torture. You were still engaged to Klaus."

Carina shuddered, drawing close to Loki as if to hide herself in his presence. "He would have done just what I described. Do you know how many women have warned me about the wedding night?"

Loki chuckled. "How could I possibly know that?"

Carina laughed with him, wrapping her arms around his waist and peeking up at him. "My point is you are so very different from what I thought was the typical male." She paused, furrowing her brows slightly, then continued, "I'm sure there are other men who think the same as you do about respect and love, even on Midgard, but they must be few and far between. That's part of what I love about you. I feel safe and treasured with you."

"I hope you always do," Loki murmured, holding her close to him, content for the moment to have her in his arms. "Do you just want to sleep then?"

She stroked his cheek with her hand again. "No, Mr. Black. I do believe I'm ready to be your wife in every way."

"Mrs. Lukas Black," he sighed, leaning in to her touch. "It has a nice ring to it."

"What about Mrs. Loki? Or Mrs. Odinson?" she inquired. "Is that right?"

"No, we use patronymic last names for everyone on Asgard. You would be Carina Josephdotter, Princess of Asgard," Loki corrected her, brushing a few tendrils of her hair away from her face.

"Your mother said the woman you marry would be a princess," Carina remembered. "I think I would be an unwelcome one."

"Maybe they would come to accept you. If I were king, I could make them," Loki asserted.

Carina stepped back, her eyes fearful. "I don't think I would be a very good queen."

"In my heart, you are already my queen," Loki declared, taking her hands and drawing her back to him.

Carina's brow furrowed with worry, but Loki kissed away the little grooves in her skin until she giggled. "I suppose we have other things to focus on, don't we?"

"I'm all yours, my star," he whispered.

When she lifted her face trustingly to his, he kissed her with everything within him. Carina was right; something felt different. There was no internal battle, no doubt, no fear that she would accuse him of taking advantage of her, no question of what was appropriate or not. There was simply his beautiful bride and the freedom to love her in a way he had only imagined.

As his kiss grew more demanding, she suddenly broke away and studied him coyly. "Is this still just a taste of the happiness Baldur hinted you would give me as your bride?"

"Am I not moving fast enough for you?" he growled impishly.

"You're doing just fine," she purred. "But I'm definitely ready for more."

"Oh, Carina," Loki groaned, his voice husky. "There's so much more I want to give you."

"Show me," she whispered, leading him over to the bed.

Loki's heart leaped into his throat, that familiar hunger surging through his veins yet again. But this time, because it was good and right, what had previously been painfully denied longing blossomed into holy passion, pure and deeply fulfilling. Time and any sense of urgency faded. The newlyweds simply allowed themselves to be swept away by the natural progression of it all as they willingly and gladly gave themselves to each other. An incredibly powerful soul connection took form through the physical expression of their love. And after they had fully satisfied each other, Loki held Carina tightly in his arms, never wanting to let her go, his heart brimming over with joy. He had never felt closer or more bonded with anyone.

He whispered in her ear, "*Now*, we are lovers."

"In every sense of the word," she whispered back. "Was I worth the wait?"

"Without question," he affirmed as she sighed with contentment and snuggled into his chest. "Although we really didn't have to wait long at all."

"No, we didn't. Less than twenty-four hours ago, I thought we might be apart forever. And now, we are one … for life."

"One for life," Loki agreed, kissing her nose softly. "It all happened so fast."

"I hope we won't come to regret that," Carina responded sleepily, her eyes beginning to close.

"I've never been so sure of anything," he assured her. "And I've never been happier."

"Me either," she sighed.

Her breathing became rhythmic, and he knew she had fallen asleep. He gently removed his arm from where it cradled her head, then propped himself up on one elbow, watching her sleep until he could no longer stay awake himself.

Still, he woke up first as the first rays of sunlight brightened the room. He opened his eyes to see her still lying there beside him, though she had changed positions. He gently massaged her back until she opened her eyes and smiled shyly at him.

"Good morning, beautiful," he crooned. "Did you sleep well?"

"Mm-hmm," she murmured, snuggling into him again. "Did you?"

"I could barely sleep for watching you," he answered truthfully.

"Well, that won't do, Loki," she scolded. She checked the clock on the wall, then stroked his hair. "It's early yet. Lie here with me, and go back to sleep."

He let her touch relax him, feeling his eyelids grow heavy as he muttered, "What about breakfast?"

"They'll have a dining car on the train," she said softly.

When Loki opened his eyes several hours later, Carina was sitting beside him on the bed, fully dressed, watching him.

"Now, I understand why you stayed up to watch me sleep," she said gleefully.

He sat up and looked around the room. "Did you already pack everything?"

"Yes, we need to hurry," she told him. "You slept longer than I expected, but I couldn't bring myself to wake you."

"So much for round two," he teased, winking at her.

"Don't get fresh, Mr. Black," she giggled, pushing him playfully. "You'll just have to wait until we get to Bergen."

"Must I?" he challenged her, his voice low and alluring.

"Loki!" she scolded, lightly smacking his chest as he pulled her to him. "Kristoff will be furious if we miss that train!"

He groaned, knowing she was right. "Fine, Mrs. Black, you win this time," he whispered, but he kissed her hard before he reluctantly let her go and got ready to leave.

They made it to the station with ten minutes to spare. As they settled into their seats for the seven-hour train ride to Bergen, Carina laid her head on Loki's shoulder. "I'm so glad we're doing this, Luke. It'll be so nice to just relax and see the sights."

"You're going to confuse me if you keep switching names like that," he teased her. "I won't know who I am."

"I don't think I should call you your real name in public," Carina pointed out. She brought her voice to an intimate whisper as she continued, "Tonight, when we're alone again, you will be Loki."

He chuckled, laying his head on top of hers. Together, they watched the lush green scenery go by their window for a while, then explored the train. They stopped in the dining car for lunch, then returned to their seats, where they talked and enjoyed each other's company.

Several hours into the trip, Carina suddenly pointed out the window as they crossed a particularly gorgeous ravine. "Beauty like that makes me think there has to be a god out there somewhere. It's like a living painting. Someone or something must have designed all this."

"Maybe it just fell into place," Loki suggested. "Some cosmic accident."

"Do you really think so?" she asked.

"I honestly never thought about it much. Not since Paris, anyway," Loki admitted. "I really don't know."

"Do you think I was a cosmic accident?" she pressed him. "Something that just had all the right pieces fall into place?"

Loki frowned. He did not know the right answer or what she wanted to hear, but he sensed she was troubled and needed reassurance.

"You're far too complex for that," he told her. "But I will say that if some god somewhere designed you, maybe even Gustave's God, He knew what He was doing."

She kissed him on the cheek, clearly pleased by his answer. "Do you think we'll see the northern lights?"

"Probably not on this trip," Loki answered. "Kristoff said it's the wrong time of year. I've heard the sky has to be clear and dark. The sun still shines into the night right now."

"If the conditions are just right, maybe it could happen," Carina countered. "I can hope, right?"

"Sure, but I'd hate for you to be disappointed," Loki cautioned.

"I could never be disappointed when I'm with you," she insisted, then frowned. "It will be over far too soon. Then we have to face my father."

"What do you think he'll say?"

"I think he'll be angry and insulted that you married me without asking him first," Carina replied. "And he's probably right to feel that way."

"What?" Loki felt anger and hurt rising up in him. "Second thoughts already?"

"Of course not," she replied, her voice testy. "But if you had a daughter, wouldn't you want to be asked? Isn't it a matter of respect?"

"You specifically asked me not to," Loki defended himself. "I was willing."

"Well, you didn't exactly fight me on it," she retorted.

"Did you want me to?"

"I don't know," she exclaimed in exasperation, staring grumpily out the window with her chin on her fist. "It's too late now."

Loki fell silent, confused and irked by her sudden change in disposition. He had no idea what to say. She seemed to think he had let her down. And he felt her disappointment in him keenly. The oneness between them brought a deeper, sharper element to the altercation that took him completely by surprise. Perhaps it was because that unity had been threatened. Regardless, he desperately wanted to please her but could not ascertain how. And he did not like the way she had spoken to him. But rather than stew any further, he decided to dig a little deeper and find out how to make things right.

"I ... I don't understand, Carina," he said cautiously, though he could not hide his own frustration. "We were in agreement about your father. Why the sudden change?"

"I didn't change," she huffed, continuing to stare out the window.

Loki felt even more confused. "Yes, you did," he argued. "You said we should get married first, then talk to him."

"I know what I said," she retorted.

She's not making any sense! he thought. "Why won't you just tell me what I did wrong?" he demanded.

"I shouldn't have to," she muttered.

Loki clenched his jaw. Now she was just being stubborn and unreasonable. Not wanting to argue with his new bride anymore, especially in front of the other passengers, he got up and wandered down the narrow aisle, making his way to the open-air gondola. He stood at the rails and stared out at the picturesque scenery, allowing his anger and frustration to dissipate. He imagined the time alone would also clear her head. Then maybe they could talk it out.

When the soot in the air from the coal-burning engine became too much for him, he returned to his seat.

"You do not want to go out there," he told Carina playfully. "I think my face is as black as my hair now."

She glanced at him contemptuously, then turned back to the window. "It's not."

"Please tell me what's wrong, my star," Loki requested tenderly, ready to try a different tactic.

To his surprise, she started furiously wiping her face.

"Are you crying?" he asked, aghast.

She did not answer but turned her body away from him pointedly. He gently turned her back toward him and hugged her. She cried silently for a few seconds, then gasped for air as she pulled away.

"You're right. This is my fault," she whimpered. "Please don't be angry with me anymore."

"Carina, I never said anything was your fault," Loki told her gently. He was thankful most of the people had already gone to the dining car for dinner. "And I'm not angry with you."

"Well, why did you storm off if you weren't angry?" she demanded.

"I didn't storm off. I just stepped away."

"You still left. You've never done that before."

He shrugged. "It seemed the honorable thing to do. I didn't want to take my frustration out on you. I came back, didn't I?"

"Yes," she admitted quietly.

"Carina, I won't always say or do the right thing," Loki told her. "I'll even get angry at times. So will you. But I won't stop loving you. I'm yours for life, remember?"

She nodded. "I'm sorry I got snippy. It's just that the fear of my father's reaction looms over me like a storm I cannot escape."

"That was quite poetic." Loki chuckled but grew serious when she glared at him. "I'm sorry too. I should have asked what you really wanted before we got married. I just assumed—"

"I didn't know what I wanted when it comes to my father," she interrupted. "I still don't. But that's not your fault."

"Do you wish we had waited to talk with him first?"

"Maybe a little but only because I'm afraid. I don't regret marrying you. Not one bit."

Loki sighed with relief, then said gently, "Carina, I was terrified to tell you who I really am. That's why it took me so long to do it. And when I finally did, your reaction was exactly as I feared it would be. Nothing I did differently would have changed that or how much it hurt."

Carina grimaced. "What are you saying?"

"Well, I had to hide my identity from everyone at first, so it wouldn't have mattered when I told you the truth. You had to come to terms with it on your own, in your own time. And that's exactly what your father will have to do."

"I never thought about it that way," she responded, her face brightening a little.

"I really think everything will be fine. Even if it's not, look at what we've come through already. We will face this together."

"And what do you think our life together will be like?" Carina asked softly, laying her head on his shoulder again.

"Wonderful," he answered confidently, kissing her lightly between words. "Exciting. Adventurous."

She snuggled closer. "Once again, your way with words serves you well."

"You asked me how I would want to be treated if I had a daughter," Loki pondered her words aloud. "I can't even imagine it, honestly, but I will make an effort to treat Joseph Green with more respect since he is your father."

"Thank you," she said. "That gives me hope there won't be a fistfight, at least."

"Oh, Carina," Loki laughed, "there's no question who would win that one."

She punched him playfully on the shoulder, then poked him right under the ribs, which made him involuntarily squirm.

"Are you ticklish?" she gasped.

"I'm not answering that," Loki muttered, hoping she wouldn't poke him again. He was unbelievably ticklish. Thor had tortured him to no end with tickling bouts when they were children.

"Then I'll find out for myself," she whispered suggestively. "Tonight."

He grinned. He rather liked the sound of that.

"Are you hungry? We should probably eat before they close the dining car," he suggested, noticing many of the other passengers were coming back to their seats.

"I am, but I don't see how you could be," she laughed. "I'm not sure how I'll be able to keep you fed if you always eat like you did at lunch."

"I have an incredibly fast metabolism," Loki defended himself, feeling a little embarrassed. "We did skip breakfast, you know, and I'm unusually hungry today. Besides, you should see Thor eat."

"I have," she reminded him. "It was quite the spectacle. Whoever marries him will be hard pressed to keep up with him."

"What did you mean, 'keep' me 'fed' anyway?" Loki asked, helping her across the couplers as they moved toward the dining car.

"Don't you expect your wife to cook for you?" she teased him.

"You cook?"

"Quite well, I'm told."

He held out her chair, then seated himself. "I'm surprised your father allows that, as wealthy as he is. Don't you have servants?"

"We weren't always wealthy, you know. My mother was a fine cook," Carina explained. "She left behind a recipe book her mother used to teach her. I taught myself as a way to be close to her."

After they had ordered, Loki watched her curiously, for her demeanor was slightly downcast. "Tell me about your mother."

"She died when I was only three," Carina began sadly. "She was very beautiful, but my memories are hazy. Father once told me I have her eyes and his hair. Her arms were as soft as cotton but as strong as steel. I always felt better when she was near."

"What happened to her?" Loki reached across the small table and held her hand, caressing it with his thumb.

"She got sick when she was pregnant with my baby sister. She just ... never got better. Then she delivered the baby far too early. Neither of them survived," Carina answered, her eyes filled with sadness. "At the time, Father just told me my mother and my sister went to a better place. I cried until I ran out of tears because I didn't understand why I couldn't go too. I probably made it harder for him."

"When did you finally understand?" Loki asked.

"I honestly don't remember. My whole world flipped upside down," Carina answered. "My father was a kinder man in those days. He was only a few years older than I am now, but he never remarried. He just threw himself into his work. Even when he started mixing with questionable people, he's always tried to give me the best of everything."

"I'm so sorry," Loki said empathetically. "I was quite miserable when Baldur died. Only, he wasn't really dead."

"How old were you?"

"I'm not even sure. Between two and three hundred?"

"I don't know if I'll ever get used to that," Carina remarked. "What?"

"How old you are," she answered. "You could be my great-great-great-great-grandfather."

"Asgardian age is completely different than human age," he protested, releasing her hand to take a few bites of the food that had arrived. "At two hundred, I was just a gangly, awkward thing, though I grew faster after that."

"That's funny to imagine. Like a teenager?"

"I suppose. Now it seems hard to believe I couldn't remember what Baldur was like. I think I'm still angry he put us all through so much. Especially Mother."

"You mentioned he faked his death, then disappeared? Why?"

"He didn't want to be king, I guess. He says he fell in love, though she must have died centuries ago. Hod says Baldur has been through that cycle multiple times."

"I think he may be cycling again, then. He certainly seems fond of Helga," Carina pointed out. Then she grew serious. "You'll outlive me then."

"Not if I have any say in it," Loki growled.

The night Loki found out Baldur was still alive, he mentioned he was working on something to prolong human life. But Loki had never asked him to expound or explain. He knew it was a subject he needed to broach with his oldest brother eventually, but for now, it was something he could not bear to discuss with her or anyone else.

"Do you think you would fall in love again when I'm gone?" Carina asked. "Like Baldur?"

"No, I'd be more like your father," he insisted, scowling at the rest of his food. He had completely lost his appetite. "Can we not talk about this, please?"

She smiled tenderly, her eyes soft and knowing. "Is it painful to think of losing me?"

He shuddered. "You have no idea."

"I'm sorry. I won't bring it up again," she promised, pushing aside her own plate and reaching across to grab his hand. "I'm here now, and as long as I live, I'm yours."

They made their way back through the other cars and took their seats once again. Loki put his arm around her shoulders and held her more tightly than ever, shaken by their conversation. The rhythm of the train on the tracks lulled Carina to sleep, leaving Loki alone with his thoughts. Could he work with Baldur to find a way to prolong her life? He briefly considered seeking an answer from his father or mother but banished the fleeting thought immediately. He desperately wanted his parents to accept her, but he knew neither of them would without significant motivation. He had three months to form a plan, though he really could not fathom which way to go. Should he attempt reasoning with King Odin? Should he pursue kingship to force acceptance of his bride? Should he keep her hidden on Midgard and embrace the image of a bachelor prince in front of his people? Just how would he figure this out? He forced all morbid thoughts out of his mind, choosing instead to enjoy her presence.

17

Bergen was as majestic as the train ride had been. Situated on the west coast, the city was somewhat warmer than Christiania. The fjords and mountains contrasted each other in a picturesque landscape that was panoramic in its scope. Though broken up by islands, there seemed to be no end to the ocean beyond, something quite new to Loki, although not to Carina, who had already crossed the Atlantic several times.

They settled into their hotel the first night without seeing the northern lights. Carina asked the locals about the odds of seeing the phenomenon. They all confirmed that the couple's visit to Bergen was too early and suggested they might have a chance further north in about a month.

For four days, Loki and Carina explored the city, toured the fjords, hiked in the mountains, and attended several shows, including a magnificent concert by the Bergen Philharmonic Orchestra. And Carina stubbornly watched the skies each night, once it grew dark, holding onto hope.

But still no sign of the northern lights.

Their final night, they wandered down to one of the wharfs after seeing a play at Den Nationale Scene.

"Hasn't it been nice to watch other people perform?" Carina asked Loki, leaning back against him as they sat on the rough wood of the old dock and looked out on the water. "And for absolutely no one to know who we are?"

"Mm-hmm," Loki grunted absentmindedly, not really focused on her words. His mind had already left Bergen and flown to Stuttgart. Joseph Green had surely arrived by now.

"What are you thinking about?" she asked, looking up at him.

"Just wishing it wasn't over already," Loki sighed.

"We still have the rest of tonight and the long train ride back to Christiania," Carina reminded him.

"Mm-hmm," Loki murmured.

"You're so distracted, Loki," Carina teased him, kissing him just below his ear. "What do I have to do to get your attention?"

"That was fairly effective," he murmured, kissing her back. It was finally growing dark, which meant it was nearing midnight.

"Do you want to go back to the hotel?" Carina asked him.

"Why, Carina, have you given up on your quest?" he teased her.

She shoved him playfully. "It's our last night. I don't want to waste it on my foolish notions."

He grinned. "Oh, are you suggesting something other than sleep?"

"Why not? Are you too tired?" she taunted.

"Even if I am, we'll have seven hours to make up for it on the train tomorrow."

She giggled, then suddenly grabbed his arm and cried, "Loki, look!"

She pointed excitedly to the rippled surface of the fjord, where reflections of green and blue light swirled on the dark water lapping slowly at the wooden pillars holding up the wharf. They looked up at the navy blue sky at the exact same time to see a rare display of the aurora borealis dancing there in all its splendor.

"It's almost like someone put it there just for us," Carina breathed in awestruck wonder.

"I've never seen anything like it!" Loki exclaimed, pulling Carina onto his lap to be as close to her as possible in the moment.

"I have," she murmured. "It reminds me very much of what you do with light, only bigger."

He chuckled, honored by the comparison, then kissed the top of her head as they watched the colors snake in and out of each other.

"I think this might become my favorite memory," Carina sighed. "It's the perfect ending to our little honeymoon."

"No, it's the perfect beginning to the rest of our lives," Loki corrected her.

They watched until the colors began to fade, then reluctantly headed back to their hotel. The whole experience had been so magical, neither of them felt the need to talk. Instead, they enjoyed each other with a passion unlike any they had experienced up to that point in their young marriage. And as they drifted off to sleep, nestled close to each other, Loki thought to himself that three months was far too short a time. He finally understood Baldur's choice and seriously considered never returning to Asgard.

As they settled in for the return train ride the next morning, Loki tentatively brought up the subject to his bride, speaking in low tones to avoid being overheard by the other passengers. "Carina, do you remember when I told you I would renounce everything for you?"

"I asked you to stop talking like that," Carina reminded him. "I could never ask you to be less than you are."

He sighed deeply, looking over her head at the scenery passing before his eyes. "I don't want to go back."

He could feel her staring at him, but when he dared to look at her, her expression was unreadable.

"If we were discovered by Odin or Heimdall ..." Loki continued quietly so none of the other passengers would overhear, then trailed off.

"Are you having second thoughts now?"

"About marrying you? Never," Loki reassured her, kissing her forehead. "But there are serious complications if I go back."

"Like what?"

"Once I return to Asgard after the allotted rite of passage time, it will be harder for me to come back to Midgard. I'll be expected to be at Thor's side most of the time. And then there's my mother with her matchmaking schemes," Loki thought aloud. "I don't know how I'll explain things to her. Not yet, anyway."

"And don't forget your father's expectations," Carina added.

"Yes. I could try to wear down their resistance," Loki said wistfully. "But that would take time, and I can't be in both places at once."

"How have you managed up to this point?"

"A lot of sneaking around and manipulation," Loki admitted.

"And that won't work anymore?"

"It might, but if I get caught, there'll be hell to pay, far worse than Kristoff would have had from Joseph over you. Faking my death like Baldur did and just disappearing with you seems like the best option."

"Is that what you want?" Carina asked softly.

"You're what I want, my star," Loki responded, hugging her close to him. "And if that's the only way to be with you, then so be it."

She did not answer but sighed deeply and pulled away, staring out the window.

"Isn't that what you want? To always be together?" Loki asked, suddenly irrationally fearful.

"Of course it is," she said slowly, thoughtfully, as she turned back to him. "I don't want you to go back either. But I also know you love Asgard and your family and your people. I don't ever want you to resent me for keeping you from what you love."

"I could never resent you," Loki argued. "I love you more than any of that."

"You can't live with a heart that's torn," Carina replied.

"That's exactly my point," Loki countered. "When I'm on Asgard, I'll long for you. And when I'm with you again, our time together will be tempered by the fact that I eventually have to go back. If that's not living with a heart that's torn, then what is?"

"If you leave Asgard because you truly want to leave Asgard, then I'm glad. I can't bear the thought of being separated from you for days or weeks on end. It's just that ..." Her voice trailed off.

"What?" he prodded her.

"If the roles were reversed and being with you meant I had to leave my singing career and never see my father again …" She still did not complete her sentence.

Loki desperately needed to know. "Would you?" he asked her, staring at his fingernails.

She turned his face, forcing him to look at her. "Yes, I would."

"Then it's settled," Loki pronounced with finality. "I'll go back one more time to fake my death as Baldur did, then return to be with you forever."

"I do like the sound of that," Carina admitted. "But I'll support whatever decision you make."

"I've made my decision," Loki insisted, then abruptly changed the subject. "Now, what about this American tour Kristoff has been planning with Kathleen?"

Carina brightened, her beautiful smile transforming her face. "I can't wait! Besides singing at the Opera House in Paris or Buckingham Palace in London, touring America has been one of my wildest dreams. So far, I've only performed in New York, and that was with Klaus."

"I wonder how that mongrel is holding up in his jail cell," Loki snorted.

"I couldn't care less," Carina scoffed. "At least we know he won't bother us again."

"I'm not entirely certain of that," Loki remarked.

"I thought you took care of everything!" Carina gasped. "Are we still in danger?"

Loki frowned. "There's no real way of knowing. The man who shot Kristoff was fairly frightened, and with no hope of getting paid, any other threats from hired guns should fall away. Kristoff can look to himself. And I'll protect you. What we really need to worry about is when Klaus gets out of prison. A man like that will most certainly hold a grudge."

"That has to be at least several years away," Carina said. She had relaxed considerably. "Let's not borrow trouble."

"Back to the tour then," Loki replied. "What do you look forward to the most?"

"Showing you New York," Carina asserted.

"That's not part of the tour," Loki laughed. "I meant which city?"

"Oh, I don't even know where they'll schedule us," she mused. "But I do hope they at least choose New Orleans and Chicago."

"We could make sure they do," Loki suggested.

"We could," Carina agreed, winking at him. "Can we stop in to see Kristoff, Helga, and Kathleen when we reach Christiania?"

"I don't see why not," Loki answered. "They're probably expecting it. We can spare a few hours before we head to Stuttgart."

"Have you thought about what you'll say to my father?" she pressed him. "I'm so nervous about the whole thing."

"Courage, my star. Everything will be fine," Loki reassured her, gently drawing her head onto his shoulder so she could sleep.

Though he was tired himself, he did not sleep but thought through every possible scenario for the conversation he dreaded, until a coach attendant announced the dining car would be closing soon.

Carina stirred beside him. "Can we just stay here?"

"We can eat in Christiania if you would rather," he told her. "But we still have three hours to go."

She looked up at him sleepily. "Are you hungry?"

"Yes," he admitted. "But I can wait."

"It's okay," she yawned, stretching. "I'm awake now."

"So unselfish," he praised her, kissing her forehead.

"You may not always find me so," she teased him as they made their way to the dining car.

After lunch, Loki was finally able to sleep with his head resting on the back of the seat, but he felt as though he had just dozed off when Carina shook his arm violently. The train had pulled into the station.

"I just saw my father on the platform," she gasped, her face white. "And I'm fairly certain he looked right at me!"

"What?" Loki exclaimed, trying to see out the window. "Are you sure?"

"Yes!" she cried. "He's here! What are we going to do?"

"Why is he here?" Loki muttered to himself. This was a scenario he had not considered.

"What are we going to do?" Carina repeated frantically, a demanding urgency in her tone.

"Carina, calm down," Loki soothed her. "We are going to do exactly as I said before. We'll face him together."

Carina clutched Loki's arm, almost hiding behind him as they followed the line of people getting off the train. He still did not see Joseph Green, and Carina had lost sight of him. Loki was beginning to think she had only imagined seeing her father.

Suddenly, his stern, commanding voice sounded from a few feet away. "Carina!"

Carina whirled around, facing her father. But he was not looking at her.

Joseph stared at Loki with anger and disdain. "You have a lot of explaining to do, Lukas Black."

"Hello, Joseph," Loki said, holding his hands up as if requesting a truce. "I'm perfectly willing to speak with you but not here."

"You're in no position to set terms, boy!" Joseph spat. "Do you have any idea the danger you've put her in?"

"The danger I've put her in?" Loki retorted, his body tense. "I've been the one protecting her ... from the scoundrel you tried to force her to marry!"

Joseph took a menacing step toward Loki. "Carina, get behind me while I teach this disrespectful whelp a lesson. And then, I'm taking you home."

"No, Father," she objected quietly, stepping behind Loki instead. "I belong with him."

Joseph took his angry gaze from Loki to throw a puzzled look at his daughter. "I admit I made a mistake with Klaus, sweetheart, but now is not the time for rash decisions. You need time to recover." When Carina opened her mouth to protest, Joseph waved his hand to silence her and continued, "I know you think you're in love with Lukas here. But in time, you'll see he's just not right for you, dear."

"I've already married her," Loki blurted out. This was not the way he had envisioned telling Joseph the news.

"What?" Joseph blustered, his face reddening with suppressed anger. A vein stood out in his forehead as he clenched his fists tightly at his side and stood toe to toe with Loki. "You dare to rob me of my daughter?"

Carina was visibly distraught, tears streaming down her face as she looked from her father to her husband. People streamed around them, glancing furtively at them with concern and curiosity.

"Look at your daughter, Joseph," Loki prompted quietly, as respectfully as he could muster. "For her sake, can we please not do this here?"

Joseph glanced at his daughter. She buried her face into Loki's chest as he protectively placed his arm around her. The fight went out of Joseph instantly.

"Very well," he sighed. "I am incredibly relieved you are safe, Carina."

She released Loki's arm and embraced her father tightly. "Thank you, Father."

Joseph glared over her head at Loki. "Where did you want to do this, Lukas? I don't know this town."

"Kristoff's house is as good a place as any," Loki answered. "We had planned to stop there before going to Stuttgart to see you."

Joseph nodded.

"Father, why are you in Norway?" Carina asked as they walked off the platform. She stayed as close as she could to Loki, with a tight grip on his hand.

"I came to find you, naturally. I thought you'd have come home by now," Joseph answered, his face twitching a little when he noticed Carina's firm grasp on Loki's hand.

"I would have arrived tomorrow," Carina stated. "Didn't Kristoff tell you that?"

"I haven't heard from him since I left New York. I had no idea where you were, but I figured he knew something."

"We just returned from our honeymoon," Carina said enthusiastically. When Joseph did not respond, his face twitching again, she added, "He might not have known exactly what day we were coming back."

An uncomfortable silence stretched between them for several minutes. Finally, Joseph asked, "Kristoff knows you're married?"

"Yes," Carina admitted quietly. "He was there."

"Then I have a few things to say to him too," Joseph growled.

18

The three of them waited at the front door of the quaint townhouse as Loki knocked firmly. The taxi ride over had been unbearably silent. Loki went over what he wanted to say to Joseph in his mind, then moved to knock again, just as Helga opened the door.

She smiled warmly at Loki and Carina, but her words of welcome died in the air when she spotted Joseph, who suddenly seemed incredibly uncomfortable.

"Helga!" he exclaimed, doffing his hat and shifting it from hand to hand. "You're the *last* person I expected to see."

"I happen to live here," Helga stated, her tone hostile, and her blue eyes icy. "And it's Mrs. Anderson, if you please."

"You're married now?" Joseph asked.

"Widowed," she corrected him.

Loki looked from Joseph's unreadable face to Helga's tense one. He had never seen either of them behave this way.

Joseph turned to Loki and accused, "You've brought us to the wrong house. You said this was Kristoff's house."

"You're at the right house, though it's actually mine. Kristoff just happens to live here on occasion," Helga interjected. "He should be back from Lillehammer soon."

Joseph peered at her with sudden realization. "I can't believe I never made the connection. You never told me you had a son."

"He's my baby brother," she corrected him dryly. "I'm not quite old enough to be his mother, thank you." Then she addressed Loki and Carina. "Is everything settled between you three?"

"No," Carina said, drawing the word out slowly. "Father, what's going on?"

Joseph Green did not answer. He shifted his hat again and looked down at the doorstep.

"Well?" Helga demanded. "You might as well come inside."

"Helga—" Joseph started to speak, but she cut him off.

"Mrs. Anderson," she corrected him.

"I'm not calling you that," Joseph growled.

For the first time, Helga's haughty demeanor softened. "Inside, all of you."

Helga led them into the living room, then left her three guests alone. Joseph sat down in an armchair, rested his head in one hand, and stared at the floor. Carina and Loki settled on the sofa together and exchanged nervous glances.

Helga came back into the room with tea and cookies. She set the tray down and handed each of them a cup.

For the first time, Joseph smiled as he took the cup from her. "Helga, you haven't changed a bit."

"You have," she observed, as if she was softening again.

Loki could not stand the suspense any longer and blurted out, "Just what happened between you two?"

"I believe we have other things to discuss," Joseph reminded him, his voice warning Loki not to pry.

"I'll leave you to it, then," Helga stated. She left the room again, leaving the tray behind.

"Alright, Lukas, you've got what you wanted," Joseph acknowledged, grabbing a cookie. He took a bite, momentarily distracted by its decadence. "Helga always did make the best cookies. Now, start by explaining why you completely disregarded my instructions, then married my daughter without my permission."

"Your instructions?" Carina repeated warily.

"The night we met, he told me to stay away from you," Loki informed her. "He said it was in your best interests."

"Really, Father?" Carina was clearly irritated.

Joseph did not bother defending himself but fixed Loki with his gaze and waited for him to speak.

"I felt it was in her best interests to marry her right away," Loki explained.

"Why? Did you get her pregnant?"

"Father!" Carina scolded him. "Luke never dishonored me."

Loki shoved down his rising anger, remembering his promise to treat her father respectfully. "In my culture, men protect the purity of the women they love."

"Impressive," Joseph murmured. "What exactly is your culture? I checked with some of my contacts in Iceland, and they've never heard of you."

"Yes, I lied about that," Loki admitted. He glanced at Carina, who shook her head slightly.

"What else have you lied about?" Joseph asked in a maddeningly patronizing tone.

"Quite a bit," Loki replied defiantly. "But I speak the truth when I say how much I love your daughter. I will protect her and provide for her, just as you have."

"Are you some sort of con artist?"

"No," Loki answered, then smirked. "Well, maybe a little, but not professionally."

The edges of Joseph's mouth twitched under his slightly graying mustache as if trying to suppress a smile. "Are you in trouble with the law?"

"Not yet."

"Do you plan to be?" Joseph's attempts to hide his amusement were proving futile.

"Does anyone?" Loki smirked. When they first met, Joseph had liked him. Perhaps he could win that back. He continued, "Come now, Joseph, we've all done things we aren't proud of. But I have no intention of doing anything that would jeopardize Carina's safety."

"I will grant that you have kept her safe thus far," Joseph admitted. "How do you expect to provide for her as I have?"

Loki grinned. "I'm actually quite wealthy. I've made quite a bit of money on tour, but I'm also royalty in my home country."

Joseph raised an eyebrow at Loki. "Royalty? You actually expect me to believe that?"

"It's true, Father," Carina insisted. "I've been there. He's a prince."

"You still haven't told me where," Joseph pointed out, leaning forward and staring Loki down.

"Does it matter?" Loki asked with a shrug, refusing to be intimidated. "We've chosen not to live there. Carina and I would like to have a second wedding in Stuttgart so you can be a part of it. Then we plan to go on tour together."

"As Lukas Black and the Shooting Star," Carina added.

"I've seen the papers," Joseph replied, leaning back in his chair and stroking his chin. "In Europe?"

"In America," Carina corrected, her eyes sparkling with the thought of it. "Father, can't you see how happy I am?"

Joseph sighed deeply. "You're not old enough to know what makes you happy."

"Mother was my age when she married you!" Carina huffed indignantly.

"Leave her out of this," Joseph warned, though a flicker of pain, mingled with realization, passed over his face.

"Klaus made me miserable, Father," Carina reminded him. "You admitted you made a mistake. Isn't it time you let me make some choices of my own?"

"You already have," Joseph said with resignation. "Time will tell if you've chosen wisely."

Loki frowned, thinking, *Now I know where Carina gets her stubbornness.*

"There's something else that's really bothering me," Joseph remarked thoughtfully, then continued without waiting for a response. "The timing doesn't add up. I left New York three days after you did, Carina. How did you find Lukas, manage to visit his homeland, get married, and go on a honeymoon in such a short time?"

Loki glanced at Carina. She shook her head yet again. He really did not want to reveal his true identity to Joseph either, so he thought up a veiled truth. "We have more advanced technology in my country, which enables me to travel places faster."

"You mean aircraft?"

Loki paused. "Similar, I suppose, but faster. I followed Carina to New York and rescued her from Klaus."

"You stabbed him?" Joseph asked.

"No, I did, Father, in self-defense," Carina admitted. "After I stabbed him, Luke knocked him out."

"Why did you run away?"

Carina started to cry. "I was so afraid of what you would say and what you would do. I didn't want you to hurt Luke over the whole thing or make me marry Klaus anyway."

Loki put his arm around her to comfort her. Joseph stood, then knelt in front of his daughter.

"Do you really think I would make you marry a man who beats you?" His voice was quiet but filled with hurt. "I didn't know, Carina. Not until Kristoff told me. Why didn't you tell me before you left Paris, before Klaus hired those thugs?"

Carina sighed. "I didn't think you would listen."

Joseph's face was truly troubled. "I never meant to cause you so much pain. I only wanted you to be provided for when I'm gone."

"I will be," she assured him, drying her eyes. "Please, Father, I beg you to accept Luke. I love him!"

"And you? What do you want from me?" Joseph asked, turning to Loki.

"I'm not one for asking permission," Loki replied. "I never was. And it's too late for that anyway, but I would like to ask for your blessing. I love your daughter more than my own life. I will take care of her, I swear."

"Am I to understand from all of this that you have renounced your title for the sake of my daughter?" Joseph asked.

"I have," Loki affirmed confidently.

"You really love her that much?"

"With all of my being," Loki stated firmly.

Joseph stood again and extended his hand to Loki, who also stood and grasped it firmly.

"I still don't like this," Joseph admitted. "But I give you both my blessing."

Carina started to cry again, this time with happy and relieved tears. She threw her arms around her father.

Joseph addressed Loki again. "I suppose you're expecting me to pay for this second wedding?"

Loki grimaced to himself at the distasteful comment. Would Joseph make this as difficult as possible?

"Well, Joseph," Helga interjected from the doorway, where no one had noticed her until now. Her voice dripped with scorn. "In some ways, you have not changed."

Joseph looked at her with a pained expression, then walked over to place his hand gently on her shoulder. "Now, Helga, don't be cruel."

Helga coldly pushed his hand away from her, narrowing her eyes. "I am not the one who is cruel."

"Are you ever going to forgive me?" Joseph sighed.

"Have you ever asked me to?" Helga snapped.

"Point taken," Joseph muttered, taking a step backward.

To break the awful tension, Carina spoke up, "Most of the wedding is already planned and paid for, Father. If we have it the same day as originally planned, it won't be wasted."

"I'll cover the rest if funds are a problem for you, Joseph," Loki offered, allowing a snarky tone to creep into his voice. He could not resist the opportunity to return the insult of moments ago.

Joseph whirled around and glared at Loki. Then he began to chuckle. "I have to admit, I do admire your pluck. And I think you'll find money is no problem for me."

From the doorway, Helga scoffed, "That entirely depends on your perspective."

"I see time has made you no less witty, Helga." Joseph smirked, his eyes sparking with something Loki had never seen in them. "Since I'm obviously not welcome here, I think I'll go see about a hotel room."

Helga made no move to stop him. Loki and Carina glanced at each other. Loki felt extremely uncomfortable with the whole situation and did not know what to do.

Before leaving the room, Joseph squinted at Helga, who had moved aside to let him pass. "I *am* sorry, Helga. I hope you'll think better of me someday."

Loki grabbed Carina's hand and pulled her with him to follow Joseph.

Just as Joseph reached the front door, Helga spoke, "Joseph, wait."

Joseph paused with his hand on the doorknob, but he did not turn around.

"Didn't you come to see Kristoff?" Helga asked.

Loki could tell that was not what she had planned to say.

"Originally, yes," Joseph admitted, finally turning. "I can stop in tomorrow before the three of us leave for Stuttgart."

"Actually, Father," Carina interjected, "Luke and I had planned to leave for Stuttgart tonight."

"Why don't the three of you stay for dinner?" Helga suggested. "There's time before the last train leaves."

Joseph responded first. "I do believe I'll take you up on that, as long as you don't poison me."

Helga laughed and motioned for them to follow her back to the living room, though the tension remained.

The front door burst open, followed by the sound of laughter.

"C'mon, Kat, let's find Helga," Loki heard Kristoff suggest.

Loki smirked at Helga. "Have you decided to give Kathleen a chance?"

"She's growing on me," she whispered.

The couple walked hand-in-hand into the room, then stopped short when they saw everyone.

"Did somebody die?" Kristoff quipped, his high spirits unchanged by the lingering uneasiness in the room.

"Kristoff, you never told me Helga was your sister," Joseph reprimanded him.

"Why would that matter?" Kristoff asked with a shrug. He looked from Helga to Joseph with a puzzled frown. "You two know each other?"

"I'd better get dinner started," Helga announced, abruptly leaving the room.

"Carina, why don't you catch up with your father?" Loki suggested. "I'll give Helga a hand."

19

Loki quietly entered the kitchen. Helga was busily gathering ingredients and dabbing her eyes with her clean apron.

"Are you alright?" Loki asked softly.

She was startled but quickly recovered. "What are you doing in my kitchen, Luke?"

"Giving my wife a chance to catch up with her father," Loki replied nonchalantly, pausing as he inwardly relished calling Carina his wife. "I thought I'd help you with dinner."

"You don't fool me, Luke. Curiosity is written all over your face," Helga laughed as she wound her long blonde braid into a bun at the back of her head to keep it from falling over her shoulder while she cooked. "Besides, I rather doubt you'll be any help."

"Give me a job to do, and I'll do it," Loki offered gallantly.

Helga smiled, setting a bowl of freshly washed potatoes and a paring knife on the table. "Wash your hands, then peel these," she instructed him. "And don't cut yourself."

Loki grinned to himself as he obeyed. He had never peeled a potato before, but he was quite adept with knives. How hard could it be? He cut a huge chunk out of the first one, his normally agile fingers suddenly awkward and clumsy.

"Like this," Helga laughed, showing him how to hold the potato to avoid chopping off his fingers.

He copied her swift movements and mastered the proper angle quickly, stopping the knife against his thumb as curls of the potato skin fell onto the table. He held up his first peeled potato for her to inspect, feeling quite proud of himself.

"Good," she praised him. "Now do the rest."

She began slicing onions, which made his eyes swell and water. Unable to see what he was doing, he put down the paring knife.

"Doesn't that bother you?" Loki demanded.

"I've been chopping onions for almost thirty years," she informed him proudly. "Whatever you do, don't rub your eyes. Just open them widely and blink all the tears out until you can see again."

She poured a little oil into a big iron skillet, then began to sauté the onion slices. An amazing smell replaced the irritant in the air, making Loki's stomach growl. He went back to peeling potatoes. Helga set aside the cooked onions and sat down at the table, slicing the potatoes Loki had peeled.

They worked together in silence for several minutes. Then Helga suddenly spoke, "I had been living in London as a nanny and cook for about a year when I met Joseph."

Loki was delighted. He had given up thinking she might confide in him. "That explains why you speak English so well. Was Joseph in London on business?"

"Yes, he was staying with his business partner, who happened to be my employer. We interacted here and there, but I knew next to nothing about him. One day, I was playing with the children in the nursery when I saw him watching us from the doorway. I had been instructed to make sure the children did not bother him, so I asked if we had been too loud."

"What did he say?" Loki continued peeling, engrossed in her story.

"He insisted we hadn't disturbed him but said the little girl reminded him of his young daughter, your Carina. He complimented me on how I handled her, then explained he needed a good nanny since his wife had died the year before. He wanted me to consider working for him."

"You turned him down, I take it?" Loki preempted her.

"At first, yes. Politely, of course. But he persisted. He would wander into the kitchen and talk to me while I baked, always stealing at least one cookie." She smiled fondly at the memory. "And he would walk with us when I would take the children to the park. And every time, he asked how he could snatch me away from the Chestertons."

"Sounds like he was interested in more than just employing you," Loki observed thoughtfully.

"It seemed that way, but I told myself I was imagining things. He's only a few years older than I am, but losing his wife seemed to have aged him even all those years ago. Of course, I understand that fully now." She paused, her sadness over her own loss apparent. "Still, there was a playfulness under all his grief."

"I can't imagine Joseph as playful," Loki admitted.

"Perhaps it's gone now," Helga remarked with some sadness. "But I could see it when he laughed or smiled, which happened more and more often when he spent time with me."

"Did he spend time with you a lot?"

"Yes. Sometimes, he would even make himself late for his appointments because he was too busy talking to me," she chuckled.

"I'm sure that didn't sit well with his business partner," Loki observed. "Did they know he was trying to steal you away from them?"

"I don't think they took it seriously. Joseph made it sound like a joke to them, and I always said I had no intention of leaving. They would laugh, but they certainly didn't like how he always seemed to be in the kitchen."

"Did you?"

"Did I what?"

"Did you like him being in the kitchen?" Loki clarified.

"Yes. I actually looked forward to his visits. And I started to seriously consider his offer."

"To work for him?"

"That was his only offer, Luke. But he did everything to make it sound better and better … more money, my own living quarters, paying for all my expenses …" she remembered, her voice trailing off.

"Why did you keep saying no then?" Loki pressed, almost afraid she would not continue.

"Because of the one thing he would never say," she murmured, her eyes on her knife as she adeptly sliced her pile of potatoes.

"Meaning?" Loki prodded. He was not slicing nearly as quickly as Helga, but he did not care.

"I felt we were becoming friends, maybe even more than friends. He would sometimes share deep, personal things with me. A few times, I caught him looking at me like …"

Her voice trailed off again, her cheeks flushing. "Well, it doesn't matter."

"At the risk of being too bold, how did you feel about him?"

Helga peered at him as if she would scold him for prying. Then she sighed. "I've already told you so much, but you're strangely easy to talk to. And I've kept it all bottled up for years."

"Were you in love with him?"

"I don't know," Helga admitted. "I definitely thought him handsome and wise. Part of me wanted him to see me as more than a potential nanny, but the rest of me was terrified he might."

Loki chuckled. "I know that feeling. It's awful."

"Well, I told myself it was all in my head, mostly because I really was tempted by his offer, and I soon found out I was right."

"Why, what happened?"

"Mrs. Chesterton called me into her husband's study after breakfast one morning. She proceeded to lecture me on how inappropriate it was for a working-class woman like myself to entertain romantic notions toward a wealthy widower like him."

Helga's face contorted, clearly still feeling the sting of the woman's words. She pulled the iron skillet back onto the stove and started plopping the sliced potatoes into it, adding bits of spice and more oil as she stirred it all vigorously.

"That doesn't explain why you decided you were wrong about him after all."

"She went on to tell me he was courting a debutante in London who was more suited to his social status. That's why he had been there so long. She said he was so embarrassed his intentions had been so grossly misunderstood, he went to stay somewhere else and was no longer interested in hiring me."

"That's highly suspicious," Loki remarked as he focused on peeling the last of his potatoes. Once he had finished, he began slicing them since Helga was occupied. "Why would he not tell you that himself?"

"I assume because he was utterly humiliated and couldn't face me after having led me on, even if it was unintentional."

"Sounds like you think it was intentional," Loki observed.

"Only because of something that happened that I prefer to keep to myself. It was a small thing ... but still ... something ..."

Loki sensed not to push her this time, though his curiosity was hard to squelch. Instead of pressing her, he pointed out, "Joseph doesn't strike me as the kind of man who would let someone else do his talking for him."

"Well, I had no chance to defend myself or ask questions. And I hadn't seen him since ... until today."

"Helga, I think that woman lied to you," Loki stated.

Loki looked up when he heard her sniff. His eyes widened, and he cleared his throat, for Joseph Green stood in the doorway.

"She did lie to you, Helga. I never knew any of this," Joseph interjected quietly.

Helga whirled around, bits of onion flying off the wooden spoon she held in her hand. A few escaped tears glistened on her cheeks. "How long have you been listening?" she demanded.

"I'm sorry," Joseph muttered sheepishly. "The girls disappeared upstairs, and Kristoff went in his study. I ... uh ... I thought maybe we could talk."

"So you just stood there and eavesdropped?" she snapped as she grabbed the remaining sliced potatoes and threw them into the pan.

"I'll go see what the girls are up to," Loki announced, standing and stretching a little too casually.

"You sit right back down, Luke," Helga commanded him so sternly, he did exactly as he was told.

Joseph took a few steps into the kitchen but gave Helga a wide berth, for she had grabbed a carving knife and a large ring of sausage. He leaned against the wall and watched uneasily as she viciously cut into the meat.

"And I suppose you didn't know they fired me either?" she spouted suddenly.

"What?" Joseph exclaimed indignantly. "William told me you quit because of me."

"When did he say that?" Helga asked.

"After I told him I couldn't go through with the inheritance scam," he answered.

"What inheritance scam?"

Joseph sighed. "At this point, I shouldn't be surprised you don't know. It's a bit of a long story, Helga."

"I think she deserves to hear it, Joseph," Loki prompted quietly.

"Does he need to be in here?" Joseph spouted, jerking his thumb at Loki.

She raised the knife, making Joseph flinch. "Luke stays."

Joseph sighed again, even more deeply this time, and sank into the wooden chair opposite Loki at the table. Whatever he was about to say seemed to truly pain him.

"William Chesterton was an attorney friend of mine, Lukas. He had a client, a young woman, who stood to inherit a fortune once she married a man who matched her family's social status. Naturally, he approached me with the idea of marrying the girl."

"Naturally," Helga grumbled.

Joseph shot her a grieved look. "The plan was to split the fortune three ways, then annul the marriage. It seemed like easy money."

"Do you mean to say the girl was part of it?" Loki said incredulously.

Joseph nodded. "It was her idea."

"Great Odin's Raven, gold diggers are everywhere!" Loki exclaimed, then silenced himself when Helga raised an eyebrow at him.

"I came to London to court the girl, just to maintain appearances, but everything changed when I met you, Helga. I visited her several times as planned, but she was cold and selfish. I could have lived with that for the brief time we would have been married, but you were so …" Joseph's voice trailed off, and he gnawed his lower lip.

Loki found his new father-in-law's sudden vulnerability painful and stared at the table. Helga offered Joseph no encouragement, her silence weighing heavily in the air. She had finished cutting the meat but seemed frozen in place.

Joseph took a deep breath and continued, "When I told William I couldn't go through with the plan and why, he was livid. I offered to help him find someone else to take my place, and he reluctantly agreed. I thought that would be the end of it."

"Is that why you left?" Helga finally asked. "To find someone else?"

"Yes, but I was planning to come back and explain every-thing to you."

"But you never did," she accused him bitterly.

"I tried, but you were already gone," he contended. "William said you found out what we were planning and were so disgusted and offended by both of us, you quit immediately."

"And you believed him?"

"I didn't want to believe it," Joseph admitted, his face reddening slightly. "I ran to the train station to try to catch you, but it was too late."

"I was on my way back to Norway in disgrace. I'd lost everything," she stated, though her tone was not as bitter as her words.

"I would have followed you, but I didn't know your address or how to find you," Joseph asserted. "When I returned to William's house, he wouldn't tell me anything I wanted to know. He said you told his wife you weren't interested in me anyway and that I should let it go." He paused for a moment, a flash of pain crossing his face, then softly added, "As if that was supposed to make me feel better."

Helga quietly stirred the cut sausage into the pan, then washed her hands and sat down at the table. She did not look at Joseph, but her face was much changed. The anger and hurt was gone, replaced by something that made Loki itch to exit the kitchen as quickly as possible.

"Helga, it seems we were both lied to," Joseph said gently. "They probably thought getting rid of you would make me change my mind."

"Did it?" she asked quietly, without looking at him.

"No, I found someone else as I promised, then ended my partnership and any relationship with them immediately after," Joseph replied, staring at his hands.

"Several years ago, Kristoff mentioned you were still unmarried, but I didn't know why." She stated it as an unspoken question.

Joseph did not answer her directly. "You've kept tabs on me through your brother all these years? I've always wondered what happened to you. Why didn't you write me a letter or something?"

"Why would I, Joseph, after what I was told?" Helga retorted. "Besides, by the time Kristoff started doing business with you, I had already met and married my Erik."

"Did he make you happy?" Joseph lifted his chin and fixed his green eyes on Helga's face.

"Yes, he did," she whispered as tears filled her eyes. "He's been gone a little over a year now."

"I'm very sorry for your loss," Joseph murmured, reaching out his hand to grasp Helga's and smiling slightly when she did not pull away.

They were the kindest, most tender words Loki had ever heard the man speak. The two of them seemed to have forgotten Loki was still sitting there, which increased his discomfort. Just as he thought he could slip out, Kristoff poked his head through the kitchen doorway.

"Is something burning?" he asked playfully.

Helga snatched her hand from Joseph's at the very first word out of Kristoff's mouth. But her brother did not see the movement and seemed cheerfully oblivious to the tension in the kitchen.

"Oh, my goodness!" Helga exclaimed as she rushed to the stove and slid the pan off the burner.

"There are three of you in here," Kristoff teased. "How did none of you notice?"

"Never, not once in my life, have I ever burned dinner!" Helga wailed. "Joseph, look what you made me do!"

Joseph walked over to inspect the pan. "It's not too bad. Just a few burned potatoes. We can pick those out."

"Everybody out of my kitchen!" she cried.

"If anybody can fix it, you can," Joseph encouraged her.

"Out!" she repeated, grabbing the carving knife again for emphasis.

All three men hastened to obey, almost knocking each other over in their hurry to avoid her fury. Back in the living room, Joseph wearily sank back into the armchair, heavily laden with his own thoughts.

"Lukas, I'm not really feeling up to going back to Stuttgart tonight," he sighed. "It's a long trip, and today has been rough for me. You two can go ahead if you wish."

"I'll ask Carina what she wants to do," Loki replied.

"You're welcome to stay in the guest bedroom, Joseph," Kristoff offered.

Joseph's eyes widened with alarm. "I don't think that's a good idea. I'm not entirely certain I'm going to make it out of here alive as it is."

"What's that supposed to mean?" Kristoff asked peevishly. "My sister is the kindest woman anyone could ever want to meet."

Loki was shocked to see Joseph's face completely transform from his usual stern expression to a wistful, almost dreamy, smile as he murmured, "She really is."

"Oh no," Kristoff gasped, meeting Loki's eyes as if to ask if he had just seen what he thought he saw.

Loki made a helpless face and nodded, silently communicating to Kristoff he had read the man's face correctly.

Kristoff smacked his forehead with the palm of his hand. "You've got to be kidding me!"

"What?" Joseph asked, having not seen the silent exchange between the two men.

"Oh, I ... uh ... kind of forgot about Kat," Kristoff lied. "What are those girls doing up there?"

"I'll go find out," Loki offered. "I have to ask Carina if she wants to go back tonight or wait until tomorrow anyway."

"I'll go with you," Kristoff suggested hurriedly.

Joseph was not even listening anymore. He stared out the living room window with a distant look on his face. Loki and Kristoff exchanged looks, then ran up the stairs in search of the girls.

They found them sitting on a bed in a small sewing room, surrounded by scattered magazines and leaflets.

"I would love to see you on stage in that one," Kathleen was saying to Carina as she pointed to a dress in a fashion magazine.

"Girls, we have a major problem," Kristoff burst out.

"Are you being dramatic, Kris?" Kathleen teased him. "We're working on tour plans."

Loki raised an eyebrow at Kristoff at the nickname, thinking, *Well, these two sure got cozy fast.*

"This is serious, Kat," Kristoff insisted, ignoring Loki's questioning look. "Carina, I think your father is in love with my sister!"

"What?" Carina exclaimed, standing up suddenly and spilling the magazines onto the floor.

"So?" scoffed Kathleen. "I think that's sweet. Love can be just as wonderful the second time around."

Carina acted as if she would dash out the door and down the stairs, but Loki stopped her with gentle hands on her shoulders. "Carina, don't. You need to hear this."

When she nodded and sat back down, Loki told them what he had heard. When he finished, Carina slumped forward with her head in her hands and tears in her eyes.

"Wow," Kristoff muttered, shuffling his feet and staring at the carpet. "When she came home unexpectedly, she told our parents and me that she just couldn't bear to miss our birthday."

"You and Helga share a birthday?" Kathleen asked.

"Yeah, it was my tenth. She was thirteen when I was born and always called me her birthday present," Kristoff reminisced. "Anyway, she made a really big fuss over me that year, but I knew she was sad about something. And she never did go back to London. Now I know why. I wish I didn't."

"It's utterly heartbreaking," Kathleen sighed. Then her face brightened. "Maybe this is their chance to start over!"

Carina suddenly spoke up and voiced the problem Loki had been pondering but had not dared to address. "What about Baldur?"

"Like I said," Kristoff groaned. "We have a real problem."

"It's a problem, but it's not our problem," stated Loki. "They're grown adults. Let them sort it out."

"How can you say that?" Carina gasped. "Baldur is your brother. He's going to be crushed."

"Only if my sister feels the same way about your father," Kristoff stated curtly. "It was a long time ago."

Judging by how Helga had looked at Joseph, Loki assumed any thought of Baldur had been driven from her mind, but he kept that to himself.

"It's probably time to eat," Loki remarked instead. "Why don't we head downstairs and leave it alone for now?"

As they left the room, Loki whispered, "Carina, Joseph doesn't want to leave tonight."

"Why not?" she whispered back.

"He said he's too worn out," he replied.

"Rubbish," she sighed. "I know my father. He already lost her once. He won't let it happen again."

The table was set. The food was out and ready to be served. But neither Joseph nor Helga was anywhere to be seen.

"What is this?" Kristoff asked somewhat angrily. "Where did they go?"

Loki saw movement out of the corner of his eye. He glanced out the kitchen window, which was still open to let in the air and sunlight. The curtains had moved slightly in the summer breeze, but beyond them, Loki could see Joseph and Helga walking in the small but beautiful garden, deep in conversation.

"I found them," Loki announced dryly.

His eyes widened when he saw Joseph take Helga in his arms. Loki quickly shut the curtains to block Kristoff's view as he rushed over.

"Never mind! Nothing to see here!" Loki blurted out.

"You're actually encouraging this?" Kristoff exclaimed, starting to head for the kitchen door.

Loki grabbed his arm. "Kristoff, give them some privacy. They went outside for a reason."

"That's what I have a problem with," he growled.

"You never fussed this much about Baldur," Loki pointed out.

"Baldur's different. He's playful and loving. Joseph is a hard, ruthless—"

"Hey!" Carina spouted indignantly.

"Don't get me wrong. I admire your father, Carina. But he's broken her heart once already," Kristoff continued. "I won't let him do it again."

"You might not like this, but you need to let your sister make her own choices," Loki told him, tightening his grip on his friend's arm. "Helga is wiser than you think."

Kristoff started to jerk his arm away from Loki but calmed down when Kathleen gently grasped his other arm.

"Kris, Mr. Black is right. Let them be," she advised.

"Just call me Luke, Kathleen," Loki suggested. "Everyone else does."

She nodded, then gestured to the table. "Let's just eat before the food gets cold. Helga's outdone herself again."

Kristoff relaxed, though he kept looking from the window to the door as they all helped themselves. Helga had fixed the sausage and potato dish so well, there was no trace of any burnt pieces. Wheat rolls and buttered peas completed the meal. Helga had even thought to set out German beer and, of course, Norwegian coffee.

Loki sampled the main dish, a perfect blend of taste and texture that was even more delicious to him because he had helped make it himself.

"Carina, do you think you could learn to make this?" Loki asked out of the side of his mouth.

"Only if you peel the potatoes," she teased him.

"I can do that," he bragged.

"And slice the onions," she added.

He groaned as she snickered at his clearly expected reaction. He had already told the others how the onions had irritated his eyes while Helga sliced them. As an experienced cook herself, Carina had found that part of his retelling hilarious.

The kitchen door opened, and Helga stepped through, her blue eyes sparkling and her cheeks flushed. Joseph had held the door for her and followed her inside. Loki noted the twinkle in his eyes and the grin on his face.

Ah, there's the playfulness Helga mentioned, Loki thought. In fact, years had melted off of them both.

"Oh good, you didn't wait for us," Joseph observed.

"And just what were you doing out there?" Kristoff demanded, then shook his head as Joseph opened his mouth to speak. "That was a rhetorical question, Joseph. I actually don't want to know."

"Father," Carina spoke up, "Luke says you'd rather leave in the morning?"

Joseph shuffled his feet, looking at the ground but still grinning. "Actually, I … uh … I'm going to stay here for a while."

"You're not staying here," Kristoff stated flatly.

Loki grinned to himself. Kristoff had once described Joseph as a man who never takes no for an answer. Kristoff's consternation over this new development must have given him boldness. And sure enough, Joseph narrowed his eyes at Kristoff's rudeness.

Helga had been helping herself to her own plate of food, but in a quiet, no-nonsense voice, she interjected, "Have you forgotten this is my house, Kristoff?"

"Helga, may I speak with you privately?" Kristoff growled through clenched teeth.

Helga cocked her head at her brother. "Not if you're going to act like a child."

Kristoff stood abruptly, stomped over to the sink, and set down his dishes with a jarring clatter. "I'll be in my study."

Loki gestured for everyone else to stay in the kitchen and followed his human friend. He caught the door just before it slammed in his face.

"Kristoff, talk to me, buddy. What's going on with you?" Loki asked as he stepped into the small office and gently closed the door.

"I wouldn't expect you to understand. You're not human," Kristoff muttered grouchily.

Loki pushed down his irritation over Kristoff's rude comment, watching as he slumped into the chair behind his desk. When his friend avoided his gaze to carefully run his finger over one of his dust-free bookshelves, Loki knew Kristoff was stalling.

"Try me," Loki urged dryly.

"Baldur is your brother," Kristoff snapped. "If I feel a sense of responsibility over this, you definitely should."

Remembering Frigga's strategy of using silence to extract information, Loki raised one eyebrow and waited for the room to grow heavy and uncomfortable.

Kristoff began to squirm. "What do you think Baldur will do to Joseph when he finds out he's moved in on Helga while he's gone?"

Loki still said nothing.

"Alright, fine!" Kristoff spouted, throwing his hands up, just as Loki had with his mother when she used that trick on him. "I haven't seen Helga like this since before Erik died, not even with Baldur. And I'm very concerned she's just jumping into whatever this thing is."

"Love?"

Kristoff scowled. "That's exactly what I'm afraid of. I do business with Joseph, but that doesn't mean I trust him."

"You know, Helga didn't trust Kathleen at first either," Loki reminded his friend. "But she gave her a chance. Maybe you need to show her the same courtesy. And if Joseph stays here, you can at least keep an eye on things."

Kristoff groaned, running his hand through his sandy hair in angst. "Do you realize that if she marries him, Joseph will be my brother-in-law?"

"He's already my father-in-law," Loki chuckled. "We'll commiserate together."

Kristoff cracked a slight smile, then frowned again. "That would make you my step-nephew-in-law or something. It's just weird."

"Uncle Kristoff, eh?" Loki grinned. "It isn't any stranger than some of my family issues. Baldur doesn't even know who his real mother is."

"And now we've come full circle," Kristoff said with irritation. "What do we do about Baldur?"

"Why should we do anything?" Loki commented casually. "Baldur is a reasonable fellow, and he falls in love easily. He's also dealt with loss before. Honestly, and I can't believe the words coming out of my mouth, I'm rooting for Joseph on this one."

"Why?" Kristoff asked incredulously. Yet, under his peeved tone lurked a genuine curiosity.

"You didn't see what I saw," Loki pondered aloud. "Helga looked at Joseph the way Carina looks at me. And ..." He held up his hand as Kristoff began to sputter. "The way Kathleen looks at you."

Kristoff grinned. "How does she look at me?"

"You haven't seen it?" Loki teased. "I'm not going to imitate it, so you're on your own. But I do want to know how you two went from all business to holding hands in less than a week."

A knock interrupted the conversation before Kristoff could answer or really do anything more than grin even more widely. Helga softly requested permission to enter.

Kristoff seemed in much better spirits. "Yeah, come on in, sis."

Helga walked in breezily. She shut the door firmly behind her, then stated, "This concerns both of you." She addressed Loki first. "I'm assuming you told Kristoff my history with Carina's father?"

Loki nodded.

"Kristoff, I can tell you're concerned, and rightly so," Helga began.

Kristoff looked surprised, his body relaxing instantly. But he was not fully ready to relinquish whatever hurt feelings he was battling and asked, "Why didn't you ever tell me? You knew he was ... is ... my best customer!"

"I never wanted what happened between us, or what I thought happened, to affect your business relationship with him. I realize this is a shock to you, and you must be wondering how this will affect your business now."

Shame passed over Kristoff's good-natured face. "That isn't my only concern, Helga."

"I know," she acknowledged. "You also don't want me to get hurt again. And you're worried about Baldur."

"Were you eavesdropping?" Kristoff accused her.

"I'm a woman, Kristoff, and I know you," she chuckled. "I don't have to eavesdrop to know what's going on in your head."

Loki smirked to himself. She was so much like Frigga. Kristoff frowned and crossed his arms on his chest, looking every bit like a boy who was not getting his way.

"As far as getting hurt again, it's a risk I'm willing to take. He's asked me for a second chance, and I've already agreed, on my own terms," she told him. "And since this is my house, it's my right to invite him to stay here."

"This isn't like you, Helga," Kristoff protested. "You've always been the first one to insist on decorum. You threw a fit when I asked if Kathleen could stay in your sewing room."

Helga narrowed her eyes. "And I only allowed it because you promised me you'd behave yourself."

"Why *is* Kathleen staying here?" Loki asked innocently.

"The bathroom in her hotel room flooded," Kristoff answered distractedly.

"Oh sure," Loki laughed. "How convenient for you!"

Kristoff turned his attention to Loki and asked indignantly, "Are you suggesting I took advantage of the situation?"

"You'd better believe I am," Loki retorted gleefully. "Maybe you even created the situation."

"Well, it just so happens it really did flood, along with several other rooms," Kristoff insisted, his eyes twinkling. "Something got stuck in one of the pipes, I guess. The hotel was already overbooked, so they offered to put her up somewhere else. She thought she'd just stay up in Lillehammer, but I didn't like that idea." He paused thoughtfully. "I guess I did take advantage of the situation."

"And now I'm taking advantage of your situation," Helga laughed. "With you and Kathleen here, everything will be quite appropriate."

Loki spoke up. "Helga, you said this concerns both of us. What exactly does this have to do with me?"

"Well, for one, you and Carina will be on your own in Stuttgart, though I rather doubt you'll mind that," Helga answered with a warm smile. "Secondly, since Baldur is your brother, I don't think he would mind if I told you about our last conversation."

Kristoff looked up suddenly. "You've seen Baldur since he and Hod left for Paris?"

"Yes," she affirmed. "Just two nights ago, he came alone to tell me goodbye."

"Through the Paris Bifröst portal?" Loki asked.

"No, he had other technology. Apparently, when he returned to Paris, an Asgardian named Tyr told him someone was looking for him."

"Who was it?" Loki asked.

"This is where it gets very strange," Helga admitted. Then she chuckled. "Although, perhaps not as strange as having a house full of Asgardians. Anyway, it was a royal messenger from Baldur's mother's planet."

"Alfheim?"

Helga shook her head.

"Baldur said his mother was from Alfheim," Loki insisted.

"That's what he had been told when he discovered his mother was not Frigga, no doubt to keep him from learning the truth," Helga explained. She paused as if to end her story there.

"Go on," Loki urged, his insatiable curiosity getting the better of him.

"His mother was Athena, the daughter of Zeus," she stated quietly.

"My father had a child with Zeus's favorite daughter?" Loki groaned. "What next?"

"Well, Zeus is dying, and Baldur is next in line for the throne."

"Of what, Olympus?" Kristoff quipped.

"Yes, exactly," Helga confirmed.

"Helga, I was joking," Kristoff remarked dryly. "But then, why am I surprised? Next, you'll say Jupiter and Neptune are real."

"Those are just other names for Zeus and Poseidon, his brother," Loki said. "You should know that."

"Of course, silly me!" Kristoff spouted sarcastically. "Where is this Olympus?"

"Mount Olympus is in Greece," Loki informed him. "The planet, where the Olympians returned after the humans drove them out, is in the Andromeda Galaxy, the next major galaxy over from ours."

"Humans drove out the Greek gods?" Kristoff asked sarcastically.

"Why do you think Asgardians live in hiding here?" Loki asked ironically. "You lot are incredibly powerful when you band together. And they aren't gods any more than we are. I've never met an Olympian, but I recognized some of the names from Greek mythology."

"Greek mythology is even more twisted than Norse mythology," Kristoff mentioned. "Surely Kvasir didn't write those stories?"

"No, they've been around far longer. It's more likely he read the Greek stories and modeled his writings after them," Loki mused. "And judging from Zeus's reputation on Asgard, I have no doubt he's at least somewhat like the humans described him."

"Zeus had a lot of offspring, from multiple women, including humans," Kristoff pointed out. "How is Baldur next in line for the throne?"

"Apparently, anyone with human blood is automatically disinherited," Helga explained. "Baldur says Zeus is incredibly protective of his throne. He drove out most of his children centuries ago."

"How's that working for him now?" Kristoff remarked sarcastically.

"It's put Baldur in a bad spot. Athena died six years ago. They've been looking for Baldur ever since, mostly because Zeus has become paranoid and unreasonable in his grief," Helga answered. "The Olympians will make Baldur king by force if he doesn't find a closer heir."

"How did the Olympians find him?" Loki asked.

"He didn't tell me," Helga replied. "And I didn't ask."

"You suffer from a deplorable lack of curiosity, Helga," Loki chuckled.

"Wait just a minute," Kristoff exclaimed. "If Olympus is in Andromeda, how would anyone even get to Earth from there? Or vice versa? It's physically impossible."

"Maybe humanly," Loki told him. "But the Olympians have developed some quite impressive technology. Olympus was an ally of Asgard's once, so we have some of the earlier tech ourselves."

"Once? Are they enemies now?"

"No, they just have nothing to do with each other these days. Zeus had been a good friend of my father's, but they had a falling out over two thousand years ago that almost resulted in war. It must have been over Baldur's mother."

"Did Baldur take Hod with him on this quest of his?" Kristoff asked.

Helga nodded.

"And what about you?" Loki questioned her. "You said he came to say goodbye."

"He did," she affirmed, with a surprising lack of sadness. "He said he dared not ask me to wait for him, knowing my life would be shorter than his and not knowing how long he would be gone. I believe it was a harder parting for him than for me. I had already decided a relationship with him was not what I really wanted, once all the excitement died down. I much prefer a simple, quiet life with my kitchen and my garden. We agreed to be friends only, although I'll always have a fondness for him."

Kristoff grumbled something to himself.

"What was that?" Helga asked innocently.

"Never mind," he answered. "Now what?"

"Baldur really doesn't want anyone else to know about what I just told you," she informed them. "This has to stay between the three of us."

"I don't keep secrets from my wife," Loki objected. "At least, not anymore."

"Of course, you may tell your wife," Helga conceded, winking at Loki.

"And I don't plan to keep secrets from my fiancée," added Kristoff, standing and stretching.

"Your what?" Helga gasped.

Loki turned on Kristoff at the exact same time. "Fiancée? What happened to not rushing things?"

"Oh, you're one to talk," Kristoff snorted.

"I leave for just shy of a week, and everyone's getting married!" Loki exclaimed.

"I'm certainly not getting married," Helga retorted.

"When were you going to tell me about this, Kristoff?" Loki demanded.

"You? He didn't even tell me!" Helga huffed indignantly. "His own sister."

"I just did. Besides, when would I have had a chance to tell you? Either of you?"

"We've been in here for thirty minutes," Loki retorted furiously.

"Talking about other stuff," Kristoff defended himself.

Loki folded his arms across his chest, not caring that he was pouting. "When did this happen?"

"Less than a few hours ago," Kristoff confessed, now grinning from ear to ear. "I drove her up to Lillehammer and met her family. We stopped at the lookout on the way back. I asked her there."

"You've known her for three weeks," Loki pointed out dryly. "And you didn't see each other for two of those weeks."

"They were the most miserable weeks of my life," Kristoff countered. "Especially when I had to watch you and Carina in London while missing Kat so much, I could hardly breathe!"

"We tried to be considerate of you," Loki grumbled.

"I know, I know," Kristoff admitted. "I don't blame you. It was just rough. When she showed up here ... Anyway, I've dabbled around enough to know she's exactly what I want. And I've always gone after what I want with little to no hesitation."

"That's for sure," Loki agreed with a wide grin. "However did you get her to agree to marry you so quickly? I thought she had better sense."

Kristoff shot him a look. "Thanks a lot, buddy. I thought you were supposed to be my best friend."

"Oh, am I? That's nice to know," Loki quipped. Though he had made light of it, he was delighted by Kristoff's words.

Helga was listening with great amusement.

"Anyway, I suppose it was my near brush with death," Kristoff stated with a dramatic air.

"You mean getting shot in the shoulder?" Loki scoffed.

"Yes!" Kristoff exclaimed. "It reassorted my priorities, thank you very much. And hers. Besides, we won't be getting married the same day we got engaged like you and Carina did either. I'll let you hold that record."

"Technically, it was night on Asgard when I asked her," Loki corrected him defensively, "and morning on Asgard when we got married."

"Oh, excuse me," Kristoff teased. "Let me rephrase that. We won't be getting married within twelve hours like you two."

Loki scowled, but Helga burst out laughing. "You two sound like a couple of roosters in a cockfight!"

Loki and Kristoff laughed with her, breaking the remaining tension.

Loki crossed the room and shook his friend's hand. "Congratulations, old boy. When's the wedding?"

"Tomorrow," he jested, then laughed uproariously at the looks on their faces. "I'm kidding. We don't have a date set yet. With all the traveling we both do, a longer engagement just makes sense. It will take time to figure everything out."

Helga hugged her brother tightly. "I have to admit, I'm a little surprised you asked her so quickly and even more surprised she agreed, but I saw this day coming. I'm happy for you both."

"Thanks, sis," he responded, returning her embrace. "It was a little impulsive, I'll admit. I just wanted her to know how I felt before she left again. I didn't want to dance around the subject like you and Carina did, Luke. And I certainly didn't want some other guy to swoop in."

"You didn't even know how she felt?" Loki probed.

"No, I took a huge risk. I've never been more nervous in my life. I wish I'd been a little more romantic," Kristoff admitted. "I think I phrased it more like a business proposition."

"Somehow, I imagine that appealed to her," Loki bantered.

"Was she surprised?" Helga asked.

"You'd have to ask her," Kristoff answered, a sly grin sliding across his face. "I'm not sure she would want me to say much more."

"Oh, Kristoff, tell me you didn't," Loki groaned, misinterpreting Kristoff's rakish grin.

"No, I didn't," Kristoff assured him. "I'm doing things the Asgardian way, as far as that goes."

"Do you need me to step out so you don't have to speak

in such cryptic language?" Helga demanded, somewhat annoyed.

Loki laughed. "Sorry, Helga, it's just something we talked about on my wedding night. Man stuff."

"Very well, keep your secrets," she sighed.

"Speaking of secrets, have you told Kathleen who I am?" Loki asked Kristoff.

"Are you kidding?" Kristoff scoffed. "She's an American journalist. She'd react worse than Carina did."

"No secrets from your fiancée, huh?" Loki mocked.

"That's your secret. You deal with it."

"You told Helga," Loki pointed out.

"No, he didn't," denied Helga. "And I gave him what-for over it. Baldur was the one who finally explained everything."

"I guess I'll just tell Kat that Baldur left on family business and it didn't work out between the two of you," Kristoff decided. "I don't see any reason for her to know about Asgard."

"Joseph either," Loki warned Helga. "Carina didn't want me to tell him, and I quite agree with her. There's no need, especially since I am not planning to go back, at least not after I fake my death."

"Wow," Kristoff breathed. "Has it come to that?"

"I don't want a double life anymore," Loki stated. "I've decided to do what all the other Asgardians on Earth have done."

"You'll get no objections from me," Kristoff offered with a grin.

Helga, on the other hand, grasped Loki's shoulders with her soft hands. "Luke, dear, are you sure? What about your family?"

"If Carina has no place on Asgard, then neither do I," Loki insisted. Then he grinned mischievously. "Besides, you're a lot like my mother, Helga. And if things work out between you and Joseph, you'll be my mother-in-law."

Her eyes grew quite swimmy. Then she hugged him as tightly as she had Kristoff. "I hope you know what you're doing."

Loki frowned, thinking, *Why would anyone think otherwise? I've handled things just fine thus far, haven't I?*

He put those thoughts out of his mind, but even as he and Carina bid the Norway household goodbye and traveled to Stuttgart by rail, he could not dispel all his doubts.

21

Carina knocked on the giant doors of her father's mansion in Stuttgart and smiled cheerfully at Loki. "The last time you were here, did you ever imagine you'd come back as my husband?"

"Not in my wildest dreams," Loki chuckled. "And I've had some crazy dreams."

The doors swung open. The butler ushered them inside, where the housekeeper greeted them excitedly in German, chattering on about how excited she had been to receive Joseph's phone call that morning, informing her to prepare for their arrival.

The robust woman took Carina's arm and patted her hand. "Oh, my little duckie, look at you. You are positively glowing!"

"I'm just so happy, Mrs. Wagner," Carina gushed.

The woman dipped her head respectfully at Loki and remarked, "And no wonder, with this handsome man as your husband! Mr. Green was very clear you were to be treated with no less deference than he is, Mr. Black. We are happy to serve you."

Loki bowed and replied in perfect German, "Thank you, Mrs. Wagner. I trust you will find me an easy guest to please."

The woman flushed, pleased by his gallantry. "Please follow me. We've saved supper for you in the dining room."

As Loki followed his wife and the housekeeper, he remembered the last time he had walked down this hall and through the great dining room doors. The room looked forlorn without all the guests. The newlyweds did not talk much as they ate their late supper, weary as they were from the long train ride.

"This place seems so different," Loki remarked, pushing his empty plate aside to stand and stretch.

Carina nodded, looking around her, then stated, "It's usually like this. Tomorrow, we'll eat in the kitchen."

"Will I finally get to taste your cooking?" Loki teased her.

"We'll see," she said slyly, as if she was already planning something.

She also stood and stretched, then took Loki's hand to lead him back to the main hall and the curved staircase where he had seen her for the first time. He stopped at the base.

"What are you doing?" she demanded, pulling at him to follow her up the stairs.

"Remembering the first time I saw you," he answered softly.

"Well, I'm right here, silly," she laughed. "You don't have to remember. I still have the dress. I'll go put it on."

Loki grinned rakishly at her, suddenly feeling wide-awake and quite mischievous. "I'm more interested in taking it off."

Carina blushed deeply. "Stop it! The servants will hear you!"

"So what?" he argued, taking her in his arms. "We're married now. Surely they know how newlyweds behave."

"That doesn't mean they want to hear about it," she taunted, but she allowed him to kiss her there at the bottom of the staircase. "Shall I show you to your quarters then, Mr. Black?"

"Only if I'll be sharing them with you, Mrs. Black," he whispered.

She merely giggled, then took him on a tour of the upstairs. Joseph's living quarters and a second office comprised the west wing while Carina's bedroom, sitting room, and music studio made up the east wing.

As soon as she opened the door to her room, which almost rivaled his room on Asgard in size, a black ball of fur shot across the lushly carpeted floor and attached itself to Loki's thigh. Loki gently removed the kitten's claws and held the squirming fuzzball up to inspect him.

"Well, my feisty namesake, you have indeed grown," Loki chuckled, turning to Carina as the cat nestled into his arms and purred loudly. "I'm surprised he remembers me."

"Sometimes, I think you're the only person he actually likes," she scoffed as she opened one of the suitcases the servants had hauled to her room during dinner.

"Doesn't he like you?" Loki asked in surprise.

"Well enough, I suppose," she answered, sitting down on her large bed and brushing her wavy hair. "But he's never been as affectionate with me as he is with you."

As if to prove her a liar, the kitten jumped down from Loki's arms and onto the bed. He cocked his head at her, then sniffed her, acting more like a dog than a cat. The small animal then nudged her stomach and settled into her lap.

"Well, I'll be," she murmured. "He's never done that before. Do you think he understood me?"

"Maybe. Cats sense things," Loki remarked with a shrug. He sat beside her on the bed, taking care not to disturb the cat. "Perhaps he senses how much I love you." He kissed her shoulder softly. "He does present a problem … two, actually."

"What's that?"

"You need to give him another name," he laughed.

"I'll work on that," she promised, her eyes shining. "What's the other problem?"

"Whatever-his-name-is will have to move, whether he likes it or not," he growled, taking her into his arms.

Disturbed by the movement and Carina's low gasp, the kitten opened its green eyes and seemed to smirk at Loki. He stretched himself as if he had not a care in the world. Then he jumped off the bed to explore some other part of the room, as if he owned the place. He glanced back just once and twitched his tail as if he was offended by their presence, stalking off to sulk when they laughed at him.

Loki tenderly drew Carina to himself, successfully turning her attention away from the kitten. She melted into his kiss and surrendered to his touch gladly. Neither of them cared where the cat had gone, focused as they were on each other. But soon after Carina had fallen asleep, Loki felt the kitten return to the bed, settling as close to Carina's waist as he could. It was a little strange, but he knew cats could be peculiar. He rubbed the kitten's little black head and listened to Carina's rhythmic breathing until he suddenly woke up and realized not only was daylight pouring through the windows, he was alone in the room.

He hurriedly dressed, then went searching through the house for his bride. Though he had not seen all of the mansion, an amazing and familiar smell led him straight to the kitchen.

He spotted Carina immediately, bustling around the servants as they went about their regular morning routines. Her hair was pulled back from her face, where a smudge of flour added to her beauty and charm. She wore a plain dress with short sleeves and a white apron spattered with foodstuff.

"Luke, you're up earlier than I expected," she scolded him, trying to shoo him out. "Breakfast isn't quite ready yet."

"We're eating in here anyway," he protested. "Can't I stay and watch?"

"Oh, alright," she conceded, "but don't get in the way."

He sat down at an elaborately carved oak table and watched the activity around him with amusement. The kitchen itself seemed to feature all the latest gadgets and innovations but still held a quaint and charming appeal. He wondered if the room bespoke Carina's feminine touch or her mother's, assuming Joseph had not hung up the lacy curtains or carefully arranged the collection of ceramic teapots lining the tops of the cabinets.

When she noticed him inspecting the teapots, Carina said softly, "Those were my mother's. I brought half of her collection here from New York." She wiped her hands on her apron, then drew near to kiss him on the cheek. "Good morning, by the way."

"You don't get off that easily," he laughed. He pulled her onto his lap and kissed her soundly, right in front of the servants. "Good morning!"

Several of the kitchen crew rolled their eyes as they continued about their work. They certainly did seem to hurry more, as if eager to exit the kitchen as quickly as possible. A timer sounded shrilly. Carina hurriedly extracted herself from his embrace to take a pan out of the oven and set it on a wire rack to cool.

"I knew I smelled cinnamon buns!" he exclaimed, reaching out to grab one.

She smacked his hand as he touched one of the pastries, scolding, "They're not ready yet!"

He stuck his thumb and forefinger in his mouth, sucking off the hot bits of cinnamon sugar. "You are far too eager to smack people, you know that?"

"Well, don't be greedy!" Carina laughed as she set a plate in front of him, laden with cheesy scrambled eggs, crisp bacon, and fried potatoes. "Start with this."

The rest of the servants left them alone in the kitchen. The sunlight streamed in through the open curtains, creating a warm and intimate setting, despite the large size of the kitchen. She sat down beside him with a smaller portion for herself, eagerly watching for his reaction as he took his first bite. He chewed thoughtfully, exaggerating his movements and making grotesque expressions to poke a little fun at her obvious desire for his approval. He swallowed as if with difficulty, then tentatively took another bite.

Impatiently, she demanded, "Well? Do you like it or not?"

"I don't know, Carina. It's just ..." he trailed off as anxiety spread over her face, then burst out laughing. "It's just so delicious, I might never eat at a restaurant again!"

She punched him lightly and whined petulantly, "Why were you toying with me?"

"Because it was funny," he laughed. "Should I resign myself to getting hit all the time?"

"Yes, if you're going to act like that," she shot back playfully.

"I love how witty you are," Loki praised her. He finished the rest of his breakfast quickly, then helped himself to a cinnamon bun. One bite of its gooey richness immediately transformed his expression into one of absolute delight. "Ohhh, my star, you put that fat Norwegian baker to shame."

Carina wrinkled her nose in confusion. "What fat Norwegian baker?"

"The day I met Kristoff, I had a cinnamon bun in a bakery in Christiania. It was the first Midgardian food I had ever tasted. They're my second favorite food. How did you know?"

"I heard you mention them to Helga, so I asked for her recipe," Carina replied. "What's your favorite food?"

"Ice cream," Loki answered without hesitation.

She laughed. "You have quite the sweet tooth. You'll be as fat as your Norwegian baker if you keep that up."

"Not likely," Loki snorted, looking down at himself and flexing his muscles. "I've kept this physique for a thousand years. Of course, I've never enjoyed cooking as amazing as yours. If I get fat, it's your fault."

She laughed with delight. "I'm glad you're pleased."

She took their empty plates and silverware to the large kitchen sink, adeptly washing and drying them. Loki watched with fascination, astounded by her skill and willingness to tackle menial household chores when there were clearly enough servants to manage things. Before he could comment on it, she turned to him with an expectant face.

"Shall we get started on our second wedding planning?" she asked.

He groaned. "Do you really need me for that?"

"Well, you do plan to be there, don't you?" she spouted indignantly.

"That's all I thought I had to do," he protested.

Carina laughed, then grabbed his hand and led him out of the kitchen into a parlor cluttered with decorations and assorted accessories. He looked around the room in dismay. The sheer number of things he did not recognize overwhelmed him.

"What is all this?" Loki demanded.

"I bought most of this for the reception," Carina answered, then pointed to a large white lattice arch. "We'll set this up in the main hall to take our Midgardian vows."

"Will people stand?" Loki asked, suddenly slightly interested in the details.

Carina pulled out a bolt of shiny white material. "No, we'll be renting chairs since we really won't need them afterward. One of the maids will sew bows for the chair backs out of this satin. After the ceremony, the men will move the chairs into the ballroom, where we'll host the reception."

"Is a reception like a banquet?" Loki asked, watching her move things around.

"Somewhat, but more like my debut party," she answered. "We'll eat food and mingle with our guests, maybe do a few wedding traditions."

"What traditions?" he queried curiously. "What kind of food?"

"Not cinnamon buns and ice cream," she teased him. "We'll have to plan a menu with the cook. And you'll have to be surprised about the traditions. You left me in the dark about yours, after all."

"I honestly thought Sigyn would tell you," Loki said sheepishly.

"She just told me to trust you, so I did," Carina answered with a warm smile. "Anyway, we will definitely have a wedding cake."

"Why do we have to have cake?" Loki complained.

Carina looked up in surprise from the white candles she was counting. "Don't you like cake?"

He made a face. "Not at all! On Asgard, they always put dried fruit and nuts in it."

"That sounds like fruitcake," she laughed. "And I quite agree. It's disgusting. I think I'll bake the cake myself, just to add a little personal touch. I'll make sure it's moist and decadent. No nuts or fruit."

Loki grinned, looking over her shoulder at all of the boxes of frilly things. "If you make it, I'll try it. What else do we need to do?"

Carina's hands suddenly flew to her mouth, her eyes wide with panic.

"What's wrong?" Loki asked, truly alarmed.

"We sent out the invitations already, with Klaus's name on them! Some of his relatives might show up to the wedding!"

"What?" Loki growled. "Can't we send letters? Or print an announcement in the newspaper?"

"I'm sure Father will print an announcement, but there's no guarantee everyone will see it. And I'm afraid letters might not arrive quickly enough either."

"Joseph has a phone. Why don't we just call everyone?"

"I can call almost everyone, including mutual friends, but I only have addresses for Klaus's guests," Carina informed him, looking pale. "We'll have to handle those personally, door to door."

"Wouldn't Klaus's parents have additional information?" Loki suggested.

"His parents are dead, and he was an only child," Carina stated, her voice strained. "His old, widowed aunt is likely too weak to come, but his cousin might. Other than that, there are just a few of his father's friends."

"Do any of them know Klaus was arrested?"

"I don't know," Carina admitted. "But we shouldn't take any chances. Besides, it's common courtesy."

"It really isn't too many people," Loki remarked. "What are his two family members like?"

"His cousin is nothing like Klaus. He's actually quite nice," Carina replied, leading Loki out of the room and into Joseph's office where they would be able to make phone calls to most of the wedding guests. "His mother, Klaus's aunt, on the other hand, is a dreadful woman. I am not looking forward to that visit."

"I'll protect you from the witch, my star," Loki promised, kissing her forehead.

Carina smiled at him, then flipped through a small box filled with handwritten address cards and calling cards. She selected one, then picked up the phone and dialed her first guest. For the next hour or so, Loki listened idly while Carina called everyone she could. He shamelessly manipulated the sound to hear both ends of every conversation. Carina seemed to find his presence comforting and spoke with confident enthusiasm.

She could be a queen, he thought to himself, impressed with her ability to address concerns and steer the conversations wherever she wanted.

When she hung up the final call, she informed him, "Everyone has been so nice! I guess our mutual friends liked me better. They'll all come anyway."

Loki nodded as if he had not already heard. The two of them went down to the kitchen, where Carina quickly fixed them a few sandwiches for lunch.

When he had finished eating, Loki wiped his mouth with his napkin. "Shouldn't we let your father know we've arrived safely?"

"I completely forgot!" Carina gasped. "Maybe the staff told him? I'm surprised he hasn't already called here about ten times."

"Well, I'll call Kristoff just to make sure. I need to speak with him about the wedding anyway," Loki stated as he stood and took his dishes to the sink.

Carina thanked him for doing so then inquired, "What else is there to talk about? They already know the date."

"I read somewhere that most grooms have a best man, and I'd like him to do it."

"Oh," Carina said quietly. "I didn't mention it to you because I don't have anyone to be my maid of honor."

"What about Sigyn, Kathleen, or Helga?"

"Kathleen makes the most sense, but I don't know if she would do it. We don't know each other very well," Carina mused. "Would you ask her for me?"

"Why not ask her yourself?"

"I have some cleaning up to do here. I'll join you when I'm finished."

Loki ambled back to the study to make his first phone call. He found Kristoff's card in Joseph's box of contacts, picked up the receiver, and told the operator the phone number for the house in Norway, just as he had observed Carina do before lunch. The operator connected him quickly. After several rings, Kristoff answered the phone. He promised to let Joseph know all was well, then filled Loki in on the happenings since they had left, which were not extensive. After Kristoff heartily agreed to stand as Loki's best man, he called Kathleen to the phone so Loki could ask her to be Carina's maid of honor. She sounded pleased and readily consented.

Loki placed the receiver back on the hook. He stood and stretched, thinking he had better go find his wife, but she entered the study at that moment.

"How are things in Norway?" she asked.

"Sounds rather boring, but Kristoff says Joseph and Helga are getting quite cozy."

"Of course they are," Carina snorted grimly. "I wouldn't expect anything less."

"You don't sound happy about it," Loki observed.

"It's bittersweet," she said shortly, as if she was not ready to talk about it. "What did Kristoff and Kathleen say?"

"They would be honored," he answered with a grin, pleased to see her face brighten. "Are you ready to make house calls?"

"Almost," Carina replied as she took out a pen and a piece of paper from her father's desk and jotted down a few notes. She handed Loki the paper. "These are just the things I need to do myself. Everything else, the servants can do."

Loki read aloud, "Finalize with florist, buy wedding dress, meet with officiant, settle menu with cook, bake and decorate cake." He looked up from the paper. "Why do you need a second dress? What's wrong with the other one?"

"I'd like you to see me in something different," she replied.

"Do we have to do all of this today?" he complained.

"No, of course not. But I would like to at least visit the florist and look at dresses after we finish the house calls."

He grinned mischievously as he remembered one thing that could redeem their potentially boring excursion. "Joseph showed me his collection of cars the day I met him. Could we take one of those? I rather fancy the Rolls Royce."

"I suppose," she granted. "The chauffeur has the day off, so I was planning to drive."

"You can drive?"

"Why? Can't you?"

"Well, I never have," he admitted. "But I'm quite good with an airship. How hard could it be?"

She playfully tweaked his nose. "Would you like me to teach you?"

"I don't need you to teach me," he grumbled, following her outside to the freestanding garage that housed her father's cars.

"Fine then," Carina retorted with a smirk, gesturing to the sleek, black Rolls Royce. "Have at it."

After about thirty seconds of sitting in the driver's seat of the Rolls Royce, staring at the controls, Loki swallowed his pride and turned to his grinning wife. He should have paid more attention to how Kristoff operated his car.

"Okay, fine," he grumbled. "How do you start the blasted car? Kristoff had keys for his."

She handed him the key, barely able to contain her laughter. "Put the key in the ignition, that little slot there, and turn it … no, the other way."

He narrowed his eyes at her as the engine roared to life, though his lips twitched with amusement at her little joke. "You deserve to be smacked for that."

"But you won't do it," she taunted in a singsong voice.

"There's more than one kind of smack," he teased. He leaned over to kiss her cheek. "Now what?"

Carina quickly showed him how to operate the controls, pedals, and brake. Getting out of the garage was rocky, to say the least, with several lurches forward and screeching halts. Once Loki had maneuvered the car onto the street, he started to get the hang of it, enjoying the vibrations he could feel through the steering wheel. Managing the powerful vehicle gave him a thrill that almost equaled flying an airship. Instead of viewing the car's inability to leave the ground as an annoying restriction, Loki embraced it as an interesting challenge. The car ride became smoother and more rhythmic. Carina eventually released her death grip on the inside handle of her door. She no longer looked like she might jump out of the car.

"You're a natural," she praised him. "Are you always such a quick learner?"

"Only when I have a good teacher." He winked at her, accidentally jerking the wheel when he took his eyes off the road.

"Road!" she yelled, then relaxed when he immediately straightened the car. "Maybe a little practice is in order."

"What do you think I'm doing now?" he teased her, undeterred by her nervousness. "You'll have to tell me where to go."

She directed him to their first stop—an impressive, old stone manor house set with many windows, which were shadowed by dark drapes to prevent even a fleeting glimpse of the inside.

"Who lives here?" Loki asked, following Carina's instructions to park the car.

"The dreadful aunt," Carina warned with a shudder, getting out of her side and starting up the walkway. "I figured I would get the worst one out of the way first. She only speaks German and does not allow English to be spoken in her presence."

They rang the doorbell and were admitted by a sad-looking maid, who led them to a dark room with closed drapes. A fragile woman with crisp white hair sat in an armchair next to a table, where a colorful glass lamp shed light over the book she was reading. The air smelled strange, like sickness and medicine. Loki instantly felt a pressing need to run out of the house, but he resisted for his wife's sake.

"Carina Green," the woman acknowledged in a raspy voice. "What brings you here? And who is this handsome young man?"

"This is Lukas Black, Mrs. Mayar," Carina replied respectfully.

The old woman nodded in Loki's direction, her gaze one of disdain mixed with a strange interest.

"I've come to tell you personally that your nephew and I are no longer getting married next Wednesday," Carina stated.

"And why is that? He couldn't tell me himself?" she asked coldly.

"I'm afraid he's been arrested and detained in New York," Carina informed her quietly. "I'm sorry to be the one to break the news to you."

Klaus's aunt drew herself up in her armchair, straightened her shoulders, and glared at Carina. "You abandoned him in his hour of need?"

Loki gritted his teeth. The woman's haughty manner grated on him, reminding him of Sigyn's aggravating mother. Carina dropped her mouth in shock and consternation at the widow's audacity, apparently at a loss for words.

"She did nothing of the sort," Loki defended her gruffly. "Your nephew deserves everything he got. He not only robbed a bank, he treated Carina shamefully, even dared to hit her."

The old woman pondered this, and when she spoke to Loki, her voice was kinder than it had been to Carina. "And you were her savior, I take it?"

Even in the dim light, Loki saw Carina's eyes darken dangerously.

"I know that look. Let me handle this," he whispered to her. Then he addressed the old lady again. "Yes, I rescued her since Joseph wasn't there. I am truly sorry your nephew is such a disappointment, but Carina has suffered enough. She does not blame you for your nephew's actions. I trust you will not blame her either."

The frail widow regarded Loki with a knowing look. "I see," she replied simply. Then she directed her last cutting remark at Carina. "I believe I would have chosen this man over my nephew as well, but I am still very disappointed, young lady. Then again, without a mother to teach you refinement, I shouldn't be surprised you would jump so quickly into another relationship."

The snide remark about her mother sent Carina over the edge. Loki's restraining hand on her arm was not enough to stem the outpouring of her anger.

"How dare you?" she seethed at the woman, who merely stared at her haughtily. "You weren't happy about my engagement to Klaus in the first place. And now you aren't happy it's ended? Well, now that I'll no longer be related to you, I can tell you exactly what I think of you."

Carina hesitated, her anger abating, but the old woman motioned her hand to encourage her to speak. "And what is that?"

Carina stared at the frail old thing and furrowed her brows, as if contemplating. "You are a sad, lonely old woman who takes no pleasure in life but to make others feel less important. And for that, you have my pity."

The woman sat there in shock, her mouth slightly agape as just a tiny bit of moisture shone in her eyes. She recovered quickly, coldly commanding, "Get out of my house."

Carina stepped toward the woman, but Loki took her arm and urged, "Let's go, my star."

At the front door, Carina turned to the maid. "Would you please let Gunter know the wedding with Klaus is off?"

"But Miss Green, he is out of the country on business," the maid protested. "We do not expect him to return until next Wednesday afternoon."

"Did he plan to attend the wedding?" Carina asked.

"I do not know, miss," she answered hurriedly, her face growing white when she heard the old lady call from down the hall. "And he did not tell us where he was going either."

The maid slammed the door behind them in her rush to attend to her mistress.

"Are you alright?" Loki asked Carina, switching to English again.

"Yes, but I wish I hadn't said that," she answered thoughtfully. "The maid might bear the wrath meant for me."

"She'll be fine," Loki assured her. "She wouldn't still be working for her if she couldn't handle it. Meanwhile, what do we do about the cousin?"

"We've done all we can," Carina replied. "We'll just have to hope he didn't plan to attend or that someone can get word to him."

As he got into the car and started the engine, he grinned wickedly at Carina. "I can't believe someone married that woman and gave her a son."

"Her husband died many years ago in the Abushiri revolt on the East African coast."

"Perhaps that was a better fate," Loki quipped.

"That's a terrible thing to say," Carina scolded him. "Gunter never even knew his father. If his mother had always been so awful, he wouldn't have turned out so well."

"As rudely as she spoke to you, you defend her?" Loki asked incredulously.

"I just think there's more to her than I thought," Carina mused. "I do pity her."

"I don't think she wants your pity," Loki chuckled.

Carina fell silent, lost in her own thoughts. She furrowed her brow and stared out the window as Loki pulled away from the house.

"Carina," Loki prodded her gently, "you need to tell me where to go next."

Carina became more cheerful as she directed him, seeming to put the altercation with Klaus's aunt behind her.

And Loki enjoyed his time behind the wheel of the magnificent car. The remainder of the visits went quickly since none of Klaus's father's friends were home. They left messages with the house staff at each residence.

"Flowers or dresses?" Loki asked his wife after their last visit.

"Flowers," she answered without hesitation.

Loki pulled up to the florist shop, scowling slightly as he saw the colorful flower arrangements in the window. He expected to be exceedingly bored.

Why does she need me for this? he complained to himself, but he forced himself to get out of the car and follow her into the store.

The sweetly scented air inside was warm and heavy with moisture. Every square foot seemed to be bursting with botanicals. Carina moseyed through the labyrinth with a tight grip on Loki's hand, as if she sensed he was about to bolt.

A stocky man with spectacles approached them. "Miss Green!" he gushed in German. "Have you come to finalize your order? The wedding is next Wednesday, yes?"

"Yes, Mr. Busch," Carina answered with a smile. "But there has been one significant change."

Loki snickered inwardly at the irony of the man's name but kept his face composed and friendly as the florist turned to him.

"A different groom, no?" Mr. Busch guessed with a knowing grin. "Your magic is good, Mr. Black. I am pleased to see you did not give up."

"What do you mean?" Loki asked curiously.

"I was there at Miss Green's debut party," the florist admitted. "I work with many couples and could not help but see you two seemed made for each other. I am very happy for you both. But come, it should not take long to finish the arrangements."

Carina turned to Loki. "We'll have white roses, of course, but I could never decide on a secondary color. What would you choose?"

"Definitely not red or yellow," Loki chuckled. He pointed to a purple-blue bloom that reminded him of a star. "What is that flower over there?"

"Ah, Centaurea cyanus," replied the florist.

"That's a mouthful," Loki muttered.

"It's common name is cornflower or bachelor's button. It is often worn by young men in love, the beloved flower of Germany. It even has ties to royalty, as it was the favorite flower of Kaiser Wilhelm the First," the florist recited proudly.

Carina smiled brightly. "Luke, it's the perfect flower for you!"

Loki puffed out his chest, quite pleased with himself. "Actually, I chose it because it reminds me of you, my star."

The florist paid them no heed, already gathering flowers together to show them a sample. "Yes, cornflowers and edelweiss with the white roses will be perfect." He held up a small bouquet he had thrown together, adding, "Larger, of course."

"It's beautiful," Carina breathed as Loki nodded his approval. "I trust you, Mr. Busch."

After finalizing all the flower arrangements, including the corsages and boutonnieres, Loki and Carina left the florist shop and sauntered down the sidewalk toward a quaint dress shop. He dreaded this visit even more than he had the florist shop, especially when he saw the elaborate, lacy wedding gown in the window. To his relief, Carina made a face at the dress.

"Definitely not my style," she informed Loki. "I hope they have other dresses. There isn't time for a custom one."

"Can you make modifications to the one you already have?" Loki asked innocently.

Carina shot him a sharp look, then softened. "You really like that dress, don't you?"

"I do," he admitted, then added in a mournful tone, "but I know how important this is to you, so I'll suffer through it."

Carina lightly smacked his arm. "Suffer through it?"

"That's it! I'm making up a new rule. Every time you hit me, you have to kiss me," Loki commanded.

"I'll agree to that," she murmured, kissing him on the cheek.

"I expect back pay," he whispered as he held open the door for her. "I figure you owe me at least four."

"Very well," Carina giggled. "But later."

As they entered the dress shop, three women recognized Carina and instantly surrounded the couple. They gushed over her and repeatedly complimented her singing ability before finally leading her to several racks of white dresses. She selected a few, then headed to the dressing room area with the women trailing behind her. Feeling forgotten, Loki frowned and settled himself down on a couch in front of three floor-length mirrors clustered around a short, pink pedestal.

What is taking so long? he grumbled to himself as he listened to the women chattering in the dressing rooms.

One stayed with Carina while the other two went back and forth with different gowns for her to try. No one had seemed to notice Loki until one saleswoman paused on her way to the front of the store.

"Aren't you Lukas Black, the magician?" she asked. "Miss Green's new groom?"

"Yes, I am," he answered with a smile, pleased to have a break in the boredom. "Don't I get to see her in any of these dresses?"

"Oh no!" she chided. "The groom doesn't see the bride in her dress until she walks down the aisle on the day of the wedding."

"Then why am I here?" Loki asked impatiently.

The woman stifled a laugh. Clearly, this question did not surprise her. "She has it narrowed down to three. I think she will want your opinion, but we'll show you the dresses on their hangers."

Loki frowned again. "I don't know how much help I'll be."

He liked to dress well and often noticed attractive clothing, but he wondered why he should be involved at all. He did not have to wonder long, for just as the woman had grinned and scurried off, Carina appeared in her regular clothes, followed by the other two women. They each carried one bridal gown.

"Luke, I can't decide. Would you please help me choose?" Carina asked sweetly.

"Sure, show me the ones you narrowed it down to," Loki instructed, making a show of great interest as he leaned back and linked his long fingers behind his head.

She had asked nicely after all. If he must be subjected to

such things, he could at least do his best, just as he had when his mother solicited his help for his birthday banquet.

The first saleswoman held up a white satin gown with thin straps and a sheer overlay that would drape over the chest, shoulders, and upper arms. Silver scallops threaded with white gems adorned the bodice of the elegant dress like criss-crossing necklaces falling to a point just above the waist.

Loki nodded his approval, imagining his wife in it, then turned to the second saleswoman, who held up a similar gown with sheer, capped sleeves. Strings of white pearls embellished the bodice and waist in a pattern that reminded Loki of a spiderweb. Below the hips, the strings of pearls fell in pleasing lines, almost to the hem of the gown. The design was sassy but not quite right for Carina.

"Show me yours, Carina," Loki requested, for she had held it close to her, as if guarding her favorite.

When she held it up, he was speechless for a brief moment. The dress looked uncannily similar to a yellow gown his mother had worn for Thor's rite of passage celebration banquet. A delicate lace jacket formed a V at the waist of the satin gown and fell in soft folds around the layered skirt. Tiny white beads lined the edges of the jacket in an oddly Asgardian style. Loki shook his head vehemently, wondering if some exiled or hidden Asgardian had designed the gown.

"You don't like this one?" Carina asked, her tone disappointed.

"I do like it," Loki protested. "But it's too much like a dress my mother wore once. Is it your favorite?"

"No," she admitted. "I didn't hold the one I liked the best, just to make sure you gave your honest opinion."

Loki grinned at her cleverness. "I like the jeweled one best. The first. It suits you."

"Well done, Luke! I was leaning toward that one," she admitted with a pleased smile that told Loki how truly delighted she was.

Carina went back into the dressing room for a quick alterations fitting, then joined Loki at the front of the store, where he had been browsing the men's formal wear in the catalog at the counter.

"We won't have time to order anything for you," Carina reminded him, pulling him out the door.

"Well, I'm not wearing anything Asgardian," Loki replied as he opened the car door for her. "Would you mind if I spin an illusion?"

"What about that white suit you got for our first official performance together?"

Loki smiled sheepishly. "It was an illusion."

Carina smirked at him. "Why am I not surprised? Well, we'll need to get you a real one for the tour. But for the wedding, do something in navy blue."

"Why navy blue?"

"It will make the cornflowers stand out more," she replied.

Loki shrugged. "I got some ideas from the catalog. I'll give you something you'll love, but if I don't get to see yours before the wedding, you don't get to see mine."

Carina shrugged. "I suppose that's fair."

"Where are we going next? Back to the house, I hope? My back pay is long overdue," he teased.

"You'll just have to wait," she answered with a wink. "I have a surprise for you. Take that road right there, and drive until you see something magnificent."

"Like what?"

"You'll know."

Before long, Loki spied the "something magnificent"—a large city square in front of a grand palace that stretched over the grounds like the palaces in London.

"What is this place?" he asked.

"Schlossplatz. And beyond the square is Neues Schloss Palace," Carina replied as she showed him where to park. "We're eating dinner here."

"Are there restaurants here?"

"Yes, in the Königsbau over there," she said, pointing toward the enormous buildings. "But I packed us a picnic."

She proudly pulled out a picnic basket she had hidden in the back of the Rolls Royce.

"When did you sneak that in there?" Loki asked in wonder.

"When you were on the phone with Kristoff," she boasted.

"But how did you know I would choose the Rolls Royce?" He was impressed she could know him so well already.

"I grilled Father after his first meeting with you," she confessed. "He told me how much you admired the Rolls."

"My clever minx," Loki whispered, kissing her while he tried to peek into the basket. He found he was quite hungry, especially for more of her cooking.

"Not yet," she laughed, holding the basket out of his reach.

She led him to a soft, grassy spot under one of the trees, somewhat secluded from the other people enjoying the grounds. Loki watched hungrily as she unpacked cold fried chicken, soft white rolls, deviled eggs, green grapes, and pickled cucumbers.

Loki picked up one of the pickles. The smell made his mouth feel tangy. "I've never tried one of these before."

"Why not?" Carina looked at him curiously as she bit into one herself.

"They scare me," he laughed.

"I love them! I canned these myself last fall. Try one."

Loki tentatively bit one. It was crunchy, both sour and sweet, with a hint of garlic and vinegar. He mustered all of his effort not to spit it out. She laughed at the look on his face as he forced himself to swallow the bite.

"I guess that's a no, then," she observed. "Unless you're toying with me again."

"It's too sour," he admitted, handing it back to her. "I'm sorry."

"We don't have to like all the same things," she reassured him. "And you don't have to like everything I make."

When they had finished their leisurely dinner, Carina's face grew serious. "Klaus brought me here a few times." Then, since no one was close by, she switched to his real name. "Thank you for coming here with me, Loki, and giving me this memory with you."

"Let's make it an even better memory." He drew her onto his lap and kissed her, then grimaced.

"What's wrong?" she asked.

"I can taste that pickle," he complained.

She burst out laughing, then took several bites of a roll. She kissed him again, then asked, "Is that better?"

"Much," he murmured against her mouth, deepening the kiss as he caressed her face with one hand.

"People are watching," she whispered, suddenly pulling away.

"So? I don't care," he argued.

"Well, I do. You don't like kissing me after I've eaten a pickle, and I don't like kissing you like that in front of other people," she teased him. "We'll have plenty of time at home later."

"I'll hold you to that," he bantered, rising to his feet and brushing off his pants. "I did enjoy your surprise."

"Oh, we're not done." She smiled brightly and gestured toward the palace. "There's a charity gala here tonight."

"In the palace?"

"Yes, almost the entire first floor is a fairly new museum," she informed him. "Tonight, they're raising money for an orphanage. Over one million German children were orphaned during the war. Even though it's been a number of years, the need is still great. "

When Carina's eyes misted over, Loki felt a responding tenderness well up in his own heart. He easily recognized her giving and loving spirit, which complimented her feistiness, but this newly revealed soft spot for children fascinated him.

She would make a wonderful mother, he thought fondly. "How do we get in?" he asked aloud.

"Father had two invitations. I found them in his study and brought them. He probably forgot all about it," Carina responded. "The doors open at seven."

"It's already half past six. We don't have time to go home and change, do we?" Loki asked, checking his watch.

"I thought you might enjoy designing our attire for tonight."

Loki's eyes gleamed with excitement. He had never had the opportunity to cast a clothing illusion for someone else. He grabbed the picnic basket and Carina's hand, then almost ran to the car. He hurriedly threw the basket inside the Rolls and locked it again, then led Carina to a spot with more privacy. Since no one was around, he took the opportunity to kiss her deeply while he transformed her simple day dress into a rich, purple gown he had seen in a magazine. He stepped back to admire his work, then made an illusion of her so she could look at herself without a mirror.

"Do I really look like that?" she breathed, her eyes shining.

"It's how I see you," he answered, admiring her again. Then he transformed the more casual clothes he had been wearing into an elegant black suit with tails, complete with a purple bow tie that matched her dress. "How do I look?"

"Dashing, as always," she sighed.

Loki held out his arm. "Shall we, my star?"

Together, they walked confidently to the entrance, where they handed their invitations to the attendants and entered the grand palace.

Loki soon found himself truly enjoying the charity gala. He held Carina's hand during the fundraising presentation. When tears began streaming down her cheeks, he handed her his handkerchief. They both pledged a large amount of money to the orphanage, the first time Loki had ever donated to such a cause. Helping these children brought him a warmth he had not expected, though he would likely never meet them.

After many of the other guests had left, still they lingered, mingling with people Carina knew, including several who would be attending the wedding.

On their way out, the two of them drew near the elegant staircase leading to the restricted areas on the next floor. Carina tugged at Loki's arm when he paused and cocked his head at the ropes blocking off the stairs.

"Loki, no," she whispered fiercely, apparently noting the mischievous glint in his eyes.

"No one's around," he whispered back. "Come on, just a peek? I want to see what's up there."

"Boring government offices," she insisted. "You want to see something incredible? Follow me."

Loki cast a reluctant glance upstairs but followed her into a side room, where a magnificent fresco caught his eye. He forgot all about the higher floors.

"This is just one of three," Carina informed Loki, triumphantly noting his interest in the art. "Josef Anton Gegenbauer painted them about seventy years ago to portray some of the history of the Duchy and the Kingdom of Württember."

"This *is* incredible," Loki murmured. "You asked me once if there was anything I can't do. Well, I could never do this. An illusion, maybe, but not by hand."

Carina smiled up at Loki, then admired the scene with him. After several minutes, she whispered, "I need to iron my shoelaces."

"What?" Loki asked incredulously. He had never heard that expression and could not begin to guess what it meant.

"As you would put it, nature calls," Carina rephrased, laughing slightly. "I'll be back in a few minutes."

Loki chuckled to himself at the absurd expression, then turned his attention back to the art, listening to her heels echo down the hallway. When he remembered her illusionary clothing would fade if she got too far from him, he pulled himself away to follow her.

Suddenly, a muffled scream sounded from the direction Carina had gone.

A man yelped and swore, as Carina cried, "Luke, help m—" Then her voice was cut off again.

"Carina!" Loki shouted.

He took off running, catching just a glimpse of her red hair and vivid purple dress disappearing behind a small side door. Frantically, Loki ran out into the deepening night. Just as he caught up to them, Carina's captor whirled around with his gun against Carina's head and a firm grip on her upper arm.

"One more step, and she's dead," the man snarled at Loki. Then he sneered at Carina. "The lady is going with me for a little ride, Black."

"Is it money you're after?" Loki seethed, his tone hard and menacing.

"Oh, you needn't worry yourself about that. I'm getting paid plenty." The man's eyes narrowed as Carina struggled against him. He removed the gun from her head and aimed it at Loki. "One more move out of you, sweetheart, and I'll shoot him."

She glanced at Loki, who nodded almost imperceptibly. He quickly formulated a rough plan in his mind and discreetly signaled to Carina. When she smiled slightly then tensed, Loki knew she understood his silent message to attempt to fight off the man.

"Carina, no," he warned her, winking at her to communicate the opposite.

She stomped one heeled shoe into the man's boot, surprising him for a second. She quickly slipped off the heel and tried to stab him with it, but the brute was too fast for her. He grabbed the arm that held the shoe, knocking it to the ground. He shot Loki in the leg, then threw Carina over his shoulder.

"Loki!" Carina screamed, forgetting to use his human name in her distress, for he had crumpled to the ground in a pool of blood.

At least, that was how it was meant to look.

But while the thug was distracted, Loki had vanished and shifted his stance, maintaining the illusion of his original position. The bullet hit a sculpture and ricocheted into a tree, but Loki hid its true arc and changed the sound to that of a bullet penetrating flesh and bone. Then, as the bleeding replication of himself wallowed on the ground, the real Loki grabbed the fallen shoe, so as not to leave any evidence behind, and silently crept after Carina and her kidnapper. By the time any bystanders arrived, all of the illusions would disappear.

Loki had just gathered the energy in his muscles to spring at the man when a black car screeched to a halt in the street. The goon holding Carina threw her into the back, then spoke quickly with the driver.

Loki enhanced the sound.

"Where's Black?" the driver asked.

"I shot him in the leg," answered the first thug, pointing to the still visible illusion. "He's probably bleeding out over there."

The driver groaned in exasperation. "Mayar specifically said not to kill him!"

"Did you really think he'd let us just take her without a fight? Besides, there are too many people around. I did what I had to do."

"Where'd he go?" the driver demanded, for the illusion had finally dissipated.

The thug whirled around, paling when he saw nothing in the spot he had left the fake, bleeding Loki. "He can't have gotten far!"

The driver got out. "You take her back to the hiding place. I'll go after Black. You're liable to shoot him again."

Loki heard no more. The delay had given him just enough time to dash over to the Rolls Royce. He slid across the hood to the driver's side, unlocked the car, and started the engine as quickly as he could. He stayed invisible, speeding after the black car as it quickly accelerated. Loki guessed the thug knew he was being followed. He grinned, imagining the man's reaction to being chased by a seemingly empty car. He wondered if the goon had noticed Carina's change of clothing since he had not been able to maintain her purple dress illusion.

Loki stayed close enough to the other car to see Carina peering out the back window, her face concerned but hopeful. Loki assumed she had guessed he was the invisible driver behind the wheel of the Rolls. The speeding caravan raced past the city limits. Then the lead car suddenly veered off the road and crashed into an abandoned brick building.

Loki braked hard. He leaped out of the car before it had fully stopped and rushed toward the other vehicle, but a violent explosion threw him to the ground.

"No!" Loki howled.

The roar and crackle of the ensuing flames erupted from a fire with such intense heat, it was nearly impossible to approach the car. He attempted it anyway, terrified of what he might find.

Frantically searching for anything to smash the car window or protect his hands from searing metal, he suddenly stood still. His sharp ears picked up a grunt followed by a loud curse and a thud sounding from behind the building. He paused, uncertain. He could not see inside the car. He heard a woman's muffled cry from the same direction, then silence. He stealthily slipped behind the building and came upon a scene that relieved him and made his blood boil with rage all at once.

Carina huddled fearfully on the ground, alive but with her hands tied and her mouth gagged. The thug stood over her with his gun cocked, panting heavily as some blood trickled out of nasty looking scratches on his face.

"Stop!" Loki shouted, revealing himself.

The man turned ghostly white but kept the gun trained on Carina. "Black! Where did you … How did you—"

His words were cut off as Loki hurled himself at the man, throwing them both to the ground. As they wrestled on the cold, hard-packed dirt, the thug desperately tried to prevent Loki from grabbing the gun. Loki nearly had the upper hand when the pistol suddenly went off. The man slumped to the ground, his eyes glassy and empty. Blood welled up from the bullet hole in his chest.

Loki jumped away from him. He drew one of his daggers and cut Carina's bonds, suddenly aware of police sirens in the distance. "Are you alright, my star?"

"Is he dead?" she asked, her body shaking.

"Yes, you're safe now," he answered softly, helping her to her feet and holding her close.

She winced, shuddering as she looked over at the corpse. "Did you kill him?"

"Not on purpose. The gun went off while we were fighting,"

he said shortly. "We need to get out of here before the cops arrive. Can you walk?"

"Not very fast," she admitted. "I lost my shoes. And I hurt my knees when he pushed me to the ground and tied my hands."

"I'll carry you then." He scooped her up and took her to the Rolls Royce, gently setting her down on the passenger seat.

"Loki?" Carina whispered as he started the engine and peeled away from the scene.

"What?" he asked, his voice terse with anxiety.

"I love you," she said. Then she slumped over with her head on the window.

"Carina?"

When she did not answer, he stopped the car and frantically patted her cheek to wake her.

Her eyes fluttered, and she stared at him almost fearfully, as if she did not really see him. "Where am I?"

"We're going home," Loki soothed her. "Everything's okay."

"Home," she repeated drowsily. "Good. I'm so sleepy."

"Carina, did you hit your head?"

"I don't know."

"I think I'd better take you to a hospital," he insisted.

She shook her head. "No, no, I'm okay. I just blacked out for a minute. I need some sleep."

"You need to stay awake for a little while longer, just in case you have a concussion," Loki told her, pulling back into the road. "I'll take care of your knees when we get back. And I'll check your pupil dilation. If it's normal, I'll let you sleep. For now, tell me everything that happened."

Loki listened attentively as Carina recounted her harrowing experience. He chuckled approvingly as she described biting the man's hand at the gala when he covered her mouth. She seemed to be improving in mental clarity and spoke with more enthusiasm. Loki burst out laughing at her imitation of the goon's reaction to her sudden change of clothing, as well as the invisible driver.

"How were you not hurt in the crash or explosion?" Loki asked curiously.

"Right before he crashed, he told me to get down and brace myself, then pulled me out when the door to the Rolls flew open. He pushed some sort of detonator to set off what must have been explosives in the back seat. I've never seen anything like it. When they went off, he dragged me behind the building."

"I thought you were dead for sure. I've never been so scared in my life," Loki sighed as the panic he had experienced finally eased.

"Well, I thought he had really shot you, even though I told myself it must have been an illusion. It looked so real."

"It was supposed to," Loki chuckled. "I saw the marks on his face. How did you manage that?"

"He was watching the car when the explosives went off, trying to figure out who yelled since we couldn't see you. I grabbed his hair and got my other hand free enough to scratch his face, but he shoved me to the ground and pulled my arms behind me, then tied and gagged me."

"If he weren't already dead, I'd kill him," Loki seethed. "*Nobody* treats my wife like that!"

Carina grinned at his declaration, then sobered. In a worried tone, she pointed out, "But now we don't know who he was or why he tried to kidnap me. And the police might trace it back to us, thinking we murdered him."

"He must have been one of Klaus's hired guns. Either that first gunman in Norway didn't do what he said he would or Klaus hired other people. We'll have to be more careful," Loki urged. "If the police come calling, I'll handle it. The cops I've dealt with have been reasonable enough, though they ask some unpleasant questions."

Carina sighed, her eyelids drooping slightly. "Are we almost home?"

"Yes, we're here," Loki assured her. "Stay awake just a little longer, my star."

He carried her inside and upstairs to her room. Concerned his own light manipulation would be too strong for her eyes, Loki instructed the worried staff to bring him a pocket-sized electric lamp Joseph had shown him at one point. While he waited, Loki washed her knees. He did not need his sealing kit but slathered the scrapes on her skin with Asgardian ointment, which assisted with bruising as well as injuries ranging from minor cuts to lacerations. As soon as one of the maids brought him the small light, he inspected her pupils, relieved to see they contracted evenly when he shone the light and dilated evenly when he removed it.

"Please don't disturb us for the rest of the evening," Loki instructed the maid. "She'll be just fine, but she needs to rest."

Carina spoke up. "Shouldn't we have Mrs. Wagner call my father tonight? Or would you rather call him?"

Loki felt a little peeved. Her father did not need to know everything that happened in their lives. And Loki certainly did not need a lecture from Joseph regarding his daughter's safety.

"No, he'll be here early next week with the others," he replied. "We can fill him in then. There's nothing he can do from Norway anyway."

"I guess that makes sense," Carina agreed sleepily.

"Very well, sir. Ma'am." The maid nodded and curtsied. "I'll inform the housekeeper."

When the maid had left, Loki helped Carina change into her nightgown and settle into the bed.

"Sleep now, my star," he whispered, caressing her cheek with one hand until her eyes drifted shut and her breathing became deep and rhythmic.

He settled in next to her, then grinned when he felt his furry namesake take the same position by her stomach as he had the previous night. He absentmindedly patted the cat's little head and finally fell asleep with a determination to better protect his beloved in the future.

23

The telephone in Joseph's study started ringing for the third time in less than twenty minutes. Loki threw his book down and stalked out of the library, angry at being torn from Leo Tolstoy's *War and Peace* when he was so close to finishing it.

They'll wake Carina, the dolts, he thought as he threw open the study door.

At his insistence, Carina had gone upstairs to take a nap hours ago. Since the altercation with the two thugs the day before yesterday, the newlyweds had not left the house. Loki spent the first day focused on Carina's recovery, which kept him from growing bored and gave him ample time to read while she rested. But this morning, despite his warning that she not overdo it, she wore herself out planning the reception menu with the cook. After ensuring she was asleep, Loki had settled down with his book in the library adjacent to Joseph's study. He had ignored the ringing phone long enough, hoping a servant would answer or, at the very least, that the person on the other end would abandon his quest to speak with someone at the Green residence. But apparently, he was alone on the lower level. And, of course, the mystery caller persisted.

He stepped into the study and lifted the receiver. "Green residence," he uttered with annoyance. "Lukas Black speaking."

"Oh, Mr. Black," responded a stern voice. "I'd actually hoped to speak with you as well, but first, is Joseph Green in?"

"I'm afraid not," Loki answered.

"When do you expect him? It's most urgent," the man on the other end stated emphatically.

"I'm sorry, but you haven't identified yourself," Loki pointed out. "What's this all about?"

"This is Franz Werner, chief of police," responded the man. "I need to ask Mr. Green some questions about his whereabouts the night before last."

"He's been out of town," Loki informed him, hoping that would be the end of it.

Loki recalled briefly meeting the man at Carina's debut party but knew very little about him—only that he was a personal friend of the Greens. When Carina called his wife about the wedding change, she had neglected to mention that her father had stayed in Norway. They had run into her again at the gala but were interrupted before she could ask about Joseph's whereabouts.

"Regardless, I need to speak with him," Chief Werner persisted. "Do you have an alternate number for him?"

Loki recognized the determination in the chief's voice and changed tactics. "Oh, you're in luck, Chief Werner. I believe he just walked in the door. Wait a moment, please."

Loki placed the receiver on the desk, then made the noise of footsteps entering the room as he called, "Joseph, there's a phone call for you."

"Who is it, Lukas?" Loki asked the air, imitating Joseph's voice.

"Chief Werner," Loki answered in his own voice. "Something about your whereabouts the night before last?"

"You know very well I was out of town," Loki barked in Joseph's gruff tone.

"Yes, I told him," Loki responded normally. "He wants to speak with you anyway."

Loki picked up the receiver. "Franz? This is Joseph. What can I do for you?"

"Ah, Joseph, old friend!" the chief bellowed, making Loki wince at the volume. "I'm glad you found Carina. And I hear she's marrying the magician instead of Klaus?"

"Yes, she is," Loki affirmed in Joseph's voice. "You and Sylvia aren't canceling, are you?"

"Oh no, not at all. We wouldn't miss Carina's wedding for anything, even if she had married that good-for-nothing Klaus Mayar."

"Then, what's this all about? Lukas said you wanted to know where I was the other night?" Loki asked in Joseph's voice.

"You were supposed to be at the gala," the chief pointed out. "I missed it myself. Had to investigate a mugging."

"Sorry to hear that," Loki grunted.

"Sylvia said your future son-in-law brought Carina instead. Did they happen to mention the shots fired on the plaza?"

"Shots on the plaza?" Loki, as Joseph, exclaimed. "This is the first I've heard of it! Was anyone hurt?"

"Early reports were someone had been shot on the plaza, but we didn't find any evidence to support that," explained the chief. "But witnesses did see a black Rolls Royce speeding away from the plaza in pursuit of another black car, which we found charred to a crisp at an abandoned flour mill a few miles outside the city. The driver had been shot dead not far from the car. There were signs of a struggle, including some cut ropes."

Loki thought desperately. They had too much information. Should he come clean? "Are you suggesting I had something to do with it?" he asked nonchalantly. "Lukas said he told you I was out of town."

"No, not you, Joseph. But I do have some questions for your future son-in-law," the chief stated. "Do you know which car he drove to the gala?"

"Lukas, did you drive the Rolls?" Loki asked the room.

"Yes, I did. Why?" Loki asked, making his voice sound distant.

"You'd better talk with the chief then," Loki instructed in Joseph's voice, as if speaking to Lukas Black. Then he spoke into the receiver. "I'm putting Lukas back on."

"Chief? It's Lukas Black again," Loki stated. "Yes, I drove the Rolls the other night to the gala and back to the Green residence."

"Were you aware there was a shooting?"

"We heard shots, but I didn't want to worry Joseph, so I didn't tell him. I did see two suspicious characters lurking around. Did I overhear you say there was a fatality?"

"Yes, likely one of the men you saw. Did you pursue the other vehicle?"

"It might have looked like it to any bystanders who saw us leave. I was probably driving too fast. I'm sure you understand I was eager to get Carina home as quickly as I could."

"Can you give me a description of the men you saw?"

"Certainly. Would you like me to come down to the station and give you a statement?"

"That would be helpful, Mr. Black," the chief acknowledged. "As soon as you can manage it, please."

"Of course," Loki responded. "Carina is resting at the moment. We'll come in about an hour."

Loki hung up the telephone and collapsed into Joseph's desk chair with relief, assured he had successfully allayed suspicion.

Just then, Carina poked her head into the study. "Father? Are you in here?" she asked, then spotted Loki. "Loki, weren't you just talking with my father? Where did he go?"

"Your father's still in Norway," Loki answered wearily. "You must have been hearing things."

Carina shook her head. "I hope I didn't hit my head hard enough to hear phantom voices!"

Loki frowned. Had he really just blatantly lied to his wife? "No, you didn't. I'm afraid I've been lying to the chief of police just now, pretending to be Joseph. And I just lied to you too."

"You lied to Chief Werner? You lied to *me*?" Carina gasped but kept right on firing questions without pause. "You can imitate my father? What other voices can you do?"

Loki laughed. "Slow down, my star! I'm sorry I lied to you. It just sort of slipped out."

"I forgive you. Just don't do it again," Carina scolded. "Was it about the other night? Does the chief suspect you?"

"I'm not sure. I think I just skated by. We have to go down to the station in an hour to give a statement about the men we saw."

Carina sighed. "Oh, joy. I suppose you'd better fill me in. But first, what about the voices?"

"You've heard me mimic voices," Loki reminded her. "I can imitate anything I hear."

"I thought you were just good at doing your family's voices and random sounds," Carina admitted. "Can you do me?"

"Of course I can," Loki scoffed. He changed his voice to hers and trilled, "My name is Carina Black, and I enjoy slapping people."

Carina grinned but punched him in the arm, then squealed with delight and tried to squirm away when he grabbed her around the waist.

"Oh no, you don't," Loki scolded her playfully. "You know our agreement."

Carina's eyes widened with realization, and she hit him again. "You wanted me to hit you? Just to get a kiss?"

"That's two," Loki counted, his smile growing. "Shall we make it three? I could say something really awful."

"No need," she protested. "I still owe you several from the other day."

"Indeed, you do," he bantered. "And from before that."

"Do we have time for all those kisses?" Carina bantered back.

"How about I let you off easy? Just one really good one?"

Carina sat gingerly on his lap. "Very well, Mr. Black. I accept your counteroffer."

She kissed him deeply, making his head spin. But he kept his wits enough to take the opportunity to tease her further.

In Kristoff's voice, Loki remarked, "Why, Carina, whatever will Luke say if he catches you kissing me like that?"

Carina scrambled off his lap, wiping her mouth furiously. "Don't you *ever* do that again!"

Loki burst out laughing. He attempted to grab her again, too overcome with hilarity to be effective.

"I'm not kidding, Loki. That was an awful trick to play!" Carina spouted, though her lips twitched as if she resisted her own laughter. "You ruined one of my best kisses!"

"Oh, come here," Loki gasped when he could breathe again. "I'll make it up to you."

"No," she pouted.

She moved toward the door, but Loki was out of Joseph's chair in a flash and chasing her through the floor level of the manor. He caught her easily and scooped her up in his arms as their laughter blended together in an almost musical harmony.

"I guess you're feeling better," Loki observed. "But let's not overdo it."

"I certainly wasn't chasing myself," Carina protested indignantly, though she draped her arms around his neck and rested her head on his shoulder.

"Let's have a look at your knees," Loki suggested, setting her down on a sofa in the now-clean parlor.

She obediently bared her legs. Loki looked at the scabbed-over scrapes and light bruising with a critical eye, then applied a little more Asgardian ointment.

"You'll be as good as new in a day or two," he told her. "Just in time to bake that cake."

"Gold, silver, or chocolate?" she asked with a smirk.

"What?" Loki squinted at her in confusion. He had no idea what she meant.

"Have you never had chocolate?" she asked incredulously.

"Of course I've had chocolate," Loki scoffed. "I've been to Paris, haven't I? You can make wedding cake with chocolate?"

"Yes, Loki, it's delicious! Gold cake is yellow. It tastes like buttery vanilla. And silver cake is a white cake with a touch of almond flavor."

"I can't even imagine any of them," Loki admitted.

"I'll make a layer of each then," Carina offered.

Just then, the doorbell rang. Since none of the servants appeared, Loki strode to the large foyer to open the door with Carina following close behind him. And there stood the chief of police and a lower-ranking officer.

"Mr. Black, Miss Green," Chief Werner greeted them. "May we come in?"

"Of course!" Carina exclaimed, nudging Loki.

"How convenient," Loki responded quickly. "You've brought the station to us."

Carina led the three men into a small sitting room reserved for formal visits. "Would any of you care for tea or coffee? Perhaps something colder?"

"Iced tea for me, please," Chief Werner stated. "Hans?"

Loki snickered inwardly to himself as the other man also asked for iced tea. *Hans and Franz. Sounds like a dime store detective novel*, he thought.

Carina nodded and started for the kitchen. Loki called after her, "Carina, maybe I should do that? I don't want you to overexert yourself."

"I'm fine, Luke," she insisted through clenched teeth, her eyes warning him not to say anything further about her injuries. "It will only take a minute. Chief Werner, Constable Weber, please make yourselves comfortable."

Loki stifled a chuckle as he thought, *Werner and Weber? That's even better. What a pair these two must be.*

"Has Carina taken ill?" Chief Werner asked Loki.

"Oh, she just had a rigorous tour schedule. Then we traveled extensively after that," Loki answered casually. "And with the wedding planning, she's somewhat worn out."

Chief Werner watched him very closely, his dark eyes narrowed and his face contemplative. Loki had an eerie feeling much did not escape this man's notice.

Chief Werner suddenly changed the subject, gesturing to the other policeman. "I don't believe you've met Constable Hans Weber. He's one of the best detectives on the force here in Stuttgart. He was on night patrol the night of Miss Green's debut. Or is it Mrs. Black now?"

"Beg pardon?" Loki almost stuttered.

Even Constable Weber looked strangely at the chief at that last comment.

"The two of you interact very differently than you did the night of the debut," Chief Werner observed. "The tension is gone, replaced by a level of intimacy usually shared by married couples. And then, there is the matter of the unusual rings you both wear."

"Most astute," praised the constable. "I had noticed the rings but not the rest."

"Well, naturally, you wouldn't," stated the chief. "This is your first interaction with Mr. Black, besides his street performances."

"Impressive powers of observation, Chief," Loki answered. "You are correct. We married in secret just over a week ago, but that's not common knowledge. We're doing a second wedding, for Joseph's sake more than anything, although Carina is quite excited about it."

"Ah, you aren't?" Constable Weber guessed.

Loki shrugged. "If it makes her happy, I'm glad to do it. But I'm more or less along for the ride."

"Speaking of rides," Chief Werner interjected somewhat abruptly, "we'd like to take a look at the Rolls."

"Whatever for?" Carina asked sweetly as she entered the room, bearing a tray of four frosty glasses filled with deep amber liquid.

She handed one to each man, who all thanked her. Then she sat down close to Loki with her own. Loki lifted his glass to his lips and sipped his first taste of iced tea. It was flavorful but somewhat bitter, although not as harsh as coffee. He would have liked to add some sugar. He grinned to himself, remembering Carina's teasing about his sweet tooth.

"We'd like to examine the tires, Mrs. Black," answered Constable Weber.

"Mrs. Black?" Carina asked innocently. "The wedding isn't until Wednesday, Constable Weber."

"They know we're married, Carina," Loki informed her, then addressed the two men. "But please, gentlemen, let's keep that amongst ourselves."

"What else have you told them?" Carina whispered fiercely. "The chief may be my father's friend, but they're still cops."

"They figured it out themselves," he whispered back, smiling charmingly at the policemen, who merely sipped their tea and watched the exchange with amusement. "They're *extremely* observant."

"Speaking of your father, has Joseph stepped out again?" Chief Werner asked.

Carina paled when she realized the chief had overheard her, but he just winked at her.

"Yes, he has," Loki answered quickly.

"Curious," the chief responded with a knowing smirk. "Especially since he was never actually here."

Loki groaned. "Let me guess, he doesn't call you Franz?"

"Oh no, he does," Chief Werner affirmed, his grin widening beneath his mustache.

"Was my timing off?" Loki pressed him. "I know the voice was right. Inflections, perhaps?"

"Your imitation was flawless," the chief assured him. "Most impressive skill you have there. You would have fooled me, but Joseph called my wife from Norway this morning to make sure the new wedding announcement is printed in the paper as scheduled. She happened to mention it after I finished speaking with you."

Loki groaned. "You didn't call him, did you?"

"No, I haven't," Chief Werner answered. "I haven't even told my wife anything. I noticed it was only after I asked for another number that you began your deception." He leaned forward intently, stroking his clean-shaven chin. "The question is why?"

"Perhaps this has something to do with it?" Constable Weber suggested, drawing something charred and twisted from his pocket and holding it up for them to see.

"What on earth is that?" Carina gasped.

"I suppose it's hardly recognizable to the untrained eye," admitted the constable, tapping the object as he spoke. "It's what's left of a high-heeled shoe. These things are surprisingly durable."

"Where did you find it?" Loki asked.

"In the back of the ruined car, which, as you might have guessed, was stolen," answered the constable.

Loki glanced at Carina. She shook her head almost imperceptibly. But this time, Loki knew continuing to lie would only make the situation worse.

Before he could say anything, the chief asked, "You should know we found decelerating scuffs and skid marks from a second car near the scene of the explosion. Would you like to change your story about what happened after the gala, Mr. Black?"

Loki opened his mouth to speak, but Carina interrupted. "Are you here to arrest him?"

"No, my dear," Chief Werner reassured her. "But we are investigating a homicide, which means we question everyone involved. Now, if the two of you are willing to cooperate, everything will go more smoothly for everyone."

"Aren't we cooperating?" Carina asked sweetly.

"Not exactly," the chief responded, staring pointedly at Loki. "Your husband hasn't been entirely forthcoming. Have you, Mr. Black?"

Despite Carina's cool composure, Loki saw she was frightened. He could keep quiet no longer, for her sake.

"It was an accident," Loki declared. "I didn't kill him."

"We know that," piped up Constable Weber.

Chief Werner shot him an annoyed look, then raised an eyebrow at Loki. "So … you were there!"

Loki sighed and nodded.

The chief smiled to put him at ease. "Relax, Mr. Black. As my esteemed colleague stated, we know you didn't kill the man." He stood up, walked over to the window, and peered out the drapes. Then he placed his hands behind his back as if to begin a lecture and faced the sofa where Loki and Carina sat. "The deceased man matches the description of a known criminal from Berlin who had several warrants out for his arrest. The fingernail scratches on his face, the woman's shoe in the wrecked car, the cut ropes at the scene, and a handkerchief on the ground, which was probably a gag, all indicate an attempted kidnapping. Obviously, Carina, whatever your husband did was to protect you, though I suspect you were injured despite his efforts."

"Now, how do you know that?" Loki demanded.

"She favored one leg when she brought in the tea, as if she had injured her hip," Chief Werner answered.

"I did hurt my hip!" Carina cried excitedly.

"You never told me that!" Loki exclaimed indignantly.

"It only started hurting a little while ago," she defended herself. "It's just sore."

Loki frowned but turned back to the chief. "Why are you calling this a homicide investigation if you know I didn't kill the man?"

"Even self-defense cases are investigated as homicides until we can determine no crime was committed," the chief explained. "But we should be able to close this case fairly quickly. We do have to wait for an official autopsy, but I could clearly see the bullet entered through the lower abdomen. That, combined with the powder burns on his skin and clothing, tells me the gun went off at extremely close proximity. The autopsy should tell us the path of the bullet, but I suspect it went up through the chest cavity into the heart. You couldn't have shot him."

"If you knew this already, why are you here?" Loki asked.

The chief sighed, as if dealing with a small child who needed an unnecessary explanation. "Until now, we only suspected you were involved, but we needed more information. And now, we need you to tell us what really happened."

"Very well," Carina relented, then launched into her perspective, leaving out Loki's illusions.

Loki filled in where necessary, briefly including what happened in Norway and ending with, "And there you have it. Do you still want a look at the tires?"

"We'll just take a few photographs for the official report," the chief stated. "Do you happen to have the clothing you wore that night, Mr. Black? And Carina, do you have the match to this ruined shoe?"

"I'll go get them," Carina offered. "Meanwhile, Luke, why don't you take the chief and the constable to the garage?"

Loki nodded and gestured for the two policemen to follow him outside. He silently watched them examine the tread and snap a few photos.

Once back inside, the chief remarked, "If we can catch the other man, he'll be arrested for attempted kidnapping at the very least. And you said you think Klaus Mayar hired them?"

Carina reentered the room with the items the chief had requested and handed them over to him to inspect.

"That's my best guess," admitted Loki. "This latest attack fits with what the first gunman said."

"If you're correct," commented the constable, his icy blue eyes glittering with excitement, "that makes him even more dangerous than we thought."

He began to take pictures of the shoe as the chief held up Loki's shirt.

"You must have been severely underdressed, Mr. Black," the chief stated. "Would you like to try again? My wife told me what you were wearing that night."

"That really is what I was wearing when it happened," Loki corrected him. "We'd had a picnic before the gala, so we changed back into more comfortable clothes afterward." When the chief raised an eyebrow, Loki insisted, "I have no reason to lie."

The chief squinted at him but relented and went back to inspecting the clothing. "No powder burns," he observed approvingly. "Good sign. I just wish you hadn't washed it."

"By the way, I meant to mention earlier that we heard Klaus is a suspect for robberies here," Loki said, ignoring the chief's lament.

"We have yet to find much evidence for the thefts here, but what we do have points to him," the chief acknowledged.

Carina dropped her head in her hands, her voice filled with shame and dismay. "And to think I almost married him!"

"He fooled us all," the chief comforted her. "But I really do wish you had involved us sooner. We could have helped."

"Have you heard about the bank robbery in New York?" Loki asked.

"Joseph wired me that news," the chief said grimly.

The constable sighed heavily, scratching his receding, light brown hairline. "Everything is further complicated by the American charges."

"Meaning?" Loki asked.

"Klaus is an exceptionally clever criminal and a master at allaying suspicion. Every time we get close, he slips through our fingers yet again. We didn't even know who we were chasing until several weeks ago. But the Americans got him first."

"He must have made a mistake to have been caught in New York," Loki observed.

"Perhaps, but something about that doesn't add up," the chief mused. "We suspect he has ties with some unscrupulous characters both here and in New York. He should have been protected, unless he was a scapegoat they simply disavowed. But that would have been a dangerous move on their part."

"Regardless, I'm glad they caught him," Carina sighed.

"As long as he's held in New York, he's untouchable," Constable Weber informed them. "And he might have ways to communicate with confederates while in jail."

"Couldn't he be extradited?" Carina asked.

"That can take years, if it happens at all. It's up to the government on whether or not they want to retrieve him," the chief explained. "And only after he serves his American sentence, which could be months or years."

"What if they set him free?" Carina asked, her hands trembling ever so slightly.

"Let's just hope he can't do any more harm for a while. Meanwhile, if you've already had run-ins with several of his associates, there may be more," the chief warned, his tone ominous. "How do you plan to keep your wife safe, Mr. Black?"

Loki's blood boiled at the thought of someone attempting to hurt her again. A murderous rage flooded his mind, though he kept it well-hidden.

Even if someone else has to die to end this, he thought to himself. He finished his thought out loud through clenched teeth. "I will protect her at all costs."

"Excellent!" the chief exclaimed as he took out a little notebook. "Now, the last thing we need from you is a detailed description of the other man."

"He was a little taller than Carina," Loki described. "I'm fairly certain his hair and eyes were dark. Tweed suit, no hat."

"Any unusual features?" the constable asked. "That could be anyone."

"He had a mole over his left eyebrow," Carina interjected.

Loki stared at Carina in surprise. "I didn't even know you saw him!"

She winked. "It's amazing what you can see when you're slung over someone's shoulder."

"Most helpful," the chief stated, flipping his little notebook closed. "We'll leave you to the rest of your day."

Loki showed the two men to the door. "When will you close the homicide case?"

"We'll notify you," the chief said vaguely. "Hopefully we'll catch the other man quickly and be done with the entire thing."

Loki nodded and shook their hands, then thanked them and bid them goodbye. He waved in acknowledgment when the chief called from the walkway, "See you at the wedding!"

After they were gone, Loki drew Carina into wedding plans, eager to distract her from worrying about further danger or altercations with the police.

There was still so much to do.

Loki inspected himself in front of the floor-length mirror in the guest room allocated for him to dress for the wedding. The women had kicked him out of Carina's room earlier that morning.

The Norway crowd had arrived the day before, just in time for lunch. Kvasir and Sigyn had also traveled from Paris to attend, but the absence of Baldur and Hod was a slight damper on all of the excitement. In the whirlwind of wedding activity, Loki had passed up several opportunities to tell Joseph about what had happened the night of the gala. Carina had not broached the subject either, focused as she was on last minute details. And now, just as the timing had seemed perfect, as Loki was about to speak, Joseph had been called to take his place with the bride. The staff would come for Loki shortly.

Loki sighed. It would just have to wait until after the wedding.

"What's wrong, Luke?" Kristoff asked. "Are you nervous?"

"Yes," Loki readily admitted, thankful Kristoff rarely called him Loki since servants bustled about just outside the room.

"Why?" Kristoff joked. "You already took the plunge. What's left to be nervous about?"

"Everything about today is foreign to me," Loki confessed, not caring to discuss the gala incident with Kristoff, though he knew it was inevitable. "It means so much to her."

Kristoff affectionately patted him on the shoulder. "I'll be there for you ... to make sure you don't mess it up."

Loki grinned. "Thanks a lot. Now, how do I look?"

"Carina will approve," Kristoff answered with a sly grin. "But I think you look better in black."

Loki threw a lazy punch, which Kristoff easily ducked. They both laughed but quieted instantly when they heard the soft knock on the door for which they had been waiting.

"It's time," Kristoff observed solemnly.

Loki took a deep breath, then followed Kristoff and the servant to take his place under the beautiful white arch laden with white roses, cornflowers, and edelweiss. True to Carina's wishes, candles glowed all over the great room, which had been transformed into a wonderland of flowers and shimmering white fabric. The florist and the servants, under Carina's able instruction, had truly outdone themselves.

The music began, and the guests immediately dropped their voices to an expectant hush. Kristoff winked at the beaming Kathleen as she slowly walked up the aisle in time to the music, her blue dress enhancing the color of her eyes. Loki wondered if she imagined the day she herself would walk a similar aisle as a bride rather than a bridesmaid. Kristoff nudged Loki's shoulder, reminding him to look to the closed doors of the ballroom, from where his own bride would make her entrance. Helga, also arrayed in blue, winked at Loki and stood as the doors flew open right on cue, leading the rest of the audience to their feet. For a moment, several people blocked Loki's view as they strained to see. Then Carina and Joseph stepped onto the long white fabric leading to the arch.

Loki sharply drew in his breath. Though it was their second wedding, nothing could have prepared him for how stunning she looked. The dress was perfect for her, perhaps even more so than the one she had worn at their first wedding. This time, she also wore a sheer white veil over her face and held a large bouquet of flowers at her waistline. She smiled radiantly at him and nodded in approval at his snappy, navy blue, three-piece suit. He blinked twice, feeling frozen in time. Then she was standing beside him as the guests settled into their seats. The sweet aroma of her bouquet reached his nostrils as the officiant asked Joseph to give the bride to her groom, a human tradition Loki found strange. Though he barely registered the words, he did not fail to notice the mist in Joseph's eyes or the way he clenched his jaw before he sat down beside Helga in the front row.

Carina smirked at Loki when he almost missed his cue to repeat his vows, which were longer than his Asgardian vows but similar. She repeated her own vows perfectly, never taking her sparkling brown eyes from his. They had removed their rings in favor of a second set, Midgardian in style, which they placed on each other's fingers when prompted. Loki reminded himself he still needed to find the perfect ring for her to match the one she had given him at their Asgardian wedding. He would need the signature ring he had given her that night for his plan to fake his death on Asgard.

The officiant looked out to the audience and uttered the words Loki had scoffed at when Kristoff had warned him about them. "Should anyone here present know of any reason that this couple should not be joined in holy matrimony, speak now or forever hold your peace."

To Loki's shock, a tall, dark-haired man stood to his feet and cleared his throat.

"Gunter!" Carina exclaimed.

"Apologies, but I couldn't help but notice ... it appears you have the wrong groom," Gunter observed.

"I can assure you, she does not!" Loki growled, noting the man's resemblance to Klaus.

"You didn't get our message?" Carina cried in dismay.

Several titters and stifled snorts sounded throughout the audience. Klaus's cousin glanced around the room, his face stoic and unreadable. "I did not. But it appears I am the only one present who did not know."

"I am so sorry, Gunter. We left a message at your house," Carina informed him.

"I have not been home or spoken with my mother since she had not planned to attend," Gunter explained. "I am truly sorry to have interrupted, but I thought it rude to interject at any other point."

"Do you then withdraw your objection so we may continue?" the officiant pressed him.

Gunter nodded. "I do indeed. And I will also respectfully take my leave."

Loki cocked his head as he discerned the man was indeed nothing like his renegade cousin. "Mr. Mayar, it would honor us if you would stay," he invited gallantly.

Gunter bowed his acceptance, then sat back down in his seat. He was quiet for the rest of the ceremony. But as Loki and Carina mingled with their guests during the reception, Gunter cautiously approached them.

"I apologize, Mr. and Mrs. Black, for interrupting your wedding. And I thank you for inviting me to stay," the man began, his dark eyes gleaming with grave intelligence.

"Think nothing of it," Loki insisted.

"This is a fine party," Gunter continued. "I see your touch in the menu, Carina."

"Thank you," she responded graciously. "I hope you will not let what happened between your cousin and me stop you from visiting us in the future."

"My lady, I confess I don't know what happened," Gunter stated solemnly. "But I do know your reputation. And whatever reason you had for calling off the engagement, I am sure it was sound."

"You haven't heard then?" Carina asked.

"Heard what?"

"Klaus was arrested in New York for armed robbery," Carina informed him softly.

"Was he? I wish I could say I'm surprised," Gunter replied. "I thought perhaps your influence had changed him, but I suppose that was naiveté on my part."

"Had he shown tendencies toward theft and violence before?" Loki questioned him.

"When we were children, his favorite pastime was throwing rocks at birds and small animals," Gunter reminisced. "And he would brag about pilfering things from the dry goods store. He always had to be the best at everything. I never saw such a sore sport."

"I wish I had known this before I ever agreed to marry him," Carina confessed.

"I should have warned you," Gunter sighed. "But I was out of town the night he asked you. When I returned, I thought I saw a change in him and did not wish to disrupt either of your happiness. I am truly sorry."

Carina stepped close to him, then abruptly hugged him, which seemed to both shock and delight him. "Don't blame yourself," she admonished. "Sometimes, we only see what we wish to see."

Gunter pulled away quickly, then shook Loki's hand firmly. "My congratulations to you both. I am sure I will call again, but for now, I must truly take my leave."

"But we haven't served the cake," Carina protested.

"I am sorry, but my mother is expecting me," he stated with finality, then retrieved his belongings from the servant manning the coatroom.

Loki and Carina watched him leave but were soon distracted by several other guests gushing their congratulations. After several minutes, Loki gently tugged Carina away from a talkative woman with snowy white hair since the newlyweds had not yet taken the opportunity to eat.

Just then, Joseph directed them to the three-tiered wedding cake Carina had spent hours perfecting. White buttercream icing adorned with sugary decorations and a few real flowers hid which layers were which flavor. Loki smiled to himself, remembering how he had stolen a fingerful from each bowl of batter, eliciting several protests from his wife. It seemed a shame to cut into the culinary masterpiece now, but he knew she would want to know which flavor was his favorite.

A photographer set up his camera and snapped several pictures of different angles as Loki placed his hand over

Carina's to make the first cut. As instructed, he placed a small piece of the yellow cake in her mouth as she did the same for him.

He savored the flavor thoughtfully, which did indeed taste like buttery vanilla, just as Carina had described. He whispered, "Not bad."

"Would you like another bite?" she whispered back.

When he nodded, she shoved another piece into his face and smeared it around, laughing as she did so. A flash of light flared in their eyes as the photographer captured the moment on film.

Kristoff cupped his hands over his mouth and yelled, "Get her back!"

Loki grabbed a fistful of cake and smeared it on Carina's face as she shrieked, "Not on my dress!"

Amidst the roaring laughter of the guests, Loki wiped off some of the cake and kissed her soundly, which brought several hoots and hollers. She used the opportunity to smash just a little more cake on top of his head, delighting the audience even more.

Once they both had cleaned up in separate washrooms, they came back together for the last of the events, still having not eaten.

Carina tossed her bouquet to all the single women present, who jumped and pushed each other out of the way to catch it. A teenage girl snatched it out of the air just before Kathleen's attempt to grab it. The other women groaned in disappointment but congratulated her and teased her about being the next bride while Kathleen just shared a secret smile with Kristoff.

Then the single men lined up with raucous smiles for the garter toss, which Loki had never heard of until Kristoff had told him about it.

"Why are we doing this?" Loki whispered to Carina.

"People used to think it good luck to have a piece of the bride's dress, so the guests would accost her and rip her gown to shreds to get a piece," Carina informed him as she sat down in the chair allocated for her. "Both these traditions came from trying to avoid that. You saw how the women went after the bouquet. Imagine if they came after me that way!"

"Barbaric," Loki grunted.

"More barbaric than tying a groom to a tree?" she teased him.

Loki chuckled, then knelt in front of her. He could feel the heat in his face and the tips of his ears. He slid his hands under Carina's dress to find her garter as the men heckled and catcalled. Thankfully, she had placed it close to her knee, making it easy for him to locate. He gently pulled it off, then flipped the lacey thing over his shoulder. He could hear the mad scramble before he even turned.

Kristoff held it up with a surprised look on his face. "I wasn't even trying! It practically landed on my hand."

The rest of the men jostled him and laughed uproariously as Kristoff exchanged another secret smile with Kathleen. The two seemed to be attempting to move toward each other, but Loki lost sight of them as several guests approached to say their goodbyes.

With perfect poise, Carina thanked each guest for coming. Kvasir and Sigyn were the last guests to leave.

"I wish we could stay longer," Kvasir declared, "but we have a train to catch."

"And a house to finish," Sigyn added. "You'll come visit us in Norway, won't you?"

Carina nodded, hugging them both briefly. Kvasir clapped Loki's shoulder and nodded just once in a silent message of respect, then led his own bride through the doors and out into the lovely Stuttgart afternoon.

Carina turned to Loki wearily. He suddenly noticed how pale she was.

"You need to eat, my star," Loki directed.

He beckoned to one of the staff members cleaning up and instructed him to bring them each a plate of food and some cake. Carina sank into a chair at one of the abandoned tables.

Joseph rushed over. "Carina, what's wrong?"

"I'm fine, Father," she yawned. "I just need food. And a nap."

Joseph hesitated, scrutinizing her carefully, but finally turned to Helga. "Would you care to take an afternoon stroll with me? We'll take a late supper tonight."

She nodded, then took Joseph's arm. Kristoff and Kathleen quickly followed suit, leaving the newlyweds alone in the great hall amidst the busyness of clean-up. The servant returned with two plates of wedding food and several slices of cake.

As they ate, Loki tentatively admitted, "I still haven't told your father about the gala. And I noticed you haven't either."

"I've been so distracted, Luke, I hadn't thought about it much," Carina said between bites.

"Maybe we don't need to tell him," Loki suggested.

"Maybe not," Carina mumbled. "We haven't had any trouble, so maybe the danger has passed. But he won't be happy if he hears about it from someone else."

"Wouldn't the chief or constable have said something today if they planned to?" Loki asked.

"Oh no, that would hardly be an appropriate subject at a wedding. But it's bound to come up sooner or later."

Loki finished his food, then dug enthusiastically into one of the slices of cake, eager to find out if the other two flavors were as tasty as the gold cake.

"Better than Asgardian fruitcake?" Carina teased. She had also finished her food, then helped herself to a bite of the silver cake Loki had just sampled. "I hope you're willing to share."

"This is nothing like Asgardian cake," Loki agreed. "Better hurry if you want more. I'm about to eat the whole thing."

Carina held up a forkful of the dark brown cake. "Try the chocolate one first."

Loki ate the offered confection. His eyes lit up as his taste buds seemed to dance with delight. "That one is the best yet!"

"I knew you'd think so," Carina laughed. "Why don't you eat the chocolate and leave the silver for me? That one's my favorite."

Loki did not answer. He was already digging into the rich, decadent dessert. He finished it before she had taken two bites of hers. He reached for the last slice, which was gold cake, but she put her hand over his to stop him.

"Whatever will we do about this sweet tooth of yours?" she demanded, her voice rich with laughter as she tried to keep the cake away from him. "You'll make yourself sick!"

"Not likely," Loki snorted. He succeeded in getting the cake away from her and wolfed it down almost in one bite. "And now that I've satisfied my sweet tooth, how about that nap you wanted?"

But before they could retire upstairs, Joseph Green suddenly burst into the room, followed by Helga, Chief Werner, and Constable Weber.

"Is there something you forgot to tell me, Lukas?" Joseph demanded through clenched teeth. "Maybe the little incident when my daughter was *kidnapped*?"

Loki quickly rose to his feet, immediately on the defensive and unsure of what to expect. On instinct, he guarded Carina with his body.

"Joseph, please control your temper!" Helga begged him.

"I'm sorry, Mr. Black," Chief Werner interjected. "I assumed you would have told him by now."

"As well you should have," Joseph thundered. "There's no reasonable explanation for keeping something like this from me! And that goes for you, too, old friend!"

"Joseph, I understand you're upset, but there's no need to start pointing fingers," the chief admonished sternly. "I assumed your son-in-law had already told you. And it's not exactly something one brings up at a wedding."

"He *should* have told me!" Joseph growled. "*You* should have. Or even my own daughter. Someone should have!"

"You're right, Joseph," Loki interjected. "It was my responsibility. I should have told you."

Joseph raised an eyebrow at Loki, clearly having expected a battle, at least in words. The humility in Loki's answer quenched Joseph's anger, though his eyes still smoldered at his son-in-law as he stated, "Well, now is your chance."

Kathleen and Kristoff entered the room at that moment but stopped short at the palpable tension.

"What's going on?" Kristoff asked warily.

Loki quickly summed up what had happened at the gala, adjusting the retelling where needed so as not to compromise his cover.

"How could you have let this happen, Lukas?" Joseph sighed, though his tone was more reasonable. "You said you would protect her!"

"And I did," Loki snapped, his own temper rising again as he gestured to his wife. "Look at her! She's just fine."

Carina sat slumped in her chair at the table, warily watching the scene unfold. Loki glanced at her again, feeling uneasy at the slight pallor of her cheeks.

"Fine? She doesn't look fine," Joseph snorted. "I want my physician here within the hour to examine her!"

"Father, please, no!" Carina blurted out. "I recovered from the incident days ago. It's the wedding that has me so exhausted. As beautiful as it was, I'm glad it's over."

"Do you realize you could have been arrested, Lukas?" Joseph persisted. "Where would that have left her?"

"There was never any real danger of that, Joseph," the chief interjected. "We'd already ruled out probable cause. Oh, that reminds me, Mr. Black—"

"Luke or Lukas is just fine," Loki interrupted.

"Lukas, then," the chief acknowledged. "You'll be glad to know the autopsy confirmed he died by his own hand. And thanks to my wife, that's all the papers will print. You'll get an official letter stating the case has been closed soon."

Kristoff spoke up, "Was the dead guy the sniper who shot me?"

Loki shook his head as Joseph exclaimed, "Someone shot you?"

"Yes, in Norway, a few weeks ago," Kristoff confirmed non-chalantly. "Just a little deeper than a shoulder graze, really. What about the guy Carina knocked out at the house?"

"What?" Joseph blustered.

"I think he was the one who got away this time, but as surprising as it sounds, I didn't get a good enough look at him in Norway to be completely sure," Carina answered.

"You didn't notice if he had the mole over the left eyebrow?" the chief interjected.

"Honestly, I have no idea why that stood out to me the night of the gala," Carina admitted. "I can't remember if the man in Norway had it or not. He was dark-haired and dark-eyed though."

"What else have the two of you not told me?" Joseph asked irately.

"Joseph, relax," Helga soothed. "Luke paid off the first hired gun to put an end to all this. Now we know that didn't work, so we'd better be on our guard."

"You knew about this?" Joseph asked her, the expression on his face pained.

"I only knew about what happened in Norway, but it wasn't my story to tell or my place to tell it," Helga admitted quietly.

"Well, someone had better tell me exactly what happened in Norway," Joseph demanded.

After Loki summed everything up for him, Chief Werner exchanged another look with Joseph and asked, "Did the second man ransack Kristoff's study?"

"No," Kristoff answered. "Everything was just as I left it."

Joseph groaned. "They tapped your phone. That's how they knew Loki and Carina were in Stuttgart."

"One of the goons was watching the house here. Maybe they just followed them after they arrived," Kristoff objected.

"Maybe," Joseph grunted. "But I'm checking my own phone, just in case."

"So we possibly have four men out there to worry about now?" Kristoff asked.

"Where do you get four?" Kathleen interjected. "The guy who shot you said there were only three."

Kristoff held up his fingers, ticking them off as he counted, "The guy who shot me, the other two he mentioned, and the guy who got away this last time. Four."

"The dead man is probably one of the original three, the associate in Germany, perhaps," Loki guessed. "And Carina thinks his accomplice was the other one in Norway, remember?"

"But we don't really know," Kristoff pointed out.

"I'm afraid there's more," the chief spoke up. "That's what we came to tell you all when we ran into Joseph outside, but we never actually got that far. A message was waiting for me when I got back to the station after the wedding."

"That's right. You did mention you had word on one of Carina's kidnappers. I apologize for my outburst. Please fill us in," Joseph requested.

"Well, we had put out an all-points bulletin in surrounding countries for the man who escaped. Someone matching his description was spotted boarding the RMS *Berengaria* in Southampton."

"Does that mean he's headed for America?" Loki whispered to Carina.

"I'm surprised a man of your extensive reading even has to ask, but yes," she whispered back playfully.

"I haven't exactly studied all the shipping routes," Loki growled under his breath.

"We've sent word to New York. Hopefully, they'll apprehend him there for questioning," the chief said. "But you know how it is, Joseph. We're operating with our hands tied behind our backs."

"So he's jumped the country," Kristoff observed, not caring he had just stated the obvious.

"There might be a reason he went west," the constable suggested ominously.

"The warrant for his arrest?" Kristoff guessed sarcastically.

"That would be a better story. But no, hiding in Europe or even Asia would have been less of a risk," the chief said. "Especially since he must know he missed his mark."

"Enough with the riddles," Joseph barked. "Speak plainly, Franz!"

"Quite honestly, Joseph, he could just be an American taking refuge in his own country," the chief said hesitantly.

"But you don't think so," Loki stated.

"No, Mr. Black, I don't. And neither does the constable. Why wouldn't he have hid somewhere, then attempted to finish the job? We believe he has been summoned back to New York, which would mean he has a way to communicate with Klaus Mayar. Perhaps they plan to regroup after this last failure."

"Doesn't anyone else think this is all a little over-the-top?" Kristoff asked.

"He did say he would kill me if I stole his woman," Loki remarked dryly. "But you're right, Kristoff. This does seem a bit much."

Joseph and Chief Werner exchanged a quick, almost imperceptible look. Loki immediately sensed they were keeping something from the rest of the group, but he had the prudence not to force the issue.

"Well, regardless, I would imagine this changes your travel plans," Joseph said matter-of-factly to Loki and Carina.

"Why would it?" Loki asked, narrowing his eyes.

"I'm with Luke," Kristoff quipped.

"I don't think this American tour is such a good idea with all of this danger," Joseph insisted.

"Father, I refuse to live my life in hiding," Carina protested, though she lacked her usual feistiness. "We could stay locked up here for years and have nothing happen. Or we could walk out the door tomorrow and get hit by a truck."

"That actually supports my position, Carina," Joseph said dryly.

"You would rather I die of boredom?" she shot right back.

"Are you suggesting throwing caution to the wind, knowing there are still hoodlums out there who could harm you, one who is headed for New York as we speak?" Joseph cried.

Loki spoke up again. "Considering the thugs did nothing until they were able to get Carina alone—"

"Don't even get me started on the fact that you let her walk off by herself," Joseph interrupted.

"She's a grown woman," Loki retorted. "Should I follow her into the bathroom as well? This discourse is not helpful. I'm trying to say the tour might be the very way to end all of this."

"How so?" Joseph demanded.

"I don't relish the idea of living in hiding either. If we continue with the tour, they're likely to think we've let our guard down. It might force their hand or cause them to make a mistake," Loki explained. "Maybe we could draw them out. There will be too many people around to present any real danger."

"That's actually not a bad idea," interjected the constable.

"What about snipers?" Joseph asked pointedly.

"If they had wanted to kill us, we would already be dead," Loki declared.

Kristoff nodded his agreement.

Kathleen interjected, "If it's any comfort, Mr. Green, New York is only a small part of the tour."

"Where else do you plan to perform?" inquired the chief. "And when do you plan to release this information to the public?"

"Boston, Philadelphia, Washington DC, Richmond, Charleston ..." Kristoff answered, then looked to Kathleen as if unsure of the rest.

She finished for him, "New Orleans, Memphis, St. Louis, Chicago, and Cincinnati. Each city is already advertising and selling tickets, so the word is out."

Loki's eyes widened at the prospect of seeing all those places with Carina, even more delighted when she perked up at the mention of several of the cities.

"You've laid out a breadcrumb trail!" the constable exclaimed. "Why, they could lie in wait for you at any city they choose!"

"Which is why they'll think we don't expect an attack," Loki informed him. "If we make it easy enough, I doubt they'll wait long to strike. And we'll be ready."

"This is either madness or genius!" the constable muttered.

Joseph quietly contemplated this information. Loki did

not miss the silent question Carina's father sent Chief Werner or the chief's responding nod.

"I see the wisdom in your plan, Lukas," Joseph relented. "But who exactly is traveling this tour?"

"Luke, Carina, Kat, and myself," Kristoff answered.

"Actually, Kris," interjected Kathleen, "I thought I would return to Chicago after the New York shows, then join back up with you there for the rest of the tour. I've been away far longer than I intended."

"Now, wait just a minute, Kat," Kristoff protested. "When were you planning to tell me this?"

"I just did."

Loki grinned to himself over the irony that Kathleen used the exact same words Kristoff had less than two weeks ago, when Loki and Helga had challenged him about not telling them about their engagement. Despite the storm simmering between the two, it was one more confirmation they were perfect for each other.

"Kathleen, I'm not okay with this!" Kristoff retorted. "It's too much of a risk."

Loki's eyes widened as he registered how upset Kristoff must be. He had not called her by her full name since the night they met.

"Oh please, Kristoff," Kathleen scoffed, resorting to his full name as well. "I've been on my own for years, reporting in some very dangerous places. I can handle myself."

"I know, but—"

"And no one involved in this even knows I exist, right?" she continued. "No one bothered us in Norway all this time. Besides, if they're after you three, I'll be safer in Chicago, won't I?"

"I suppose," Kristoff grumbled. "But I still don't like it."

"All this risk!" Joseph interjected. "We don't know who or what they know. I don't think anyone should go off alone. Including you, Helga."

"Oh, Joseph, I'll be just fine in my house, doing what I've always done," Helga insisted.

"Absolutely not," Joseph growled. "What if that first hoodlum is still in play, laying low in Norway, waiting to strike? No one knows what happened to him."

"Joseph has a valid point, Helga," Kristoff declared. "You can't go back right now. Not alone."

"Well, just where am I supposed to go then?" Helga huffed. "You have business in New York, Joseph. And I'm certainly not gallivanting around America on this tour! Who will take care of my garden?"

"I could send a few servants up there so you could come with me to New York," Joseph suggested softly.

"That would hardly be appropriate," Helga answered a little too quickly.

"And why is that?" Joseph asked innocently, causing Helga to blush deeply.

"You know why," she murmured, her blue eyes down as if something of great interest were on the floor.

"Nonsense," Joseph retorted. "The New York house is fully staffed and large enough for several house guests. There will be no appearance of anything scandalous. Besides, didn't this Baldur character you told me about stay at your house after the first wedding? And I've been staying there as well. That hasn't bothered you."

"That's not what I meant, Joseph. Do we have to discuss this in present company?" Helga pleaded.

The other two couples and the policemen all exchanged uncomfortable looks. Loki wondered what was bothering Helga. And why did Joseph look so confused? She seemed to think he should know what she was not disclosing.

"Helga, please consider going with us," Loki prodded. "You could help the plan work if it looks like we've all fled Europe and believe we're safe in America. And Kristoff, Kathleen's return to Chicago could make our play more convincing."

Kristoff shot Loki a skeptical look but remained silent.

"Well, then," Joseph announced, "it appears Helga and I need to finish our walk."

Helga's face brightened considerably as she took Joseph's proffered arm.

Carina's father turned to Chief Werner. "Are we still on for lunch tomorrow?"

"Yes, indeed," the chief replied with a grin. Then he gestured toward the constable as he suggested, "Joseph, I would feel a lot better about all of this if you would reconsider letting Hans stand guard here overnight."

Loki stared in surprise at Joseph, wondering why he would turn down the offer of an armed guard when he so often coddled his daughter.

"It's not necessary, Franz," Joseph insisted. "We have plenty of capable men here to protect the women. The constable's time would be better served on the investigation."

"Very well. We'll see ourselves out," the chief replied.

Joseph and Helga meandered off in the direction of the rose garden. Carina strained her neck as if trying to see the older couple through one of the windows overlooking the atrium.

"Well, I have no problem bringing up what no one seems to want to talk about," Kristoff quipped. "Anyone have any idea what's bothering Helga?"

"She's your sister," Loki returned. "I figured you might know."

"All I know is she seems very self-conscious about her relationship with Joseph," Kristoff observed. "She didn't want to miss the wedding, but she was nervous about coming here. I heard her say something to a neighbor about how people talk."

Loki frowned, remembering the hurt on Helga's face when she told him about her former employer's harsh words about her station compared with Joseph's.

Does she not realize her own worth? he asked himself.

Carina chimed in softly, "It could be because the last woman who lived there, besides me, was my mother."

An awkward silence fell over the great room.

Kathleen finally broke the tension. "Kris, weren't you going to show me around town?"

"Right," he muttered. "Well then, we'll see you at that late supper Joseph mentioned."

After they had gone, Loki lifted Carina into his arms and carried her upstairs. "Are you alright, my star?"

"Just tired," she answered. "I'm glad we'll have some peace and quiet, even if it's only for a little while."

Loki helped her change out of her wedding dress, then settled next to her on the large bed. The black kitten curled up in his usual spot by Carina's abdomen, his purring somewhat raspy. Expecting a quiet, lazy afternoon, Loki allowed his mind to wander, wondering what it would be like to visit the American cities Kathleen and Kristoff had mentioned. They had a week to finalize the rest of the details before they would embark on Loki's first trip across the Atlantic on the famed and newly refitted RMS *Mauretania*. Though Kristoff had given him a brochure, Loki found Carina's description of the vessel and its history more interesting.

Still unable to rest, he got up quietly so as not to disturb his wife or the cat. He perused the stack of books near Carina's armchair. The title, *Anna Karenina*, jumped out at him from the spine of an unusually thick book.

Ah, Tolstoy, Loki thought as he picked up the novel. *War and Peace was exceptionally good. Let's see how this one compares.*

Before long, he was completely immersed in Russian society and culture, captivated by the characters and the intricate weaving of their lives in the deeply engaging but tragic tale.

25

"I just finished *Anna Karenina*," Loki told Carina.

The morning had dawned with a bright and beautiful sunrise, but Loki's heart was still heavy with the weight of the magnificent novel.

"I didn't even know you were reading it. When did you have time for that?" Carina asked curiously.

"I started it during your nap yesterday," Loki confessed.

"You read eight hundred pages that quickly?" Carina gasped.

"What can I say? I read fast. And I didn't sleep. I would have finished it sooner, but I reread a few parts to really absorb it all."

"I take it you enjoyed it then," Carina observed, as she sat at her vanity and brushed her long red hair.

He stood behind her, watching her until she met his gaze in the mirror. He wanted her to know it had affected him deeply but was not sure he was ready to tell her he had actually been brought to tears. Several times.

At the look on his face, she spun herself around on her cushioned stool, giving him her undivided attention. "What's wrong?"

"No other book has ever affected me like this. Not here, and certainly not on Asgard. Not even *War and Peace*, though that came close."

"Affected you how?"

"It's hard to put into words. I both hated and loved how it forced me to think deeply about certain things."

"I can understand that. Some say it was the greatest work of literary fiction ever written," Carina remarked. "It's even been made into a film in America. Betty Nansen starred in it."

"Who?"

"She's a Danish actress, quite talented."

"Oh. Well, I've never seen a film, so I wouldn't know," Loki declared.

"No? I've seen a few. Maybe we'll have time for one between tour stops. But what didn't you like about the book?"

"I can't say it was a matter of not liking anything. It was just … so painfully real," Loki explained. "It certainly wasn't a happy ending for most of the characters."

"I've always appreciated the raw beauty of life that Tolstoy captured," Carina mused. "Happy endings aren't real, you know. In life, what really ends? I don't think death itself is even an end but a doorway to another chapter."

"Really?"

"I just think the soul is far too complex to simply cease to exist."

"In my culture, we teach that souls travel to Valhalla or Hel after death," Loki declared. "I've always secretly doubted the existence of such places." Uncomfortable with the side topic, he forced a chuckle and asked, "Do you dislike happy endings?"

"I don't mind them in most stories," she replied as she walked to her wardrobe to choose a dress. "But think about it. If something were to end, would that be a happy thing? It's a bit of a paradox, really."

A rush of emotion suddenly hit Loki like an avalanche. He grabbed Carina's arm as she passed him again and spun her around to face him, causing her to drop the dress she had chosen. Before she could scold him or pick it up, he crushed her body against his in a fierce hug.

"You're my everything! Do you know that?" he whispered against her hair.

"Loki, what's gotten into you?" she gasped.

"Just promise me you will never forget or doubt my love," he pleaded.

"I promise," she responded softly. "But maybe no more late-night reading for you, my dear husband."

Loki chuckled, releasing her so she could finish getting ready for the day. He was a little embarrassed he had reacted so strongly but was thankful Carina seemed to understand. He still did not want to share his deepest fears with her. What if another man drew her eye like Vronsky had tempted Anna? Her husband, Karenin, had seemed oblivious to his wife's unhappiness until it hit him squarely in the face, in all its devastation and ugliness. Could Carina grow unhappy with him, disillusioned by the ever-moving currents of life? Or might he himself stray from her after years of marriage, as had Oblonsky from Dolly, and doom Carina to misery, poverty, and humiliation? No, he could not think this way. He shook his head to free himself from dreary thoughts, assuring himself he shared a deep bond with his wife, beyond jealousy or betrayal. And there was no sense in borrowing trouble or worrying over things likely to never happen. It was just a story, after all. And yet, the struggle Levin had experienced over his faith had also been deeply compelling. He definitely needed to ponder that more.

"Loki, come here," Carina called softly. She stood at the window, fully dressed and looking out through the floor-length, cream-colored curtains.

He joined her at the window. She pointed to the oak tree reaching proudly into the sky just outside. Loki's sharp eyes could make out the shapes of several domed bird nests tucked neatly into a large hollow, as well as several more attached to a few branches. Small grayish-brown birds flew in and out, depositing fat insects or berries into the open beaks of red-throated baby birds. He noticed one adult bird with black markings sitting quite still in one nest, watching the flurry of activity centered around the little bird community. Another bird, plain and slightly larger, soon relieved the jaunty little fellow. Loki caught a glimpse of a few speckled eggs before the second bird, which he guessed was the mother, settled into the nest.

"Looks like that couple got off to a late start," Loki observed, watching as the male flew off to get his own breakfast.

"See how they share the load, both male and female? Most people consider house sparrows to be pests, but I love to watch them," Carina sighed happily. "They're one of the species of birds that mate for life."

"Oh really?" Loki feigned casual interest, wondering why she was explaining the habits of these rather plain birds. When she first pointed them out, he thought perhaps she changed the subject because he had made her feel uncomfortable. But after that last comment, he wondered if she had figured out what was really bothering him.

"They mate for life, Loki," Carina repeated, turning to him with a smile that shined light into his soul and dispelled any darkness there. "Other couples might wander away from each other, but we will not. We are like the sparrows."

Loki blinked away the hot tears pricking his eyes and wrapped his arms around his wife as together they watched the sparrows tend to their young. How had he found such a gem, such an incredible woman of empathy and insight? He had never before prayed, never believed in any higher power than himself. But in that tender moment, he sent silent gratitude to the heavens, in case someone might be watching and listening, as Tolstoy had seemed to believe. A strange peace filled his heart, making him want to stretch a minute into a thousand.

Carina's voice broke the spell. "We should probably join the others for breakfast."

"Must we?" Loki murmured.

"We said we would," Carina reminded him as she pouted playfully and pulled him toward the door. "Besides, I'm hungry!"

When they reached the large dining room, Kristoff sat alone at the long table, staring at his hands.

"Where is everyone?" Carina asked.

"No idea," Kristoff muttered glumly, not bothering to look up.

"What's wrong?" Carina pressed him. "Where's Kathleen?"

Loki grimaced. He knew the despondent look on Kristoff's face all too well and guessed the two had quarreled.

"She went for a walk in the rose garden," he stated flatly.

Carina looked about to speak, but Loki suggested, "Why don't you go keep her company, Carina?"

She caught his meaningful look, nodded, and hurried toward the atrium.

Loki sat down beside his gloomy friend. "Want to talk about it?"

"What for?" Kristoff grunted. "I don't think things are working out between us, so why bother?"

"Guess that's it then," Loki remarked dryly, knowing full well he would get further with a cavalier attitude than by pushing Kristoff into revealing anything.

"How am I supposed to protect her when she won't let me?" Kristoff suddenly spouted. "All I wanted was to keep her safe. And what do I get in return?"

Loki waited for him to answer himself.

Kristoff threw his hands into the air as he stood and paced around the table. "I get accused of acting like an old, banty rooster and interfering with her career!"

Loki suppressed a grin. "Wow, she has a sharp tongue."

"Well, I did say she's as stubborn as a mule," Kristoff admitted sheepishly, running one hand through his hair, as he often did when agitated.

"Did you really?" Loki snickered. "I don't think I'd have the nerve to say that to Carina, although it's just as true of her."

"We've got ourselves a couple of strong women, don't we?" Kristoff relaxed somewhat, his easy grin sliding across his face again. "Have you and Carina fought?"

Loki laughed. "Sure, we have. She called me a conceited high-hat once."

"Ouch! Why?"

"I snapped at her for putting trash in a priceless vase," Loki confessed. "Seems so trivial now."

Kristoff chuckled, then grew sober again. "Astrid was my most serious girlfriend, but we never quarreled. And I had no idea she was fooling around with other men until she left me."

"I don't think that relationship was very healthy. If you never argued, then someone was getting stifled," Loki pointed out.

"Yeah, me," Kristoff agreed, slumping into the chair nearest him. "I think I'd rather be stifled than feel like this."

"I don't think you really mean that. Settling your differences can be very rewarding, you know," Loki informed him.

"He's right," Helga announced as she swept into the room with Joseph close behind her.

"You two really enjoy eavesdropping, don't you?" Loki teased them.

"We didn't hear much," Helga laughed. "But having been married for a number of years, I can easily predict this won't be your last quarrel. Wouldn't you agree, Joseph?"

Carina's father grinned unexpectedly. "Oh, sure! Once, when Carina's mother was pregnant with her, she got so angry with me, she threw a pan of dirty dishwater at me."

Kristoff raised his eyebrows in surprised amusement. "What did you do?"

"Absolutely nothing! I just stood there sputtering and gasping, soaking wet and utterly shocked. She laughed so hard, I thought she would deliver the baby right there." Joseph's eyes misted over suddenly. "I don't even remember what we were fighting about. You just never know which moments might be the last ones."

Helga squeezed his arm gently, as if to communicate she understood what it was to grieve. Joseph placed his hand over hers and smiled warmly at her. Loki witnessed the silent exchange with delight, encouraged by the reminder of the tenderness Joseph hid under his rough exterior.

Kristoff stood abruptly. "I'm going to go get my girl."

He strode out of the dining room as the servants bustled in to serve breakfast. Carina joined them a few minutes later.

"How'd it go with you?" Loki asked quietly.

"I found her sitting on the bench, crying," Carina answered.

"Kathleen was *crying*?" Loki repeated in surprise.

"She might be tough as nails, but she's still a woman," Carina pointed out. "She was embarrassed I caught her like that, but she did tell me they argued again about her going back to Chicago alone, so I tried to help her see it from Kristoff's perspective. She was about to go back inside to apologize when Kristoff came out."

"They'll just have to figure it out," Helga commented. "With the nature of both their careers, they are bound to have different conflicts than the two of you will."

"I don't envy them," Joseph added. "Relationships are hard enough without all the distance and conflicting schedules. They're wise not to get married right away."

At that, he looked pointedly at his son-in-law, much to Loki's annoyance. He stuffed down his irritation, but Carina had also noted Joseph's unspoken judgment.

"Father, how can you be so wise and yet so blind?" she huffed. "Every couple is different. Luke and I almost lost each other a few times, and we didn't want it to happen again, especially permanently. Perhaps we didn't do everything perfectly, but our commitment to each other will see us through the tough times."

"I'm glad you realize more is needed than just love," Joseph acceded, glancing over at Helga. "I do believe you're right. Commitment will see you through."

Loki had a strong sense Joseph was no longer speaking to his daughter, especially when Helga looked away from Joseph's intense gaze. Carina raised an eyebrow and frowned slightly. But when she began eating her breakfast, everyone else followed suit. The dining room grew uncomfortably quiet. Finally, Kristoff and Kathleen reentered, hand-in-hand, their cheery manner lightening the aura in the room. Conversation turned to plans for the day, but the doorbell interrupted them before they could discuss anything at length.

"Now, who could that be?" Joseph asked everyone and no one.

The butler appeared. "My apologies, sir, but the chief of police is here. He says it's urgent."

"Show him to my study. I'll be there shortly," Joseph instructed, wiping his mouth and rising to his feet.

"This concerns all of you," the chief spoke up as he entered the dining room, having followed the butler.

"Sir, allow me to show you to the study," the butler protested.

"No, it's alright. Thank you, Charles," Joseph said, dismissing the disgruntled butler with a wave of his hand. "What is it, Franz? This couldn't wait until our lunch appointment?"

"There was a jailbreak in New York three days ago," the chief stated grimly. "Klaus has escaped."

"What?" Joseph thundered, his face ashen.

Carina clutched Loki's arm fearfully but remained silent. Helga and Kathleen also paled noticeably. Kristoff exchanged a worried glance with Loki as the chief continued.

"The New York police cabled the news yesterday in response to our message about our mystery man headed their way," the chief explained gravely. "I wasn't informed until this morning. Heads are already rolling at the station over the delay."

"Is that why there's no constable today?" Loki asked.

"No, he had a family emergency," the chief responded distractedly. "And this couldn't wait. Four of the five men were recovered, but they're not talking. The police there think Klaus left New York and either headed west or back here."

"But they don't know," Kathleen insisted. "Even if he were headed this way, he couldn't possibly arrive for another two or three days."

"Kathleen is right! This is no time for any of us to panic," Joseph declared, but the color did not return to his face.

The doors burst open and Gunter Mayar rushed past the butler, who was trying to prevent him from entering.

"Someone should tell *him* that," Kristoff said dryly, but everyone ignored him.

"My utmost apologies, sir!" the butler cried. "I told him to wait in the foyer."

"It's fine, Charles," Joseph assured him. Then he addressed Klaus's cousin, who was hurriedly composing himself. "You've never been one for rudeness, Gunter. What's the meaning of this?"

"Good morning, Joseph, ladies, gentlemen … I do apologize." Gunter bowed, his tone polite but strained. "Ah, Chief, you're here as well. Then, you must already know the news."

"Good morning, Gunter," the chief replied as everyone else nodded in response. "You've heard from your cousin, I take it?"

"Yes, just this morning. These were delivered to my office," Gunter explained, holding up four yellow Western Union envelopes. "I only read the one addressed to me."

The chief impatiently gestured for Gunter to hand him the telegrams. Once he had done so, the chief looked over the envelopes. "One is addressed to Lukas Black and the other two to Joseph and Carina Green."

The policeman handed each of the addressees their own envelope. He quickly scanned Gunter's telegram. "It says 'Free at last STOP Will return to claim what is mine,' signed Klaus Mayar. Not much here. It could be a smoke screen to make us think he's coming to Germany. Surely he would not be foolish enough to announce his real intentions."

"That may be, but I am certain Carina is in danger," Gunter urged. "I know him. He'll stop at nothing."

"So … is now a good time to panic?" Kristoff interjected, ducking slightly when Kathleen punched his arm.

Gunter only glanced at him before continuing, "I do not know why he sent these all to my office."

"More than likely, the thug contacted Klaus before he left the country and told him you're all in Stuttgart," remarked the chief.

"But he knows Joseph's address," countered Gunter. "Why not send them here?"

"Probably because he knew he could trust you to deliver them," the chief suggested. He winked at Joseph. "Unlike you, old friend. Now, let's hear the other telegrams."

"Mine doesn't make any sense, just that it's some sort of threat," Carina pondered aloud, peering at her telegram again.

"I think I got the wrong one," Loki agreed. "Joseph, does yours seem right?"

"Yes, though it doesn't tell me anything I don't already know," Joseph answered.

"I'd certainly like to hear them," the chief prompted, as if he were patiently dealing with small children.

"I'll go first," Loki offered. He read, "Will win your love despite everything STOP You belong with me." He paused, gritting his teeth at the possessive words. "I think this was meant for Carina."

The chief nodded. "Sounds like it. Carina, what does yours say?"

She read aloud, "Framing me fatal error STOP Prepare to lose everything."

The chief looked at Joseph, who cleared his throat and said, "That one's mine, which means this one was meant for you, Lukas."

Carina and Loki exchanged glances at the cryptic message meant for Joseph, but Loki took the telegram Joseph held out to him as Carina handed hers to her father.

Loki quickly and silently read the message. His heart rate quickened, and his mouth went dry.

"Well?" Carina demanded. "Don't leave the rest of us hanging!"

Loki sighed. He did not want to reveal what was on the paper but knew withholding the information would be worse for him at this point. He read, "We know who you are STOP Will end your charade."

Carina gasped. Kristoff and Helga stared at Loki with concern.

But Loki fixed Joseph with his gaze and challenged, "Clearly, this applies to you as well."

"It could have," Joseph answered, his sly grin indicating he was pleased with some past cleverness.

Before Loki could question him further, Kathleen blurted out, "How could someone so dangerous mix up the messages that way? Did he hire some goon to send the telegrams for him after he left the States, perhaps to throw us off the trail?"

"That would be my conclusion," Gunter answered. "My cousin doesn't make those kinds of mistakes."

"It would seem logical," the chief mused, stroking his dark mustache with his thumb and forefinger. "But no, this was a more devious gambit, carefully laid by a worthy opponent."

"Worthy?" Joseph scoffed. "Hardly!"

"I warned you not to underestimate him, Joseph," the chief scolded. "And now, here we are."

"Bah!" Joseph growled, pacing the floor beside the dining room table.

"What does all of this mean?" Helga questioned softly.

Joseph answered, "Klaus seems to think he can win Carina back once he gets me and Lukas out of the way. And if he somehow discovered Lukas isn't who he claims to be, he must intend to expose him."

"And just who are you?" the chief asked Loki pointedly.

Loki clenched his teeth, annoyed that his tactic to deflect attention away from himself had proved completely ineffective. Everyone stared at him, waiting for his answer. The large grandfather clock ticked maddeningly, the only sound disturbing the heavy silence. It seemed to drone "out of time" over and over.

Joseph ran out of patience. "Oh, come now, Lukas, there's no shame in it! You're a prince who no longer has a country. What possible harm could exposing that do to you?"

Loki breathed a sigh of relief that he had not been forced to reveal his Asgardian identity. The few who knew him as Loki relaxed considerably. Those who did not continued to stare at him, their eyes wide with expressions of shock and admiration.

"You're a prince? That's what's different about you!" Kathleen suddenly rose from her chair, moving around the table toward Loki as if she were about to burst out of her skin with suppressed excitement. "The press loves stories like this! If you told your story first, it could actually bring you more crowds and fame. A prince turned performer, who fell in love and broke free from the shackles of—"

"Kathleen, please," Loki interrupted, holding up a hand to stem her flow of words. The last thing he needed was a journalist researching or writing about his fake heritage.

To Loki's surprise, the chief, who had been eyeing him with suspicious interest, interjected, "I appreciate your enthusiasm, Miss Jones, but approaching the papers could be disastrous indeed."

Kathleen pouted slightly, folding her arms across her chest. "And why is that?"

"You'd be playing right into his hands," the chief answered.

"How so?" Kathleen persisted.

"I imagine that is exactly what he wants you to do. If Klaus planned to go to the press himself, he wouldn't send a warning to be read by the wrong person. There's a calculated method here," the chief expounded.

"Do you mean he sent an empty threat to ensure Joseph was the first to read it, with the assumption he would go to the press about Luke when he figured it out?" Kristoff asked, rising to join Kathleen, who leaned against the walnut sideboard with her arms crossed. "Why would he think you'd do that, Joseph?"

"Because I would have, but only to make sure they printed what I wanted," Joseph admitted. "It's easier to distort than silence."

"How would that benefit Klaus?" Gunter asked.

"If Klaus's intention is to win Carina back, he might be hoping a spotlight on Luke would overshadow Carina and drive a wedge between them," Kathleen suggested.

The chief's dark eyes narrowed. "Or it's a distraction. Increased crowds could make it easier for Klaus or one of his men to grab Carina, especially if Lukas becomes distracted by his growing fame. And if he succeeds, local police might believe there were political motivations for the kidnapping, drawing the investigation away from the true culprit."

"I suppose that scenario makes sense," Kathleen conceded, though she looked unhappy about it. "But if nothing shows up in the press, surely he would assume we're on to him and report it himself. I just don't understand why he hasn't done it already!"

"It's not likely the press would take Klaus seriously if he did come forward. And I'm sure he knows that," the chief stated.

Loki watched the chief carefully. Why had the policeman protected him from Kathleen's prying? The chief winked subtly at him and jutted his chin toward Kathleen, who still looked as if she would press the issue. Loki decided to add another compelling reason to keep her from any investigative journalism where he was concerned.

"I agree. We can't go to the press. I left my homeland and my title for a reason, but I do have a vested interest in protecting my people," Loki informed her. "We have remained hidden from the world for centuries and prefer to keep it that way."

"But—" Kathleen started.

Loki cut her off before she could object any further. "To dredge up the whole story could cause serious problems for my country politically. Then Carina might be in further danger if my countrymen or enemies found out about her."

"You said you'd been there, Carina, to this mystery country," Joseph pointed out somewhat accusingly.

"I have! But I wasn't there long, and Luke kept me hidden," Carina replied.

"And you said you renounced your title," Joseph griped at Loki.

"Personally, not publicly. My father wouldn't have accepted my abdication. Very soon, they will all be led to believe I am dead," Loki declared. "Otherwise, they might find me here in the outside world and force me to return. And they could abuse my attachment to Carina to do so."

"Why haven't they done so already?" Joseph demanded, red mottling his face.

Loki deduced his father-in-law was close to losing his temper, no doubt at the implied danger to Carina caused by Loki's actions.

"In my culture, we have a period of time when a man goes off on his own, into the wilderness, to prove he is a man. I used it as a chance to escape a life I no longer want," Loki explained, delighting in the convenience these half-truths lent him and the obvious fascination of everyone in the room who did not already know the full truth. "Once they believe I was killed during my time in the wilderness, they will mourn and move on. I'll be free to pursue my own way, and Carina won't be in danger anymore." When Joseph relaxed, Loki continued, "That being said, can we all agree that no one is going to the press? And no more questions?"

Everyone in the room agreed readily, even Joseph. But Kathleen narrowed her eyes at Loki. He saw the questions there and knew how hard it was for her to resist her curiosity and her training.

But she finally nodded in retreat, her disappointment evident on her face. "I surrender, though I might use your story as inspiration for a novel someday, Mr. Black, with fictional names, of course."

Loki grinned. He knew she was somewhat angry with him since she had switched back to addressing him formally. "I just might allow that, Miss Jones."

She relaxed and smiled back at him, then addressed the chief. "Do you suppose a member of the press traveling with the performers might persuade this scallywag that a story is forthcoming?"

"Yes, I think it might," the chief replied with a grin and a wink in Kristoff's direction.

"You mean it?" Kristoff exclaimed, grabbing Kathleen around the waist and lifting her into the air.

She giggled, something Loki had never heard her do, as she looked down at her fiancé with shining eyes and firmly gripped his biceps. "Well, it seems the right thing to do, don't you agree?"

"I do," Kristoff murmured, setting her back on her feet. He looked as though he would kiss her. "And all the more so because it benefits me."

Carina nudged Loki and whispered, "They'll be right as rain."

Kristoff whispered something in Kathleen's ear, bringing an instant rosy hue to her cheeks. She pushed him away slightly but kissed him on the cheek before she turned her attention back to the chief.

"Moving away from that, have any of you noticed the most significant word of all three telegrams?" the chief was saying. When no one offered an answer, he sighed and continued, "Klaus says '*We* know who you are.' There are others."

"We already know there are others," Joseph huffed in frustration.

"We know Klaus hired thugs, yes," the chief acknowledged.

But they didn't know who I am, Loki thought with a start. Aloud, he exclaimed, "Mayar is taking orders from someone! He's a pawn himself."

"That's quite a jump," Kristoff protested.

"Not at all. Consider the facts, Mr. Schmidt," the chief encouraged him. "First of all, where has Klaus Mayar obtained enough money for these goons to operate, even while he's been locked up?"

"He robbed a bank," Kristoff pointed out. "He could have easily stashed the money somewhere before he was caught, then given someone access to it."

"Ah, but wouldn't they have just double-crossed him and taken off with all the money, especially after he was arrested?" the chief prompted.

"I'm not a criminal," huffed Kristoff. "How should I know?"

"Klaus could have inspired enough fear on his own to prevent a double cross, but he couldn't have funded everything," Gunter interjected. "His financial state was in disarray when he went on tour with Carina. He even tried to borrow money from my mother, but she turned him down."

"And he stole money from me," Carina added.

The chief rubbed his chin thoughtfully. "It is far more likely someone with money and authority controlled and funded the entire operation. We could go back and forth with scenarios all morning. I'd like to know whether he broke out on his own or had help. I would assume the latter."

"Why?" Carina asked.

"Because he was probably smart enough not to reveal where he stashed the money," the chief answered. "Which would keep him useful to his current boss."

"If you're right and someone broke him out, why did this mysterious benefactor wait so long?" Kristoff queried. "Especially if Klaus was the only one with access to the money."

"To distance himself," the chief suggested. "And precisely because a quick breakout is what most people would expect."

"But wouldn't that someone have protected him from being arrested in the first place?" argued Carina.

"That's a good point. There's a fierce loyalty in organized crime," mused Kathleen. "They watch out for their own."

"Maybe he was a rat they needed to get rid of … or a scapegoat," Kristoff offered.

"That occurred to me, as well, when he was first arrested," replied the chief. "Carina and Lukas may remember, I mentioned it during our interview. But no, rats and spies are dealt with quickly and usually gruesomely. If he were one of those, they would have just killed him. A scapegoat is possible.

Regardless, we've suspected Klaus is involved with the New York Mafia for a while now. All of this lines up with that."

"Well, it doesn't make sense to me. Why would he rob a bank if someone else, especially the Mafia, is funding him?" Carina interjected.

"That could have been part of the agreement," Helga suggested. "He does their dirty work, and they take out a few enemies for him."

Joseph stared at Helga with delighted shock as Loki nodded his approval of her insight.

"Do you really believe the Mafia would expend resources for a personal squabble over a woman?" Kristoff scoffed.

"It's not out of the realm of possibilities," stated the chief. "Either your sister is indeed correct or there's a far more sinister game afoot."

"I think perhaps we are all missing something," Gunter interjected. "It seems quite odd to me that a German would be welcomed into the New York Mafia. I don't mean to offend those present, but I was under the impression Germans are looked upon with disfavor in America since the war. And isn't the Mafia mainly Italian?"

"There is some validity to that," Joseph agreed.

"I wonder if perhaps someone loaned Klaus money, which he used to pay the thugs, then robbed the bank to replenish his resources," Gunter pondered aloud.

"Judging by their engaging conversation," Loki commented sarcastically, "none of the men I encountered had been paid yet. But they did speak as though Mayar is in charge."

"Common thugs often work for later payment," Kathleen pointed out. "Klaus could have made big promises based on his plans to rob the bank, which he can likely fulfill now that he's free and able to access the money himself."

"No, the chief is right. They couldn't have had the means to cover their own expenses while he was in jail," Kristoff countered.

"Exactly, Mr. Schmidt. And they wouldn't need to with an overarching crime boss," agreed Chief Werner.

"But the Mafia?" Gunter repeated doubtfully.

"Well, how else do we account for the 'we' in Klaus's telegram?" Carina asked. "Those thugs did not know Luke's true identity, so he must have meant someone else."

"There are other crime organizations," Kathleen pointed out. "Perhaps he was recruited by a different one."

Loki had been watching Joseph closely during this discussion, which he found rather pointless. Joseph met his gaze and narrowed his eyes in return.

"Has anyone considered that Klaus might not have robbed that bank?" Loki queried, keeping his eyes on his father-in-law.

"Come to think of it, Joseph, you haven't explained the meaning behind your own telegram," Kristoff pointed out. "Klaus claims you framed him. And you didn't seem at all surprised."

"Naturally," Joseph answered smoothly, tearing his eyes away from Loki's to meet Kristoff's. "I suppose it's time I reveal my own secret."

"Father?" Carina whispered. "Did you frame Klaus?"

"Of course not!" Joseph harrumphed. "But I know why he thinks I did."

"Joseph, perhaps you shouldn't … What about her?"

Chief Werner protested, pointing toward Kathleen. "She's a journalist!"

"You're worried about that now?" Joseph scoffed.

"Don't worry, Chief, I'm getting used to being sworn into silence when it comes to Kristoff's friends," she replied, glancing with some angst at Loki. "I'll keep all of this to myself."

"Helga and the chief already know this," Joseph began, "and I trust everyone else not to let it leave this room."

Loki tried to catch Carina's eye, but she did not see. Instead, she gawked at her father with a vexed expression on her face.

"A number of years ago, I was recruited by the Pinkerton Agency to infiltrate the Mafia through legitimate business contacts," Joseph continued. "But now that Hoover is running the FBI, they've taken over quite a bit of that arena. There's little need for me, so I'll be retiring soon."

"You're a paid informant? A spy? A mole?" Kristoff asked quietly, though his voice rose a little when he added, "A Pinkerton?"

Joseph shot him an annoyed look. "Are you quite finished?"

"I think I might retire myself," Kathleen muttered, "if I have to keep secrets like these."

"I'm not opposed to that," Kristoff commented with a wide grin that grew even wider when she slugged him.

"I see you're not the only girl who likes to hit people," Loki joked to Carina out of the side of his mouth, but she ignored him as her eyes bored into her father.

"Kristoff knows I started investigating Klaus when the chief wired me his suspicions about Klaus's involvement with the robberies here," Joseph continued. "Honestly, I wanted to prove his theory wrong, but I also help the German police when I can, given my background and training."

"And we are very thankful for that," the chief interjected.

Joseph acknowledged him with a slight nod, then continued, "By the time Klaus arrived in New York, I had been able to deduce he was involved in something, but not what. He was every bit the perfect picture of a heartbroken man. When he described how Lukas Black had swooped in on Carina with his charisma and skilled manipulations—"

"Thank you," Loki interrupted.

Joseph shot him a dirty look. "Anyway, I believed him. And trusting in his integrity and love for my daughter, I sent the telegram instructing Carina to come to New York. In the interim, I asked him candidly about the robberies."

"How did he respond?" Kristoff asked, riveted by these new revelations.

"I expected him to fully deny everything despite the evidence I had against him," Joseph replied.

"He didn't?" Gunter asked in surprise.

"No, he looked at me for a long time without speaking, then quietly informed me he loved my daughter and had left that all behind him when he lost her. He swore he'd win her back and threatened to remove anyone who stood in his way, including me," Joseph answered. "He said he had known about my work as a Pinkterton for some time and if I continued to pry, he would be forced to reveal said information to both my daughter and the Mafia."

Kristoff let out a low whistle as Loki exclaimed, "Blackmail again!"

"He went on to assure me he would do everything in his power to protect Carina if I cooperated," Joseph continued.

"I knew his threat would endanger Carina's life, so I played my part and agreed to his terms simply to allow myself time to find a way to take him out."

"You mean have him killed?" Kristoff remarked dryly.

"Nonsense!" Joseph protested. "I'm not that kind of Pinkerton. I find that practice highly distasteful."

"Effective though," muttered Loki. He expected Carina to smack him for such a remark, but she merely sat there in a stony silence that worried him.

"When Klaus insisted on picking Carina up from the docks alone, I used the opportunity to report the danger to the agency and was told they would handle it without bloodshed," Joseph finished. "But when he returned with Carina, there was a new dilemma. She told me quite happily they had made up on the way home and were proceeding with the marriage."

"Because he threatened to kill Luke and Kristoff if I didn't," Carina burst out furiously.

"I didn't know that at the time or that he had abused you in Paris, which Kristoff told me later," Joseph defended himself. "You can't imagine the panic I felt when I heard a scuffle upstairs the morning you disappeared. And then to find him stabbed, unconscious, but not a trace of you?"

Carina fell back into stony silence.

"The Pinkertons framed Klaus?" Kristoff asked.

"So it would seem," Joseph answered. "They kept me out of the whole thing. And I was too focused on finding my daughter to think much more about it."

"I hate to say it, Joseph, but it will not matter one bit to Klaus that you did not actually arrange it," advised Gunter.

"You alerted the Pinkertons, so in his mind, it might as well have been you."

Before Joseph could answer, Helga tentatively asserted, "Joseph, you told me Klaus really did rob that bank."

"I thought he had until today, when I heard that telegram," Joseph defended himself. "It was perfectly feasible to think he got himself into trouble before the Pinkertons could get to him."

"Then you lied to yourself! But why does that surprise me?" Carina blurted indignantly, pointing at Helga as she almost shouted, "You lied to *me*, but you told *her*!"

"Watch your tone, Carina! What does Helga have to do with—" Joseph sputtered.

"Father, how *could* you?" Carina cut him off and, bursting into tears, ran from the room.

"Perhaps I should go after her?" Helga suggested softly, though the look on her face told Loki she was wounded to the quick.

"No, I'll go," Loki offered. "It's better you speak with her when things are calmer."

Just as he was leaving, he overheard the chief saying, "I meant to ask if you checked your phone yet, Joseph."

Loki paused.

"Yes, I did. No taps. But I'm concerned about Helga's house," Joseph replied.

"Isn't she going to New York with you?" the chief asked.

"I haven't decided," Helga interjected.

Loki desperately wanted to hear the rest of the discussion, but he had already lingered too long.

His wife needed him.

Loki ran up the stairs and tried the door to the room he shared with Carina, but it was locked.

"Carina, please let me in," Loki pleaded, fiddling with the locked door again. He could easily pick the lock but wanted her to open the door of her own volition.

"Go *away*, Loki!" she wailed, her voice quavery from crying.

"Don't make me pick this lock," he threatened, growing impatient to get back to the dining room.

No answer. A tiny black paw darted out from underneath the door, then disappeared.

"I beg your pardon, Lukas, but might I have a word?" The voice of the police chief sounded from a few steps away.

Loki cursed himself inwardly for not noticing that the chief had followed him up the stairs. There was little chance the policeman had not heard Carina call him by his real name.

"Not now, Chief," Loki growled, knocking on the door again.

"This will only take a moment," the chief insisted. "I really must be getting back to the station, but I must speak with you first ... regarding your *actual* identity."

When eerie silence grew heavy behind Carina's door, Loki knew she was listening. Footsteps and voices echoed in the great hall, moving toward the front door. A small click sounded as Carina's door opened. Carina reached out, grabbed both men by their sleeves, and yanked them inside.

"Really, my dear girl, I must protest!" the chief exclaimed, visibly embarrassed. "This is hardly appropriate!"

"If you wish to discuss my husband's identity, you will do so in absolute privacy," Carina stated with finality. She had composed herself so well, only a little red around the eyes hinted at her outburst.

The cat, whom they still had not renamed, rubbed his flexible little body against Loki's legs, almost tripping him. He scooped up the kitten, allowing him to settle between his neck and shoulder.

"Very well," conceded the chief, whose sharp eyes had already taken in everything about this new environment, as if he simply could not help it. "I might as well get to the point. Your story doesn't quite add up, and I want to know what's really going on."

"Is that why you dissuaded Kathleen from going public?" Loki inquired.

"Yes, I could tell you were quite uncomfortable with the idea. And now, you owe me," the chief replied with a congenial smile.

"I do indeed," Loki agreed. "But what about my story do you not believe?"

"It seems rather far-fetched," the chief declared. "What prince studies stage magic and abdicates his throne to be a mere performer?"

"For one, I'm not the crown prince," Loki responded. "For two, I didn't study stage magic. I simply used the abilities I was born with to dazzle Europe."

To emphasize, he allowed several rays of green light to shoot from one palm to the other.

The chief scrutinized Loki's face, then studied Carina's. "You're really telling the truth! But I don't understand. I sensed you weren't being totally honest in front of the others."

"No, I wasn't," Loki confessed. "I only told a partial truth. Very few know where I come from and what abilities I possess."

"Are you a witch, Mr. Black?"

"Witches are female," Loki informed him dryly. "I think you mean a warlock or a wizard."

"Well, are you?" the chief persisted.

"Why, do I look like one?" Loki asked playfully.

"I really couldn't say," admitted the chief with a smirk.

"Well, rest at ease. I'm not," Loki proclaimed. "I don't conjure or cast spells."

"And is your name Loki, as Carina called you?" the chief asked.

"Loki is my cat's name," Carina interjected quickly.

"Do you mean to say you were so angry with your husband, you called him by your cat's name?" the chief questioned dryly.

"It's alright, Carina," Loki reassured her, noticing how she bit her lip in vexation. Then he answered the chief, "Loki is my given name. But it's highly unusual, so I took the name Lukas to remain incognito as much as possible."

"Is that another partial truth?" the chief demanded, crossing his arms and lifting his chin. "I'm still finding something unbelievable in all of this."

"Believe me, Chief," Loki chuckled, "the full truth is even less believable."

"Try me," the chief challenged him.

"Very well, but do resist the urge to shout," Loki instructed him, then disappeared.

The chief stared at the spot Loki had been, mouth gaping.

"Really, Loki?" Carina groaned. "Why didn't you try that trick with me? Instead, you put me through all that—"

"I didn't want to scare you!" Loki exclaimed, reappearing behind the chief.

The policeman nearly jumped out of his skin but still did not shout. His face was pale but composed as he whispered, "What are you?"

Instead of answering him, Loki walked over to Carina and nuzzled her nose. "Even if I had gone invisible, it wouldn't have mattered. You were being just plain stubborn. I had to work the hardest to convince you."

"Convince her of what?" the chief demanded.

"Everything I said was true to a point, but the detail I left out was that I'm not from Earth," Loki told him. "I'm from a planet called Asgard, where the inspiration for your Norse gods came from."

"Are you saying you're the actual Loki from Norse mythology?" queried the chief.

"That Loki was based on me, but inaccurately," Loki explained. "I'm much older than I look."

"As a learned man, I would not have believed a word of this if I hadn't seen you vanish with my own eyes," the chief admitted. "What else can you do? What do you want on Earth?"

"Nothing more than to blend in and be as human as you are," Loki declared. "I can give you a demonstration and more of an explanation another time, as I have something to discuss with my wife. And you have to get back to the station."

"Would you kindly indulge me just a few more questions?" the chief asked shyly, not once taking his eyes from Loki's.

"If I must," Loki responded, but he was not prepared for the volley of words that came out of the chief. He answered them as quickly as he could, unable to keep the delighted laughter from his voice. "Yes, I can be killed. Yes, I really look like this. No, Joseph doesn't know. And no, you can't tell anyone else."

The chief's final question sobered Loki instantly. "Does Klaus know your alibi story or does he know the full truth?"

"I don't see how he could possibly know the full truth," Carina retorted.

"If he regained consciousness just for a few seconds, he might have seen us vanish right before I took you through the portal to Asgard," Loki speculated. "I only saw Joseph rush over to him, but I could have missed something."

"But all he would know then is that you aren't human, unless he met someone later who knows you," Carina insisted.

"Which is possible," Loki advised her. "There could be Asgardians or Vanir in New York."

"There are more of your kind here?" the chief exclaimed.

Loki winced at his choice of words. "And you wonder why we keep our true selves a secret?"

"Forgive me," the chief apologized. "I am simply at a loss. In all my years on the force, I have never encountered someone like you. Knowing there are others as extraordinary is quite humbling."

Loki was pleased. "Thank you, Chief. You really are a capital fellow."

"Are you two quite finished fawning on each other?" Carina demanded. "I believe my husband came up here for a reason."

"Oh yes, of course," the chief assented. "I'll leave you to it, then. May I enlighten the constable? He's such an asset to the force. I think he could serve you better with this knowledge."

"Do you trust him?" Loki asked.

"With my life," the chief confirmed.

"Very well, you can tell him but no one else. Not even your wife," Loki said, feeling a slight pang of guilt at that last remark.

"I couldn't tell her this," the chief assured him. "She'd think I'd gone crazy. I don't even know how I'll tell Hans. But that's my problem. Good day to you both."

The chief bowed and left them to themselves.

27

Karina walked to the window and gazed outside. "It seems our marriage has gotten off to a rocky start, Loki. Will we ever have peace and quiet?"

"I can't see the future," Loki answered her quietly, joining her at the window. "But I wouldn't want a future without you in it."

She turned to smile too brightly at him, shimmering tears welling up in her eyes. "I'm afraid for you. If Klaus does know who you are and succeeds in his plan, I might be facing a future without you."

"That's not going to happen," he soothed her. "I won't let it."

"Are you that powerful?" she questioned.

He drew back, hurt by the doubt in her eyes. "Don't you trust me?"

"Of course I do," she sighed. "But even you have limitations. Neither of us can make things as we want them to be."

"Perhaps not," Loki conceded, setting aside his wounded pride to heed the deeper meaning underlying her words. "But together, we can face them as they are and work toward making them better."

Carina did not answer, but she closed the remaining distance between them and laid her head against his chest.

"Now, will you tell me what's been bothering you about Helga and your father?" Loki prompted her.

Carina shook her head adamantly, causing some of her hair to fall across his shoulder. The kitten, who had somehow remained perched on Loki's other shoulder the whole time, batted at it playfully. She clicked her tongue in irritation at the animal, then sat down at her vanity to fix her hair.

"You need to talk about it, my star," Loki gently reproached her. "If you keep it bottled up, you'll hurt yourself and everyone else."

Carina's shoulders dropped. "Everything's changing, Loki! Do you know what it's like to be caught between two worlds, between two loves?"

"You know I do," Loki acknowledged softly, gently massaging her shoulders from behind. "Literally."

"Well, I am figuratively," she said, relaxing into his touch. "I love you so much, I can't breathe from it at times. But I've loved my father longer. I'm caught between his world and my life with you, which is just starting. And as I'm slipping away from the world I've always known, it seems like he doesn't even care. I feel like I'm losing him. No, worse, that I don't even know him. I can't believe he didn't tell me the truth."

She rose to her feet in agitation, threw herself on the bed, and hugged a pillow tightly, attempting to bury her emotion in its downy plumpness.

Loki cautiously sat beside her. "He kept the truth from you to protect you, Carina. You were probably too young to handle it."

"I'm not now. And he still told Helga first," she murmured angrily into the pillow. "She will never replace my mother."

"Do you think she wants to?"

Carina sat up and threw the pillow away from her slightly, then grabbed it again. "No."

"Do you think Joseph told Helga because he loves her more?"

"Yes!" she spat, but when Loki raised his eyebrows at her, she sighed. "Well ... no, not really."

"Nothing he could say or do would ever make you not his daughter, right?" Loki continued.

"I suppose," she growled, squeezing the pillow so tightly, her knuckles turned white.

"But what do you think would have happened if you knew and Helga didn't? If she found out the way you did, in front of everyone," Loki asked. "What if Joseph had lied to her?"

Carina glared at Loki and wrapped her arms around her knees. "She would have left him, I'm sure! And I would have been very angry with her for doing so, if that's your next question. I've already told myself all of this. It just ... hurts, Loki. Am I allowed to hurt?"

Loki felt helpless at that moment. He had been so sure logic would overcome the emotions his wife was experiencing, that she simply needed to change her perspective. Why did she not want his insight or advice?

"No, no, don't you dare look like that," she chided him, taking his face in her hands. "I'm sorry. I'm not trying to hurt you. Please ... just be here with me, let me hurt, and don't try to fix it."

He nodded, gathered her in his arms, and kissed the top of her head. The kitten jumped on the bed and nudged Carina's arm. When she lifted her hand to pet the cat, he crawled up to her chin and settled his little body between her chest and shoulder, purring loudly. They sat in silence for several minutes, but when Loki realized she had fallen asleep, he allowed himself to doze off as well.

A knock on the door startled Loki. Carina awoke as well and upset the cat. She rushed to her vanity to smooth her disheveled appearance while Loki answered the door.

"Is everything okay?" asked Helga, who stood there wringing her hands. "You've been up here for quite some time."

"I think so," Loki replied. "What did I miss?"

"Everything's settled, but I'm sure Kristoff can catch you up. May I speak with Carina privately?"

Loki almost suggested that might not be the best idea when Carina appeared at his elbow with a warm smile and answered, "Of course, Helga. Please come in."

"I'll go downstairs," Loki declared awkwardly. He really wanted to stay and listen but sensed this was a conversation on which he must not eavesdrop. He would ask Carina about it later.

He jogged lightly down the stairs and found the dining room empty and cleared of all evidence of breakfast. He checked his watch. Almost noon.

Joseph must have kept his lunch appointment with the chief, Loki thought. *What else could they possibly discuss?*

He decided to enjoy the atrium for a while but accidentally walked in on Kristoff and Kathleen locked in a passionate embrace. Though Loki tried to exit gracefully, Kathleen had heard his footsteps and broke away from her fiancé quickly.

"I'm so sorry," Loki gasped.

"It's alright, old boy," Kristoff laughed, waving Loki over.

Kathleen, on the other hand, turned crimson and mumbled something about freshening up before lunch.

After she disappeared, Kristoff turned to Loki with a wide grin. "We'll just say that was a little payback."

"For what?" Loki asked.

"All those times I had to endure with you and Carina."

"We never behaved like *that* in front of you," Loki protested.

"No, I know," Kristoff agreed. "It's probably a good thing you interrupted. We were getting a little carried away."

"You're welcome, then," Loki mumbled, still embarrassed by the incident.

"In all seriousness, Luke, I don't know how much longer I can wait," Kristoff admitted. "However did you do it?"

"Well, I didn't have your experience, but it still wasn't easy," Loki replied.

"You've got to have more for me than that!" Kristoff pleaded.

"I reminded myself in the moment that she wasn't mine for the taking," Loki explained, "and that I loved her too much to use her for my own needs. Without the commitment we made to each other, how was she to know whether or not I'd love her and leave her?"

"But you knew you wouldn't," Kristoff objected.

"I didn't plan to, no, but can a man really know his own heart or how things could change?" Loki mused. "So I chose to put her before me. Next time you're tempted to push it, take yourself beyond the realization of your desires to the aftermath. Then ask yourself if that temporary pleasure is worth it. Follow it through to its logical conclusion."

"I've never done that," Kristoff admitted.

"How have you resisted thus far?"

"Lack of opportunity or sheer discipline," Kristoff confessed. "But it's gotten more difficult, especially because we haven't really talked about it. There's always this tension there."

"Avoiding opportunities helps. And sheer discipline is needed. But it will only take you so far if you don't think about it differently," Loki expounded. "And you can help each other if you discuss your wishes to wait until you're married. Just think of what you have to look forward to."

"Wouldn't that just make it harder?" Kristoff asked.

"Follow me," Loki commanded him with a sly smirk.

As Loki led Kristoff to the kitchen, they passed several servants on their way to the dining room with trays for lunch. Loki quickly pulled out a plate of freshly baked chocolate brownies from its hiding spot in the pantry.

"How did you know those were there?" Kristoff gasped.

"Carina baked them last night before bed," Loki answered, his green eyes dancing with mischief. "Do you know what she would do to us if we each ate one now?"

"Then you'd better put them back," Kristoff urged, looking around as if he expected Carina to pop out of nowhere.

"But look at how moist and perfect they are," Loki suggested. "Can't you smell how delicious they must be?"

"Why are you torturing me?" Kristoff demanded. "Just put them back! I have no quarrel with Carina, and I don't want one."

"If we each just took a tiny corner off two brownies, she would never know," Loki tempted his friend. "Just a little taste."

"No thanks!" Kristoff spouted. "It's not worth the risk. Besides, I bet they're for lunch or dinner. I'd rather wait and have a whole one without any guilt on my conscience. Why spoil things …" Realization dawned on Kristoff's face. "Ohhh, I get it!"

Loki smiled broadly as he put the brownies back. "Delayed gratification. You're not saying no to yourself or to her for forever. Just for now, so you can really enjoy it when it's good and right."

Kristoff peered at Loki. "And that's been your experience?"

Loki grinned one of the most roguish grins of his entire existence as he recalled some of his moments of intimacy with his wife, but there was also a strength and purity in his smile that did not escape Kristoff's notice.

"Never mind," Kristoff muttered. "The look on your face says it all."

"What are you two doing in here?" Carina demanded, stomping into the kitchen.

Kristoff burst out laughing as the look on Loki's face immediately changed to the expression of a guilty schoolboy.

"If you're hungry, the servants just served lunch in the dining room," Carina announced, eyeing Loki suspiciously. "If I've found you've gotten into my brownies—"

"We didn't, I promise!" Loki exclaimed.

"Then why do you look so guilty?" Carina accused him as she pulled out the plate and inspected it. She smiled with relief. "Not a crumb out of place!"

"How could I rob you of your joy by tasting them without you?" Loki reassured her, wrapping his arms around her waist and kissing her cheek from behind. "I know you like to see my reaction."

"Please tell me we're actually talking about brownies right now," Kristoff grumbled, shoving his hands in his pockets.

"What else would we be talking about?" Carina asked innocently.

"Oh, nothing. I just used the brownies as an object lesson," Loki told her. "But I promise, we didn't touch them."

"You'll have to tell me about it sometime," Carina asserted, not noticing Kristoff frantically shaking his head at Loki or how his face flushed.

Loki just winked at him and suggested, "You should probably tell Kathleen lunch is ready."

"Oh, she's already in there," Carina informed them hurriedly, already out the door with the brownies. She called back, "Better hurry, you two. We ladies don't like to be kept waiting."

Loki was delighted to see her spirits so obviously lifted. He hoped she would tell him later about her conversation with Helga.

"Oh, Helga said you'd fill me in on what's been settled," Loki mentioned to Kristoff.

"Well, she finally agreed to go to New York with Joseph."

"Surprising, but I'm relieved," Loki replied.

"I'll tell you the rest over lunch," Kristoff replied. "Carina's right. We'd better not keep the ladies waiting. They might eat all the brownies."

28

Loki and Carina lounged on the bed in their room, propped up against the headboard as they talked late into the evening. Loki had just finished telling Carina about his brownie analogy for Kristoff's dilemma.

"I'm impressed he wants to wait until marriage. I honestly didn't think he had it in him," Carina mused. "Maybe before Astrid, but not after. He must really love Kathleen."

"He's doing it because of my example," Loki bragged.

Carina snickered. "Don't get too big for your britches, husband. He'll need more than that for motivation, especially with a long engagement."

"He has what he needs. He may just require some encouragement along the way," Loki remarked. Seeing Carina nod thoughtfully in agreement, he teased, "Not from you, wife. You can't reveal what I told you."

"No, but maybe I'll have a chance to talk discreetly with Kathleen," Carina suggested.

"Only if she brings it up," Loki warned. "It's technically none of our business."

"I know what to say and what not to say," Carina argued. "I just want them to experience the same joy we do, so maybe

I can help a little. After all, when you first told me you wanted to wait, I thought maybe there was something wrong with me. Then I thought there was something wrong with you."

"You mean like you weren't attractive enough, or I wasn't able to perform?" Loki pretended to be offended.

She punched him playfully. "Something like that. But I understood fairly quickly. I felt so much more loved knowing you respected me that much."

She started to kiss him, but he stopped her. "Ah-ah, you're not getting out of it that easily."

"Don't I owe you a kiss?"

"Later. For now, it's your turn," Loki prompted.

"My turn for what?" Carina asked, feigning innocence.

"Don't get coy with me," Loki teased. "You know very well you promised to tell me about your chat with Helga if I told you about mine with Kristoff. And now, I want to know why my beautiful wife is so much happier. A great weight has been lifted off your shoulders."

"Loki, what are you saying?" she gasped mockingly. "We've only been married a few weeks, and you're already talking about my weight?"

Loki dropped his mouth open and stared at her. He had no idea how to answer and, despite his limited experience with women, he sensed that topic was dangerous ground.

She laughed delightedly at his reaction, then taunted him, "Besides, I think it's you who's put on weight anyway, with all the sugar you've eaten lately."

"What?" Loki exclaimed, surveying his own physique. "I have not! And I don't eat *that* much sugar!"

"How many brownies did you eat after lunch?"

"Four," he admitted sheepishly.

"And how many cookies after dinner?"

"Six," Loki grumped. "But they were small!"

Carina laughed so hard, she fell over on her side. "I'm only teasing you, my husband. You still look as lean and handsome as the day I first saw you."

Loki grinned. "If I pulled a stunt like that with you, you would cry!"

"Yes, I would," she agreed. "But you're such a tease yourself, Mr. Trickster, you deserve some of your own medicine sometimes."

"I haven't teased anyone or played a prank in so long, I'm becoming downright respectable," Loki quipped.

"Oh, Loki, we can't have that," Carina stated sarcastically. "Heaven forbid you be respectable!"

"Just for that, I'll think of a really good prank to play on you," Loki proclaimed. "But you're still not getting out of your promise."

"Okay, fine!" Carina whined playfully. Then she grew serious. "It wasn't an easy conversation, and it's not easy for me to talk about, even with you."

Loki drew her close and quietly waited for her to work through her emotions and figure out what to say.

"I've seen how important Helga is to my father. I didn't say anything to her, but I think he wants to marry her," Carina began. "And that brings a family dynamic I've never had to face before. If it hadn't been for those despicable, meddling Chestertons, I probably would have grown up with Helga as my stepmother and not known any differently."

"Perhaps, but that would have changed many other things, including Kristoff's business and how we even met," Loki pointed out. "We might not have met at all. I kept coming back to Midgard because of Kristoff, you know. Until I met you."

"I hadn't even thought of that," Carina gasped. She hugged Loki suddenly. "I don't like the idea of a reality where I never met you. And having you makes me realize how amazing it is that my father found Helga again. He might be rough around the edges, but I can tell he's completely in love with her."

"Yes, I can see that, though not as clearly as you do, I'm sure," Loki acknowledged.

"Well, when Helga came up to talk to me, I apologized for my outburst before she could say anything. She understood how much it hurt that Father told her his secrets but didn't share them with me," Carina continued. "Then she suggested I speak with him about it, without offering any excuses for him, which was refreshing."

"Have you spoken with him?"

"Not yet. By the time I came back downstairs, he had already gone to lunch with the chief, and once he got back, he was focused on leaving for Norway with Helga," Carina replied.

"I'm still surprised they went all the way up there," Loki remarked. "Joseph could have just bought everything she needed for the trip."

"She didn't want him to," Carina reminded him with amusement. "And she wanted to make sure the servants who went with them understood exactly how to take care of her garden."

"You know, she really is a good match for your father," Loki observed, chuckling to himself.

"I know," Carina sighed. "She can go toe to toe with him if she has to. And he'll listen to her."

Loki laughed at that mental picture. "Do you think he'll listen to you?"

"I hope so," Carina murmured. "Since we're meeting them in Hamburg, at least I'll have time to think about what to say."

"Speaking of that, I wish Kristoff would stop pushing us to perform in Hamburg this trip," Loki remarked.

"Is it such a bad idea?" she asked.

"No, but I want some peace and quiet before life gets crazy again," Loki admitted. "And you know it will once we cross the ocean."

"As long as you don't get bored," Carina warned him. "You tend to get into trouble when you're bored."

"I really don't want to do it," Loki sighed. "Not this trip, anyway. I'd rather have the extra time here."

Carina laughed. "Okay, we won't do it!"

Loki heaved a sigh of relief, then reminded her, "Are you going to finish telling me the rest of your conversation with Helga?"

"Well, we talked about my mother for a long time," Carina replied. "Helga wanted to know what I remembered about her. I guess my father had talked about her a lot with Helga, and she talked to him about her late husband, Erik. She actually knew more about my mother than I did, which was strange. Helga suggested I talk with Father about that too."

"That's going to be a lengthy conversation," Loki predicted. "Why don't I sit with Helga on the train to Calais so you can have all the time you need?"

"Thank you, Loki," Carina uttered softly, kissing his cheek. "Helga asked me how I felt about her relationship with my father. I told her I had mixed feelings. Bittersweet, like I told you. She said that was natural. All in all, she was warm and compassionate. And she assured me she had no intention of trying to be my mother. She knew that place was taken in my heart, but she hoped there would be room for her in a new place."

"What did you say to that?" Loki asked.

"I told her she was already my friend," Carina answered, "and she said that was enough. Then we hugged and came downstairs."

"You seem to feel better about the whole thing," Loki observed.

"I really do," Carina confirmed. "But I'm nervous about talking with my father."

"It can't be worse than when we had to tell him you ran off and got married to some no-account magician," Loki teased.

"You are many things, Loki of Midgard," Carina whispered, taking his face in her hands, "but a no-account is not one of them."

With that, she kissed him with such fervor, he was positively dizzy when she let him go.

"What brought that on?" he breathed.

"You listened to me," she declared. "When you truly connect with my heart, you hold a key that unlocks the door to the rest of me."

"I'll remember that," Loki murmured, quite ready to step through that door. He pulled her close and spent the rest of the evening knitting his soul with hers once more.

But the next morning, he awoke before she did, itching for mischief as he remembered his promise to play a special prank on Carina. Not wanting to disturb her or the cat, who had taken up his usual post, Loki lay there thinking through his repertoire of tricks. Whatever he chose had to be funny but not cruel, which ruled out bugs and snakes.

Or did it?

He suddenly had a brilliant idea, both naughty and nice. He gently extricated himself from under the arm Carina had thrown over him in her sleep and got dressed, then quietly sneaked down to the kitchen.

Loki located Carina's recipe book and flipped through it, wrinkling his nose at a few of the recipes. He had never cooked or baked anything in his life, besides helping Helga that one time, but he had watched others do it. How hard could it be? He read page after page. The only recipes that interested him took too long. The kitchen staff trickled in and started breakfast preparations. Loki began to worry Carina would wake up before he could execute his plan. He abandoned the recipe book and searched his memories for the times he had watched the Asgardian palace cooks make his favorite breakfast. If he had seen enough, perhaps he could replicate it.

He gathered ingredients to attempt making the dish. He asked for help just a few times from one of the kitchen maids, who was delighted he was trying to fix breakfast in bed for his bride. She happily pointed out where things were and took the time to show him how to measure correctly. Within the hour, longer than he had hoped, Loki mastered the dish and proudly carried the result of his kitchen endeavors on a decorative tray up to Carina's room. She was just beginning to stir when he opened the door.

"What's this?" she murmured, shifting positions and upsetting the cat.

"I made you breakfast!" Loki proudly proclaimed, bringing the tray over to her to show it off.

Her face turned a slight shade of green when she saw everything arranged on the tray. "Oh, Loki, you're so cute," she sighed, her nose wrinkling slightly in disgust, though she tried to hide it. "You really shouldn't have. You'll spoil me."

Loki stifled a snicker as he admired his illusions. All of the food looked either burned or half-cooked, with several items in unsightly colors. He had even made the flowers he placed on the tray look wilted. But the best part was the illusion he would cast as soon as she took her first bite.

He pasted a sorrowful look on his face. "It's the first time I've ever cooked anything, besides that time at Helga's. I worked really hard on it."

Carina swallowed hard and motioned for him to give her the tray. She picked up what looked like a partially burnt muffin, which was the least scary item on the tray, and gingerly took a small bite from the least charred part.

Her eyes widened in surprise. "This tastes really good! What's this crunchy stuff inside? It's so flavorful!"

She looked at the rest of the muffin and shrieked when she saw what looked like half of a cockroach sticking out right where she had bitten it. She threw the muffin at Loki, who burst out laughing and easily caught the flying food. He expected her to attack him, but since she had already swallowed the first bite, she was frantically trying to rinse out her mouth with the glass of murky water on the tray.

"Look again, my star," he commanded when he had caught his breath. He transformed the tray to its true form.

And not a moment too soon. She looked like she might be about to heave into the wastebasket by their bed. She glanced at the tray and the muffin he held out to her, which now looked like the delicious concoction it was—a biscuit-like pastry baked like a muffin but filled with egg, cheese, red peppers, and crumbled sausage, which the kitchen maid had suggested adding. The flowers were now bright and cheery. The fruit was plump, ripe, and vibrant in color. And the strips of bacon were not quite Helga-caliber, but definitely better than the undercooked mess Loki had made them appear to be.

"Is that the real one or an illusion?" she whispered, though her eyes had a murderous look in them.

"The real one." Loki polished off the breakfast muffin himself to reassure her.

He expected her to hit him or something, but she just sat there, as if deep in thought. Loki revealed a hidden basket of his special muffins and brought it over to her.

She finally spoke as she took one. "That was a very clever trick. I don't know whether to laugh or cry. I might still throw up, actually."

Loki joined her on the bed. "I had hoped you'd laugh. I thought you'd at least hit me."

"And give you the satisfaction of a kiss?" Carina scoffed. She picked up a ruby red strawberry and bit into it viciously. "I can't believe you made me think I ate a cockroach. Making the food look gross wasn't good enough?"

Loki chuckled. "A lot of the pranks I played as a boy involved bugs or animals. I couldn't very well justify doing something with a real bug."

Carina shuddered. "Thank the heavens! At least you have some decency! I don't know how I'll survive if I ever give you a son."

"A son?" Loki repeated, his heart filled with wonder at the thought. "I don't know if the world could handle another one of me."

"Well, he'd be mine too, you know," Carina teased him.

"That's true," Loki admitted. "And if he's more like you, he'll be just fine."

"Trying to butter me up so I won't get you back?" Carina laughed.

"Get me back?" Loki asked, astounded. "No one's ever done that."

"Maybe they were too afraid or lacked the desire or knowledge," Carina mused. "I have none of those problems. You, sir, apparently do not know who you are dealing with."

"I shall consider myself warned," Loki chuckled.

Carina merely winked at him as she finished her breakfast. When she complimented him on the food, he understood her eagerness to please him with her cooking, for he felt pride well up inside him at her praise. Loki ate the rest of the muffins as she got ready for the day. With Joseph and Helga gone, the other two couples planned an early picnic to a little lake not far from Stuttgart. Loki stayed on guard throughout the entire morning, waiting for Carina's retaliation. But she spent all her time preparing for the picnic, insisting on preparing some of the food herself. Once they arrived at the lake, Loki carefully examined his food to make sure she had not tampered with it. All was well, and she did not seem to notice his trepidation. After they packed up the leftovers,

Loki grabbed the picnic basket as the foursome sauntered around the peaceful body of water, which was surrounded by bulrushes and rife with plentiful wildlife.

"We have some leftover grapes. Why don't we feed the ducks?" Carina suggested, pointing to several of the waterfowl swimming away from the shore. "Oh, Luke, see that little mama with her ducklings? Maybe you could catch her attention if you got closer and tossed a grape out."

Loki smirked knowingly. "You expect me to fall for that? You'll push me in!"

"I will not!" Carina protested. "Here, take half this grape, and I'll stay right here."

"How do I know you didn't get Kristoff in on this? Maybe he'll push me in," Loki protested.

He eyed Kristoff, who burst out laughing, for Carina had told them about Loki's prank that morning, though she described it as a magic trick so as not to reveal Loki's identity to Kathleen.

"As gratifying as that would be, I was going to teach my city girl fiancée how to skip stones," Kristoff informed him.

"Oh, teach me too!" Carina exclaimed. "But after we feed the ducks, or we'll scare them."

Carina cut the rest of the grapes in half and held out a portion to Loki. He took the treats but gave her a wide berth as he approached the shore and tossed one to the mother duck, who dove quickly to grab it with her strong bill. Carina rolled her eyes but chose another spot to throw some of her grapes to a few drakes with metallic green heads. There were several types of ducks and other waterfowl on the lake. Quite a few swam closer to gobble up the grapes thrown out to

441

them. Loki found the experience quite relaxing, especially when he escaped joining the ducks after all.

Once they finished with the ducks, Kristoff led the group to another section of the lake, where he picked up a smooth, flat stone and chucked it into the water. To Loki's surprise, it hit the water with a plinking sound, then ricocheted across the surface three times before finally sinking.

"Show me how to do that!" Loki exclaimed.

"You've never skipped stones?" Kristoff asked. "Not even as a boy?"

"That's not really something princes do in my country," Loki chuckled.

"No? What a pity," Kristoff mused. Then he straightened his shoulders and instructed, "Well, my little class of eager stone-skipping enthusiasts, find a smooth, oval, flat stone that isn't quite perfect. Then I'll show you what's next."

"What *did* you do as a boy, Luke?" Kathleen asked as they scoured the ground for the perfect skipping stones.

"Mostly learned how to fight and studied all the things a future king needs to know," Loki answered. "I wasn't the crown prince, but I still had to learn it all."

"That must be hard, knowing what it takes to be king but never really having the chance," Kathleen observed, inspecting a stone she had just picked up.

"That one's perfect, Kat!" Kristoff exclaimed before Loki could respond. "Let me show you how to throw it. Luke and Carina can take a turn once they find a suitable stone."

He showed them how to tuck the stone into the webbing between the thumb and forefinger, making sure the other fingers were tucked out of the way. Then he helped Kathleen take a sideways stance with feet apart. He instructed her to throw from the waist with a quick snap of the wrist as she released the stone. They all counted as the stone hopped five times.

"Way to go, Kat!" Kristoff whooped, jumping in the air with one arm extended.

She bowed playfully, then stepped back to let Carina try. But Carina's stone only sank into the lake with a *thunk*. She groaned in disappointment.

"That happens," Kristoff reassured her. "Next time, don't worry about throwing it hard. It's about motion, not velocity."

She nodded, then went looking for another stone. Loki sent the stone he had found skimming across the lake.

"Yeah!" he hollered when it jumped eight times. "Best yet!"

Kristoff made a wry face. "Of course, Mr. Anything You Can Do, I Can Do Better."

"Sounds like a song title," Loki quipped.

"Not one I've ever heard," Kathleen countered.

"Kristoff can write it, and we'll sing it," Carina joined in laughingly.

"Yeah, no thanks," Kristoff scoffed. "Did you find another one, Carina?"

She held up her stone for inspection. When Kristoff approved it, she threw it more gently this time. It jumped four times.

"I did it!" she exclaimed happily, bouncing in place.

"Outdone by a bunch of novices," Kristoff griped. "I'm going again."

They spent the next several hours happily skipping stones, trying to best each other, and talking about little things. Loki never could get higher than eight, but Kathleen shocked them all when one of hers skipped ten times.

"Wow, you really know how to pick 'em," Kristoff praised her.

"Yes, I do," she agreed softly, kissing him on the cheek. "And not just stones either."

Kristoff grinned. Loki and Carina smiled at each other, then started toward the car to give them some privacy.

"I'm glad to see Kristoff so happy," Carina remarked. "Kathleen too. She's hard to get to know, but I like her."

"They're good for each other," Loki agreed. "But I do wonder how we're going to manage all these weddings."

"It's only two more, and I don't think they'll be anytime soon," Carina replied. "Oh, here they come."

Kristoff and Kathleen joined them at the car, hand-in-hand.

"Are you two ready to head back?" Kathleen asked. "I'd like to wash up before we do anything else."

"You and me, both, girl," Kristoff quipped. Then he immediately stuttered, "I—I mean, not together. I just meant ..."

His face turned scarlet, and he dropped his head as the other three laughed.

"I knew what you meant," Kathleen reassured him.

"Well, I think I smell like fish and lake water by now," Loki laughed. "I could definitely use a wash."

Once they had arrived home, Kathleen and Kristoff headed for their rooms, while Carina and Loki went upstairs.

She started the water in the bathroom, then asked him to fetch two towels from her linen closet. Just as he opened the double doors to the stand-alone closet, he was baptized with a deluge of frigid water. He hollered in shock, narrowly avoiding being hit by the tin bucket tumbling down.

Carina shrieked with laughter as he stood there dripping and gasping. She had apparently hidden herself by the door to watch him spring her carefully laid trap. "You said you wanted a wash!"

"When did you set this up?" Loki asked, impressed by her ingenuity.

"Before we left," she admitted. "Didn't you notice I took just a little longer than you did to come down?"

"It didn't seem like very long," Loki replied. "You're a fast, clever minx, you are. I had actually forgotten your threat to get me back."

"Ah, you let your guard down," she mocked, slipping back into the bathroom. "We'll still need those towels, by the way. And do be a dear and put one over that mess you just made."

"The mess I made?" Loki retorted incredulously.

Carina just laughed. "Come along, husband," she teased him. "We're even now."

Oh, we are, are we? I'll have to remedy that, he thought with a devilish grin.

He already had the perfect payback in mind, but he would need Kristoff's help to pull it off. And quite conveniently, after they had all reconvened in the great hall, Kathleen asked Carina to show her some of the dress shops in Stuttgart, with the idea of getting some costumes made for their American tour. As soon as they were gone, Loki shared his plan with Kristoff, who was practically giddy at the prospect of being Loki's partner-in-crime. The two of them embarked on their own little shopping trip, then spent the rest of the afternoon preparing their snare and eagerly awaiting the women's return.

"You know this will affect Kathleen, right?" Loki pointed out. "Are you sure you're okay with that?"

"Oh, I'm all in," Kristoff replied jubilantly. "I want to see how she reacts."

Finally, when the wait had grown unbearable, the two men heard the car pull up to the garage. Like renegade school boys, they peeked out the window and snickered as the women approached the main doors of the house.

Kristoff and Loki took their positions. As one of the front doors opened and the women stepped through, Loki yanked the strings he held, which dumped two open honeypots they had suspended above the doorframe. Since Carina was a little farther away than they had anticipated, she did not get gooped as squarely as Kathleen did, but she screamed just as loudly. Just then, Kristoff pulled his strings to release the pin in a bag of feathers, which rained down in a flurry of white and stuck to the honey all over the girls.

"Well, looks like you walked into that one, honey," Kristoff guffawed.

Carina groaned at the terrible pun, but Kathleen stomped over to them so quickly, both men instinctively took a step back.

She moved too fast for them, however, and smeared Kristoff's face with feathery honey, spouting, "You just sealed your own fate, *honey*!"

Loki laughed uproariously, but Kathleen spouted, "Don't think you're off the hook, Luke!"

Carina used the momentary distraction to scoop a glob of honey off the floor and lob it at Loki. Her aim was better than he expected. The sticky mess hit him on his left cheek and oozed down to his shoulder, leaving a nasty feeling trail of scratchy goo. Before he knew what was happening, the women were bombarding the men with honey and feathers. Loki and Kristoff laughed helplessly and tried to fend off the onslaught.

"Run!" Kristoff finally gasped.

"No, man! Stand and fight!" Loki commanded.

Within minutes, honey and feathers covered all four of them from head to foot as the ruckus echoed in the great hall. A startled gasp and a disapproving harrumph interrupted their child's play. Mrs. Wagner and Charles, the butler, stood just a few feet away with arms crossed and faces indignant, surveying the damage.

"What have you done?" Mrs. Wagner wailed in German. "Oh, my clean floors and the doors … and …"

"We'll clean it up, Mrs. Wagner," Loki offered penitently.

"You'll do no such thing!" she retorted. "Enough damage has been done. See to yourselves!"

"Outside!" Charles ordered. "You need to be thoroughly hosed off before you even attempt to wash in the bathrooms."

"I call the hose," Carina yelled with a wicked edge, already on her way to the outside entrance of the atrium.

Even though Carina reached the garden hose first, Loki and Kristoff wrestled it away from her quickly. A water fight ensued, leaving them all soaked and bedraggled. A few staff members watched the scene from the windows with almost wistful expressions on their faces. Once they had washed off most of the honey and feathers, the foursome traipsed inside and helped themselves to the towels left for them by the door, just inside the house. They mopped up as much water as possible, then parted ways to finish cleaning themselves up for dinner.

During the meal, they discussed plans for the tour, including the dresses Carina and Kathleen had ordered, which would be ready just in time for the group to leave for Hamburg.

After dinner, Kathleen suggested, "Boys, why don't you two go out tonight? We have some rather girly things to do."

"Trying to get rid of us, Kat?" Kristoff remarked suspiciously.

"Fine, stay here," Kathleen replied with a shrug. "But expect to be bored."

"I don't think it would hurt to go out for a little while," Loki told Kristoff with a wink.

"Oh, Luke, that reminds me! The tailor needs your measurements for that white suit I ordered for you," Carina informed Loki. "The shop is closed by now. Could you stop by his house?"

"Is there some nasty surprise waiting for me there?" Loki asked.

"No, of course not," Carina assured him. "Do hurry though. We need that suit before we leave Europe. I can't believe I forgot!"

"I can," Kathleen quipped. "Getting attacked with honey and feathers would drive rational thought from anyone's mind."

Loki and Kristoff exchanged glances and chuckled somewhat sheepishly.

"We'll be back later," Loki stated. "Don't get into trouble while we're gone."

As the two men passed through the main hall, Loki noted how clean everything was. "Mrs. Wagner is a wonder. You'd never know what happened here a few hours ago."

Kristoff nodded. "You know those girls are up to something, right?"

"Yes, I'm sure of it. We'd better not stay out long," Loki answered. "And I think we should be prepared with retribution for whatever they pull."

"You've started an all-out prank war, old pal," Kristoff observed.

Loki laughed. "Well then, we do whatever it takes to win."

29

Kristoff parked the car out of sight down the street. They had wanted to sneak back earlier to spy on the girls, but their adventures took longer than expected. First, Loki's fitting at the tailor's was not a quick visit. Then Kristoff ran into several friends at one of the bars. He had even scheduled an impromptu sales appointment for the following morning.

The men hurried to the servants' entrance and sneaked into the Green home, so as not to alert the women to their presence. Loki quietly instructed one of the manservants to retrieve the car. Then he and Kristoff tiptoed through the house, shushing any servants who spotted them.

A burst of feminine laughter from the parlor alerted the men to the women's whereabouts. They peeked inside, unnoticed, then looked at each other in confusion at what they saw. The girls were hand sewing, surrounded by assorted fabric and tiny, sparkly things. The sound of the car approaching the garage slowed their activity as they both cocked their heads to listen.

"Sounds like they're back," Carina observed.

"We're almost done," Kathleen replied. "Maybe they'll read or play games in the library so we can finish."

She laid aside the garment she was working on and stood. Carina did the same. Loki and Kristoff scurried away to the side door leading outside to the garage to give the appearance they had just arrived.

"What do you make of it?" Loki asked Kristoff.

"Looked like they were working on tour stuff," Kristoff guessed. "Whatever they're planning has to be in the library or upstairs. Be on your guard."

"How'd it go?" Carina called as she and Kathleen approached.

"Oh, just fine," Loki answered casually. "I have another fitting tomorrow afternoon. How were things here?"

"Well, we thought you'd be gone longer. We didn't quite finish our project," Kathleen hinted.

"Not a problem," Kristoff responded with a grin. "How about a backgammon rematch, Luke?"

"Only if you want to get beat again," Loki crowed. He had not missed the secret, triumphant smile between the two girls. "Ladies, forgive me for being so bold, but would you mind accompanying us to the library and entering first?"

"Whatever for?" Carina asked innocently.

"I think you know," Loki retorted.

"That's ridiculous," Carina spouted. "This afternoon was fun, but we have work to do!"

"Hiding something?" Kristoff prodded.

"Oh, have it your way!" Carina sighed in exasperation. Her tone grew mocking. "We'll escort you sweet little boys to the library, then get back to work. And maybe, when we're done, we can tuck you in for bed."

"I'd like that," Loki quipped, undaunted by her teasing.

"So would I," Kristoff chuckled, winking at Kathleen, who blushed.

"Come along, little ones," Carina taunted, leading the way to the library.

She entered the room and turned on the lamp. Everyone else followed her inside.

Nothing happened.

Loki surveyed the room. Nothing seemed amiss or out of place. He retrieved the backgammon set and sat down at the game table. Kristoff joined him and helped set up the game.

"Well, if you young lads require anything else, we'll be in the parlor," Carina offered, her tone still mocking.

Loki rolled his eyes, and Kristoff snorted. Once the girls disappeared, they played three games of backgammon, two of which Loki won. Then they switched to chess. As they played, they discussed ideas for retaliation after Carina and Kathleen made their next move. Finally, the women returned to the library to announce they were finished and ready for bed. The couples went their separate ways and settled in for the night without even a hint of mischief or pranks. Carina even offered to massage Loki's head and shoulders with some special oils she wanted to try.

As a result, Loki slept so deeply, he did not dream, though he was conscious of a strange tickling sensation as he grew aware of the sun. He woke to Carina bustling about the room.

"Good morning, sleepyhead," she chirped. "Hurry, it's time to go down for breakfast already."

"What's the rush?" Loki yawned, easing himself out of bed. "Are we going somewhere?"

"Kathleen and I have more tour things to do today,"

Carina informed him. "And I'd like to have breakfast with my husband since I might not be seeing much of you."

"Oh," Loki sighed, disappointed by the thought of most of the day without her. "Well, I'll just comb my hair then."

"Just run your fingers through it like you usually do. It looks fine," Carina insisted. She held out some of his clothing. "Here, throw this on, and let's go."

Still too groggy to argue, Loki ran his fingers through his hair, put on the proffered clothes, and followed her downstairs. He entered the dining room and almost missed a step when he saw who awaited him there. A strange-looking man who bore a vague resemblance to Kristoff sat in a chair by Kathleen, whose eyes widened with suppressed mirth when she saw Loki. The Kristoff look-alike stood up so quickly, he knocked over the chair. He raised a pair of dark eyebrows that matched his dark hair, his oddly colored lips twitching with amusement.

"Luke, did you look in the mirror this morning?" the man asked in Kristoff's voice.

"Kristoff, is that you?" Loki asked just as incredulously. "I don't think you looked in the mirror either."

The girls snickered.

"I just got dressed and came down," Kristoff explained. "Kathleen says the girls have things to do, so I had to hurry."

Loki shot Carina a wry glance. "How convenient! Carina said the same to me."

"Okay, girls, what did you do to us?" Kristoff demanded.

"Well, your hair is about the same color as mine now, for one thing," Loki pointed out.

"It's pink?" Kristoff yelped, reaching up to feel his hair.

"Pink?" Loki shouted, grabbing at his own hair.

The girls howled with laughter. Kristoff rounded the perimeter of the table and dashed into the hall to find a mirror. Loki followed right on his heels, which gave him a perfect view of the huge, sparkly flower attached to the bottom of Kristoff's suit coat.

"I really hope that flower on your backside isn't permanent," Loki commented.

Kristoff stopped abruptly and pulled the back of the coat forward to look at it. Then he grabbed Loki and twirled him around to look at the back of his suit coat.

"You've got one too," Kristoff informed him. "It's bigger than mine. Looks like Carina even added a little bee."

Loki shrugged off his suit coat to look at the art, which was more elaborate than the red, abstract flower on Kristoff's clothing. Loki's flower was purple, and just as Kristoff said, there was a small yellow insect close to it. The little scene actually impressed him, though not enough to want it on his suit coat.

"What are these things?" Loki asked, fingering the tiny, shimmering discs forming the flower design.

"Sequins?" Kristoff guessed. He turned to the girls, who had followed to watch. "Was this what you were working on last night?"

They nodded, breathless from laughing so hard.

Loki suddenly spotted a bizarre reflection in a nearby mirror and remembered why they had rushed into the hall. He grabbed Kristoff by the sleeve and yanked him over to the large mirror near the coatroom. They stared agape at themselves, then at each other. Loki's hair was a mottled pink. A black substance rimmed both men's eyes. Their cheeks had been smeared with a gaudy, orangish-pink powder, and their lips were tinted ruby red. As they touched their hands to their faces in shock, they both noticed a translucent pink sheen on their fingernails.

Almost as if on cue, they both bellowed the respective names of their lady loves. Carina and Kathleen glanced at each other with amused, mock horror and took off running down the hall. Loki and Kristoff caught up with them in the dining room, where the servants were setting out breakfast. The two maids and the butler gasped when they saw the two men and quickly exited, their peals of laughter drifting behind them.

"What did you do to me, Kathleen?" Kristoff demanded. "I have a sales appointment in less than an hour!"

"I didn't know that!" she gasped. "You didn't tell me!"

"I forgot," Kristoff admitted, calming down enough to grab some food. "At least you used a somewhat normal color for my hair."

"Why exactly was I the one honored with pink hair?" Loki demanded, arms folded across his chest as he glared at his wife.

"That was an accident!" Carina defended herself as she filled her own plate and settled into her seat. "We tried to switch your hair colors."

"That wasn't massage oil you used on my head last night, was it?" Loki sighed as he grabbed a hot, flaky biscuit.

"That was her excuse, eh?" Kristoff commented, scarfing down the last bite of his first helping. "Kat told me I still had honey in my hair and offered to wash it for me with a special soap since I couldn't see or feel where it was."

"Nice one, Kat," Carina praised her.

Kathleen looked up from her food and winked ostentatiously at Carina.

They must be getting close, Loki thought, noting Carina's use of Kathleen's nickname. Aloud, he stated, "I still don't understand why my hair is pink."

"I borrowed the supplies from a chemist I know," Carina explained. "He's been experimenting with different formulas for coloring hair. But, Luke, your hair didn't respond the way I expected at all. I really can't explain it."

"Better tell your chemist friend he needs to keep working on it," Kristoff muttered, forking more scrambled eggs and pan-seared ham onto his plate. "This stuff washes out, right?"

Carina and Kathleen exchanged worried looks.

"The makeup will," Kathleen answered. "We can get that off fairly quickly. And we have normal suit coats ready for you both."

"What about our hair?" Kristoff prodded. "I can't go to a sales appointment like this. I'd be a laughingstock!"

"We were planning to just dye it back to your normal color," Kathleen admitted. "But there isn't time right now."

"I've got an idea, buddy," Loki reassured Kristoff when he groaned in exasperation. "I'll just go with you."

"How will that help?" Kristoff asked worriedly. "May I remind you that your hair is pink?"

"We'll keep our hats on, and I'll use one of my magic tricks to distract from whatever shows through," Loki replied. "Then the girls can fix this when we get back."

"What about my eyebrows?"

"That's makeup," Kathleen said quickly. "I can wash that off."

"Well, then, let's get to it, you vixen!" Kristoff commanded, his good humor returning. "And no special soap this time."

As soon as breakfast was over, Carina and Kathleen fixed the men up as best as they could and sent them on their way.

Since Kristoff had requested to drive the Rolls Royce, Loki clambered into the passenger seat and huffed, "Forget keeping our hats on. I'll just spin an illusion."

"I was hoping you'd say that," Kristoff sighed in relief as he pulled out onto the street. "Now, what are we going to do about those girls?"

Since none of their previous ideas seemed drastic enough, they bounced around a few others on the way to Kristoff's appointment, then picked up right where they left off during the ride back to the mansion.

"What about the classic ink-in-your-tea trick?" Kristoff suggested.

"What does that do?" Loki asked.

"Oh, it turns your teeth black," Kristoff explained. "Just until you brush them again."

"It's good but not quite enough," Loki mused. "We need something else with it."

"We could do that and make them think that's it, then strike again soon after with a worse trick," Kristoff proposed. "They'd never see it coming."

"Yes, but what?" Loki exclaimed in frustration. "I don't want to hurt them, frighten them, or make them sick."

"What if we moved all of the furniture out of their bedrooms?"

"I share a bedroom with Carina, remember?"

"Oh yeah," Kristoff grunted.

"I've got it! Why don't we steal all of their clothes and hide them?" Loki suggested excitedly. "I did that to Thor once. I even took the towels and made sure the servants were all busy elsewhere. He came down to breakfast wrapped up in his window drapes."

Kristoff laughed. "I like it! Tea at lunch and vanishing wardrobes right before daybreak?"

"I wish we could do the second one sooner," Loki declared. "The girls might retaliate tonight."

"It can't be helped," Kristoff stated. "Can you distract the girls with an illusion while I put the ink in their tea?"

"Sure, I'll make it look like you never moved," Loki agreed.

They arrived at the mansion just after the women, who claimed they were almost finished with their tour shopping, with only two appointments left that afternoon. But Loki wondered if they were also planning more mischief.

Lunch was quick and fairly uneventful. The ink-in-the-tea trick went off without a hitch. The girls did not even notice the stains on their formerly perfect teeth.

The doorbell rang right after lunch. The butler introduced Miss Frank, a small, well-groomed hairdresser who eyed Kristoff's and Loki's hair with amusement.

"I see why you called me," she remarked dryly to the women, who were smiling at her with blackened teeth. "And I see they got the last laugh."

"What do you mean?" Carina and Kathleen asked at the same time, as the men controlled the urge to laugh.

"You girls can figure that out on your own," Miss Frank replied with a smirk. "Gentlemen, I understand we haven't much time. We'll start with you, blondie."

She pointed at Kristoff and motioned for him to follow her to the kitchen. A servant traipsed behind them, carrying a bulging leather case. The hairdresser opened it to reveal several foreign items and different-colored bottles. She lathered Kristoff's hair with a gooey substance and covered it with a cap, then instructed him to wait at the table while she did the same to Loki.

"Your hair is unusual," she commented as she worked the product into Loki's hair with strong fingers. "Soft, but incredibly strong. If we weren't going dark, this could take days."

While Loki's new color was setting, Miss Frank tutted disapprovingly as she rinsed out Kristoff's hair. "What on earth did you girls use?"

"Um, it's a secret," Carina answered sheepishly.

"I can guess what that means. Leave it to the professionals next time, ladies," the hairdresser lectured as she repeated the application process with Kristoff. "Let's hope it lightens enough this time. Any more in one sitting might destroy his hair."

"Yeah, let's not do that," Kristoff quipped.

But she need not have worried. When she was finished with both men, they looked almost as they had before the prank. Before she left, she informed them the rest would have to fade or grow out.

Strangely enough, the girls still had not noticed each other's teeth or looked in the mirror. Loki and Kristoff made arrangements to meet the women for dinner at a German restaurant, then left for Loki's fitting without even a hint that anything was amiss. But they laughed and joked about how the girls might discover their new "dental work" on the way to the tailor's shop, which was small and unassuming. Only one dress and a suit graced the display in the spotless window.

The tailor made a few quick adjustments in his back room, which was comfortable but practical, and assured Loki his suit would be ready in a day or two. Once Loki had chosen a hat to match the suit, the two men took their leave of the tailor. Since there was still quite a bit of time left until they would meet the women, they moseyed into a nearby store to browse hunting equipment and fishing tackle.

"I haven't been fishing since I was a boy," Kristoff commented with a nostalgic air as he fingered a wicked-looking, gleaming hook attached to a small, painted wooden fish.

"I've not gone myself for at least two hundred years," Loki murmured, keeping his voice low.

"What are we doing tomorrow?" Kristoff asked. "Maybe we could have a go."

"With or without the girls?" Loki asked.

"I don't relish another day without them, do you?"

"Not really, but the last time I went fishing with a girl, she scared all the fish and let the bait loose," Loki grumbled.

"Let me guess … Sigyn?"

"Yeah," Loki mumbled. "She followed me and Thor down to the river. He thought the whole thing hilarious—until she knocked over our bait can. Then he made her cry, and when her father found out, he convinced Odin to whip us both."

Kristoff snickered. "What was the bait?"

"Crickets and caterpillars," Loki answered. "The crickets weren't easy to catch either."

"Well, I vote for taking the girls but surprising them," Kristoff declared. "We'll just tell them not to scare the fish or dump the bait."

They purchased the supplies they needed for the fishing trip, including a container of live crickets, then spent a good hour discussing fishing techniques and locations with the store owner. Once they left the store, they stashed everything in the trunk, confident the women would not see since they had driven separately.

When they finally moseyed over to the restaurant, they were still a little early.

The women arrived a short time later and flashed shining white smiles at the men as they took their seats.

"Very nice prank, boys," Kathleen remarked. "I'm a little underwhelmed though. I thought you'd go a bit more glamorous than that old trick."

"When did you finally notice?" Kristoff chuckled.

"Soon after you left, but never mind that," Carina answered. "No pranks in public. Are we agreed?"

"Agreed," the men replied in unison.

They talked, ate, and enjoyed each other's company without further incident, then went for an evening stroll before returning to the Green mansion to play games. Loki did not want to leave the crickets in the car overnight, so he placed the container in a somewhat hidden spot on one of the kitchen counters, where he was sure they would be undisturbed until he retrieved them in the morning.

After a few games in the library, Carina went to the kitchen to grab some snacks. Suddenly, an earsplitting scream pierced the air. Loki bolted from the library and skidded into the kitchen to see Carina standing frozen in place, almost hyperventilating. The cricket container lay on its side at her feet where she had dropped it. A few crickets clung for dear life to her skirt and blouse. Several crawled on the counter. More hopped all over the kitchen floor.

"Nobody move!" Loki exclaimed as Kristoff, Kathleen, a maid, the butler, and the housekeeper crowded behind him.

"I hate crickets!" Carina shrieked, barely moving her mouth. "One of them jumped in my mouth when I screamed!"

Loki fought the urge to laugh.

"I'll get the pesticide," the butler sighed.

"No!" Loki protested. "I need them alive. We have to catch them all!"

"Why?" Kathleen spouted. "Can't you see how frightened she is, you big lug? You took it too far."

"This isn't a prank, Kat," Kristoff told her.

"I bought those for live bait. We planned to take you girls fishing tomorrow as a surprise," Loki explained. "I thought I put it in a safe place. Why did you open it, Carina?"

"I didn't know what it was!" she cried. "You should have warned me! You knew I was coming in here to get snacks."

"How was I supposed to know you'd even go over there?" Loki defended himself, no longer amused at the situation when he saw how truly distressed she was. "I didn't know you were afraid of crickets."

"Please, just get them away from me," she pleaded.

Loki gingerly stepped over to her, grabbed the container, scooped as many crickets as he could into it, including the ones on her clothing, and replaced the lid. Kristoff caught a few at the door as they tried to escape and took the container from Loki. There were so many crickets jumping or crawling around, it was nearly impossible to avoid stepping on some. Carina winced with each sickening crunch, still frozen in place. Loki gathered her in his arms and carried her out of the kitchen into the parlor. He checked to make sure no crickets were still attached, set her down on the sofa, and left her there with Kathleen to comfort her. When he returned to the kitchen, the maid and the housekeeper had disappeared. Loki helped Kristoff and the butler chase down the rest of the crickets, carefully putting them back in the container to avoid another breach. Within the hour, the three men had captured as many crickets as they could find and cleaned up the dead ones.

"I'm using the pesticide if I see any more," the butler warned Loki.

"Fair enough," Loki responded. "I'm awfully sorry about this."

"Yes, well, if it's all the same to you, Mr. Black, I think perhaps it's best we leave your bait can in the atrium over-night," the butler stated.

"A wise suggestion," Loki agreed, handing over the container.

When Loki and Kristoff returned to the parlor, it was empty. The two men bid each other goodnight. Neither of them felt inclined to pull their next prank after what had happened.

Loki trudged up the stairs to Carina's room, nervous about how she would respond to him after her fright. To his relief, she was dressed for bed and curled up in her armchair, contentedly reading a book.

"I'm really sorry, my star," he offered, coming over to kiss her cheek.

"I know you didn't mean to," she replied, smiling up at him. "You look tired. Why don't you lie down?"

"Are you coming?" he asked as he stripped down and changed into his usual nighttime attire.

"In a minute," she affirmed. "I just want to finish this chapter."

Loki pulled back the covers and flopped backward onto the bed, without looking, then screeched and scrambled off again. His bare back and arms itched all over with a fiery sensation.

"What did you put in our bed?" he cried in dismay. "Carina, I told you it was an accident!"

"They're stinging nettles," she chortled wickedly. "And they're actually revenge for the tea. Kristoff should have gotten it too, by now."

"Why would anyone grow such a plant?" Loki asked, wincing as the burning sensation increased.

"Oh, they're good for lots of things," Carina insisted. "People eat them, and they attract butterflies and beneficial insects for the vegetable garden out back. And did you know they made German uniforms out of nettle during the war?"

"No, and I don't care," Loki grumped. "This really hurts!"

"Oh, come on," Carina soothed him, setting aside her book and taking him by the hand. "You won't have to suffer much longer."

She gently washed his back and arms with soap and water, then told him to soak in a tub of lukewarm water she had prepared. "I put some baking soda in there. When you're done, we'll have one more step. I'm going to go change the bedding."

Loki soaked for a while, already feeling better. Her tender care was almost worth the pain. He knew the prank war had gotten out of hand, but if he stopped now, he would lose. And he simply could not allow that.

When Carina finally returned, she applied some crushed leaves to his back and arms.

"These are dock leaves," she informed him as she rubbed the leaves into his skin. "Some people say they don't work, but they did for me when I got into the nettles as a child."

"Then you know what this feels like?" Loki asked petulantly, feeling like a boy again.

"Yes, and I also knew I could make it better fairly quickly," she replied.

"It was still mean," Loki pouted. "I wonder how Kristoff fared."

"I told Kat what to do. And I checked in on them when I took the linens outside to shake them out. I warned the maids and the housekeeper, of course, in case any nettles remained. Mrs. Wagner was not happy," Carina told him. "But Kristoff is fine. He apparently only put his hands down on his bed before he realized what was there. And I don't think he sleeps without a shirt on, anyway."

"He doesn't," Loki confirmed. He frowned. "But how do you know that?"

"I just assumed. Kat was soaking his hands when I went in his room. He was wearing pajamas," Carina answered nonchalantly. "How do you feel now?"

"A little peeved that I got it worse than he did," Loki growled.

"Well, I didn't know you were going to flop backward like that," Carina defended herself.

"It is a lot better now," Loki admitted gratefully as she brushed the leaves off.

"Good, then put on some pajamas and your robe," Carina instructed. "I'll put some more dock leaves on you if you need them later, but Kristoff thinks we should lay down some ground rules before this prank war goes any further. And I think he's right."

"So do I," Loki confessed.

He put on his best pair of pajamas and his robe, then followed Carina to Kristoff's room, where the foursome hashed out acceptable boundaries for any pranks moving forward, including no bugs or animals or dangerous plants. They also agreed the prank war would end the night before they left for Hamburg to meet Joseph and Helga.

Before leaving to return to his own room with Carina, Loki pulled Kristoff aside and whispered, "Operation Vanishing Wardrobe starts in two hours."

"Got it," he whispered back. "I'll meet you in the hall outside your room."

Loki settled into the remade bed with his wife but kept himself awake even as her breathing became deep and rhythmic. When he eased himself out of bed to start emptying her wardrobe and dresser drawers, the kitten ran over to investigate and batted at a few articles of clothing.

Carina stirred in her sleep. Loki froze. When she sighed and turned over, he relaxed and continued with his mischief. Once he piled everything near the door, he opened it and began chucking armfuls of clothing into the hallway. He did not see or hear Kristoff until he hit him squarely in the face with one of Carina's nicer dresses.

"Sorry, buddy," Loki whispered.

"No problem. But I think I just saw Carina's cat run out."

"Oh no!" Loki gasped. "We still have to get Kathleen's clothes. And now we have to chase down that blasted cat?"

Kristoff eyed the huge pile of clothing in the hallway. "Kat doesn't have nearly this much. She only packed about a month's worth. I can handle it. You track down the cat."

"Thanks a lot," Loki grumbled.

"You're the one who let him out," Kristoff chuckled. "Where are we hiding everything?"

"I thought it would be funnier to throw it all over the staircase into the great hall," Loki suggested.

"That might mix up their clothes," Kristoff warned. "What a mess that would make."

"The girls can sort it out," Loki assured him. He grinned impishly. "Or the maids can."

"Shame on you!" Kristoff snickered. "You sound like a pampered palace brat."

"Aren't I?" Loki shot back playfully.

He suddenly glimpsed the kitten's tail under another of Carina's dresses, but before he could catch him, the cat scampered down the hallway, right through Kristoff's legs. Loki almost knocked Kristoff down in his attempt to grab the small animal.

"This might be a long night," Kristoff pointed out as he grabbed the nearest section of wall to keep himself from falling.

And he was not wrong. By the time they caught the cat and finished throwing all the women's clothing into the main hall, dawn was much closer than they realized. Loki was immensely grateful to fall back into the bed and drift off to sleep, but morning came far too soon.

"Loki," Carina cooed, playing with his hair and stroking his face to wake him. "I thought we were going fishing!"

"Oh, go without me," Loki groaned, flipping over onto his stomach.

Carina laughed. "Well, fine! I was going to suggest a little fun before I get dressed, but never mind!"

Loki groaned again, too tired to protest. He allowed his eyes to drift shut and started to dream.

Suddenly, Carina pounced on him.

"Where are my clothes, you beluga?" she hollered, yanking away his pillow and the sheet he tried to throw over his head.

"Did you just call me a big lug again?" Loki mumbled.

"Kathleen called you that, not me," she corrected him. "And no, I just called you a beluga."

"Is that better?" he muttered, finally opening his eyes.

"No, it's way worse!" she exclaimed. "Now, where are my clothes? I have nothing to wear!"

"After all the shopping you've been doing?" Loki teased.

"Very funny! I'll just go down to breakfast in my under-garments, then," Carina spouted.

"Oh no, you won't," Loki growled.

He grabbed her and tickled her, keeping a firm grip on her arms with one hand so she could not tickle him back. She squirmed, squealed with laughter, and begged him to stop. He ignored her and soon regretted it, for she managed to get her toes in his worst ticklish spot. In seconds, she gained the upper hand, tickling him mercilessly and rendering him helpless.

Unable to stand the onslaught any longer, he gasped, "I surrender!"

Carina released him, still slightly breathless herself. "Since you refuse to tell me where you put all my clothes, I'll just have to steal some of yours."

They were interrupted by a rather unhappy-sounding knock at the door, as if someone had rapidly struck it four times with two knuckles. Carina hurriedly wrapped herself in a blanket while Loki grabbed his robe and answered the door. The housekeeper stood there, looking stern, disgruntled, and determined.

"Would you care to explain the mountain of women's clothing in the hall, Mr. Black?" she demanded, hands on her hips.

"Carina was just asking me where all her clothes were," Loki answered flippantly, then spoke over his shoulder to his wife. "Sounds like they're downstairs, Carina."

"And we all know very well who put them there," Mrs. Wagner huffed indignantly. "Poor Miss Jones cannot even leave her room until we sort out this mess."

Loki smirked unrepentantly. "Alright, I confess. Kristoff and I did it last night."

"For all that's decent, Carina, please show us whose clothes are whose so we can put them away and Miss Jones can get dressed," the housekeeper pleaded.

"Maybe Kristoff and I should clean it up," Loki suggested.

"It's bad enough you rifled through their clothing once. I won't stand for it again." Mrs. Wagner shook her finger in Loki's face, then looked past him at Carina. "I'm still very unhappy with you regarding the nettles in the bed linens, young lady. And now this?"

"I'm sorry, Mrs. Wagner," Carina offered sheepishly. "I know the pranks have gotten out of hand. We set some rules last night, but we didn't think about messes or how it affects the staff. We'll be more considerate, but it will all be over when we leave for Hamburg, anyway."

"Will it, indeed?" she retorted dryly, narrowing her eyes.

"Yes," Carina confirmed. "I'll come down and separate Kathleen's clothes from mine."

"Very good," Mrs. Wagner replied with an approving nod, her features softening slightly. "You'll have two maids at your disposal. We won't be serving breakfast until everything is back where it belongs."

"Thank you, Mrs. Wagner," Carina called to her retreating form. Then she commanded Loki, "You stay here, Mister."

Loki got dressed, then absentmindedly stroked the black kitten, trying to think of a suitable name for him besides Loki-Cat. Carina finally returned, followed by two maids and the housekeeper, all of whom carried stacks of clothing. They sent him down to the dining room to wait with Kristoff and Kathleen.

"You boys really upset the staff," Kathleen laughed. "I, for one, found it quite clever."

"Why, thank you," Loki replied, quite pleased. "But I guess we have to amend our rules to include avoiding huge messes now."

Kristoff and Kathleen nodded. Then the three of them turned their conversation to fishing. Kathleen was surprisingly knowledgeable on the subject, having fished with her cousins every summer until her parents moved her family to Chicago for her father's job.

"Does he still work in Chicago?" Loki asked casually.

Kathleen's face dropped.

Kristoff answered for her, "Her parents died under suspicious circumstances ten years ago."

"I'm terribly sorry," Loki murmured.

"It's part of why I became a journalist," Kathleen stated matter-of-factly, though tears formed in her eyes. "But I never did uncover even the faintest clue, so it's still a mystery. I guess I just wasn't cut out for private detective work."

"Don't give up yet, Kat," Kristoff encouraged her. "No one

would take you seriously, remember? It won't always be that way."

"Maybe," she muttered.

Carina came into the dining room at that moment, followed by the staff carrying the breakfast trays. The group ate quickly, then packed one of Joseph's less luxurious cars with sandwiches, cookies, fishing poles, buckets, nets, and a tackle box. Loki tucked his bait can far away from Carina's seat. Once he and Kristoff strapped a rowboat to the top of the car, the foursome headed to a lake with a reputation as an excellent fishing spot, according to the store owner who sold them the fishing gear.

The drive was somewhat long but relaxing. Once they arrived, Kathleen strode over to a rickety, wooden bait shack to buy some night crawlers, her bait of choice. Loki and Kristoff unloaded the rowboat, packed it with the rest of their gear, and dragged it across the small, sandy beach to the water. The sun cast tiny shards of brilliant white light onto the rippling surface of the lake. When Kathleen returned, Kristoff got into the rowboat first. He kept his body low and gently stepped into the center to avoid tipping, then sat in the rowing station closest to the bow, facing the stern. Loki steadied the stern to allow the women to climb in and settle themselves in the center. He got in last, then gently pushed one oar against the shore to release the boat into the water.

"What do you boys say to a little contest?" Kathleen suggested when they reached their chosen fishing spot near the middle of the lake.

"What did you have in mind?" Kristoff asked with a grin. He could barely take his eyes off Kathleen, who looked almost boyish in knickerbockers and one of Kristoff's shirts, sleeves rolled up above her elbows.

Carina was dressed the same, in one of Loki's shirts. Loki had to admit there was something appealing about the sporty look, which they had adapted for safety and convenience more than anything. Heavy dresses or skirts would not do if they happened to fall into the water. The men had opted for swimming shorts and long tank tops.

"We have two buckets. We could do biggest fish caught or most fish caught. Girls against boys," Kathleen replied.

"Hardly seems fair," Kristoff quipped.

"And why not?" Kathleen huffed, placing her fists on her hips. "Because we're women?"

"Well, yeah," Kristoff said hesitantly. "We have more experience, we're stronger …" His voice trailed off as Kathleen's face grew stormy and Carina raised her eyebrows at him. "Help me out here, Luke. Don't you think a couples' contest would be more sporting?"

"Oh sure, that would be super convenient for you, wouldn't it?" Loki protested. "I heard how much experience Kathleen has fishing. You just want her on your team. Carina and I wouldn't stand a chance!"

"Oh, I see how it is," Carina spoke up indignantly. "You don't think I can hold my own just because I'm afraid of crickets."

Loki stuttered a bit, knowing his face betrayed him. He raised his eyebrows at Kristoff, who snickered as if he knew something Loki did not.

"Give me one of those night crawlers, Kat," Carina demanded.

Loki watched in amazement as she expertly baited her hook, dropped it over the side of the boat, and maneuvered the line to make the bait dance and dangle below the surface of the lake.

"I'm impressed," Loki admitted with wonder.

"Give it a few more minutes, and you'll owe me an engraved apology," Carina responded, so intensely focused on what she was doing, she did not look at him.

"Well, that's a bit much," Loki grumbled.

He carefully removed one of his squirming crickets and pushed the sharp hook through a hard spot near its head to prevent losing the bait. Then he dropped his own line from the other side of the rowboat. Within minutes, he had a tug. He quickly reeled in the line and pulled up a small, rather disappointing fish with spikes fanning out down its spine.

"There's not much to him, but first catch has to count for something," Loki announced, holding the fish up for the others to see.

"Sunfish love crickets," Kristoff laughed. "Catch about four more of those, and you just might have enough for a plate."

"Should I throw him back?" Loki asked doubtfully, carefully removing the shimmering fish from the hook to avoid getting poked by the spikes.

"No, put him in the boys' bucket," Kathleen told him. "You'll probably catch a few more."

Just then, Carina let out an excited squeal and started reeling in her line. In moments, she pulled up a magnificent, thrashing brown trout.

"Look at the size of that fellow!" Kristoff exclaimed.

Carina unhooked him, plopped him into the other bucket,

and grinned proudly at Loki. "First catch belongs to you, but I bet no one catches a bigger fish."

"Maybe I'll have to make you eat your words. Literally," Loki teased. "Catfish like crickets, and they get fairly big."

"More fishing, less talking," Kathleen spouted.

Soon, she reeled in a lovely perch, then a striped bass, several panfish, and a decent-sized walleye all in a row. Just as Loki began to think all of the fish were magically drawn to Kathleen's hook, Kristoff landed a largemouth bass almost as big as Carina's trout.

"He's obviously not full-grown," Kristoff pointed out. "But maybe his parents are down there."

Loki caught another sunfish, bigger than the first, just as Carina caught a walleye bigger than Kathleen's. The girls' bucket was looking quite full when Loki yanked up a bullhead catfish that was about two-thirds the size of Carina's trout.

"Still not as big as mine," she taunted in a singsong voice.

Loki reached over and playfully nudged her shoulder, harder than he intended. The movement shifted her center of gravity, causing a chain reaction as she tried to readjust herself. The boat rocked slightly, disturbing Kathleen's balance as she reeled in yet another fish. Kristoff grabbed her arm to steady her, but this only added to her precarious position. She fell into the water with a shriek, pulling Kristoff with her and causing the boat to dip in the other direction. In seconds, the boat capsized and deposited everything, including Loki and Carina, into the lake.

By the time Loki shot back up to the surface, sputtering and soaked, Kathleen and Kristoff had already righted the boat. Carina was treading water, her water-laden red hair slicked back away from her face, with the ends floating around her in the water. If Loki had not been so concerned for her safety, he would have been content to just watch her and imagine her as one of those elusive mermaids he had read about in a fantasy story. Instead, he quickly swam over to her.

"Are you alright?" he asked.

"Yes, I can swim quite well," she laughed. "What about you? Are you quite happy with what you've done?"

Her words were harsh, but her tone was playful.

Kristoff did not hesitate to jump into the good-natured teasing. He splashed Loki from where he held the boat and hollered, "Yeah, they wouldn't have come so close to beating us if you hadn't pulled that stunt, Luke!"

"What do you mean? We did beat you!" Kathleen exclaimed, splashing water over the boat at Kristoff. "Largest fish to Carina and most fish to me!"

"Where's your proof?" Loki asked with a gleeful, impish grin.

Carina narrowed her eyes, gripped both his shoulders, and to his shock, shoved him underwater. When she pulled him up, he had not quite regained his wits after how quickly she had bested him.

"Did you capsize us on purpose?" Carina demanded.

"No, of course not," he growled. "But this is definitely on purpose!"

With that, he grabbed Carina around the waist and threw her. Shrieking, she soared several feet away from him and fell into the water again with a huge splash. Kathleen came to her defense and tried to dunk Loki, unsuccessfully. Carina swam back and joined in the effort to submerge him. Kristoff pulled the women away and found himself their new target. They were all laughing, splashing, and hooting with delight, completely unaware as the boat floated away on the resulting waves.

"Do you young people need rescuing?" called a voice from an unusually large, beautiful canoe that had approached them without their noticing.

"Not really. We can all swim," Kristoff laughed. "Sorry to have concerned you."

The rugged, salt-and-pepper-haired man in the canoe pointed toward the escaping rowboat with a twinkle in his hazel eyes. "You plan to swim all the way out there to retrieve your boat, do you?"

Kristoff and Loki groaned as the girls gasped.

The would-be rescuer chuckled. "Maybe pay more attention to your vessel next time, gentlemen. You lost your oars as well?"

Kristoff nodded. "It appears we do, in fact, need rescuing."

"Climb aboard," the man offered good-naturedly. "Ladies first, and don't capsize me while you're at it."

Kristoff and Loki held the canoe steady while the girls hoisted themselves over the side. Then they clambered in on opposite sides, so as not to throw off the balance.

"I've never seen such a large canoe!" Kathleen exclaimed.

"My father came from a large family," their rescuer replied. "He and my grandfather made it together. It's been in the family ever since."

"It's beautiful," Kathleen breathed, tracing a decorative carving.

"Well, it's a good thing it seats more than most canoes, or you boys would still be treading water," the man chortled. "We'll take the girls back to shore, then go get your boat."

"Thank you," the four said, almost in unison.

"I couldn't very well let you keep scaring the fish with all that ruckus you were making," he chuckled. He pointed to a distant shore. "My wife and I set up camp not far from there. She can help you dry off. I was heading back for a late lunch anyway. You're welcome to join us."

"Oh, we couldn't impose," Carina objected politely.

"Speak for yourself!" Kristoff quipped. "We lost our lunch and all our fish."

"I caught plenty this morning," the man stated, gesturing to the variety of fish in several buckets. "If you boys help me get a fire going, I'll share."

"We can do that," Loki agreed, holding out his hand to initiate formal introductions. "I'm Luke. This is my wife, Carina. And this is Kristoff and his fiancée, Kathleen."

"Pleased to meet you," the man stated, shaking hands first with Loki then Kristoff, and tipping his hat to the women. "I'm Finn."

Finn handed Kristoff an extra paddle. Loki insisted on taking the other to relieve their rescuer. They all chatted casually about the weather and the beauty of the lake as their new acquaintance described how he had been coming to this particular lake since boyhood. Once they reached the shore, Finn led them to the campsite set in a little clearing surrounded by tall trees.

"Sophie, look what I fished out of the lake," he called to his wife, a friendly looking woman with silver-streaked hair that enhanced her blue-gray eyes.

"My, my," she exclaimed, looking over the bedraggled foursome. "Did you turn over?"

"Yes, it was my fault," Loki answered. "But I still maintain it was a complete accident."

"It almost always is," she laughed. "I would love to hear the story!"

After a round of introductions, Loki and Kristoff gathered wood and helped Finn build a crackling fire. They left the ladies to prepare lunch and set off in pursuit of their runaway rowboat. By the time they reached it, the vessel had lodged itself in the branches of a fallen tree on the shore. At first, they tried pushing the boat loose with the canoe paddles. When that proved futile, Kristoff and Loki climbed out of the boat and waded to shore. While Finn manned his own boat, Loki planted himself at the stern and pushed as Kristoff tugged at the bow. Loki underestimated his own strength, however, and shoved so hard, the boat shot out into open water, knocking Kristoff backward. Loki tried to grab it but missed. He fell over the tree and almost impaled himself on a large branch. Kristoff kept his head and swam after the runaway rowboat. He grabbed the starboard side and held on as Finn brought the other boat around. Loki swam out to help them tie a rope to ensure the boat did not escape again. Then they towed the elusive water vessel to the right section of shore. After they secured the rowboat to Joseph's car, they got back in Finn's canoe and returned to the clearing.

Before the campsite came into view, they could smell the mouth-watering aroma of fresh fish sizzling over a hot flame, combined with a whiff of something equally tantalizing that Loki did not recognize. The now-breaded fish smoked in a heavy cast-iron skillet over the fire. Several bulging packets of foil shone brightly underneath the skillet. Sophie checked the fish, flaking the white flesh with a fork. When she pronounced the food was ready, the girls carefully removed the foil packets and opened them to reveal a steaming assortment of vegetables—chopped onions, tomatoes, potatoes, and a green squash the humans called zucchini. The tender, golden fish burst with perfect flavor, enhanced by the wholesome vegetables. Together, it was a fine meal. After they had eaten enough, Sophie brought out a package of soft and fluffy white confections. She showed them how to choose the perfect stick to impale the marshmallows and roast them over the fire.

Loki burned his first one but discovered the charred, crunchy exterior combined with the gooey, creamy center was the perfect combination. Carina, on the other hand, insisted the best ones were lightly toasted. The others preferred theirs somewhere in between, except for Finn, who declined to roast any at all and shoved them into his mouth whole. After everyone else had roasted one or two each, Sophie brought out some chocolate and a sleeve of graham crackers. She made a stacked concoction with a roasted marshmallow and a square of chocolate between two crackers. She broke it into four pieces for her guests to sample.

"What is this?" Loki exclaimed after wolfing his down. The incredible taste and combined textures of gooey and crunchy pleased him to his core.

Sophie laughed. "I don't know. I used to make it for our children, but I never named it. My daughter, who lives in America now, taught the Girl Scout troop she runs how to make them. The girls absolutely love them. They call them 'some more' in English. Who knows? Maybe they'll put it in one of their own recipe books someday."

"Did you say Girl Scouts?" Kristoff asked with great interest. "I was a Boy Scout for a couple of years. Are they similar?"

Loki tuned out as the others discussed the similarities between the scouting programs since it did not really interest him at that moment. He reflected instead on the wholesome scents of the fresh air, the strength and power in the towering trees, the warmth of the sun, and the gentle sounds of the lake. In a way, he felt connected with his boyhood, with no pressing need to be anywhere or do anything but enjoy nature and the company around him. He began to relax as he had not since he started his education. He found his thoughts turning surprisingly to Asgard. If he had chosen to do his rite of passage as expected, the last few weeks might have been just like his current experience, without the company. The sun ducked behind a cloud, and Loki shivered.

"Get closer to the fire if you're cold," Carina whispered.

"It's not that," Loki whispered back. "I was just thinking I could be doing something like this back home—but without you. Being here with you makes all the difference."

She squeezed his hand. "That's sweet, Luke. I'm glad to be here with you too."

"How long have you two been married?" Sophie asked, having witnessed the tender moment.

"Almost a month," Carina replied.

"Three weeks," Loki answered at the exact same time.

Sophie and Finn exchanged knowing looks, as if their answers signified something.

"Well, congratulations!" Finn exclaimed.

"And what about you two?" Kathleen inquired.

"Forty years this past May," Sophie responded. "Sometimes it seems it's been forever."

"Hey now," Finn protested.

"And other times, it seems like just yesterday," Sophie finished, winking fondly at her husband, whose eyes grew tender as his leathery face crinkled into a broad smile.

"You're just as beautiful as the day I married you," Finn complimented her, walking over and planting a kiss on the top of her head.

Sophie smiled radiantly at him, then addressed Kathleen and Kristoff. "And when are you two getting married?"

"We haven't set a date yet," Kathleen answered. "Perhaps sometime next spring?"

Kristoff remained strangely silent and merely shifted his pensive gaze between the two married couples.

"Spring is a beautiful time for a wedding," Sophie commented.

As the fire slowly dwindled down, the older couple regaled the foursome with comical stories about their wedding day mishaps, early marriage, and raising children. Though it was a warm summer afternoon, no one seemed inclined to move away from the extra heat from the fire. Even as the conversation lulled, no one moved.

"Well, I suppose I'd better start cleaning up," Sophie finally sighed, easing herself out of her folding chair.

The two younger women jumped to their feet and offered to help, as if eager to stay in Sophie's presence.

"Why don't I drive you boys over to your car so you can drive back here to pick up the ladies?" Finn offered.

Kristoff and Loki readily agreed and climbed into Finn's station wagon, not quite ready to part ways with their new friend. He possessed an easygoing, quiet wisdom. Loki found himself wishing he could talk to Finn any time he pleased. Once they returned to the campsite with Joseph's car, they found everything cleaned up and the women chatting amicably. Everyone seemed reluctant to part ways.

"Girls, here's our address and telephone number," Sophie offered, holding out a piece of paper with the information written in a firm, elegant hand. "Please stay in touch!"

"We will," the girls promised in unison, hugging Sophie in turn.

"Gee, I really hate for you folks to go home empty-handed," Finn remarked, scratching a slight balding spot on his head. "Why don't you take home some of my fish?"

"That's very kind of you, but we're leaving for America the day after tomorrow," Loki replied.

"America!" Sophie exclaimed. "Will you be going near Charleston?"

"Yes, actually," Kristoff affirmed. "We'll be there in early September."

"Our daughter lives there," Sophie informed them. She took the paper back and scripted another address. "Maybe you can look her up?"

"We'd be happy to, after all you've done for us," Carina affirmed. "We could even bring her a message or something from you if you'd like."

"Would you?" Sophie practically squealed. "Why, just this morning, I finished knitting a blanket for our first grandbaby, due to arrive in October, but we can't visit until Christmas at the earliest." She disappeared into their tent to retrieve the blanket, proclaiming, "This is the hand of Providence, this is!"

"Providence?" Loki whispered to Carina. "Is that her god?"

"Kind of," Carina whispered back. "It's another way to refer to the one God we've talked about. She means He's provided a need or want through us. It's actually quite an honor."

During this exchange, Finn packed up half a dozen fish with plenty of ice and handed the bulky package to Kristoff. "You'll at least have fresh fish for tomorrow. I insist."

Sophie came back outside with another handwritten note and the blanket, a perfectly crafted masterpiece of colorful yarn. Pastel blues, pinks, yellows, and greens blended together in an aesthetically pleasing pattern that engaged the eye but did not overwhelm.

Carina gasped as she reached out and fingered the soft texture. "It's beautiful, Sophie!"

"Stay in touch with me, dear girl, and I'll make one for your first baby," Sophie promised, hugging her again.

Carina giggled as a pretty pink spread over her smooth cheeks. As Kristoff put the fish into the car, Finn focused on his wife's delight over Carina's obvious interest in the baby blanket. Only Loki seemed to notice Kathleen's intent inspection of the ground. As if she felt his curious gaze, Kathleen met Loki's eyes for a split second. She looked away. He wondered at the flash of pain he saw, but she composed herself so quickly, he assumed he had imagined it. And he knew not to ask her any probing questions, though he doubted she would hesitate had the roles been reversed. For one so bold in her investigations and journalism, she maintained a surprising air of privacy and reservation about herself.

After yet another round of hugs, goodbyes, and promises to write or call, the two young couples finally pulled themselves away from the delightful camping site and their new friends. Carina held the baby blanket the entire way home, fingering it with a dreamy smile on her face.

They arrived back at the Green mansion just in time for dinner. Despite the huge campfire lunch, Loki found his hunger had returned with a vengeance. The smells emanating from the kitchen elicited a loud growl from his rumbling stomach, much to his chagrin, until Kristoff's stomach answered back. Both girls snickered, though they looked just as eager to enjoy dinner. After they had all washed and changed, they gathered in the dining room. The staff seemed especially pleased with their culinary efforts and proudly set each prepared plate in front of each diner.

The steamed vegetables were shiny, the meatloaf looked moist and tender, and the rolls were the perfect shade of light brown. The food looked so delicious, no one hesitated to start eating right away.

But all was not as it seemed.

Carina sampled the vegetables, then made a horrified face within seconds. She reached for her water glass, but the water would not budge. At the same time, Loki bit into his roll and was treated to a mouthful of some white, tangy substance. He glanced at Kristoff and Kathleen. They had both spit out their bites of meatloaf, which Loki could see was filled with small pieces of paper.

"Is something wrong?" the housekeeper asked as she bustled back into the dining room in time to see the looks on their faces.

Kristoff was poking the firm, clear substance in his water glass. "Is this some kind of gelatin?"

"Mrs. Wagner, there's something terribly wrong with the food," Carina declared. "The vegetables are horribly bitter, the meatloaf has paper in it, and I think the rolls are filled with mayonnaise!"

"I will address this with the staff immediately!" Mrs. Wagner exclaimed. "We planned a special treat for dessert. Shall we serve that now while we sort this out?"

By this time, Loki had noticed the twinkle in the house-keeper's eyes. He began to suspect they had been pranked, but he doubted his own instincts. Surely, the servants would not dare. He knew neither Odin nor Frigga would tolerate such behavior, though they treated all their palace servants with respect.

Carina nodded, looking somewhat suspicious herself. Kathleen and Kristoff silently exchanged glances. Neither of them touched the rest of the food on their plates as Mrs. Wagner hurried back to the kitchen.

When she returned, a maid followed her, bearing ice cream sundaes in frosted glasses. Loki eyed his carefully and touched the cold mound with one finger. Since it looked and felt exactly like real ice cream, which he loved, he spooned some into his mouth. The others watched him and chuckled slightly when he spat it right back out.

"Not ice cream?" Kristoff guessed wryly.

Loki shook his head ruefully. This latest trick was worse than the mayonnaise-infused roll. "It tastes like overly salty mashed potatoes and badly flavored gravy."

"Mrs. Wagner, what is the meaning of this?" Carina demanded. "My father would not—"

"But no, my dear duckie, he approved the entire operation and even made a few suggestions," Mrs. Wagner confessed gleefully, unable to hide her feigned innocence any longer. "I called him this morning and told him everything."

"Clearly we've been had," Kristoff remarked, a grin spreading across his face. "I didn't think Joseph even *had* this kind of humor."

"I can't believe it," Carina gasped, staring at the prank food. "My father was in on this?"

"Bravo," Kathleen laughed, clapping lightly.

"I'm quite impressed, Mrs. Wagner. You really are a fine actress," Loki praised her. When she curtsied at his words, he continued, "I really am hoping there's an alternative to all of this."

"Yes, my dear Mr. Black, but the real meal comes with a condition," the housekeeper warned. "Absolutely no more pranks."

"I readily agree," Loki announced. "Especially if there's real ice cream."

"There is," Mrs. Wagner confirmed, visibly pleased with the success of her elaborate prank.

"I concede as well," Kristoff stated. "I'll even say the girls won if it means I don't have to eat this."

"Let's not take it that far," Loki protested.

"Why don't we call it a draw?" Carina offered.

"Surely you boys can live with that," Kathleen added. When they nodded, she spoke for them all, "We accept your terms, noble housekeeper, and plead your mercy for our heinous crimes against the home you so efficiently manage."

"That's my girl," Kristoff whispered to Loki.

"And they call *me* silver-tongued," Loki whispered back.

The housekeeper bowed, then signaled to the waiting maid. Suspiciously merry-looking servants, who had apparently been watching and listening in hiding, whisked away the prank food and brought out the real food. The former pranksters all cautiously tried each dish, then dug into the excellent meal with relish. The servants replaced the gelatin-filled glasses with water, then served the real ice cream sundaes after dinner.

The day had been so full, no one seemed to have the energy for games or much conversation after dessert. They soon parted ways for the night. After he and Carina had gone to bed, Loki lay awake, listening to his wife's rhythmic breathing and the kitten's purring, quite content with the day. In just over twenty-four hours, they would be leaving for Hamburg. Part of him was disappointed the prank war was officially over. But with so much to do to prepare for the tour, and the danger they would most likely face soon, it was just as well.

The diversions had been fun while they lasted.

31

Beautiful German countryside, resplendent with wildflowers dancing in the morning sun, flew by Loki's train window. Despite the beauty to which he was being treated, he felt himself growing increasingly agitated as the two couples neared Hamburg to meet with Joseph and Helga.

Over the last twenty-four hours, Loki and Kristoff had fallen into a bored melancholy without the pranks to distract them. While the women focused on final preparations for the tour, the men had resorted to sparring with each other to fill the time. Loki taught Kristoff some knife-fighting tips, and Kristoff showed Loki his best street brawl moves. Since Loki was stronger, he usually won, but Kristoff surprised him a few times.

Now they were confined to the train as they sped along the tracks toward an even longer train ride, which would include a conversation Loki dreaded on behalf of his wife but knew she desperately needed. And due to the constraints of the train, he would most likely not be able to interfere if Joseph did not handle things well.

What on earth am I going to talk with Helga about? he wondered to himself.

He expected the boredom to continue. He knew he was being terribly selfish, but he felt a little jaded by the closeness developing between Carina and Kathleen. They were still jabbering on and on about dresses and hairstyles and tour details that did not interest him in the slightest.

Girls! he huffed to himself, staring grumpily out the window.

He glanced at the book he had brought but did not bother to open it. He had no desire to read. He wanted to talk with his wife, to prepare her for her talk with her father, but his conscience warned him to let her be. He was wise enough to recognize he was making a mountain out of a molehill, as the humans liked to say, but that knowledge did not improve his mood.

Kristoff set down the paper he was reading and eyed Loki with concern. "Hey Luke, let's go see if the dining car is open yet."

Loki was about to argue just for the sake of arguing but clamped his mouth shut and nodded when he saw the look on his friend's face.

Once they were out of earshot of the women, who had barely noticed their departure, Kristoff remarked, "You've been grumpy all day. What's going on?"

"Nothing," Loki muttered.

"Fine, don't tell me," Kristoff said with a careless shrug. "I'm not exactly happy either, you know, but I'm man enough to talk about it."

"Why?" Loki asked sheepishly. His own moping had made him oblivious to Kristoff's disposition.

"Do you remember when Kat told Sophie we were thinking next spring for the wedding?"

"Yes," Loki replied. "I'm surprised you want to wait that long."

"*We* don't," Kristoff corrected him. "*She* does. We've talked about it twice since then. I'd like to get married as soon as the tour is over. But she thinks it's too soon."

"Okay." Loki drew out the word, unsure how else to respond.

"Don't you get it? I think she's having second thoughts," Kristoff declared.

"Oh, I doubt that," Loki disagreed. "Maybe she has a good reason. You haven't known each other very long, you know."

"Neither have you and Carina," Kristoff pointed out. "I know what I want. Why doesn't she?"

"She's not you," Loki reminded him. "I'll tell you something. The more tightly you grasp something or someone, the more it will slip through your fingers."

"Sage advice," Kristoff acknowledged reluctantly. "Does that apply to you?"

"What's that supposed to mean?" Loki huffed.

"You think I don't know why you've been grumpy all morning? You're jealous of Kat," Kristoff stated.

"Why would I be jealous of her?" Loki deflected, while thinking, *How does he see right through me?*

"Carina hasn't paid any attention to you since we boarded the train. I've been watching you scratch and itch this whole time," Kristoff informed him.

"That's a little creepy, Kristoff. But you're not wrong. Kathleen hasn't said more than two words to you either. Why doesn't it bother you?" Loki asked moodily.

"Because I remind myself she isn't replacing me any more than Carina is replacing you," Kristoff lectured. "Women need other women. It's just the way of things. I'm actually glad they're becoming such good friends."

"Like us?" Loki murmured suddenly, surprised at the sentiment coming out of his own mouth.

"Like us," Kristoff repeated, smiling warmly as he placed a firm, but brotherly hand on Loki's shoulder. "I guess we both need to let go of some things, eh?"

"Yeah," Loki admitted. His selfish attitude vanished as he considered his wife's needs. His stomach rumbled slightly. "Are we actually going to the dining car? It must be open by now."

Kristoff laughed. "Probably. Let's check, then go get the girls. They're sure to notice if we eat without them."

Loki bit his tongue before he released the snarky comment that had popped into his mind. Instead, he followed Kristoff, determined to be more understanding and less prideful.

The dining car was indeed open. The two men retrieved the women, who continued their conversation through lunch. But now that he was thinking more clearly, Loki figured he could stew over Carina's preoccupation with the tour and her developing friendship, or he could simply ask her to spend some of the train trip with him. He decided on the latter, but to his surprise, he did not have to broach the subject.

On the way back to their seats after lunch, Carina asked, "Luke, would you mind if we talked for a while? I know you brought your book, but I was hoping we could discuss what I'm going to say to my father."

"Absolutely!" Loki affirmed. "Incidentally, so was I."

Carina smiled and took his hand, leading him to the mostly empty lounge car. She sat down next to him and leaned her head on his shoulder. "I'm sorry if you felt ignored the last couple of days."

"You noticed?" Loki was shocked.

"No, Kat did," Carina admitted, her eyes downcast. "It's been so long since I had a female friend, I got a little carried away."

Loki lifted her chin so she would look at him. "It's okay. I suppose we can't be together every second of every day. I'm glad you have a friend."

She searched his eyes, then kissed him, abruptly and hungrily.

"Don't tease me, Carina," Loki groaned. "You shouldn't kiss me like that when you know we won't have much privacy for a few days."

"Now, Luke," she purred, "where is your discipline?"

He laughed. "More people are sure to be trickling in soon. Are we going to talk about your father or not?"

The rest of the train ride to Hamburg, Carina role-played with Loki. At first, he used Joseph's voice and responded so outlandishly, Carina laughed until she gasped for air. But they soon grew serious and ironed out what points she wanted to cover. By the time the train pulled into the station, she was ready, and Loki anticipated the conversation would go well.

They found Joseph and Helga inside the station. After a flurry of hugs and excited greetings, Joseph declared, "Well, we have one answer to our puzzle."

"What's that?" Kristoff asked. "Let me guess, our phone was tapped?"

"It was indeed," Joseph confirmed. "And I found two little electronic machines I've never seen before. I didn't think the technology existed, but I think they were some sort of miniature recording devices. Not even the United States government has access to anything like it."

"Where were they?" Loki asked. "Do you still have them?"

"One in the kitchen and the other in the living room," Joseph answered, arching one eyebrow. "Yes, I still have them. I'm turning them over to the Pinkertons when we get to New York."

"I'd like to take a look at them," Loki stated.

"They're hidden in my luggage," Joseph replied. "It'll have to wait. I'm guessing they were planted long before the first attack."

"That must be how they knew when Hod left his post!" exclaimed Kristoff.

"And when Carina and I arrived," Loki added nervously.

"Which means they sneaked into the house without my knowing it," Helga commented. "I must admit, I'm glad to be going to New York now. They may have returned for those devices at the very least."

"Speaking of New York, hadn't we better board the train?" Kathleen asked just as the whistle sounded.

The conductor shouted, "All aboard!"

The group hurried to the boarding area and handed over their tickets for the conductor to punch. Once on the train to Calais, they made their way down the aisle, searching for their grouped seat assignments.

"Father, will you sit with me?" Carina asked.

Joseph beamed at his daughter. "Of course! For the first stretch anyway."

Helga winked at Loki as he settled into the seat next to her. "Don't worry, Luke. I prepared him."

Loki smiled gratefully at Helga, then peeked over the seats to make sure everyone had settled in for the first stretch. As Kristoff and Kathleen talked quietly, looking quite cozy, Carina caught Loki's glance and flashed him a confident smile.

Loki relaxed into his own seat and turned his attention partly to Helga. Since Carina had role-played with him, he saw no issue with enhancing the sounds of Carina's conversation with her father, though he knew he must not interfere. Listening to both them and Helga was a bit of a mental exercise. Once he was sure the conversation was progressing nicely, he gave Helga his full attention as she told him about her garden and a short visit from Kvasir and Sigyn.

She's nervous, Loki thought, noting how fast she was talking.

"Is something bothering you?" Loki asked cautiously.

Helga patted his hand. "Don't you worry about me, dear boy! I just haven't traveled much. But I do want to hear all about this prank war. Joseph told me a little."

Loki grinned and launched into a spectacular retelling, pleased when Helga laughed several times. Kristoff overheard and poked his head around to correct Loki once or twice on details. Kathleen also tuned in with silent amusement.

After a couple of hours, Carina switched seats with Helga, then filled Loki in on how well her communication with Joseph had gone. Her father had allowed her to be honest without interruption or defense, waiting to explain his own perspective with respect to hers. As he listened, Loki sent silent thanks—to whoever might be listening—for this new level of understanding between father and daughter.

Once Carina had finished recounting the conversation, they fell into contented silence. The train hummed along the tracks, lulling Loki to sleep. Carina woke him in time to visit the dining car. After they had eaten dinner and returned to their seats, Loki noticed Kathleen sitting alone.

"Where'd Kristoff run off to?" Loki asked her.

"He needed some air," Kathleen replied, not taking her gaze from the window.

"I think I do too," Loki announced, remembering how unusually quiet Kristoff had been during dinner.

Loki sensed something might be amiss and went searching for his friend. Loki finally found him standing on the little railed-in platform between two passenger cars.

"What are you doing out here?" Loki asked.

"Oh, hey," Kristoff responded distractedly. "Just thinking."

"About you and Kathleen?"

"No, actually," Kristoff replied. He released his hold on the short railing to his left and scratched his head, scrunching up his face slightly. "Well, sort of, I guess. I've been trying to figure out what to do after this tour."

"Whatever you want," Loki commented casually. "Isn't that what you normally do?"

"I don't really know what I want, pal." Kristoff looked down at the bits of visible ground and track rushing by in a blur under the cracks of the wooden planks at his feet.

"You did this morning," Loki pointed out. "What changed?"

"I guess I'm trying to put Kat first," Kristoff replied. "It's a new experience for me, so I'm a little thrown."

"That's a healthy thing," Loki assured him. "What does she want?"

"She only knows what she doesn't want," Kristoff sighed.

"Well, that's a start," Loki encouraged him.

"But I'm at an impasse," Kristoff vented with a grunt of frustration. "For one, she doesn't want me to go back to Europe after the tour."

"That's a dilemma, but a minor one," Loki mused.

"How is it minor? I'd lose my whole business if I relocated to Chicago to be near her. And how would I manage you and Carina?"

"How would you manage us if you got married?"

Kristoff grinned sheepishly. "I assumed she would come with me. She can write from anywhere."

"Can't you work from anywhere?"

"Not as easily," Kristoff asserted. "I would have to travel back and forth a lot. Kat doesn't seem to understand it could be weeks in between visits."

"I guess you'll have to compromise. Would it be possible for the two of you to travel with each other when you can?"

Kristoff rubbed the slight stubble on his chin. "I suppose. I do see her point about having our home base in Chicago since she already has her own place. I just don't want to live in hotels until she decides it's a good time to get married."

"Does she understand that?"

"I don't know. Maybe?" Kristoff guessed. "I really think she's just being stubborn. I wish she'd tell me what's holding her back."

"Maybe she will when she's ready," Loki suggested. "Do you want me to ask Carina to talk with her?"

"No, we'll figure it out," Kristoff declined. "Thanks for the offer. What about you?"

"What about me?" Loki repeated.

"After the tour. Where do you want to go next?"

"I haven't thought about it," Loki admitted. "Once I get back from Asgard, I'd like to see more of your world. Asia, maybe."

"I've never been that far east myself," Kristoff told him. "But I've always wanted to go."

"Do they do these types of shows there?"

"I'll look into it," Kristoff promised. Then he furrowed his brow. "Don't you think it's been too quiet lately?"

"Meaning?"

"No threats, no danger, not even a hint of anything amiss," Kristoff noted. "Doesn't that seem odd?"

"Not really," Loki countered. "I think it proves we need to be on our guard even more in America. That's likely where the hammer will fall."

Kristoff chuckled. "You're getting good at human expressions. Here's one for you. It feels like the calm before the storm, and I don't like it. Not one bit."

Loki stared at the sun lazily dipping below the western horizon. He felt convinced they would conquer anything else that came their way. He found it hard to imagine gloom and danger, preferring to think of how blissful, yet exciting, his life with Carina would be. Though small, niggling doubts tried to shove their way to the front of his mind, he brushed them away like he would a pesky fly.

"Oh, I don't know, Kristoff," Loki responded cheerfully. "I think the worst is behind us."

Kristoff grunted doubtfully, but his face brightened. He clapped his hand on Loki's shoulder. "I thought I was the optimistic one."

Loki laughed. "So did I."

The two of them stepped back into the train and made their way to their seats to join the others. In less than a few hours, they would all head to their bunks in the sleeping cars. By morning, they would arrive in Calais, where they would take the ferry to London to board the steamship to New York City.

Loki did not know what adventures lay before them in America, but with each mile closer to that much-anticipated shore, his excitement built upon itself until he felt only greatness awaited them.

Surely, nothing could stand in their way.

ACKNOWLEDGMENTS

Many thanks to all the people who have been part of the development of this second book in the series:

Jeremy Meinking, for listening to me read the entire book out loud. Ariana Meinking, for all the brainstorming sessions that pushed me through writer's block. Tammy Meyer, for helping me work through a crime plot hole. Joseph and Christie Treen, for helping me work through a motive plot hole. Sergeant Jeremy Vaughan of the New Mexico State Police, for lending a professional eye and providing information for my police and crime scenes.

Mary Cornell, for sharing her expertise in literature and helping me flesh out areas that needed a little more oomph and clarity. Michelle Ross, for encouraging me to employ more world-building and character development. Kathy Filardo, for sharing insight and information from her vast writing repertoire. D'Anne Frazier, for evaluating several areas that needed stronger writing and better scenes, as well as her painstaking attention to detail in organization, design, and email management.

Sylvia Chatham, for sending information and pictures for my London scenes. Florence Marley Bråthen, for evaluating and helping me research aspects of my Norway scenes. Kim Buchanan and Cambri Holden, for helping me handle one of my romance scenes accurately.

Jen Zelinger, for her professional editing skills and working with me to produce a richer, better book. Nick Zelinger, for his ability to capture my vision and design another beautifully compelling cover and interior layout. Veronica Yager, for her efficiency in project management and expertise in the final publishing steps.

A big New Mexico shout-out to all the friends and family who came out to support me at the Paint Nite fundraiser at Painting with a Twist.

And finally, a huge thank you to all my amazing backers from Kickstarter for helping to fund the publishing of this book.

Tara-Jo Archer	KJ Humphrey
Yaya Bardsky	Tillie Jenkins
Chad Bowden	Ryan Jobe
Shari L. Bradley	Uncle John Meinking
Jacob Brein	Owens
Kelly Brennan	Andrew Parsons
Kathy Chatel	Sharon Pettit
Deborah Ciabattoni	Kevin and Kyla Pohl
Mary Cornell	Mary Ann Raley
Yolanda R. Domínguez	Carol Jean Reynolds
Susan Early	Karyn Rybacki
Darin & Tracy Elgersma	Cindy S.
Kathy Filardo	The Southwick Family
Katy Ford	Kaitlin Teore
Robert & Florence Frank	Becky Thomson
Kelley Gibisser	Liza van der Wal

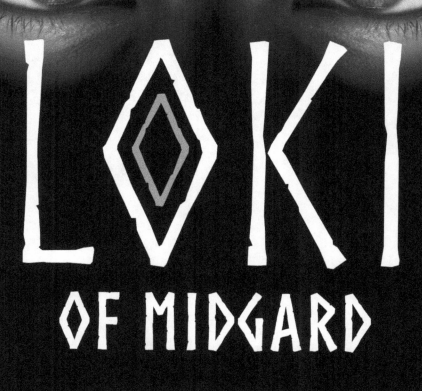

LOKI

OF MIDGARD

THE RISING OF A REBEL

Look for Book 3 of
the Loki of Midgard Series
Coming Spring 2020

Here's a preview of what's to come.
Read on …

People crowded the deck, straining against each other to get the best view of New York as the steamer approached the harbor. They would be docking within the hour. As Loki and Carina stood with the rest of the first and second class passengers, she explained that the third class steerage passengers, many of whom were immigrants seeking a new life in America, would be ferried to Ellis Island for processing. The higher-paying passengers would only have to endure a cursory inspection from the customs agents approaching the ship in a revenue cutter. Once they were approved for entry into the United States, the first and second class passengers would disembark with their trunks and luggage at the Hudson Pier.

Loki was tall enough to see over the heads of most of the people. As the ship entered the bay, the splendid feminine figure of a statue came into view, as if she were rising up from the small island on which she stood.

"There's Lady Liberty," Carina said softly as cheers erupted all over the ship, though loudest from the steerage deck.

"Who is this Lady Liberty?" Loki asked Carina as they waited for their inspections. "She looks Roman."

"She was made by the French, as a gift," answered Joseph Green, who stood nearby with Helga. "But she was inspired by a Roman goddess. She has stood there for almost forty years."

"She's beautiful," murmured Helga.

Kristoff and Kathleen were close enough to hear. They, too, gazed at the magnificent structure, taking in her noble face, her seven-pointed crown, and the torch she held high aloft. Her copper plates had begun to oxidize but still shimmered and glowed as the sun approached the highest point in the sky.

In her low, melodic voice, Carina began to recite. Kathleen joined her. "Give me your tired, your poor, your huddled masses yearning to breathe free, the wretched refuse of your teeming shore, send these, the homeless, tempest-tossed to me, I lift my lamp beside the golden door!"

"From Emma Lazarus's 'The New Colossus,'" Kathleen added, smiling warmly at Carina, then gazing back at the Statue of Liberty. "Now cast in a bronze plaque inside the pedestal. Long has Lady Liberty meant freedom and new life to people just like my parents, who came here almost thirty years ago."

They all fell silent until a customs agent finally drew near. The inspections of their luggage passed without any further delay. They were all cleared to disembark, and Loki set foot on American soil for the first time.

In many ways, New York City was like, and yet unlike, the cities Loki had experienced in Europe. The throngs of people were a diverse mixture of race and culture, rich and poor alike. The hurried pace had an undercurrent of camaraderie that reminded him of London but with artistic flair here and there that brought Paris to mind.

Joseph had sent for his limousine to fetch them in style. When it arrived, the large vehicle impressed Loki even more than the Rolls Royce had. Once the car took them beyond the docks, they passed quaint shops with Old World vibes, as well as modern stores towering above the busy streets. Joseph directed the chauffeur to take them by way of Times Square, which was quite an eye-opening sight with its heavy traffic, huge advertisements, theaters, restaurants, hotels, and stores.

"Look, Luke," Carina exclaimed, pointing to a tall building behind a giant billboard. "Times Tower was the second tallest building in New York when it was built, back when it was the home of the New York Times newspaper."

"What's the tallest?" Loki asked, peering up at the building as they passed.

"The Woolworth building, right, Father?" Carina answered.

"Yes, sweetheart," Joseph affirmed, beaming with pleasure at his daughter's knowledge. "It's almost eight hundred feet high, over fifty stories. Times Tower is under four hundred, just twenty-five stories."

Just twenty-five? Loki marveled to himself somewhat sarcastically.

Odin's palace loomed over a thousand feet high, as tall as the Eiffel Tower, yet it only had ten floors. No one had thought to include more. Loki had scoffed when Carina asked why his people did not use all the space in their spires for more levels, but seeing how packed New York was with buildings, he was beginning to understand.

Carina remarked, "As much as they build and change things, the Woolworth won't stay the tallest for long, I think."

"Oh no, there's always been someone building bigger and better ever since the Tower of Babel," Joseph agreed. "And there always will be."

"What's the Tower of Babel?" Loki whispered to Carina.

"It's an old Bible story. I'll tell you when you're older," Carina whispered back.

Kristoff had overheard and snickered. Then he suddenly pointed out the window. "Look, Kat! Fletcher Henderson's playing at the Roseland Ballroom!"

"Guess I know where we're going tonight," she laughed in response.

"That reminds me, you haven't told us where we're performing tomorrow," prodded Loki.

"We wanted to surprise you," Kathleen declared, holding Kristoff's hand tightly and grinning at him as if it were his idea.

"Now's as good a time as any. Is it one of the theaters on Broadway?" Loki prompted.

"Not this time. But you are booked at Carnegie Hall, the most prestigious venue in New York," Kathleen informed him, brimming over with excitement.

"Carnegie Hall!" Carina breathed, her brown eyes dancing. "I've never performed there."

"We're actually going right by it in a few minutes," Joseph commented.

"I thought we were going a rather roundabout way," Kathleen teased. "How on earth did you know?"

"My chauffeur told me about some advertisements he saw when I called for the car," Joseph admitted. "I'm impressed you got them in there, Kristoff."

"What can I say, I'm a decent manager," Kristoff bragged. He looked fondly at Kathleen. "But I didn't do it alone."

Loki smiled to himself, glad to see the two of them so happy together after the difficulties they had worked through in the last twenty-four hours.

As they came upon the rather square building set with arches and many windows, Carina pointed delightedly to the advertisement, which read "Lukas Black and the Shooting Star: A Magic and Music Show for All Ages" with times and prices for the matinee and evening performances. The artwork on the large poster was stunning, featuring a mysterious black-haired man standing slightly off-center behind a red-haired angel in a white dress. The two figures were surrounded by swirls of green and gold.

"It's us!" Carina exclaimed. Then she frowned. "Not a very good likeness of you, though, Luke."

"The artist is a New Yorker. He's never seen Luke, so he had to go by my description," explained Kristoff. "That's why most of the face is in shadow."

"I like it," asserted Loki. "Makes me look cunning and powerful."

"I have to admit I'm still nervous about doing two shows in one day," Carina admitted.

"You'll be fine," Kathleen reassured her gently. "It's not much different than a rehearsal and performance."

"Will one rehearsal in the morning be enough?" Carina asked Loki.

"I think so," Loki replied. "I'm a little rusty but I'll manage. Besides, we're doing the exact same songs we did in Paris and London."

"Only until Washington DC, remember?" Kathleen reminded them. "You'll have to work on a few new songs for the remaining shows. But you'll have time."

Helga had not said a word since they had climbed into the limousine. As Carina chatted excitedly with Kristoff and Kathleen about song ideas, Loki happened to catch Joseph mouthing the words "You okay?" to Helga.

She nodded but the apprehension in her blue eyes remained.

Joseph put his arm around her and kissed her on the cheek. "Everything will be fine, dove," he whispered, to which she responded with a shy smile.

Loki had never heard Joseph speak so tenderly to Helga before, though it was obviously not the first time. Certain he was not meant to have witnessed the exchange, Loki stared with interest out the car window until they reached the Green residence, an elegant brownstone mansion on Fifth Avenue.

✦✦✦

They casually walked to a small teahouse on Sixth Avenue, a front for a speakeasy called the Red Head. On the way, Loki perfected his New York accent, which he had heard often throughout the day. Hardly anyone gave them even a second glance, increasing Loki's confidence that they blended quite well with their surroundings and the other people around them.

Once inside the teahouse, Loki gave the password to gain access to the speakeasy tucked away on the secret second floor. He felt somewhat uneasy as they were ushered upstairs. With Prohibition in full swing in America, the entire aura felt different than it had in the European clubs he had frequented with Kristoff. There were only a few obvious couples in the lavish room. Everyone else seemed to be unattached young men or flappers with roving eyes, although there were a handful of gangster types and well-dressed businessmen.

Despite the smoke and dim lighting, he could tell their entrance had caused quite a stir. Loki did not like the leering looks several rough-looking men sent Carina's way, openly staring with unconcealed lust at the swell of her bustline, her round calves, and her bare arms. Loki gritted his teeth, reminding himself why they had come and how important it was not to cause a ruckus.

He scratched the itchy fake mustache Joseph had given him as one of the men sidled up to Carina, who had been temporarily separated from Loki.

Loki manipulated the sound to hear the man ask her, "Are you one of Polly Adler's girls?"

Carina shot Loki a terrified look but smoothly dismissed the man with a haughty, "No, I'm not, and I have an escort for the evening, thank you."

Before Loki could rejoin her, a well-endowed redhead approached Loki. She bore an uncanny resemblance to Carina, though her hazel eyes were lighter and lined with black to make them stand out. By the voracious look she gave him, he knew exactly what she planned to offer him. He removed his gray fedora and smiled respectfully at her, thankful he did not look like himself.

Just as she laid a manicured hand on his chest, Loki spoke first. "I believe that gentleman over there was looking for you."

She whipped her head around to look in the direction he pointed. "For me?"

"Yes, it appears he mistakenly thought my companion was you," Loki said with a soothing voice.

She snatched her hand away from him when Carina joined them and stared at her with burning eyes. The girl eyed him once more with visible disappointment, then nodded coldly at Carina and hurried off to chase down the man Loki had pointed out.

"Nicely handled," Carina whispered, taking his arm and moving with him toward an empty table. Something in her eyes told Loki she was displeased and that he had not heard the last of it. "It's a good thing I came along or you would have forgotten the whole mission."

"Not likely," he snorted. "It would have taken more than a woman like that to undo me."

"I hope so. She, unlike me, probably is one of Polly Adler's girls," Carina huffed.

"And who is this Polly Adler?"

"She owns a brothel nearby," Carina said nonchalantly. "Her girls and other such workers frequent establishments like this, looking for clients."

"How do you know such things?" Loki hissed. "I thought this place was supposed to be respectable."

"It's still a speakeasy," Carina said quietly, with a shrug. "Enough of that now, or someone will hear you."

Loki felt sickened that his wife had been mistaken for a brothel worker, but he stuffed down his disgust and remembered he had a part to play. He ordered a Brandy Alexander for himself and lobster canapés while Carina picked at the mixed nuts on the table and eyed a cheese platter at another table.

"Would you like one of those?" Loki offered.

"Yes, and shrimp cocktail. Oh, and a mint julep," she added. She smiled brightly at him, then scowled at another scantily-clad woman who had winked at Loki despite the fact he was obviously with someone.

Loki scanned the room for any sign of the person they sought, though he had been told, "You don't find Lucky Luciano. Lucky Luciano finds you."

When the food and drinks had been brought, he asked Carina, "Are you ready for this?"

512

She nodded, though there was a slight spark of fear in her eyes. Loki got up and kissed her cheek, then headed toward the men's room. As he had been instructed, he waited three minutes, then headed back to the table. A handsome, dark-haired man sat in Loki's chair, speaking with Carina, his intense, almost black eyes following her every movement. He stood as Loki approached.

"I'm in your seat, sir," the man stated with a welcoming smile. "The lady was just telling me about your recent trip to Coney Island."

Sign up for the newsletter for even more content and updates.

jennifermeinking.com

lokiofmidgard.com

email: ladymeinking@gmail.com

facebook.com/authorjennifermeinking

instagram.com/jennifermeinking

twitter.com/jenmeinking

pinterest.com/jennifermeinkingauthor

CPSIA information can be obtained
at www.ICGtesting.com
Printed in the USA
LVHW041001240721
693581LV00017B/314